THE
LOST
GIRLS
OF
DEVON

PREVIOUS BOOKS BY BARBARA O'NEAL

When We Believed in Mermaids
The Art of Inheriting Secrets
The Lost Recipe for Happiness
The Secret of Everything
How to Bake a Perfect Life
The Garden of Happy Endings
The All You Can Dream Buffet
No Place Like Home
A Piece of Heaven
The Goddesses of Kitchen Avenue
Lady Luck's Map of Vegas
The Scent of Hours

THE
LOST
GIRLS
OF
DEVON

a novel

BARBARA O'NEAL

LAKE UNION PUBLISHING

Text copyright © 2020 by Barbara Samuel
All rights reserved.

No part of this book may be reproduced, or stored in a retrieval system, or transmitted in any form or by any means, electronic, mechanical, photocopying, recording, or otherwise, without express written permission of the publisher.

Published by Lake Union Publishing, Seattle

www.apub.com

Amazon, the Amazon logo, and Lake Union Publishing are trademarks of Amazon.com, Inc., or its affiliates.

ISBN-13: 9781542020725
ISBN-10: 1542020727

Cover design by Shasti O'Leary Soudant

Printed in the United States of America

My life has been blessed by circles of extraordinary women, and yet I'm continually amazed at how powerful circles can be. This book is for the extraordinary group of writers I've grown to love through our Fiction from the Heart Facebook group: Jamie Beck, Tracy Brogan, Sonali Dev, Kwana Jackson, Donna Kauffman, Falguni Kothari, Virginia Kantra, Sally Kilpatrick, Priscilla Oliveras, Hope Ramsay, and Liz Talley. You all know why, and you are all amazing. I can't remember how I got through my writing days without you.

Life is a shipwreck,
but we must not forget to sing in the lifeboats;
Life is a desert,
but we can transform our corner into a garden.
—Voltaire

Prologue
Zoe

The day my mother left me was an overcast English morning, with drizzle moistening the air and our faces. She'd packed a bag for me that was tucked in the boot of the car, and I held a stuffed dog in my arms, because he traveled with me when I slept at my grandmother's house.

I had no sense of disaster, not then. I loved staying with my grandmother and slept there quite often—weekends and long holiday weeks when my gran and I would walk along the cliff path and hunt for shells on the beach and drink hot mugs of tea. I bloomed under the focused attention she lavished on me.

In the car on the way to Gran's, we sang along with the radio to "Walk like an Egyptian," which was one of our favorites. My mother's bracelets rattled on her arms when she made the gesture of an Egyptian dancer. I laughed and imitated her, pointing my hands like a carving on the tomb of King Tut. She hammed it up, tossing her long back curls around and dancing in her seat. She was draped in all her colors and jewelry—an india cotton skirt and a paisley-print blouse, and a scarf that wrapped twice around her neck and was still long enough to dangle to her waist. Peacock earrings shimmered coyly in her hair.

At my grandmother's house, a sprawling stone manor perched on a cliff high over the sea and the village of Axestowe, on the Devon coast, my mother carried my bag around the garden to the kitchen door. We always entered there to avoid the dark-paneled hallway hung with its somber portraits. Gran met us and gleefully swung open the door and cried out, "There's my girl! I'm so pleased." Gran was the opposite of my mother in every way—crisp slacks and pressed blouses and short white hair—but I loved her too. I found relief in her sense of order, but more in the sense that I was the center of her world, that nothing would ever take precedence over me and my needs and wishes. At Woodhurst Hall, I felt safe. Secure.

My mother must have kissed me, hugged me, but those memories vanished long ago. I turned around and saw her floating away, her sleeves fluttering from her arms like the wings of a bird taking flight, and I had the most terrible sense of dread.

"Mummy!" I cried.

She turned around and flung me kisses with both hands.

Then, she was gone.

Chapter One
Lillian

Something was going on in the village.

Not that anyone would believe her. They would tut-tut and pat her on the head and compliment the imagination that had given her more than a hundred mystery stories over the past fifty years, but once you passed eighty, no one believed you had a single thought worth listening to.

But she knew something was going on.

On the nights when she couldn't sleep, which was more often than not, as her old bones complained and the memories of nearly nine decades paraded themselves through her imagination, Lillian Fairchild made her way to the study she had created in the tower room many years before. In the dark, ensconced in the window seat her granddaughter Zoe had so loved, she sipped a soothing cup of tea and watched the sea. One of the reasons she'd refused to leave the rambling old house, despite the damp and the cold, was this view of the sea. The manor perched on a cliff overlooking the village and offered a full, unobstructed view of the coastline for miles and miles.

Tonight the waxing moon had not reached its zenith, but the light was nonetheless bright and clear, illuminating the fishing boats and yachts anchored for the night just offshore. It was the moonlight that revealed a small sailboat making its silent way toward a pair of yachts, shadows on the sea.

So many strangers these days, Lillian thought, taking a sip of tea. In her youth, tourists had been few and mostly hailed from other parts of England, or perhaps France, and the odd loud American. Now when she made her rounds of the village, there were as many tourists as locals, and they were a well-heeled lot, by the look of them. Men who golfed and brought their expensive sailboats to harbor, women in oversize sunglasses shopping the art stalls and antique shops, many of them speaking some language other than English.

She missed the days when she knew everyone.

Of course, she still knew the locals. It was her business to stay abreast of the village gossip to lend verisimilitude to her long-running series about Lady Dawood and her good friend Flora, a village baker, who solved crimes around the countryside. The pair of mild-mannered, middle-aged widows had made their creator most comfortable.

There's something going on in the village, she thought, and she watched the shadow boat slide stealthily out to the dark sea.

Suddenly she saw the scene through Lady Dawood's eyes, viewing it as if from the perch of her castle tower.

Something is amiss in the village.

Lillian stood and made her way to the computer. An idea was a terrible thing to waste.

Chapter Two

Zoe

At 7:00 p.m. England time, on the twenty-fourth of April, my friend Diana's texts ceased.

I didn't notice right away. Although we had been friends from childhood, our friendship had been under strain for more than a year; we'd been so aloof with each other that we had barely spoken. She'd sent me a handful of texts over the past couple of months, and I'd either replied curtly or not at all.

The one last Friday had gone unanswered.

This Friday night, I stood at the small dining table in my territorial adobe in Santa Fe, shoes off by the door, coat still on, and sorted through the mail. "Isabel?" I called. She didn't immediately answer, and although she nearly always listened to music on her headphones, I shucked my coat to go check on her.

I knocked and popped my head into her room. "I'm home. You hungry?"

Her long, lanky form was stretched out on the bed, one knee cocked over the angle of the other. In her hands was a paperback with an outlandish and gaudy cover that I recognized from her dad's collection of science fiction. Mósí, her giant ragdoll cat, stretched out beside her.

She held up a finger for me to wait, an established sign between us. I waited until she'd finished the scene and then tugged off the headphones. "Hi."

"How was your day?"

A shrug. "I had pizza with Dad."

I was stung. Even when I told myself that competition between parents was foolish and that being a bad husband didn't mean a man was a bad father, I hated it when Martin intruded on these rituals. "Pizza is *our* Friday thing."

"He offered, so I went." She swung her legs down over the side of the bed and smoothed her wild, curly black hair, tugging it away from her face and squeezing it tight in a gesture she'd used since grade school. "You want some eggs?"

"Sure. That's fine." The therapist said Isabel should have things to do around the house and be engaged, so she'd chosen to cook for me when I came in from work. To make sure she wasn't alone too much, she also had to eat meals with someone—me at breakfast and dinner, Martin at lunch. He'd be going on tour soon, and I'd been fretting about what to do then.

One step at a time.

"I'm going to change my clothes," I said, "and I'll join you in the kitchen."

As I padded down the hall to my own bedroom, my phone gave the old-fashioned dual ring I'd assigned to my grandmother. *Ring-ring! Ring-ring!*

With a frown—it was close to midnight in England—I answered. "Hello, Gran. Having trouble sleeping?"

"Diana has gone missing," she said without preamble. "I'm afraid she's gotten mixed up in whatever is going on in the village."

It could have been a line from one of her cozy mysteries. Things were always afoot in the village. It was how Lillian's mind worked.

"What do you mean, she's disappeared?" I shed my trousers and blouse. "Did you ring her?"

"Of course I did, Zoe. She's not answering. Poppy rang me, too, worried that Diana missed a reading."

Poppy would be my mother, who'd taken up residence in an old farmhouse outside Axestowe. She'd been trying to get back into my life, and although I was not the slightest bit interested, clearly Lillian and Diana hadn't felt the same way.

I pushed away the needle pricks of their small betrayals. "A reading?" I echoed. "Like tarot or something?"

"I don't know," Lillian snapped. "I just know she hasn't been here in a week, and she never leaves for that long."

"She hasn't been there in a week?" The first ripple of concern moved through my belly. Diana had been a home nurse for a decade but lately had been building a catering business on the side. It had been going well, but to support the kitchen and employees, she'd kept a few care jobs, Lillian being one. "Hold on, Gran. Let me check my texts."

I had my hair done in London. Quite different.

I had not replied. "I haven't heard from her since a week ago Friday," I said to Lillian. "Have you called the police?"

"Of course! They think I'm a senile old woman with too much time on my hands," she said with a humph. "They think she's just gone off with some man."

Diana *had* recently been seeing someone, a businessman from London who'd come to Axestowe for the yacht parties that had become all the rage, but despite her bohemian ways, she wouldn't have just deserted her responsibilities. I said as much to Gran.

"No," Lillian agreed. "I suspect they're just worried about their precious festival. Don't want the snooping press about, do they?"

The Axestowe Festival, an arts and folk music gathering that had been a mainstay of the town for more than three decades, had become in recent years an economic boon to the town, drawing tourists from all over England and the world. "Well, let's not jump to conclusions, Lady Dawood," I teased.

"Oh, don't you dare. I'm cross enough about no one taking me seriously."

"I'm sorry, Gran. You're right."

"I would like you to come home for a few weeks and see if you can help me sort it out."

I hesitated. I'd had a lot on my mind lately. The small graphic arts studio I worked for was slowly, inexorably going under, and I needed to figure out what to do next—not for the money so much, since my ex was as generous as he'd been unfaithful, but for my own sense of purpose.

Gran, in her late eighties, had begun to sound a little wan in her phone calls lately too. I hadn't visited Axestowe for nearly a year, not since my mother had swanned back, and now I fretted that I'd left it too long. Was Gran ill and not telling me? Was that dementia I'd heard in her slight but noticeable mental wanders lately?

But the biggest worry was my fifteen-year-old daughter, who was not only grieving the divorce of her parents but had also been caught in the middle of a brutal social media storm just over a month ago.

What that storm entailed, I had no idea. Isabel had deleted all her accounts and refused to talk to me about it. Four times now, she'd sat in a therapist's office for the full hour without saying a word. She wouldn't even talk to her father, usually her hero, and Martin's modest fame as an indie singer meant he'd been the target of social media bullying campaigns more than once. He was as worried as I was, but no matter what we'd thus far tried, she was locked up tight.

To my shame, I hadn't even realized anything was going on until Isabel was suspended from school after a fight with a girl I thought was her best friend. When she came home that day, she had simply closed up. She also refused to return to classes and instead enrolled herself in an online school, then begged tearfully for my signature to change.

I resisted signing the paper for more than a week, attempting to trade a confession for the signature, but she only hid in her room, staring at the ceiling. Fearful as ever that I was ill prepared to be a good mother thanks to my own childhood, I discussed it with her father and her therapist, and we agreed together that she needed some time. Isabel had been an old soul from the day she was born, and there were only two months left in the term. Sooner or later she'd crack with the therapist.

At least I hoped so.

In return for permission to go to school online, she'd agreed to text me every hour while I worked and to have lunch every day with her dad, who lived nearby. I didn't want her to isolate herself too much or turn to self-harm. Her cat, a gift from her father when we'd divorced, kept her company, but I'd been thinking a lot about letting her help me pick out a puppy. Dogs could wiggle their way into hearts like nothing else, and our old beloved chow mutt, Simba, had died six months before.

For now, we were taking it day by day. She ate meals and read. Book after book after book, which seemed completely appropriate to me. There'd been many times in my life when a book taking me away from my own miserable world had been the best possible choice. I'd just have to help her feel more comfortable in the real world a little at a time until she felt safe enough to come back into it.

As Gran talked on the phone about my proposed visit, Isabel's door opened, and she shuffled into the kitchen in an oversize hoodie and sweatpants, her outfit of choice the past month, as if wearing enough clothes could make her invisible.

Invisible from who? I wondered. *Or* what?

Maybe if I took her away from here, she would let down her guard and tell me what had happened. I lowered the phone. "Want to go to England?" I asked.

She turned, eyes wide. *"Yes."*

Looking into those velvet-dark eyes, so full of pain I couldn't reach, I felt my heart twist. "All right," I said into the phone. "I'll call you back when I know the details."

When I hung up, I sent a text to Diana:

Hey, is everything okay? Gran is worried about you. Text me back when you get this.

After a lifetime of shuttling back and forth between Santa Fe and the West Country of England, I should have earned a pass on jet lag. It should have been the plague of others, not a woman with dual citizenship who had half her family in New Mexico and half in England.

But as I hauled my luggage from the taxi's boot in the drive of my grandmother's rambling six-hundred-year-old Devon manor house, my very fingernails ached with weariness. It was well past midnight. Nearly thirteen hours on planes, another two to transfer to the train, three *on* the train, and we'd arrived beneath the waxing moon, faded to half in a sky scudding with clouds. Isabel, mussed and bleary eyed, unfolded herself and stared dopily at the manor. "Are we here?"

I nodded and anchored my bag more firmly over my shoulder. Gran had left the lights on, but she would have long been abed. "Come on, sweetheart. Nearly done." I remembered well how emotional I'd often been when I'd arrived at one home or the other—grieving the people left behind, eager to see the ones in the new place, never sure which emotion was more appropriate.

She allowed my hand on her shoulder, guiding her gently toward the ancient steps. In his carrier, Mósí meowed plaintively. He'd made the trip several times, but no one could make him like it.

The door flew open, revealing a small woman haloed by yellow lamplight. "Here you are!" Gran cried. "Come in, come in! Are you hungry?"

I ran up the steps, reaching to embrace my grandmother in a rush of longing and love and relief. She was made of nothing but bones and loose skin these days, but she smelled the same: hairspray and Taylor of London Lily of the Valley talcum powder, and a sweet note of lavender that belonged to her alone. I breathed it in, letting it ground me.

"Oh, sweet girl," Gran said quietly, hugging me back. "I've missed you so much."

"Me too." For one long second I let myself rest in this space, with the person who loved me the most in all the world, then reluctantly released her and turned to include Isabel, who was the person I loved most in the world.

"Hello, dear," Gran said, opening her arms. "I have had some sandwiches sent to your room, so you can go up straightaway."

Isabel kissed Lillian's cheek and for just a moment bent down low enough to rest her head on Lillian's shoulder. "Thank you."

"I shall spare you the exclamations of how you've grown. Your mother can take you to your room."

"I know where it is," Isabel said.

"Not the old room, I'm afraid. We've had some trouble with the roof, and I've settled you in the Willow Room."

Isabel narrowed her eyes. "That's the room that's haunted by the girl who was drowned, isn't it? I don't want to sleep in a haunted room."

"It's not haunted, child," Gran said. "It's the Rowan Room that's haunted."

Isabel looked at me, eyebrow raised.

"I don't think either of them are haunted, and I lived here most of my life," I said with some exasperation, "but it's the Rowan Room that gets the bad press." It had been the bedroom of a girl from the seventeenth century who'd been cast into the sea as a witch.

"Why don't *you* sleep in it, then?" she asked with a hint of her old sauciness.

"Because I have my room and I love it." I kissed her head. "Let's go up together."

"You won't have a cup of tea?" Gran asked. For a moment I hesitated, but she must have seen me swaying. "Never mind. Get yourself to bed, the both of you, and we'll chat in the morning."

Guilt plucked my heart. "No, I'll stay."

"Nonsense. Off you go. I should be going to bed as well."

In my bedroom, the fluffy white duvet had been turned back and a lamp lit in the long narrow room. I wondered who'd done the work, since much of this was beyond Gran now. I would have to find out if she'd hired some help, or needed to do so. I rubbed the spot between my brows and logged the task on my phone's reminder list.

Even after I showered in the tiny bathroom and changed into warm pajamas, I found that my exhaustion would not turn to sleep. The nightmare gremlins tossed out visions of Diana brutally murdered; of Isabel growing more and more wan, never living up to the radiant, talented woman I saw inside of her; of Gran falling down the stairs and breaking a hip.

Not helpful.

After an hour, I wandered to one of a row of windows that overlooked the sea. It was calm tonight, shimmering under the moonlight. Boats of several varieties were anchored a little way offshore. They sat as still as boulders on the mirror of water.

I rested my head on the pane, feeling myself at seven looking for my mother to return up the road, at twelve wishing my father would just leave me be in my comfortable place here in England instead of forcing me to shuttle back and forth, and at sixteen swooning in passionate teenage love.

In those days, I'd dreamed of going to the Royal College of Art in London, or perhaps Glasgow, which I'd visited on a school trip. I'd fallen in love with the MacIntosh Building, the elegant art nouveau lines and flourishes, the sheer joy of beauty for the sake of beauty in every detail.

Being in this room always reminded me of the young painter I'd been, the girl who yearned to *become* someone, to be someone important. It haunted me whenever I came home, where I'd spent so many hours dreaming of the paintings I'd create, the acclaim I would find.

So many big dreams.

Now here I was again, in my grandmother's house, my daughter in tow, and my life looked nothing like what I'd imagined it would. Instead of becoming a great artist, I was a practical graphic designer, working an ordinary sort of job in an office, divorced and unattached. Where had that girl gone?

But did any of us end up where we wanted to be?

With an impatient tsk at myself, I shoved the memories away. I didn't have time for angsty navel-gazing. I had a daughter in crisis, a grandmother growing more frail by the month, and a friend who'd gone missing without a word.

Unlike my mother, I showed up for the people who loved me. At the moment, that meant trying to find out where Diana had gone, giving Isabel a chance to heal from whatever had happened to her, and giving my grandmother a good helping of love and attention.

Where are you, my old friend? I wondered. Guilt at not responding to her last text washed through me, before I finally, *finally*, drifted off into sleep.

Chapter Three

Poppy

Jennie Cleverdon had first come to me for readings when she'd suffered a beating from a boy she'd fancied herself in love with, a brute whose father worked as a cook at the yacht club. Only fifteen and neglected by her mother, she'd had no one but me to tell her life could be different, so I brought her into the shop and settled her in the cozy nook where I did my readings. She had a bruise on her jaw and that particular sorrowful longing that often marks an abused woman. I took her hand and spread my fingers over her palm, where I discovered that untimely death lived on her small white hand. That slash of a life line, cut so short it barely qualified.

I lied, as any conscientious person would. I warned her away from the boy, but she never listened.

And now here she was, coming into my shop on a sunny May morning. "Morning, Ms. Fairchild," she said in her rolling north Devon accent. "I've come to have a reading on my daughter. Can I do that?"

The baby girl was four months old, a laughing lass with a full head of the blackest hair. She peeked out of her carrier at me and grinned, reminding me so much of Zoe that an arrow zinged right through my diaphragm. Her cheeks were red as roses, like a baby in a fairy tale, and when Jennie pulled her out and offered her with a smile as haunted as any room in Woodhurst Hall, my mother's house on the hill, I couldn't help but take her. My only granddaughter was four thousand miles away, and her mother, that very Zoe, had never let me see her.

To my surprise, the longings of a grandmother were quite different from those of a mother.

"What a beautiful little soul you are, Magdalena!" I cooed, curling her close to my bosom, where she wiggled and settled in, pursing her tiny red mouth into a coo of her own, low and sweet, like a pigeon's. "And such a big name for such a wee thing. Can we call you Maggie?"

Jennie leaned in, all collarbones and elbow joints, too young to have a baby already, cutting short so many of her options. An old story, one of the oldest, and still it repeated and repeated and repeated. My heart ached for her. She stroked the baby's cheek. "I do already, I'm afraid. I thought I'd keep it long and beautiful, but it's Maggie."

Maggie grasped my finger in her tiny fist, and I laughed when she widened those black eyes as if in first discovery. "I can't read for her, love," I said. "She's innocent and fresh, and we'll just leave that be, shall we?"

Jennie's big eyes met mine. "Are you afraid of curses?"

I smiled softly. "No." In truth, magic and readings were only ways for me to let people settle and get comfortable enough to talk so that I could find ways to offer them hope, a little healing. "She's just too young."

She nodded, twining a finger through Maggie's curls. "Now that Diana's gone missing, I'm going to have to take her up to my aunt." Diana had taken Jennie in when her drunken father had kicked her out in a fit of rage. Jennie had lived with her for eight months and had blossomed under her care. "She said she'd look after her while I look for work in Exeter. Get a fresh start, maybe."

I thought of Jennie's abbreviated life line, the tarot that predicted dire things, the rotten luck of being born into a brutal family with no money and no prospects but her own wits. She was trying to save her life. Maybe she could. "Are you going to stay with your aunt?"

Something flickered over her face. "No, she'll only take the baby. I've got to find a room on my own."

Worry slithered through me. She was hiding something. "All right, love. Come sit down. Let me make us a pot of tea, and I'll read your cards. For free."

Of course, they turned up the Tower and upside-down Cups and all manner of cautionary cards. As I took in the spread, inviting insight and intuition, all I felt was dread. "Are you sure you need to go, Jennie?"

"I am." She bounced the baby gently, letting the tiny fingers curl around her own. "Now that Diana's gone, I've got to learn to make my own way."

The dire spread on the table took on new layers, and I suddenly swept them all into a pile. Fate was never fixed. I'd make an offering to the Mother this evening, poppy seed cake and wine. I also picked out a travel amulet for her, a simple disk carved with runes, and pressed it into her hand. "Be safe, sweetheart," I said and kissed her forehead.

She hugged me hard, pressing her face into my shoulder, her arms tight. "Thank you, Poppy."

"Keep in touch, child, or I'll worry. Text me."

"I will. I promise."

When I awakened the next morning, Jennie was on my mind. I lay in bed for a little while, thinking about her, wondering if she'd made it safely to her aunt's house. I'd insisted that she leave her mobile number with me, but I knew all manner of things befell girls in a world that only wanted to exploit them. She was pretty and lost, the worst combination.

Although it was not yet light, I rose and dressed warmly for my chores. That hour of dark, so fresh and unspoiled, had always been one of my favorites, even when I was a wee girl in my parents' house, creeping downstairs to the kitchen before the staff awakened. There were only two, a cook and a housekeeper, and they each had a set of rooms off the kitchen, but as my parents never came down before ten, neither did they bother to get up only for the needs of a small girl.

I could tend to my own needs now, in my own house, Greencombe Cottage, which I had bought for myself upon my return to Axestowe not quite a year ago. The stairs were narrow from the bedroom to the kitchen, a room warmed by a Rayburn in the corner. On the counter were my masala tins, battered and no longer shiny after so many years, and the walls were hung with things collected in my travels: a pair of miniature paintings of lovers from Udaipur, a bright and cheerful Ganesha from some market stall I no longer remembered, a photo of a man in a crisply pressed linen kurta, his eyes dark and twinkling. I touched it as I passed.

The room was quiet, though beneath the silence of the modern day, I could sense the imprint of all the people and animals who'd once been housed here, hundreds of years of them. Greencombe Cottage was built in 1540 and had been occupied ever since, standing fallow for only a handful of years after plague swept the village on one of its rounds. The names of the occupants were carefully recorded in the church rolls: first the Tuckers, then the Clarkes, then the Hoopers.

And now me, Pamela Elizabeth Fairchild, known as Poppy. Student of the world, daughter of Lillian, mother of Zoe, grandmother of Isabel. My relationship was still thin and rocky with my mother, and Zoe did not claim me or allow me to meet my granddaughter, but distance did not alter the fact of our relationships. Time taught you anything could happen, even healing.

Like the others in my cottage before me, I kept farm animals. I'd learned to love them when Zoe was a baby, long ago in New Mexico, where I'd first become attuned to the rhythms of the land. Zoe's father, Ben, had tended sheep from his family herd, and goats, and chickens.

At first it had seemed romantic, rising early to collect eggs and check on the sheep to make sure there were the same number as there had been the night before.

I'd fallen in love with goats in those days, their irrepressible natures and dazzling eyes, and now had two of my own, Gandalf and Boudica, who kept the grass around the cottage clipped to manageable levels. In the crisp morning air, I strode through the garden toward their pen, next to the barn, where they bedded down in hay. They rushed out to greet me, prancing and nudging my hands and pockets. "Yes, my sweets, good morrow to you too. Was it a good night?" Boudica bleated, always the communicator. I led them to their spots—Gandalf on the hill and Boudica near the house.

The chickens heard me and came running down from the hen-house, which my handyman, Jacob, had built for me. I scattered feed and collected a nice clutch of blue and green and brown eggs. "Thank you, ladies. Perhaps I'll bake a cake today."

As I walked back up to the house through the gardens of rue and lavender, peppermint, chives, and mugwort, I thought about Sage and his ecological projects, one of which was counting the eggs of ring ouzel and cuckoo and other threatened birds. Egg poachers prized the rarest of eggs to steal and sell. Highly illegal, of course, but wealthy foodies would do almost anything to up the ante within their circle. The problem had grown more severe with all the strangers flooding in on their yachts, creating a market for the forbidden and the rare.

Sage had stopped by the shop yesterday to tell me someone had made away with a pair of striped plover eggs, and he was furious.

I'd made him a tea of tulsi leaves and honey with a squeeze of lemon and ushered him into one of the big, soft chairs sitting by the side window. Sage was a volunteer on the moor to help count not only birds but butterflies and hares and all manner of wild things. He was a bit of a wild thing himself, born and raised away from the town, spending all his time on the moor with his dogs.

Sage and I had become friends since my return, as Diana and I had. Surprisingly, both of my daughter's best friends had made room for me upon my return, unlike Zoe herself, who had displayed a remarkable talent for holding a grudge.

As the sun began its jeweled ascent over the eastern trees, I paused. *Breathe in suffering, breathe out peace.* I took in the darkness, the heat of anger, my own and that in the world, and the sorrow, and the greed, and held it.

I imagined scrubbing the dark mass into something fresh and shiny, and exhaled, letting it go.

Whether it helped the world or not was unclear. It did, however, lighten my step.

Three things were on my mind as I cracked two eggs into a bowl and scrambled them gently with goat cheese that a friend down the lane had made with the milk I'd given him.

The first was Diana. It was Wednesday. In two days, she would have been gone for two full weeks. My stomach ached with the possibilities of what had happened to her. Had she fallen from a cliff? Drowned? Been kidnapped? I didn't believe she'd run off with a man, not with Jennie living with her these past eight months.

Second, I knew that Zoe and Isabel had arrived at Woodhurst. I'd made up their beds and scrubbed the bathrooms to a shiny polish, and by now they would have arrived. Knowing that they were within a mile of where I now stood lent a certain hopeful cast to the day. Maybe, with a little luck, Zoe would thaw enough to allow me to meet her daughter at last. Failing that, I might run into them in the village or at the Tesco so at least I might get a glimpse of them. Some part of me hoped that if Zoe looked into my face, she might soften.

Though really, why would she? I kept hoping for a movie ending to our story, a big swell of Bollywood music in the background as mother and daughter embraced and broke into a big dance number. But that was highly unlikely. Zoe had rejected every overture I'd made the past seven years.

Still, I loved the vision of a Bollywood ending to our tale. Smiling gently at my fanciful longings, I sat at the table to eat my eggs and toast, drinking hot milky tea from a big mug a potter friend of mine had thrown.

The third thing on my mind was my mother and what would become of her now that Diana was missing. I had been looking after her quite a lot, but with Diana's disappearance, she would need more from me. Which I was more than willing to give, but Zoe would not want me there, and honestly, I wasn't sure Lillian would want me around the clock. Our relationship was mending, but it was not yet healed.

The trouble was, she had grown noticeably more frail in recent months. She needed a housekeeper but disliked having one in the house, although she loved the gardener, who came in three times a week to tend the vast beds of roses and figs, delphiniums and foxgloves. More than once a magazine had come to shoot photos of my mother's splendiferous gardens.

Now she mainly puttered and stopped to smell a peony or a lily carefully sheltered behind a row of tall boxwood and hawthorn trees to protect them from the hard coast winds up there on the cliffs.

Despite her advancing years and increasing frailty, Lillian did not want to leave Woodhurst Hall, however decrepit it might be, and I held that wish in great respect. I'd have to come up with a plan of some sort to keep her in her office tower with the view of the sea that she'd loved her entire adult life. My mother and I did not always get on well, but I loved her. Whatever had to be done to keep her there, I would do.

As the sun broke over that very sea, shimmering long fingers through my windows, I washed up and made myself ready for the day ahead. I'd hired a young woman to help me in the shop for the season, but there was much to be done before the festival. I needed every minute to prepare for the crowds who would soon descend on the summer village.

Chapter Four

Isabel

One of the big problems I keep having is that I go to sleep, but then I wake up and my heart is racing, or I'm all sweaty and have to take a shower, or I'm kind of awake but have just had a very bad dream. Most of the dreams are the same—I'm in the middle of a vortex that's spinning through the Milky Way, trying to grab a star or something, and I can't get a grip.

Dr. Kerry lost her shit when my mom said she was taking me to England. I thought we weren't doing anything much in those sessions, but she clearly thinks something else. The adults all came up with a deal that I keep meeting with her twice a week online, and I also have to fill out these stupid daily worksheets, and my mom has some too.

It's claustrophobic, but I'm just glad to get out of Santa Fe. I'll fill out the sheets. Journal on these dumb questions that don't have anything to do with what happened. Gigi says all writing is good practice, and she should know. My great-grandmother has written over a hundred books.

Today's prompt was an easy one: *What is your favorite subject at school? Which one is hard, and why?*

My favorite is English. It is always my favorite, because I love to read and I love words and I love writing. I love everything about it, even the things a lot of people complain about, like poetry and Shakespeare. It's the only class I really miss, and I loved my teacher, Mrs. Willow, who keeps sending me emails with poetry she thinks I'll like. She's the person who made me stay online. Mrs. Willow and Wattpad, which is my secret thing and I've never told a single other person about it. It's a writing site where I can post a chapter a week of my book, and readers comment on it.

My least favorite subject is math, which is dead boring except for Eric Healy, who sits in front of me and is one of the hottest guys in school. He doesn't talk to me. He doesn't pay me any attention at all, actually, but I sit behind him, and he smells so good it makes me dizzy.

Or, really, I *sat* behind him, because I left school. Now my classes are online and they're fine, but it's not like being in school. I kind of hate not being there, but it was too hard to even just walk down the hall and wonder who had seen . . . everything. It felt like I was wearing my skin inside out, and everything hurt. Which isn't even getting to the people who actually know what happened and didn't stop their shit even after . . . all of it.

That's what I'd write on Dr. Kerry's stupid journal sheet if I wanted to tell her what happened, but I don't. Why does anybody think they get to be inside my head? I can't stand to have anybody else digging around my life, in my soul, and that's dramatic, I know, but I hate it.

A bunch of people know what happened to me, and I hate them and hate myself for being so stupid, but the one thing I control is *who else knows*. I choose. Not my mom. It's breaking her heart, but I'm trying to get myself together so she'll stop worrying. I might have told my dad, but his girlfriend is pregnant and she's acting all step-smothery with me already, so no.

I'm not choosing Dr. Thinks She Knows Everything, either, because why should she get to know anything about me at all? And why does *anybody* think telling the story to more people will make it better anyway? I just want to forget about it. That's what I'm going to do here. Forget it. Reboot.

But I have to do those dumb worksheets. So what I actually wrote for Dr. Kerry is this: *My favorite subject at school is English because I love poetry and I love to write. I hate math because it's boring.*

And then I got on Wattpad and wrote another chapter on my story under the only name I've never shared with anybody. No one knows who I am there. It's the only place I'm free.

Chapter Five

Zoe

We woke up in England on Wednesday morning. After breakfast, Lillian wanted to go talk to the constables about Diana, and she wanted my support. In the past we usually walked to the village, but this morning it was spitting rain, and for all that she'd been a champion walker her entire life, the steep grade down to the high street—and even worse, on the way back up—had become too much for her the past couple of years. This new frailty pierced me.

Isabel was still in her room, and I poked my head in. She was cloaked in a blanket and her omnipresent hoodie, laptop open, earphones blocking the world. Mósí, as ever, sat tucked between her arm and her hip, blissfully happy. The fact that Isabel loved that cat so madly was one of the things that gave me comfort. He was her anchor, a living, breathing link to the world.

Dr. Kerry didn't think Isabel was suicidal, but definitely depressed. Every time I thought about it, which was approximately seven thousand times per day, I reviewed one or three or ten of the ideas I'd had that might help her. I imagined her being heckled, pinched, bullied. A prickling pain ran around my lower ribs, electric blue.

Kerry had prescribed a mild antidepressant, which Isabel had resisted until her dad confessed that he, too, had suffered from depression. I hoped it was episodic in her case, that talk therapy and escaping to another country would bring it to an end, but if it turned out to be more, she needed to know there was nothing wrong with treating it medically.

I waved my hand to get her attention. She pulled off her earphones, but I could see she was somewhere distant—I'd seen the expression on my grandmother's face a million times. Present but not exactly. Lost in another world.

"We're going to go down to the village. Do you want to come?"

She shook her head. "I have to talk to Dr. Kerry in twenty minutes."

"Do you want us to wait for you?"

"OMG. No." She rolled her eyes. "Are we seriously going to keep doing this forever?"

Even irritable, unbrushed, and draped in twenty tons of fabric, she was beautiful, equal parts her dashing father and my dazzling mother. My favorite face on the planet. I hated that she was so lost right now, and also holding me so steadfastly at arm's length. "Doing what forever?" I asked, but I knew.

"The mom hover. You're making me claustrophobic!"

"I have reason to be concerned, Isabel. It's my job to make sure you're okay."

She huffed. "I'm doing everything you wanted. Every single thing. I'm going to talk to Dr. Kerry, and we'll be online for an hour. You can check in by text every fifteen minutes. I just don't want to go to the village in the pouring rain and turn my hair into Jupiter."

In Santa Fe, she wore her hair in loose ringlets smoothed with various products, but it frizzed in the English damp. "Okay, sorry. I'm backing off now."

She flashed me a wry half smile.

"We might stop and get scones, if I know Gigi. Do you want me to bring you some back?"

"Yes, please. Those cranberry ones, if they have them."

"Got it." I wanted to go in the room and kiss her on the forehead, but I only lifted a hand. "You know how to reach me."

"I do." She wiggled her fingers. "Bye."

Still, it was hard to turn around, pretend that there wasn't a cord linking us together forever, and leave her in peace.

Just as the door was nearly closed, she said, "Thanks, Mom. I love you."

I smiled and called over my shoulder, as if it were casual, "Love you."

Outside it was quite wet, and it had been a while since I'd driven on the left. I gripped the wheel tightly as we made our way down the zigzagging road from the house to the top of the village and parked there.

I hurried around the car with an open umbrella and held it over Gran's head. She wore a warm cardigan beneath her raincoat, and we both clopped along in our wellies. The umbrella could have protected a small island, so I tucked Lillian's hand into my arm, and we headed into the village proper, her cane providing punctuation.

The view from the top of the high street was one of the best in the whole of Devon, so quintessentially English that Axestowe had three times been named the prettiest village in the country. Thatched buildings tumbled down the cobblestone street to the beach and the sea. Cliffs loomed on either side, the flat tops green and blown free of trees by the harsh winds that blustered through at all times of the year. Fishing boats and rowboats and yachts bobbed in the harbor. Nothing had gone out in this weather.

The tourist trade hadn't yet begun in earnest, but at high summer every parking spot for miles would be filled, the pavement packed with people shopping the quaint and the antique, eating scones and good Devon clotted cream, and getting sunburned in the supposedly mild climate.

Today Lillian was on a mission. The constable's office was tucked away in a little kink of road that dead-ended against a chalky cliff. A stream, filled to the brim, rushed by noisily on its way to the sea. We crossed a tiny bridge and went inside.

The Victorian building felt like a train station, with the same windows and a waiting area, and a big door that presumably led to offices. A woman sat at a desk in a black uniform, her russet-colored hair tightly pinned back. "Good morning, Mrs. Fairchild."

"I would like to see Inspector Hannaford," Lillian said.

"What a surprise," the woman said without any surprise whatsoever. She was middle aged and mild looking, as if she'd faded over time, her lips no longer rosy but not covered by lipstick. "He's not in this morning, I'm afraid." She tucked a manila file into a wire grid. "When's that next book coming out?"

"This is not my imagination, Mary," Lillian snapped. "Diana would not just run off with some man."

"I agree with you. So does the inspector, although you do not seem to be listening. We have all hands on deck for this one—not that it's turning up much of help."

"Oh. Well, then." Lillian folded her hands over her midsection. "Have you met my granddaughter, Zoe? She's Diana's best friend."

"We've met once or twice," Mary said, extending a hand I shook. Her grip was firm and confident. "It's good to see you."

"Thanks, you too. What have you been able to find out?" I asked.

"Very little, unfortunately. Her mother hasn't heard from her, nor any of her friends or the girls at the business."

"Who was the last person to see her?"

Mary pointed with a pen. "Lillian, here. She left her house at four p.m., and no one saw her after that."

"She brought me some meals for the weekend," Lillian said, patting down the already-sharp collar points of her lavender blouse. "A pie and some fresh rolls and butter."

I frowned. "I didn't know she was bringing you meals."

"Oh, yes, for quite some time. Not every meal, but mostly for the weekend."

Again, I felt the hollowness of missing information—both about my grandmother, who needed meals brought to her, and about Diana. Guilt plucked my belly. I should have known more about everything in Diana's life. She was my oldest friend. We had been estranged the past year, it was true, but I had never believed it would be a permanent condition. I assumed we'd have it out at some point, have a big fight over my mother, and one or the other of us—probably her, honestly—would give in, and we'd go on the way we'd always been. Her face flashed across my imagination, her big white teeth, her clear, perfect skin. She had the best laugh of anyone I'd ever known—hearty and whole body.

That I hadn't realized that she'd been making meals for Gran shamed me. At the very least, she should have been paid for the meals. She'd been pouring her heart and soul into her catering business.

"Do you remember if she had a catering job that night?" I asked. "Or maybe a date? She had a new boyfriend, last I heard."

"Last you heard?" Gran echoed. "He was all she talked about for months."

I looked away from her penetrating gaze. "We've been fighting."

"I see." And of all the people in the world, she probably knew exactly what—or rather who—we'd fought about. My mother. "Henry is his name. He's been taking her on the loveliest trips," Gran said. "But he didn't take her out that night. He had a business trip."

"Did she tell you that?" I felt a tiny twist of jealousy that she should know more about my friend than I did. Ridiculous, but there it was.

"How else would I know?" Her tone was a bit sharp. She spoke so directly sometimes that it could wound me, and the sharpness grew more and more pointed the older she got.

To cover my embarrassment, I asked Mary, "Have the police talked to him?"

"We haven't found him, in all honesty. No one seems to have any contact information. Don't suppose you've got a last name?"

I shook my head.

Mary licked a finger and took a paper from a stack. "We're having a gathering at the pub tonight to see if we can turn up any new information." She pressed the flyer on the counter between us.

MISSING: Diana Brooking, the flyer said in bold letters. *Information-gathering meeting at the Rose and Crown, 7 p.m. Wednesday night.*

Her picture, taken from a Facebook post, filled the middle of the page. I missed her acutely, all at once. It was a sunny photo, with her curly hair blowing in some unseen breeze, and she was laughing, showing off her beautiful smile.

I touched the photo, and it was all suddenly real that Diana was not here, as she'd always been before, every minute I'd ever been in England. A new layer of fear and guilt rose in my throat. "Any leads at all?"

Mary shook her head. "Not a thing. That's why we're all gathering. Maybe together we'll make some sense of it."

"I'll be there," I said.

"I'm sorry, my love," Gran said. "I know you've been best friends since childhood."

We hadn't been "best" friends for a while, but that's how things were in a village. What once had been persisted, and she meant it kindly. I nodded, steadied myself, and held out my arm to Gran. "Shall we find a cup of tea?"

"Oh, yes. I could do with a scone."

The rain had stopped, leaving behind wet streets and leaden skies and the kind of light that made every hue of green vibrate at a higher level. I caught my breath at the rolling fields, patchworked between the hedgerows that ran in unstraight lines. Pastures of green and yellow, pale fields of newly planted green, lush deep emerald along the top of the cliffs. Gorse bushes blazed yellow in clumps dotting the landscape as far as the eye could see. "It's beautiful," I said.

"Yes," Gran replied. Her pace was steady but slow, and I consciously matched my steps to hers without making it obvious. She clung to my elbow with confidence. I liked that I made her feel secure.

She paused to look in the window of a shop. The Kitchen Witch was painted a pale, pleasing green between thick, age-dark beams, and the artful window displays invited passersby to step closer.

Which I did. Bottles and jars made of blue or green or turquoise glass held displays of herbs, with dried petals and leaves in thick piles around them. I could identify spears of lavender, spearmint, and perhaps rue, along with fronds of chamomile and snapdragon, rosemary and great blowsy roses in dark-blue jars.

I wanted urgently to paint it: such a surprising and loud demand that I was startled. "Hang on, Gran. I want to take a picture." I pulled out my phone and shot the display from several directions. "This place is new," I commented.

"Less than a year," Lillian said.

"I see." I moved to the second window. This one had stacks of old wooden boxes and bags of tea with whimsical animals—hares and owls and foxes peeking out from beneath a pile of faux grass—and a row of various natural cosmetics. It was as artful and lovely as the other window display, and I shot a few photos of this one too. "Have you been in?"

Her face was blank. "Not really my sort of place, is it?"

I smiled. "I suppose not." But I made a mental note to bring Isabel back here. She would like it—all the crystals and fairies. It was exactly her sort of place.

Just as I was holding out my arm for my grandmother, a woman came into view behind the counter of the shop.

An ancient sense of loss howled somewhere in the far reaches of my brain, paralyzing me.

She wore a white tunic embroidered in white, over loose trousers, and long strings of uneven amber beads around her neck. Thick dark hair fell in tumbles of curls down her back and framed a smooth white oval of a face dominated by enormous eyes. The hair was lustrous as ever, the face unlined, and I knew the eyes were palest blue. She stood there, waiting, completely still.

For a moment I stared at her. My mother.

She was older, *so* much older. It wasn't that her skin was wrinkled or her hair turning white, though I could see it was salt and pepper, but her body had softened from voluptuous to generous, and her jawline was not so sharp. That faraway howling took long moments to fade, and then it took another long moment to cloak myself with indifference, but I managed, pulling the tatters of fury and loss and invisibility around me.

Then I tucked my grandmother's hand—the hand of my *true* mother—into my elbow, and we walked on.

"You're going to have to forgive her someday," Lillian said matter-of-factly.

"Will I?"

"You're as stubborn as your father."

"Mmm."

"It hasn't brought him any joy."

That was true enough. He lived alone on the outskirts of Santa Fe, tending a small flock of sheep and goats the same way his family had done for centuries, and drove into town daily to work his joyless but solid construction job. He loved Isabel, and they spent a lot of time together, but she was the only thing in his life that gave him genuine pleasure. Once, he'd been a gifted sculptor, but he'd given it up in the storm that followed my mother leaving him and returned home to New Mexico and the world he understood. He, too, had wounded the child I was, but at least he hadn't left me.

I shrugged. "Let's get some tea."

We ducked into a café called the Steaming Pot, with a charming mullioned window. I was surprised to find it busy at this odd hour. "Doesn't anyone work?" I asked, brushing rain off my hair.

"Hello, Lillian!" called a plump woman in a fluting voice. "Right there by the window, if you like, my dear."

My grandmother lifted a dignified hand, and we made our way through the crowded space. Gran paused twice to greet someone, a graying couple in hiking pants, hats hung on the backs of their chairs, and a youngish woman in jeans. We settled at a narrow two-top next to the window. It gave a long view of the street and hills beyond. "Do you ever write here?" I asked.

"Oh, no," she said, lowering herself carefully, leaning hard on the cane and the back of the chair. "I only write in my study. I love to sit here, though, and watch the people."

"Tourists?"

"And locals too." She set her stick aside, leaning the carved beauty against the wall. "Everyone in town passes by during the course of a day. Mothers take their children to school. The farmers bring their goods to the market."

I smiled. The secret to Lady Dawood's success was the power of her observations. "One must simply keep one's eyes open," I quoted, a phrase her character used in her mild way.

Gran's eyes narrowed. "Are you mocking me?"

"No! Not at all." I covered her hand. "Just making connections. That is what you do, isn't it? Keep your eyes open?"

"Well, yes. By observing my world carefully, I populate *her* world." She raised an eyebrow. "No one takes her seriously either."

"I take you seriously, Gran. Always have and always will."

"Thank you."

A girl came to the table with an iridescent ceramic teapot and a mismatched teacup and saucer, one with pink roses scrolling around it, the other blue. "Good morning, Mrs. Fairchild. Here's your tea. Would you like a scone? We have orange this morning."

"Oh, yes, dear, that would be lovely."

"And you?" The girl turned to me. "Tea?"

"Yes, please. Ceylon if you have it, and a scone as well. Plenty of Devon cream, if you will."

"Are you . . ." She tipped her head. "Australian?"

The accent confused anyone who heard it—Americans heard it as English, while the English guessed Australian or South African or any number of things. "American," I said, smiling. "I'm her granddaughter."

"Oh, I see! How nice." She tucked her order pad in her pocket. "I'll be right back."

I leaned in. "Tell me what you know, Gran. About Diana. And you keep saying something is going on in the village. What do you think it might be?"

She glanced to her right, into the room, then leaned in and said quietly, "I've been noticing new people around, and a lot of activity in the bay." She frowned. "Which I realize is vague, but it's a vague feeling. Something is not quite right."

"If you had to guess?"

"The cliffs are filled with caves and passageways and all sorts of pathways. It's always been a smuggler's paradise."

"I remember that." I watched as she removed the lid of her teapot and swirled the leaves within. "Isn't there a passageway to the manor?"

"It's closed off now, but there was. It leads right down to the sea on the other side of Hyrne Rock." A spindly finger of rock that stuck up out of the sea, creating a cove and semicircle of beach in front of a cave.

"What did the family smuggle?"

"All sorts of things. Brandy and arms and coin."

"Coin?"

"It still washes up on occasion," Gran said, "from a pair of galleons that wrecked eons ago, Spanish, though I suppose in those days they

33

didn't much care what government the coin belonged to—'twas all gold and silver."

The girl brought my pot, this one slightly tarnished, with pale-orange glazing on the cup and saucer. The plate of scones matched nothing else, with a woven pattern of canes around the edge. It made me wish to collect dishes again, a habit I'd fallen into as a young teen who haunted antique stores for china cups and saucers. I had imagined I'd furnish some future kitchen with them, and I wondered now what I'd done with them all.

"What do you think they're smuggling now?"

"Any number of things, I suppose." She moved her cup in a circle on its saucer. "Most likely drugs, wouldn't you suppose?"

"That's the obvious answer."

She poured a tablespoon of tea into her cup and examined it. Satisfied by the color, she poured a full measure, topped it off with milk, and with small tongs dropped in two sugar cubes. It made me think of Diana, who had loved sugar cubes from the time we were very small. She'd steal them from everywhere, since no one in the commune where we lived approved of sugar. No sugar, no coffee or black tea, nothing "unnatural," and our mothers baked fresh whole-grain bread every day. I can still get homesick for that bread if I smell a particular yeasty aroma.

Gran gestured across the street, where two fit white-haired men emerged from a building. "That's the yacht club," she said. "Douglas Wills is the commodore there. His wife is one of the Luscombe girls. I think you went to school with Gina Luscombe, didn't you? They're all such beautiful redheads."

I remembered Gina, a skinny girl with swinging red hair as smooth as the coats of her horses. We'd run in different circles.

Wills passed directly by the windows, a vigorous seventy-some-thing, with the sheen of wealth in his carefully cut hair and crisp pale trousers. Gran narrowed her eyes. "I've always wondered what he did with the first wife. She just disappeared. He always said she'd left him for another man, but just to completely disappear?"

"What?" I asked. "Murder?"

"You never know, do you?"

I had to admit that much was true in the Lady Dawood novels, but I hoped it wasn't true now. "I suppose you don't." With a sharp pain, I thought again of Diana, bustling around her perfectly orderly kitchen in a black turtleneck sweater that showed off her blonde hair. "I hope Diana is all right."

"As do I, my dear." She sipped tea delicately, settled the cup again on the saucer. "As do I."

"Has she been bringing you food for long?"

"Oh, for months. She didn't tell you?"

"No." I said this looking away from her, peering into the hilly distance in an attempt to hide my sense of guilt. "I mean, mostly we've been exchanging recipes and jokes, that kind of thing. But you'd think she would have mentioned it."

"Perhaps she didn't want to worry you. You've had a lot on your plate this past year."

I stirred my tea. "I guess. But she knows how I worry about you."

"I shouldn't fret, Zoe. It was only a good deed. She liked to cook, and I need a bit of help these days."

Maybe if we'd actually talked the past few months, rather than exchanging surface-level jokes and recipes, I would have heard more. "What did you two do that day? The day she disappeared?"

"We had tea and toast, and then she went back to town to do some cooking."

"Did she have a catering job that evening?"

"I don't know, really, but one supposes she would on a Friday night."

I nodded. "I'm sure the police checked her business logs and reservations."

"Undoubtedly."

"I wish I could see those logs," I said, watching as a girl with a backpack as big as a car struggled up the hill. "I wonder if they'd let me. Maybe I could piece together things they don't know."

Lillian gazed in the distance, her eyes as pale as cornflowers. "I wrote a book about a caterer once. It was set during the war." She paused. "I always wanted to go up in those balloons."

The non sequitur caught my attention. Gran had been a child in London during the war, moving from place to place with her peripatetic mother. I'd always thought she carried a massive amount of PTSD, but she didn't like to be coddled. Stiff upper lip and all that. "Barrage balloons?" I asked to encourage her. "What's making you think of them today?"

"I don't quite know." She frowned, her papery skin folding in soft new arrangements as she peered toward the horizon. "Perhaps it's something to do with the weather."

I frowned, watching her face. "Maybe."

When we were in the car on the way back home, I asked Gran if she'd mind if we stopped at the Tesco. "I'd like to get some things for Isabel."

"I might wait in the car, if you wouldn't mind."

"If you're tired, I can take you home first and come back down."

"Don't be silly." She yawned. "I'll nap like a proper old woman and will never even know you're gone."

So I left her in the car and hurried into the supermarket, halting just inside to get my bearings and remember how things were arranged here. It wasn't a massive store like the Albertsons in Santa Fe, acres of gleaming floors with offerings of everything under the sun. This one was more compact, only six or seven aisles, which made it easier for me to zip around to find cereal she would eat, and bananas, and almond milk and margarine, though it came packaged much more glamorously than the margarine of my youth, when everyone wanted butter, butter, butter. Isabel was insistently vegetarian, and even when she ate all day, it never seemed to be enough calories for her long, lanky frame. I gathered sweet potatoes and broccoli and piles of fruit, then swung around the freezer section to seek out whatever appropriate vegetarian fare they might stock.

A man in a dun-colored Carhartt jacket had his back to me. He opened one of the freezers and pulled out a stack of frozen savory pies. I waited politely.

"Sorry," he said over his shoulder, in the way of someone sensing the presence of another person. "I'll be right out of your way." Then he paused, stack of boxes in his hands. "Zoe?"

Damn. It was always like this the first few days, running into someone every five minutes whom I hadn't seen in ages, but to face my mother and my old boyfriend within hours was a lot. I should have recognized those curls and made a detour. Another person I've let down. "Hello, Cooper."

We didn't hug or any of the things I might have done with an old friend and lover in America. Instead, we stood safely on either side of our baskets, staring. Or at least I was staring, because as long as he'd been on the earth, Sage Cooper had been ridiculously, strikingly beautiful. When he was a boy, people stopped to take photos of him, captured by the masses of long blond curls falling around an angelically beautiful face.

Now his soft cheeks had dissolved to reveal angular cheekbones and a clean-shaven jaw, and he'd grown quite remarkably tall, but the hair was the same—loose blond curls he wore longer than was fashionable. I could smell the meadow-and-spice scent of him, which raised a sense of yearning that swamped me before I could tamp it down—not only for him, but for the moors and wild ponies and the owls hooting in the trees, a landscape unlike any other.

I found my voice. "How are you?" He'd lost his wife of three years to breast cancer eighteen months before, and although I'd sent a sympathy card (just as I'd sent a congratulations card upon his marriage), I'd not run into him on my last trip home.

"Well enough," he said. "You?"

"I came as soon as I heard about Diana. Gran and I have just been to see the police."

He placed the boxes of pies in his cart and turned back. Never many words, this one, only the sentences he found most worth uttering. He looked at me directly, taking me in, allowing me the chance to do the same. We had meant a lot to each other once upon a time. All three of us, Diana, Cooper, and I, had been part of the commune our parents had lived in on an ancient acreage that Cooper had turned back to its original purpose—raising sheep and sheepherding dogs. The farm had belonged to his family.

I couldn't remember a time before his appearance in my life, and I also couldn't imagine bridging the gulf that had lived between us for two decades. "I miss her," he said simply. "The village seems too quiet without her."

"Me too," I said.

He swallowed. "Will I see you at the pub later?"

I nodded.

"Good." He steered his cart away, around the corner, and was gone.

For one moment I allowed myself to feel the waves of grief that washed over me, grief unresolved after the loss of him, grief that our friend was missing, and—*oh, please let her be okay!*—grief over all the things that happened to a person who grew up and had to live in the world.

Chapter Six
Poppy

I'd seen Zoe pausing to admire my shop windows before she saw me. I took special care with the window displays, listening to my intuition to make each one something beautiful and inviting, not only to bring in the tourists who would soon be thronging the village but also to call those who needed me—or rather just someone to hear them, see them. My tools were tarot and rituals and crystals, but my main gift was for listening.

Like every mortal being, I had to have cash for food and shelter, for clothing and the odd pleasure, but my purpose in the shop was to be a magnet for those in pain, those seeking an outlet, relief. Hope. Humans were such fragile beings, each and every one. It had taken me a lifetime to learn that simple truth.

Zoe was fragile, too, though she'd always pretended she was not. I'd seen photos of her, of course. It wasn't hard to find photos of Zoe Fairchild, the wife of the singer/songwriter Martin Riley. In those photos, she always looked a bit apprehensive, holding her big husband's hand as he swept through one crowd or another.

As she peered through the windows of the Kitchen Witch, I had a chance to see her as she was. Looking much younger than her nearly forty years, her father's straight satiny hair sweeping down her back, cut straight across as if by a ruler, which gave it swing and flow. Such lovely, lovely hair, black as obsidian. It would be cool against my hands.

If she'd been anyone else, I would have waited for her to enter, knowing she needed to tell a story, to explore the contents of her soul, release the sorrows she carried.

But not Zoe. Once she saw me, she'd flee. I watched her with a sense of longing so enormous that it emptied my lungs. She looked well. Beautiful, and so much like her father that it gave me a pang. I'd fallen hard for him, long ago when my heart was wide open and my hungers as wild and fierce as the landscape where I found him. He had seemed carved of the desert itself, with his straight, high-bridged nose and black hair.

Zoe looked at me with his eyes, dark as the new moon, and I saw she'd still not forgiven me. That perhaps she never would.

Oh, Zoe. My Zoe.

She turned away and offered her arm to my mother, who gave me a faint smile as Zoe marched her away.

"What about the tourmaline?" a woman inside the shop asked now, tapping on the glass cupboard where I kept semiprecious stones.

"That's one possibility," I said. "Will you be wearing the necklace for any particular purpose?"

"No." Her tone was so defensive it edged on hostile. "I just want something beautiful."

Pain seeped out of her pores, almost visible if you knew how to look. It made her neck tight and stiffened her joints. She was in her late forties, with a sleek swinging pageboy of glossy brown, and she wore her sunglasses on top of her head. American, though I hadn't caught that at first. She carried some extra weight, but not so much it would burden her. I stood on the other side of the counter, waiting.

"Okay," I said mildly. "Let me see your eyes."

She raised her gaze.

"Lovely," I said quietly and then lifted a hand, letting it hover close to her cheek. "Do you mind if I touch your head?"

She shrugged, but she didn't flinch when I opened my palm over her crown chakra and gently rested it there. So much roiling emotion!

It wasn't magic or new age or anything of that nature. It was only letting myself feel her pain. "Have you lost someone recently?"

"Not to death," she said, and her face sagged. "To another woman."

I nodded. "A big loss."

"We were married twenty-seven years. Happily!" A sudden shimmer of tears brightened her irises to turquoise. "I just want to fix it."

"Mmm." A sudden image of a shattered vase came to mind. Vase and hammer. "Maybe let it be for a while." From the case, I took a moonstone necklace. The gem was elegantly mounted in the body of a tree made of pewter, and it was designed to land exactly in the middle of the upper chest. "Moonstone represents female power. If you wear this for a month, every day, you'll reclaim yourself."

Her hope blazed, and she reached for the necklace. "May I try it on?"

"Of course. Let me help you." As I fastened the clasp, I added another layer of suggestion. The art of healing mental pain was to believe it could be vanquished. "It will warm against your skin. Do you feel it? That's the energy."

Her fingers stroked the piece. "Yes."

"Good. Why don't you wear it for a little while?" Another layer of suggestion. "Look around the shop and see how it feels?"

The woman touched the moonstone around her neck again and again as she browsed the herbs, the shelves of teas for sorrow and potions for hope, and crystals and wands to call energies or heal some physical ill. Each time she touched the necklace, she almost visibly straightened just a little more, the slump of sorrow easing its grip on her.

I'd studied with gurus and monks and nuns, healers of all ilk across the world, and the best advice was all the same: listening was the thing that could cure most ills, mind or body.

No magic. Only listening.

As I busied myself behind the counter sorting empty fabric bags into various sizes, I flashed on Zoe at age five, arranging plastic beads into designs on a table. Must have been at the farm, that long wooden table where we'd all gathered in the evenings to eat lentil soup and fresh bread and tea brewed in gallon jars using herbal infusions and honey. Three families had gathered together on Will Cooper's family farm: Ben and Zoe and me; Will and his wife, Aline, and Sage; and Diana and her mother, Joan, with a series of men who didn't stick. A few others came in and out over the six years we lived there, from the time Zoe was a year old until she was seven.

Until she was seven. When I left her.

Discomfort bloomed between my ribs. I pushed it away and turned to the memory of her arranging those plastic beads on the table, at first like with like, all red and all yellow and all blue. Then red and yellow in a row, and blue with red with yellow. Sage brought in wooden blocks in more colors, and the two of them wove color with shape to create a mosaic of fields full of flowers that took my breath away. Ben was not his best self by then, drinking and smoking weed way too much to fill the hole left by being away from home, away from the landscape that grounded him. He came through the room, high on weed, and stopped. "This is good, you guys." He touched one finger to the uneven yellow beads representing flowers. "Better be careful, or the goats will think it's breakfast."

So long ago, I thought, returning to the sorting in front of me. And two minutes ago, like all of time. Our lives bent and twisted around themselves, and we never knew where the connections really were. Like sweet Diana, grown up and a bit lost, coming to me for readings in the shop, and Sage wandering in to ask about herbal remedies for the eczema that plagued his hands in the wintertime: so that two of the children from those happy years had been attracted to my realm. Even Zoe had stopped, admiring my windows before she knew they were mine.

Patience, patience. She would have to come to me. There was no other way.

Diana walked through my mind again, and a thorn pricked my heart. I'd seen trouble in her cards, the Tower, never reversed as one would hope; and the Moon; and the Shadow in my Celtic deck. She also drew the Lovers and Cups and all manner of cheering cards, so I focused there. She was so in love with her mysterious man. It glowed in her rosy cheeks and the dewiness of a woman having plenty of sex after a period of drought. It was hard to find the link between those dark cards and the joy that dripped from her, but she would not have been the first woman to have been hoodwinked by a man.

Witness the sorrowing woman here in my shop. She wandered back to me, two fingers resting on the moonstone at her throat. Already the energy around her was less agitated. The power of suggestion could cure a great many emotional ills. "I'll take the necklace, please."

I nodded. "Be right there."

It was only then that I spied a tarot card half-hidden beneath the edge of the counter. I slid it out with my foot and picked it up. It was from the Everyday Tarot, a simple deck with clear shapes, and the one Diana liked. It was the Tower, probably the very card she'd drawn the last time she was in the shop. A faint shudder sped down my spine. Warning. Or fear.

Where are you, Diana?

Chapter Seven

Zoe

Gran retreated to her bedroom for a nap when we returned. I put the groceries away in the cavernous pantry and double-wide American-style fridge. Isabel had texted me a little while ago to say she was going for a walk, which displayed about one hundred times the amount of energy she'd shown the past few weeks. It gave me a thread of hope. Maybe the wild Devon coast and the mysterious woods of my childhood would help heal her. Nature had that power at times.

My visit to Gran had been much overdue, as well. Our long chat this morning in the tea shop warmed me. I sometimes forgot just how old she'd become. Not just aging or elderly, but genuinely, undeniably old. Spending time with her should have been one of my highest priorities. How did such awareness get lost in the dailiness of things? I was grateful for the reminder.

The kitchen smelled of the dinner cooking in the Rayburn that warmed the room. A bank of windows looked to the garden tucked on the leeward side of the manor, and in the soft gray light May flowers glowed.

Feeling the drag of sadness and exhaustion, I wandered out in a sweater and wellies and allowed myself to rest my thoughts and heart in the old perennial garden where I'd spent so much of my childhood.

A drift of Queen Anne's lace fluttered against the wall, and a bank of poppies was just beginning to bud. Pinkish-purple rhododendrons had taken over an area beneath a cluster of trees near the man-made pond that shimmered silver in the breeze. A pair of blue butterflies danced from flower to flower.

I plucked stray weeds out of a patch of primroses, and some grass out of the border, feeling my nerves ease. I'd learned to garden at my grandmother's knee, following her around or playing nearby in the grass with my little family of dolls. By the time I was five, she'd allowed me a little space of my own, where I grew peas and coleus. Later, it grew to an entire section of annuals, whatever took my fancy each spring. Gran encouraged me to experiment, and I wholeheartedly did so—orange marigolds with purple phlox, daisies with foxglove. I loved the brightest flowers I could find, in outlandish combinations.

I found that space now, lying fallow as though it awaited my hands. For a moment, I considered what I might plant. Maybe Isabel would like having a garden spot of her own, though she'd never been inclined back in Santa Fe, where gardening was an extreme sport. Heat, violent rainstorms with lightning and hail, and the short season made many of my English favorites impossible, but I'd planted our courtyard anyway, with cosmos and tickseed and dahlias that would grow nearly as large as they did here.

Santa Fe seemed very far away as I came out of the shelter of the house, lured by the sea view. As I walked toward the bench beneath a twisted tree on the high cliff, I was glad of my sweater. Clouds hung low over the restless waves, heavy with more rain. I sat on the bench and looked out over the view I knew so intimately, taking comfort in its sameness—the sea, the little harbor against the cliffs on the other side, the tumble of the village in between. Diana and I had sat here often during childhood, sorting out problems, dreaming of the future, commiserating.

Without her, I felt slightly dizzy. She'd not been my anchor for a long time, but the world seemed off kilter if I couldn't just send her a text and get a reply. It felt . . . lonely.

Which was ironic, considering how little actual communication we'd had over the past year. I had been so very angry with her when she'd simply become friends with my mother as if nothing had ever happened, as if she were just a kooky lady back in the village after her travels. I had felt insanely betrayed.

Just as my mother had betrayed me. And Martin. Now Diana, who knew intimately how I'd felt about the other two. She'd listened to me cry about my mother a thousand times when we were children, and I'd leaned hard on her when I found out about Martin's affair.

But she'd been angry when I accused her of betrayal. "No one can betray you, Zoe, because you won't let anyone close enough."

I'd been too angry to even reply.

Now, I slipped my phone out of my pocket and pulled up the long, long text message thread between us, looking for anything that might help me make sense of her disappearance. With a sense of guilt, I saw that our texts in the past six or eight months had been limited to very stilted exchanges over surface things.

Two weeks ago, before she'd disappeared, we'd been talking a bit about a new movie coming out, and exercise, and recipes. She'd landed two more accounts, regulars, and was delighted by the influx of catering jobs after years of building the business, referral by referral.

I scrolled backward, looking for the first mention of her new boyfriend. I had to reload four times before it showed up, six months ago.

Met someone. We've been out three times and I think he really likes me as much as I like him!

Really?

Name's Henry. Met him when he came in to book catering for a retirement party for one of the yacht club boys.

It's a nice name.

He lives in London. Travel agent of a sort. Divorced, long time. Pretty eyes. Good smile. He's a bit older.

A bit older? How much older? At the time, I'd hesitated over how to respond to that. I'd been sitting at my desk at work in an open-concept office, a new design I honestly hated, exchanging texts surreptitiously while I pretended to design a logo for a new account. Diana had not had the best luck with men. In all other areas of life she had remarkably good judgment, but she'd been plump since youngest childhood, and her mother—a bone-skinny woman who seemed only to smoke cigarettes endlessly and never inhale a single calorie—had ridden her endlessly about it. I suffered with Diana as her mother put her on one diet after another: soup for weeks, or no fat at all. Whatever the latest craze was.

Gran hated it. When she came to my house, Gran fed her all she could eat—making crumbles with custard and special tea cakes, but also healthful meals balanced with the copious vegetables Gran loved to grow. Every variety of vegetable known to womankind—turnips and spinach and potatoes and asparagus and every other thing she could grow or others grew. As a child in the war, she'd learned to eat mainly vegetables, and she'd never lost her love for them. She passed the passion on to both Diana and me, and even now we traded recipes for the best vegetable dishes we discovered.

But all the diets and the vegetables in the world never made her into the slim swan her mother wanted, and instead she grew into a classic curvy countrywoman. She was always slightly apologetic about it. In recent years she'd taken up long walks on the South West Coast

Path, which ran right through the village—in fact, my feet practically touched it from my perch on the bench—and had toned up, dropped a few pounds, and whittled her waist a little. The main effect was that exercise gave her a sense of love for her body, which made her open to the idea that others could love it as well.

But what did "a bit older" mean? And did it even matter?

I'd texted back:

Have fun.

We're going to Lyme Regis sailing on Sunday.

She had sent a slightly out-of-focus picture of a man with thick hair and a cheery smile, completely ordinary, a little beefy but fine. I would have to show it to the police.

I had not replied. The terseness—the *meanness*—of my responses to her happy texts now made me feel ashamed of myself.

The final text in the line was the one I'd sent the night Gran called:

Hey, is everything okay? Gran is worried about you. Text me back when you get this.

It hung there, unanswered, like a warning signal. It made me feel hollow.

As if I could nag her into replying, I texted now:

I miss you. I'm home and you're not here and I'm worried.

Henry. I wondered if he'd been looking for her since she disappeared, and if anyone would know that. Had any of her friends met him?

Not that I suspected him of wrongdoing. He had seemed quite devoted, by Diana's accounts, surprising her with presents, talking to her at length about all sorts of ideas, making her laugh.

I scrolled through texts, looking for anything that might seem strange. It was all as ordinary as porridge—walks by the sea, meals consumed in her little house or on drives to neighboring villages. He wasn't in town every week, but he came at least once a month, usually twice. Several times he'd taken her on a luxurious outing—the sailing in Lyme Regis, a country inn for a long weekend, that kind of thing. It made him seem as if he had some money, which wouldn't be terrible for my friend.

To my shame, I'd only responded to one out of five texts, but she, valiantly loyal, kept texting me. For a year.

What a wretched friend I was!

Out of the corner of my eye, I caught movement and turned to see my daughter climbing the hill from the opposite direction from the house. She looked so small against the vast, dramatic landscape—a tiny figure against the big sky and endless sea and treacherous cliffs—that my heart caught in my throat. My baby.

I had not given much thought to children. Unlike many of my friends, I hadn't played with dolls or cooed over the faces of tiny babies in the streets. When I lived with my dad in Santa Fe between the ages of twelve and fifteen, I sometimes liked to play with my little cousins, but they didn't make me want to hurry up and get pregnant and have a bundle of my own. They were cute enough, but my heart didn't thrill to them. I liked nature and art and the sea.

Martin and I had only been married for six months when I found myself pregnant. When he wasn't touring, we lived in a bungalow near Old Town in Santa Fe, an adobe with thick red walls and a kiva fireplace in one corner of the tiny living room, where we burned mesquite and pine and roasted marshmallows and played with Simba, who was one of the most adorable puppies who ever lived, all roly-poly furriness and floppy shepherd ears. Often we made love, and on one of those deliri-ously happy nights, Isabel was conceived.

I knew almost instantly. Within a day, I could feel the presence of her, an Other, a Being. At first I thought I was just being fanciful, and anyway, Martin had left on tour for a two-month gig through the clubs of the Midwest. I wouldn't bother him with my suspicions until I knew for sure.

In those early days, when I didn't know and could just wander through the possibilities, I loved the idea of a child. Martin's child, who would be a multitude of bloodlines, English and Dineh, West African from Martin's father, and Swedish from his mother. I hugged the secret close.

But I also fretted. Martin was only two years older than me, and he was ambitious. Maybe he would be dismayed. Maybe it would change things between us. Maybe—

Maybe I would be a terrible mother, like my mother had been. It seemed that there was a coldness at the center of my being, a place that no one touched—not Martin or my father or my gran. Not even Cooper had reached it, although he'd tried.

In those days, I'd edged back toward painting after my big disgrace at Glasgow, and I kept a studio in the crumbling garage at the back of the yucca-studded bare-dirt backyard. For the first week after Isabel arrived in my body, I painted madly, giant flowers and sunscapes and windows.

One afternoon as I cleaned my brushes, I realized that I should not have been standing there inhaling turpentine with a baby in my belly. In fact, I really should not have been in there at all, with so many chemicals and poisons. A wave of terror washed through me, and I hurried out of the garage and closed the door. More than two years later, when we moved to a much nicer place thanks to Martin's increasing success, I had not been back. We had the movers pack everything anyway, but the boxes lived, undisturbed, until I gave the usable bits away to a local school.

I don't know why. I thought about it sometimes. Thought about my longing, the way it felt to stand and paint something, moving freely, my entire brain alight with color and hue and brushstrokes. I often looked through the adult education offerings at the local community college and imagined how I'd fit them into my schedule. Somehow, I never found the time.

But Isabel. Isabel. The day she was born, my life turned upside down. One look into her tiny face with her squished little nose and headful of blackest hair, and my heart was no longer my own, as if it had leapt out of my chest and into hers and I'd never get it back.

Her dad was as besotted as I was. No child had ever been so universally, thoroughly adored. She was the best of both of us: those big eyes and rosebud lips, the length of her fingers and the coral tone of her skin. I could not believe my good fortune.

Those early days with my daughter, when I was lost in a sea of adoration and perfect wonder, were among the happiest of my life. I had no need of painting. I'd created the most perfect thing I'd ever make. All I wanted was to keep her safe and smooth a path for her to follow toward joy and love and accomplishment.

And now she'd been bullied in some horrific way.

It was impossible to keep a child completely safe, I knew that, and I'd done everything a mother possibly could, or at least everything I'd thought of, but something terrible had happened to her anyway. She swore she'd not been sexually assaulted, but that was all I'd been able to get out of her. No matter from which direction I'd come at the problem, all I'd been able to discover was that she'd been bullied on social media. No one knew more than that, none of the other parents, none of her teachers. I even cornered one of her friends, Katrina, at a basketball game I'd attended for that express purpose, but she'd stonewalled me with her chirpy, chipper smiles.

Isabel had refused to go to school and then enrolled in the online school, which she seemed to like well enough. I had begun to worry what the summer would bring. She couldn't stay locked up in the house wearing a hoodie in ninety-degree heat. I'd worried that she might be hiding evidence of cutting or drugs, but once in a while, she arrived in the kitchen in only a T-shirt. Her arms were the same as always.

As she came closer, I saw that her expression was very peaceful, and although she *was* draped in a hundred pounds of black hoodie, like a goth version of Little Red Riding Hood, her step was lighter. She swung her arms widely, a return to an unselfconscious way of moving that I hadn't seen in at least a month.

She dropped down on the bench beside me. "Hey."

"Hi. Been for a walk?"

"Yeah. There's a forest down there that's got about a billion flowers. It's really pretty."

I smiled. "Bluebells."

"Is that what they are? I want to go back and take pictures, but—"

She was a budding photographer with a genuinely good eye, and her father had bought her a beautiful camera and an array of lenses last Christmas. Just before everything started falling apart in her life. "So why don't you?"

Her joy slid away, and she gave a one-shouldered shrug. "I deleted all my accounts."

"You don't have to *post* pictures to enjoy them."

"But what would I *do* with them?"

"Make art? Enjoy the process?"

Another shrug. "It's like they're not real unless other people see them."

"Mmm." I thought about my paintings, especially when I'd begun to imagine I might be a fine artist, and how desperately I'd wanted to have other people look at them and enjoy them. It was part of the drive of making art. "What if you made up a new name and started a new account?"

For a moment, she was still. Considering. Then she shook her head. "Maybe." She twisted her mouth. "Or not. Maybe I want an analog life."

I nodded, wondering if I should take this moment to ask again what had happened. At that exact instant she pulled her sleeves down over her hands and huddled closer into the hoodie, like a turtle withdrawing. Maybe she was remembering.

I touched her arm gently, then let go. "Millions of people survived without digital for a long, long time," I said lightly. "They managed to make art anyway."

She didn't answer, and I looked back out to the view of the sea. Maybe this would be the rebellion of the new generation—they'd go analog to reject the dehumanization of digital.

I took a breath, smelling salt and damp earth and the fishy scent of the sea, and my body eased. Against the tossing gunmetal gray of the waves, clouds scudded north, bubbles and skeins, and the wind blew over my face, my ears, tossed my hair. For the first time in months I didn't think. Just existed.

And beside me, Isabel grew still too. We simply sat for a long time letting nature heal whatever she could reach in each of us.

At last, Isabel said, "I'm getting cold."

"Me too." We stood, brushing off our butts. "I have to go to the pub for a meeting about Diana after supper. Do you want to go with me?"

"Is this one of those things where you want me to go but you won't force me?"

"No. I just thought you might want to be there."

"I didn't really know her. And I have some ideas I want to play with about the forest."

"Yeah?" A curl escaped her hoodie and blew against her cheek. I restrained myself from tucking it back in. "What kind of ideas?"

She lifted a shoulder, staring off toward the sea. That expression again. Here but not here. "Not ready for sharing."

"Okay. Let me know when you are."

"I will."

For a few more breaths, I allowed myself to look at her profile. Maybe coming here was the best idea so far.

"Stop, Mom," she said, not looking at me.

I laughed softly. "I can't help it. You're wearing my favorite face."

She rolled her eyes, but a slight smile flashed over her mouth. "You are so corny it's embarrassing."

I leaned back, pleased by the normality of her reactions. "It's my job."

It would always be my job.

Chapter Eight

Isabel

Dr. Kerry says I should be getting some exercise. Something about endorphins or serotonin or one of those brain chemicals that get out of balance. I talked to her through the computer, and it was kind of harder and kind of easier. She asked a bunch of simple questions, like how was the plane and what's it like in England, and it wasn't terrible.

But it's weird that our faces are so big. She has eyes like laser beams, and I don't want her using x-ray vision on my brain.

She's been saying all along that I should get exercise, and I didn't want to at home because of . . . well, I didn't want to see anybody. But here nobody knows me, so I promised her today I'd take a walk.

I just went wherever, walking along a trail by Gigi's house that goes all the way around this part of England, for, like, five hundred miles, all along the cliffs. You see people with backpacks on it all the time, and I saw a couple today, older than my mom, with big battered packs. Each one nodded at me, and I nodded back, wondering what it would feel like to walk five hundred miles.

The trail leads down into the valley, and I walked along the river watching some birds fishing and swimming. A sign, like a cartoon sign made of wood, pointed toward the village in one direction, the beach behind me, the South West Coast Path, and then the Drengas Hill Fort.

I was thinking it would be a fort like in New Mexico, a big wooden or adobe thing, but it wasn't like that at all.

It was just trees and flowers. Amazing, gigantic, old trees and a whole carpet of tiny blue flowers. They looked like they were floating over the grass, and it was so beautiful and quiet that it made my heart hurt. I wandered in, trying to stay off the flowers, and it felt like it was enchanted, like a fairy-tale place where you could cross through a portal if you knew where to look. The trees seemed alive, like human alive, as if they were talking to each other behind my back, making expressions.

We don't have trees like that in New Mexico.

I wandered over to one that was ancient, as wide as four people, covered in soft moss. I pressed my hands to it like it was the standing stones in *Outlander*, and I might fall through time to find my true love. It felt like moss and bark, cool, but also like something lived inside of it, something running like a river. I looked up through the branches, and there was a whole roof of leaves with this beautiful light on them, making everything in the meadow look a soft yellow-green.

It was crazy. I'd never seen a place like that before. It looked like a forest in a Disney movie, the arms of the trees wearing green felt and their leaves like long hair, like they could just go for a walk. I sat down by the foot of the Mother Tree and leaned against it and felt safe for the first time in ages. I closed my eyes and imagined there were fairies peeking out around the roots, talking to each other about this person who understood them.

As I sat there, I had a whole idea for a new book. It fell right out of the trees, a story about a girl in a forest and a magical door to a new place, and a journey to complete a quest. It was practically whole, like it had just been waiting for me to be still. I sat there and let it fill me up, every corner of my brain and body.

That was what I was thinking about as I walked home and as I sat with my mom looking at the ocean. This new idea and the people in it and how to start it.

In my room, with Mósí sitting beside me, I started a new file on Wattpad. Private, for the moment, because people don't like it if you leave them hanging for too long.

But I started, because ideas are the most fun part, and sometimes if I don't get them out, they'll follow me around like little puppies.

The thought makes me laugh. I'll have to ask Gigi if that's how it is for her, stories following her around. Maybe I'll even ask my dad. He writes songs. It must be kind of the same.

He's all awkward with me right now. His girlfriend is pregnant, maybe that's why, which is what Dr. Kerry asked me to think about, but I think he doesn't know what to say to me after everything. Even though he doesn't know anything, really. Nobody does. And I'm not going to tell them. It's my business.

Chapter Nine

Zoe

I was nervous walking down to the pub, my stomach reminding me every five seconds that this was about Diana. That she was missing. That I might hear something awful.

Breathe. Taking a long deep breath grounded me, brought me back into the moment.

The moment. This one.

It was pretty spectacular, as moments go. The clouds had cleared, leaving behind a golden glaze as thick as honey. A painter could spend a lifetime just on those hills and never fully capture them, but I considered possibilities as I walked—which paints and methods would I choose? Which brushes? How could I capture it?

When I realized what I was thinking, I was taken aback. This was the second time in a single day that I'd wanted to paint something. It had been years. More than a decade. Was it just the landscape?

My feet carried me to the pub, a half-timbered building that leaned precariously toward the street. It had been this way since I could remember and hadn't tumbled over yet, but it could make you dizzy to look at it. The mullioned windows on the second floor had been reinforced to keep them from falling out of their frames, but otherwise it remained sound. I pushed the door open.

The scent of beer soaked into the floor for centuries swamped me. Men standing at the bar swung their faces around to watch me make my way through the warren of rooms, dark and tight beneath low ceilings.

I passed a booth populated with men in golf shirts and khakis, their haircuts fresh, their faces already tan from the days out on their yachts. One of them caught my eye, and I realized it was the well-tended man my grandmother had pointed out to me. The commodore. I figured this must be where the members of the yacht club unwound.

The men at the bar who watched me walk through the room were the usual suspects, all locals who'd been bending an elbow at the Rose and Crown since they'd earned the right to drink. I'm sure I'd know many of them if I heard their names, though my gran hadn't been much of a pub dweller. A few shadier types lurked around one table, and I imagined them in the scarves and earrings of smugglers of old.

At the back of the pub, I found a much more varied crowd—more than a couple dozen people of a wide variety of ages and both sexes. I saw Diana's mother, still as skinny and dry as a broomstick, deep in conversation with a man about her age. I knew I should talk to her, but the idea met with sharp resistance. She'd make it a drama somehow, something about herself.

I slid through a group of twenty-something women decorated with tattoos and streaks of blue or green hair and gave them a nod. One of them was almost certainly Diana's right-hand woman, Cora. Diana had mentioned her a few times, but I had never met her.

I didn't really see anyone else I knew, but why would I? I'd been gone for more than twenty years, and I only popped in every six months for a couple of weeks. I looked for an empty seat that wouldn't feel too intimidating.

And then I did see a familiar face. A woman with a cloud of black hair, dressed in a white tunic with white-on-white embroidery around the hem and sleeves. My hippie mother, who still dressed like it was 1975 or as if she lived in Glastonbury. I paused for only a second, my feet stopping so abruptly I might have stepped into puddles of superglue.

She still wore bracelets, even more than she'd had when I was small. They rattled on her wrists when she talked and when she brushed her hair away from her face. I couldn't hear her voice, but I heard it in my mind, rich and husky, the way it had sounded coming through the phone lines from India for five years.

Until I refused to take her calls.

She would never dare approach me, but to be safe, I ducked around the back of the crowd and headed for a corner.

Where I found Cooper.

Of course. The place was full of perils.

He'd shed the Carhartt jacket with all its pockets and now sat in a wool sweater the color of the moor at high summer, and jeans and heavy boots. A man who walked the farthest wilds of his land and knew the names of every wildflower that grew, and every bird that called out a greeting, and every tree twisted by the harsh winds. A memory flashed through my brain—Cooper in a heavy winter coat, his magnificent hair blowing in a gale, holding my hand as we walked across the rugged ground.

A border collie with alert ears sat on the floor beside him, his white paws crossed neatly one over the other. Cooper looked up, gave a lift of his chin in greeting.

"Do you mind if I sit with you?" I asked, already pulling out the chair beside him. I saw him nearly every time I came to England, always by accident, and because the place was small and everyone knew everyone else. A decade or so of stiffness had given way to a slightly less rigid connection, but the relationship couldn't really have been called friendship. Mainly we shared a long connection with Diana, and she loved both of us, so we tried for her sake.

He gestured toward the chair.

I sat down, hiding behind the backs of the others. "My mother is here."

"I saw her."

"Diana was friendly with her."

He tilted his head to look at me, raising one brow. "You're the only one at war with your mother, as far as I know."

Stung, I said, "It's not war. I just have good boundaries."

He didn't reply because of course he wouldn't. He wouldn't take a side or have an opinion. I took a breath and pointed to the dog. We had always had dogs in common. It was a safe topic. "Who's this fellow?"

"Matt."

The dog's tail wagged ever so slightly. "Am I allowed to touch him?" The dogs weren't allowed to socialize when they were working, and while I didn't see any sheep to herd, it was better to be safe. Cooper could be prickly.

"It's all right. He's retired." He gave a command, a single syllable, and Matt leapt to his feet and came over to greet me.

"Hey, you," I said, rubbing his ears. His black and white fur was long to protect him against the harsh conditions of the land, and he had bright, alert eyes. "You're a special one, aren't you?"

He agreed, settling down against my leg and throwing Cooper a look that said, *See how this is done?*

Cooper gave him a scrub on the chest. "You're a good man, Matt, you are."

The weight of the dog against my leg eased some tangled thing along my spine. I thought of Simba, gone six months, and in the spiraling way of grief, I suddenly missed him desperately. "I lost my dog six months ago," I said.

"Ah, I'm sorry." Of all people, he would understand how a dog could take up so much space in your life. "Do you want to tell me about her?"

"Him." I stroked Matt's fur, feeling too much emotion rise in my throat. If I started crying now for Simba, I might not stop. I chanced a glance at Cooper, hoping the tears wouldn't show in my eyes. "It's still too hard."

He nodded.

Around us, people talked and murmured and greeted each other, but here in this corner it was quiet, which left space for memories to crowd their way in. When we were children, we'd spent all of our time with each other. We'd always been together, and I suppose I expected we always would be. When my mother didn't come back from India, I took even greater refuge in his company. My grandmother drove me to the farm, and we'd amble out into the moor or into the forest and follow butterflies and birds, and in the winter the cry of redwings. He cataloged birds and grasses while I drew postcards of butterflies and storms to send to my mom. Back in those days we didn't know that she wasn't coming back, just that she wasn't coming back *yet*.

All summer we wandered outdoors, taking paper bags filled with apples and cookies Sage's mother made. Our families didn't worry about us. We'd grown up there, knew every inch of our world and what to do in the event of a thunderstorm or wild winds or even a broken ankle. The sun turned us brown and walking made us strong, and we always had each other and a dog.

And I thought it would always be that way. How do you imagine not having one of your arms?

I swallowed. "How are things, Cooper?"

"You asked me that already."

I glared at him. "You don't have to be mean."

He held my gaze, and I saw that he was as conflicted as I was, both of us feeling that old connection, and the old pain. His hair caught the light, the ringlets haloed, making him look like some wild creature who'd stumbled into the pub from some other realm. Tam Lin, perhaps, already promised to the fairy queen.

At last, he relented. "I'm well enough."

"Still on the farm?"

He gave a slow nod. "Yes. It's a good life. Simple." I tried not to read anything into the answer. That farm life had looked very narrow to me once upon a time, and it had contributed to our breach.

After a moment he asked, "How are you, Zoe?"

"I'm okay," I said. "Divorced."

"I heard." He lifted his bottle of water. Even when we were teenagers, he didn't drink alcohol, a rebellion against the addiction that had run rampant through our parental group. My dad used to joke that they just said yes in the seventies, with dire consequences for a lot of them, including himself. He'd been lost to me for a couple of years. "How is your daughter?"

I paused, wondering whether to tell some portion of the truth or a social lie. I landed somewhere in the middle. "I brought her with me. She found the hill fort today and was completely enchanted."

A smile softened his face. "I reckon it's magical just now with the bluebells."

"That was the exact word she used—magical." My mother moved through the room, the pristine white of her tunic and leggings shining in the dark pub. I studiously did not look at her, thumbing my phone automatically to look at the screen. Nothing. Just the photo of Isabel I kept there, from a day a few years ago when we'd made brownies together. "She wants to shoot photos of it, but recently she canceled all of her social media accounts and doesn't know what she'd do with the pictures."

He nodded, but whether in agreement or just to be polite, I didn't know. I straightened, rubbed my hands on my thighs. "Sorry. I'll stop chattering."

"It's not chatter. And I wouldn't mind if it was."

"You always hated small talk."

"Only inane small talk," he said in his deep voice. "You have never chattered inanely."

A little more pressure in my body eased. "Don't know about that, but thanks."

"Maybe you could find her an old-school scrapbook. You might check Jacob Stone's stationery store over in Beercombe. He has things there that have been out of stock in the world since 1950."

"Still?"

"Still."

Stone's Stationery, one village over, had been the family business for over a hundred years, and it was a warren of strange and useful things. I'd haunted the place whenever I could to unearth odd papers and art supplies. "He must be a million years old."

"His daughter mainly runs it now, but I don't think she's done a thing to it."

"I'll have to check it out."

"'Check it out,'" he repeated with the faintest smile. "Very American."

"And Americans think I sound British."

"You're such a jet-setter."

I allowed a small smile to break through. It was an old joke between us, a thing he'd used to ease my sorrow at being yanked back and forth.

The group started moving into more order, taking seats, and the unrest in my belly awakened. "I'm so scared that something terrible has happened to her."

"Me too."

"What do you think happened?"

"I don't know." The veneer of politeness fell from his face, leaving behind weariness and a wreath of crow's feet etched into the weatherworn skin around his eyes. "I mean, she's been missing nearly two weeks. If she's not dead, it's worse than that."

"What's worse?"

"I don't know—kidnapped, held in some bloody awful place."

"Kidnapped! Who would do that?"

He shook his head. "Who would kill her?"

For a moment my body froze from feet to scalp, fear and sorrow winding through me in a horrified twist. I hadn't really been thinking she'd been *murdered*. But where was she, then?

"Why would anyone want to hurt her? She's so kind."

"Murder doesn't have to be logical. People do terrible things all the time."

"I know. I mean, I do know that." As a mother, I'd imagined every possible ill that could have befallen my daughter in order to try to prevent it—and that had not gone well at all. A wash of anxiety made my stomach hurt. "I just want her to be okay," I said. Talking about Isabel as much as Diana.

"So do I. I'm just trying to prepare myself."

I scowled. "I'm going to believe she's alive until I have proof that she's not."

"Have you talked to her?"

I had to say it. "No." I thought of the two unanswered texts, hanging out there in the ether, waiting. "What about her boyfriend? Maybe she really did just go somewhere with him."

"And not tell anyone? Leave your gran without notice? Leave Jennie to fend for herself?"

"Who is Jennie?"

His attention sharpened. "You don't know about Jennie?"

A bad feeling moved through my gut. "No. Should I?"

He narrowed his eyes, inclining his head slightly. "She's been living with Diana for six or eight months. Pregnant teenager."

I closed my eyes. Shook my head. "Wow."

"She didn't tell you?"

"No." I took a breath, let it go, admitted the truth. "I didn't really give her much space to tell me anything."

"What do you mean?"

"I was angry with her." I was going to leave it at that, but the reason wove through the crowd, apparently speaking to every single person there. "She made friends with my mother."

His clear eyes saw far too much, and I couldn't hold his gaze. "You probably should know I'm friends with her too."

A sharp burn pierced me. He had even more information on what my mother had done than Diana had. "Whatever," I said with effort and straightened. "What was she doing for Gran?"

He shrugged. "Little things. Shopping and the like. Checking on her."

For a moment, I absorbed that. How much *had* she been doing for Gran? Cooper lifted his chin toward the side of the room. The constable— or I supposed he must be an inspector, judging by his uniform—was a fit man in his fifties with luxurious dark hair he probably didn't notice. "Thank you for coming, everyone. I'm Inspector Hannaford, as most of you know."

The milling few settled, sitting or leaning on a wall. Waited.

"We're all here because we want to find Diana Brooking."

Murmuring traveled through the crowd.

"The facts are thin. There are no signs of violence. Her home is undisturbed. But no one has seen or spoken to her since two weeks ago Friday at about four p.m. Unless someone here has had a later contact?"

People looked at each other, hopeful. Nothing.

Inspector Hannaford consulted a notebook in his hand. "Her phone hasn't been found, and according to her carrier, no calls have gone out since roughly five p.m. that same day. Her last point of tri- angulation pinged right from the tower behind the Rose and Crown."

He paused, and his wrinkles grew deeper. "As most of you know, she was a highly social, highly visible member of our community, which leads us to an assumption of foul play. We'd like your help. Talk amongst yourselves. See if you have a bit of the puzzle that might help us put this together. Share it with us on the website we've set up, no questions asked." He waved a sheaf of printed papers. "I've the address here."

Two of the men in golf shirts had come over, including the yacht club president, and listened while they sipped their pints. A very thin woman with red hair crossed her arms next to them. I wondered if that was the older sister of Gina Luscombe, the one my gran had mentioned. "You should ask that fellow of hers," she piped up. "The Londoner."

"We'd like to," the constable said, "but he hasn't turned up."

"It must be him," the woman continued. There was something stiff in the way she held her neck, as if she'd had an injury, and it gave her a brittle aspect. "No one else would harm Diana."

A murmur rose in the room. The inspector raised his hand, and the polite group settled immediately. "It may well be that he's got something to do with her disappearance, but let's keep our minds open. Assumptions can derail an investigation."

Matt licked my forearm, and I realized that I'd been clinging too hard to his fur. "Sorry, baby," I whispered, and I kissed his head.

A few people raised their hands and asked questions, nearly all procedural, as if they'd know what to do with the information. Diana's mother petulantly asked about her daughter's bank accounts and whether they'd been frozen. I glanced at Cooper, and his mouth tightened.

Inspector Hannaford answered all the questions patiently, and when they were exhausted, he said, "We'll keep looking for her, but Saturday we're going to sweep the forest by the river. If you want to help, be at the car park at twelve noon. Thank you all for coming."

Cooper stood immediately, and Matt snapped to attention beside him. He gave me a simple nod. "Good night, Zoe."

I'd hoped he might sit and talk with me for a little while, compare notes on Diana, see what we might come up with. A small hole opened in my chest, and I watched him go, taller than every other person in the room by half a head, the ridiculous tumble of hair on his shoulders, dog faithfully trotting beside him.

Water under the bridge, that one. I stood, too, and was getting ready to make my way out when I remembered my mother was in the room. I looked around for her, afraid she'd come talk to me if she saw me now that everyone was filing out. Instead, she was deep in conversation with Diana's mom, Joan. I stared for a long moment, feeling a strange, sad thing move through my soul, deeper than I liked to go.

I pushed it away and hurried out into the night.

Chapter Ten
Lillian

Something awakened her. For a long moment she listened, but the house was utterly silent. After a long stretch lying in bed, she realized she wasn't about to go to sleep again and got up, creeping through the house like a mouse, cloaked in her thick, warm velveteen robe and slippers. Poppy had given her a pair that had rubbery soles that had a good grip on the old wooden floors of the manor, and it was easy now, too, because cell phones all had the flashlight button so you could use it that way anytime you wanted, though sometimes she couldn't remember where the button was. They'd changed it, and now it was something she had to stop and think about every time.

Tonight she shined the bright light in the hallway from her bedroom to the tower and climbed up the stairs to her office. It was cold. She used to light a fire in the office, but that had been forbidden a few years back by one of her carers. Which one? Janet? Alice? They all blurred together.

She did have a portable heater that clicked on with a button, and she turned that on, along with a lamp by her desk. Her hips were aching and her hands hurt, but they'd be better once the room warmed up.

Something was nagging her. It had awakened her, a piece of information that had helped make sense of Diana's disappearance. It was there, right on the edge of her brain when she woke up, and she scrambled to write it down, but it slipped away before she could. Something about the Romanian boy, the one who'd delivered her groceries for a while and then went to work for the yacht club.

She couldn't remember.

Frustrated, she stood by the window and gazed at the sea. Everything looked still and ordinary, but when she tried to piece together why she thought that, she couldn't seem to find the path again. It was like walking through the forest and suddenly forgetting where you were, or even that it was a forest that surrounded you.

It broke her heart to be losing her memory this way. She'd always imagined it would be a smoother thing, that you'd lose this, then that. Instead her memories had become like a box of toys tossed together—this one bumping that one in no discernible order at all. She was nine, then forty-eight, then back to twenty, all in the space of an hour. Or a minute.

Moonlight made patterns over the water, dancing bars of light that seemed solid enough to walk over. She'd been looking at this scene, those cliffs, that water, that sky, since arriving at Woodhurst as a young married woman, madly in love with her dashing Richard, the musical youngest son of the family. They'd met in London in the grim, lean days after the war, when everything was rubble and rations. They loved to dance, and he loved to play the horn, and she thought they'd live a life of excitement and adventure. He'd traveled the world and told her stories of the places they'd visit and the adventures they would experience. Lillian had only wanted to escape London and all the deprivation, have a life with some color in it.

So when he'd unexpectedly inherited Woodhurst six months after they married at the registry office, at first she'd been secretly delighted. A manor house! An old family! And they'd live in the West Country, which people said was one of the most beautiful areas in England.

Dancing on the moonlit cliffs, she thought, imagining herself spinning in a ball gown on that silvery light. They'd been happy enough, even in the provincial landscape where they'd landed, throwing parties and bringing music into the hall. For three or four years, it was fine.

And then she got pregnant.

Was that it? Getting pregnant? Was thinking about that what had awakened her? She'd been so much better a grandmother than a mother. It was one of the bittersweet truths of her life. What if she'd been better to Poppy?

Poppy. That was it.

Lillian snapped her fingers and wrote down the link between the youth at the yacht club and her daughter. Then, with the room nicely warmed, she sat down in her office chair and started to write.

Chapter Eleven

Isabel

I woke up out of a dead sleep, sitting straight up in bed so that I knocked Mósí right off me. Sweat poured off me, and I couldn't breathe. I stumbled out of bed and bent over, coughing.

After a few coughs I took in a breath, but my heart was still racing so fast it made my hands shake. I turned on the light and paced, trying to calm down, but after going back and forth a bunch of times, it didn't get any better, and I remembered this thing Dr. Kerry taught me: five, four, three, two, one.

Gasping, I looked around. Five things I could see. The window had six panes. The curtains were blue. The rug was thin and old. Mósí was looking at me like I was crazy. My sheet had flowers.

Four things I could feel. My pajamas were soft and warm. The floor was cold. I plopped down beside Mósí and stroked his soft fur. He headbutted me and his nose was a little wet, but when I kissed him and he rubbed my chin and I kissed him again, my heart started to feel a little better.

Three things I could hear. Mósí purring, really loud. That made me smile, and I kissed him again, and he crawled up in my lap and I hugged him. His purr was so loud I couldn't really hear anything else, but I guess silence is a thing. And when I listened very, very hard, I could hear the sea.

Two things I could smell. I breathed in and tried to name it, like I was one of my characters. It smelled like dampness and stone. And Mósí, who always smells clean and sweet and nice. I kissed him again, closing my eyes, and felt tears stinging my eyelids. I love him so much. He is the best cat ever in the world.

I was supposed to think of one thing I could taste, but I didn't want to get up, and anyway my heart felt better. My dad did a good thing with Mósí. My cat doesn't care what happened to me, what I did. He just wants me to love him.

So I did that. I left the light on, just in case, and crawled back under the covers with him, and he settled against my chest, purring very softly, his paw on the outside of my thumb.

I fell back asleep.

———— ❧ ~❧ ————

Despite the bad night, I woke up feeling a lot better.

The bluebell woods. My new story.

I couldn't wait to get back there, to the woods. I packed my camera and all three lenses into the vintage camera bag my dad bought me last Christmas. It's an army reporter's case, made of green canvas with leather belts. The camera itself is a mirrorless Nikon, lightweight and easy to transport, though nothing is ever as easy as a smartphone, especially now that they're getting so scary good. You can get great effects with a very small amount of effort, which means everybody is taking great shots and posting them all over the internet.

But my dad says I'm way better than everybody shooting moody selfies with filters and effects. One of the lenses he gave me is a manual focus, so you have to figure out when you want a shallow depth of field (which is the thing that makes portrait mode so great on smartphones) and how to get it, along with a bunch of other things.

Gigi was in the kitchen when I came down. She looked kind of tousled, her hair unbrushed and sticking up, and no makeup on her face. She still wore her robe and slippers, which is not the way she does things at all. "Hey, Gigi," I said, setting my camera down on the table. "Have you had some breakfast?"

"Good morning, dear," she said. "I was just thinking we might want to go over your school uniforms before you go back next week."

I wasn't sure what to say. I mean, obviously I'm not going to school here, but I didn't want to make her feel bad. My mom told me she's having memory problems, and to just go with it. "Okay," I said, like it was normal. "You want some tea and toast?"

"That would be lovely. The boysenberry jam, if you wouldn't mind."

"Got it." I filled the kettle and scoured around the pantry to find bread and jam. One jar was dark red, and I guessed that might be boysenberry, but she probably wouldn't care anyway.

My mom had picked up waffles and almond milk for me, so I poured a glass while I waited for Gigi's toast. She was sitting there at the table, looking so, so small, like a Shrinky Dink version of herself, and it made me feel sad and afraid. I sat down next to her and tried to think of something to say. "Hey, Gigi, what's your favorite part of writing?"

She looked at me, her eyes gigantic behind her glasses. "When I finish," she said, and just like that, her voice was back to normal. "It's always good to be done."

I laughed. "I can see that."

The toast popped up, so I covered it with jam, edge to edge, the way she likes, then made my waffles. We sat there eating, and finally my mom came down.

"I'm going back to the bluebell woods," I said, standing up to put my dishes in the sink.

For a second she frowned, and I thought she might be about to tell me I couldn't go. "Dr. Kerry told me to get exercise every day," I said.

"Text me every hour or so," she said, "and then I won't have to worry about you."

"You can track me on Find My Friends," I said.

She ducked her head, her hair swinging down to cover her expression, a trick she uses a lot. Mine won't do it, not like that curtain she swings down to hide behind. "I know. I'd rather you just texted me so I don't have to feel like a freak."

I drank the last of my milk. "You don't have to worry about me anyway, but I will."

"Take some good shots," she said.

So finally I escaped before the lump of sadness in my gut could grow very big. Carrying the bag slung crosswise over my body, I hiked down the steep hill that ran down to the mouth of the river in one direction, and then up to the hill fort on the other. I'd googled hill forts to find out what they were, since I'd seen zero sign of any kind of building in there. It turns out they were Stone Age settlements, like ancient forts, and the bluebells grow well there for some obscure reason I don't quite get.

I was a little afraid, approaching the grove, that I'd only imagined how amazing it was.

The first glimpse showed me I hadn't. But unlike last time, when it had been late in the day, there were quite a few people there this morning. Most of them were old, walking with canes or leaning on each other for support, and that made me feel sad all over again. Was Gigi getting senile?

I saw a bus in the parking lot and heard some of the old people speaking German. Maybe they were there on a tour. There are always German tourists in town at different times, and they park in these giant buses at the hotels along the cliff. I imagined color brochures in German grocery stores, advertising tours of the English countryside. Bluebells and seaside walks.

Avoiding the main group, I waded through knee-high grass beneath trees that stretched branches overhead, like they were fingers lacing together. I stopped to take out the camera and decide on a lens. I used the 50 millimeter and shot the fingers overlacing, the long view of the forest itself. The light was soft gold where it fell through leaves, and I shot that too. When I checked the photos, I saw that they really did look magical, and I could feel my story moving around in the back of my brain. I was already writing an Insta post, too, something clever that—

I remembered I didn't have an account anymore.

A blast of horror and shame rose through my gut, spreading like a darkness that turned my blood the color of ink. It flushed my cheeks and closed my throat, and I was just there again, standing on my porch before I went inside, realizing what my friends had done.

My *"friends."*

Emotions swamped me. I felt like I was choking, like I would die because I couldn't breathe. It was tar, sticking to everything, ruining my life.

Urgently I raised the camera, peered through the lens. That is what a camera can do—narrow the world to one thing. This frame. One shot, then another, then another. The moss on the trunk, a close-up of a bluebell, so crazy intricate and perfect, every single one the same, repeating over the entire forest. Billions of bluebells.

My heart started to slow down.

I imagined a fairy door opening in that murky space between trees over there. Shot some leaves and distant shots of blurry flowers. It made me glad I asked for the lens.

My dad is kinda famous, and very wealthy, but I try to keep my requests to a reasonable level, not like some of the girls at school who leverage the guilt of one parent or the other to get all kinds of material bullshit, and for sure my dad could afford anything I want, and he feels super guilty about having an affair.

I was mad at him for a while over it, but you'd just have to know my dad to know why I couldn't stay mad. He's just *nice*. He loves me with his whole heart and soul. I know he does. He's still in my life constantly, almost too much, even if he's embarrassed about stuff, like his girlfriend's new baby and all that.

So I could ask for anything, and he'd figure out a way to get it for me. I just don't care that much about most of it. I have lots of clothes and things, and anyway it's bad for the environment to buy stuff all the time. The camera thing has obsessed me since the year between second and third grade, when my mom and I went on tour with my dad for the whole summer. All over America, riding in his bus. My mom and I explored all the towns or stayed on the bus to read all day. My summer project was to make a scrapbook page of every state we visited, which was twenty-seven by the end of the summer, and I spent a lot of time on it. My mom carried a sketchbook and colored pencils and sketched all the trees and butterflies and sometimes birds. I loved to watch her draw.

She's very different looking, my mom, with beautiful, shiny, straight hair, not quite black, that she wears plain, parted in the middle and hanging right down her back. She's thin and lanky, kinda flat chested and boyish, with a face you can look at a thousand times and it looks different all the time. Sometimes her face looks kind of awkward, just depending. Her eyes are dark, dark, dark, and she has a really good mouth, and sharp, clean cheekbones and jaw that she got from my grandpa. I didn't get them—my face is round. Round eyes, round cheeks, round chin, even round nose. You could draw a bunch of circles and then connect them, and you'd have my face. Also, my hair. More circles, circles upon circles. My mom's face is angles upon angles. I take a million pictures of her all the time, and there's never a bad one. Not like me. The angle has to be . . .

Sprawling . . . hands . . . words . . .

Ink rushed through my veins again, and my heart sped up so fast I thought I might faint. I bent over and pressed my hands to my knees, fighting the visuals of my belly and arms and thighs . . . and for a minute, I got so sick to my stomach that I thought I might barf.

I breathed in, like Dr. Kerry said, and then out.

In. Be right where you are. Out. Only in this very minute.

In the bluebell woods, I smelled earth and something sweet that I guessed was flowers. The tourists were headed back to the bus. Birds twittered in the branches and sailed around, flashing feathers. A butterfly with blue wings settled on a flower to feed right by my knee.

I wanted to shoot the photo, but it might have disturbed him, and butterflies are in trouble these days.

I stayed still. When he moved from one flower to another I slowly, slowly, slowly lifted the camera to shoot him, zooming in on his wings where they glistened. So perfect, like the bluebells. It made me feel calm to watch him. My granddad says that's why we need nature, to remind us to be still.

Once the tourists had all disappeared, one by one as if they were zipping through a transporter, I walked down the hill. I didn't want to crush the flowers, so I found a grassy spot to lie down on my belly and aimed the eye of the lens through a frame of green blades to the flowers.

Smears of green and blue, with a single bluebell in focus, the edges of the flower frilly like a hat in an old-fashioned story. It was easy to imagine an alternative world here, a world of the fey, dangerous, and magical, a world entered by magic at a certain time of day . . . or night.

My imagination played with the idea while I shot photos. It was a relief. It was peaceful. I wasn't thinking about what was wrong with me, but only what was right.

Chapter Twelve

Poppy

The day started off on the wrong foot. I knocked a cup off the counter and it shattered on the wooden floor, scattering tiny bits of glass everywhere, which I, shortsighted as I was these days, could barely see.

I hadn't slept well, tossing and turning with all manner of things afoot in the world. I fretted that I had not been to see my mother, and Diana was missing, so she couldn't check on her either.

The meeting last night had been deeply unsettling: not only because no one knew anything but also because my daughter had been there, studiously, pointedly ignoring me. Which complicated my urgent need to see Lillian. Zoe would hate to see me at Woodhurst, which had always been her safe space.

The conflict between the two things I should do for two women I loved was causing me a great deal of restlessness, no matter how much lemon balm and chamomile tea I sipped.

And Jennie had never replied to my phone call and had never texted me. I didn't think she'd ghost me, and there was no one to ask about her. I hadn't seen her boyfriend in weeks.

The missed sleep weighted the bones of my elbows and ankles and spine. I was limping a little as I headed outside for my chores and muttering under my breath like an old woman, which I supposed I was becoming.

When I headed out to the chicken coop, I found that something had made off with one of my hens, and the others were squawking and nervous. The marauder had torn a hole in the fence, so it must have been a fox. I mended it as best I could with a square of plywood and a handful of bricks.

The goats were nervous, too, and I spent a few minutes gentling them, talking to them sweetly.

On the way back to the house, some whisper of something in the low brightening of the morning made me pause. I looked first to the house, where it sat as it always did, washed pink by the light, the windows shining. The row of trees leading into the forest showed nothing.

But when I turned toward the bluff, there stood a hare on her hind legs, paws held softly in front of her as if she were about to tell a story.

My breath caught. Hares once populated the whole of England, and it had been nothing unusual to see them boxing in the spring when I was a girl. Now they'd been chased away by encroaching development and the spread of their cousins, the rabbits—who look so much sweeter, but are not—and the dwindling habitat.

This one just stood there, extra-long ears moving slightly. I tried, truly, to meld with the air so that I wouldn't frighten her, but she didn't seem inclined to run away. Instead she simply stayed where she was, as if to give me a message, as if she were not of this earth at all, but another.

In the dark of my garden, I touched the silver hare I'd worn around my neck for forty years. I'd bought it after a wild hare had shown up to remind me that I was part of the land, that my father and his family had lived here for centuries, like the trio of hares who formed the symbolic circle of Devonshire, an ancient and sacred symbol.

The long-eared animal disappeared, as hares will do. I stayed where I was, waiting for the sunrise over the eastern hills, watching it spread slowly across the fields, divided by hedgerows as old as anything in England. It was a rare moment of peace, a knowing that whatever I'd sought the world over lived here, in a garden in Devon. In me.

It had taken such a long, long time to learn.

As I fingered the silver pendant, I realized that I must do what was mine to do. I needed to see my mother and make sure she was all right.

Chapter Thirteen

Zoe

Gran was clearly exhausted and confused after her long night of writing. I took her upstairs and helped her shower, washing her hair, then combing it out carefully afterward. She sat quietly on a plastic shower chair, wrapped in a thick terry-cloth robe, and watched my actions in the mirror. Her hands in her lap were covered with the purplish bruises and brown marks that signified great age. The bones were prominent, each joint visible, the veins blue beneath tissue-paper skin. How much longer would I have her?

"Are you eating enough?" I asked, smoothing the wrinkles over her fist.

"Plenty," she said. "I'm just old, my dear. A breath of wind leaves a bruise."

I chuckled through the ache in my chest.

"I wrote all night," she said. "I don't know that I want to be bothered for the rest of the day."

"Maybe for dinner?" I met her eyes in the mirror. We looked nothing alike, a fact that had pained me as a girl. "We can all eat together?"

"Perhaps."

I helped her into bed, made sure her phone was charged and in reach, then lowered the blinds in her room. "I'll be downstairs if you need me," I said.

She did not answer.

———— ⁛ ————

I was in the kitchen, making a cup of tea, when a knock sounded on the back door. I wiped my hands and opened it.

My mother stood there, swaddled in a big camel-colored blanket wrap. Her hair was caught under it. "Hello, Zoe. I'm sorry to bother you, but I need to see my mother."

It was so startling to see her face to face that I almost had no reaction. "What?"

She lifted a hand, palm out, like some kind of saint. "I've been here nearly every day. I know you don't want me here, so I've stayed away, but I . . . I'm worried."

Still nothing rose in my body. No anger. No disdain. No happiness. No sadness. "She's fine. I just put her to bed."

"Still," she said, looking over my shoulder as if she could see upstairs to Gran's bed, "I need to see for myself, if you don't mind."

I stationed myself squarely. "Oh, but I do mind. I'm here now. I've got it. I looked after her just fine all those years you were not even in the country."

"Fair enough." She tucked her hands under the wrap but didn't appreciably move. It was impossible to forget how large and clear her eyes were, the color of a bleached-out sky, almost crystal. "But I have been here the past year, and she is not well, a fact she has been hiding from you so that you will not worry."

Discomfort swirled through the frozenness, but I wouldn't give her the satisfaction of knowing that. "Well, I know now. And I am perfectly capable of taking care of her, whatever she needs. We don't need you."

For a long moment, Poppy only stood there. "You do," she said at last. "Both of you do. But I'm not going to knock you down to get inside."

I didn't move.

"If you would, please tell her that I was here, and that I was asking after her?"

I didn't say anything.

For one more moment my mother paused, as if waiting for me to change my mind. "All right," she said at last, "I'll leave you."

Before I could watch her walk away, I closed the door and walked away from it, focusing entirely on the tea that awaited me, and the more immediate problems in my life than my old, weary anger at my mother—on Diana, the friend I'd let down so wretchedly, and my daughter, who needed me, even if she didn't know it.

Chapter Fourteen
Isabel

By the time I finished shooting photos in the bluebell woods, I was starving. I took my camera and my growling stomach up the hill and down the other side into the town. It isn't always easy to eat as a vegetarian, but I found a takeout place that served fried cheese pies that were stupidly good. I bought one, and a can of some drink called Ribena, and carried them to a park on the bluff, where there were swings and slides and a jungle gym for kids. No kids were on them right at the moment, since it was a school day. I sat on a rock and opened the paper-wrapped pie and watched the sea.

I don't know if it was the exercise or the forest or just being out in the world again, but I felt good. I like the town, which is like Santa Fe in one way—both are quaint places for tourists. People just want to see things, my grandad says. He holds classes on traditional indigenous methods of dyeing and that kind of thing, and I sometimes help him. I love to watch him stir wool in big metal pots over an open fire. People come from all over to learn it—weavers and artists and a lot of older ladies who always flirt with Grandad, even though he never, ever flirts back.

The pie was amazing. Greasy, salty, flaky. I'd never had anything like it anywhere, and it probably had about fifty billion calories, but I didn't care.

"Hey," said a girl's voice. "Can I sit here with you?"

The girl was slim and dark haired, with thick eyeliner. She looked like Zendaya. Displaying a bag of tobacco, she said, "I'll share."

"I don't smoke," I said, "but go ahead. You roll your own?"

"Yeah, rollies are the way to go, don't you know?" The girl sat down. "God, don't you love that pie?"

"It's amazing. I feel like I could eat, like, five hundred of them, and never be too full for the next one."

"You're American!"

"Yeah. But my mom is from here."

"You're not a tourist, then?"

"No. We're here because this lady disappeared, and they want to find her. My mom knew her."

The girl nodded while expertly rolling a cigarette. I've never smoked, not even vaped, because my dad is so anticigarette. "What's your name?" I asked.

The girl had eyes like glass, very light. Mixed, like me. "Molly."

"Isabel."

Molly lit the cigarette. Took a drag and blew it out.

"Are you homeschooled or something?" I asked.

"Nah. I just don't go anymore. My mom's never around, so she don't care."

"My mom would kill me if I didn't go to school."

"You're not there now."

I shrugged. "Long story."

"I have time."

I shook my head and pointed across the roofs of the village, some thatched, some tile, to the big rambling house standing on the bluff opposite. "My great-gran lives there."

Molly turned her whole face toward me, eyes wide. "The mystery writer is your great-grandmother?"

I nodded. "We're staying with her. Where do you live?"

She pointed over her shoulder with a thumb. "In the council flats behind the Tesco. Want to walk over and have a snack?"

I'd been pretty much alone for nearly six weeks, but it was one thing to sit here on the playground and another to go to the girl's house. You just don't know with people. Who they are. What they could do. "Maybe another time," I said.

"It's all good," the girl said, standing and brushing off her rear end. She pinched the tip of her cigarette and carefully stowed the butt in her pocket. I grimaced. The smell would be awful in about six seconds, but it was none of my business. "Maybe I'll see you around."

"Maybe."

"So if you're the mystery lady's granddaughter, you must be related to the good witch."

"Witch?"

"Yeah. She has a shop on the high street. Reads cards and sells amulets and potions and things."

"She's a witch?"

"You don't know her?"

I hesitated, then shook my head. "My mom doesn't speak to her."

"Too bad. It's the best shop in the village."

For a long time after Molly left, I just sat there. Then I gathered up all my things, walked back to the trail, and headed into town.

To meet my grandmother.

Chapter Fifteen

Poppy

After the encounter with Zoe, I drove to my shop.

Where the windows had been egged.

It didn't escape me that the chickens had been targeted, and maybe these were the eggs I hadn't found. Not everyone understood me or even liked me, and mostly I didn't mind.

I minded now. Probably because I was tired. Because it felt as if the veil between worlds had grown thin and I was feeling too much of everything. Too much sorrow, too much sin, too many things gone wrong. A whisper across my ear made me turn. A pair of overly skinny European boys crossed the street toward the harbor. They had that air of hunger about them, hunger for something they didn't even know how to name. They'd come here from all over Europe—Romania and Poland and the Czech Republic, seeking a life that might offer some joy, some hope. Jennie's boyfriend, Andrei, was one of them. Maybe these two knew him.

"Hello, lads," I called. "A moment of your time?"

One looked at the other, and a signal passed between them. "Sure, all right," the first one said. He had eyes so blue they looked lit from within.

"Do you know a fellow named Andrei? Tall boy, big eyes."

"Sure, he works with us at the Harbour Inn."

"Have you seen him recently?"

The second one, slightly hunched, as if he'd been waiting for a blow his entire life, frowned. "Eh. Maybe he went off with his friend a few days ago? London? Brighton?"

"Exeter?" Despite her avowals, maybe Jennie had gone somewhere with the lad.

Blue Eyes shook his head. "No, that was Karl. I haven't seen Andrei."

I nodded, a rock weighing down my gut. "Thanks, lads. Have a great day."

They ambled down the hill, and I watched them go. Surely Jennie had not run off with Andrei? She'd been frightened of him, of his violent tendencies, and honestly, I didn't think she would have lied to me.

Once the mess was cleaned up, I tried to call Jennie, but her phone went to voice mail again. I left her a message asking for an update.

As I washed my hands with sandalwood soap, I looked up at my face in the mirror, and just like that, I was snared by the past, by a sharp, painful longing for India. It caught me under my breastbone, sudden and intense. Perhaps it was the smell of incense or some other unknown thing that my limbic brain remembered from that time— dank water that had been standing in the close, or a whisper of light breaking just so.

Whatever it was, I stepped into memories like a thousand scarves. The orange sky of sunset over Lake Pichola, the intense brilliance of the sun on the palace, the sound of Ravi laughing in that way that he had, throwing back his head and letting it pour out of his mouth, upward, like a song. My memories tossed out the sound of calls to prayer, echoing out at regular hours, so holy and beautiful. And there, in the middle of it all, was Kashmir, so beautiful and now so beleaguered. We were so happy there.

I caught my arms around my middle, holding the memory within me.

There are things you never get over. I closed my eyes for the space of a few breaths, letting it roll through me. Then I squared my shoulders and continued on.

As one must.

———— ⊘~⊘ ————

My assistant, Mia, made it in around noon, apologetic and irritable, but she was industrious and put herself to work blending spell packets for the festival, glaring every so often at a hipster pair with London accents who made sport of the tiny bottles of essential oils I had so carefully mixed and presented for all manner of purposes.

"Hippies!" the girl trilled, casting a glance over her shoulder.

"I am," I said mildly over the reading glasses perched on my nose.

Mia, carefully measuring scoops of dried calendula into a silver bowl, glowered at them. I'd only hired her a couple of months before, but she'd proven her worth a thousand times over. She had toured on the festival circuit for several years, offering tarot and henna tattoos while her girlfriend played as a violinist with a start-up band. When the girlfriend ran off with a fire dancer at Glastonbury last summer, Mia reluctantly made her way home to her middle-class parents, who were both proud of and flummoxed by their tattooed, green-dreadlocked girl. I'd adored her on sight, her fierceness hiding a heart as kind as dawn, and had only grown to love her more as the days went by.

"Be careful," she said now in a mild voice. "I've oil of toad here in my hand. Do you know what it does?"

The London girl smirked. "Give me warts?"

Mia blinked her enormous green eyes. "Ruins every selfie you ever take."

"Right."

Undeterred, Mia continued calmly. "Do you want to play a game? I guess your—"

I gave her a raised eyebrow and subtly shook my head.

"Never mind."

The two laughed and hurried out, the bell ringing behind them. Traffic was picking up this week—the street was full of people, tourists and locals out in the sunny day. Local shoppers in their sensible shoes and hats. Women in oversize sunglasses with designer bags, ramblers with their packs, and middle-aged couples on holiday from Switzerland and America and Australia.

"They're not worth your anger," I said, measuring oil of rose into a fairy-size jar the color of rubies. The jars were teardrop shaped, like something from the Arabian Nights, and came complete with glass stoppers. They cost a pretty penny even in bulk, but they more than paid for themselves during the festival. This particular one would be a love potion to draw a lusty lover and give the wearer eloquence. I would not have a single bottle left when the long weekend was over.

"I'm just sick of their type," Mia said. "Think they know everything, and all they do is gobble up every resource on the planet and then shit it out as carbon dioxide until the world is so hot it wants to explode, and then *they* make fun of those of *us* who want to live a simpler life."

I paused in my counting. "What else is happening, my love?"

She shook her head. "My parents are on me again to go to school, to cut my hair, to be"—she rolled her eyes and put the word in air quotes—"normal."

"Mmm." I waited.

"I'm stuck! Stuck in this Muggle town with Muggle people who are all oblivious to what really matters." She waved a hand toward the window. "We have to learn to live more lightly. More spiritually. I just—"

I touched her hand, feeling a swirl of longing and regret and the surge of moon-time emotions. "You aren't stuck. You're just resting between things."

She looked at me, a swell of tears making her look almost like an anime character. "I'm not running away? Because that's how it feels sometimes."

"Oh, no." I brushed hair from her face, feeling a vast sense of love for her. The world seemed so sad and lonely today. "Believe me, I've run, and that's not what you're doing. You were sent here to help me. What would I do without you just now?"

"Really?"

I thought of Zoe, standing like a medieval guard at the door to the house I'd grown up in. Thought of Diana, rosy with love, and Jennie, who still had not texted me. "More than I can say."

"Thank you." She sniffed. "I'm going to have a smoke."

She was headed out the back door just as another customer came in the front door. "Hello!" I called as the bell rang. "Come in, come in. Look around."

The girl who entered the shop was tall and willowy, with long graceful limbs and black curly hair, like mine.

I swallowed.

She paused by the door, as if her bravado had carried her this far but no farther, and then she visibly gathered herself, took a breath, and crossed the uneven wooden floors of the shop. "Hi. My name is Isabel, and I think you're my grandmother."

My heart squeezed. "I think you're right. Come in."

She hovered right there, between the door and the counter where I stood, as if she wasn't sure if she would stay or flee. "I have a question," she said.

"Please ask it."

"Why did you leave my mother?"

"Oh, my dear," I said. "That is a very complicated question. What if we start with something a bit simpler? Would you like to have a cup of tea?"

"I don't know if I should." She looked over her shoulder, toward the door. "It's going to make my mom mad if she finds out I came to see you."

I nodded, folding my hands to force myself to just wait for her, as if she were a wild thing that might startle.

She took a breath, looked back. "I would like a cup of tea. I've been out all morning."

"Wonderful. Why don't you come sit with me?" I gestured toward the back room, where I kept a kettle and a little table by the window. I filled the kettle and turned it on. "Do you like black tea? Earl Grey?"

"Just the usual." She looked around as I busied myself with mugs and such. "Do you make all this stuff?"

"I do. With help from Mia there." I pointed to my assistant, vaping as she leaned on the fence visible from the back door. "Are you interested in the magical arts?"

She shrugged. "Not sure I believe in them. My other grandma says magic is evil."

"Hmm. That would be Florence, is that right? The Catholic Mexican great-grandmother?"

"You know her?"

"I did, a long time ago. I lived in New Mexico, at the farm. Does your granddad still live there?"

"Yeah. He has sheep and goats and a big garden."

I smiled, somehow pleased that he was living that simple life he had longed for. "I'm glad." I poured milk into a small pitcher and placed it on a wooden tray. "Magic isn't evil," I said. "That was simply a way for the church to take the power of women, who were the healers and wise women."

Isabel's eyebrows rose. "Huh."

Mia came back in. "Hello," she said.

"Hi." Isabel waved a hand.

"This is my granddaughter, Isabel," I said. "We are going to have a cup of tea. Will you watch the front?"

"Sure." Mia inclined her head, smiling softly. "She's your Mini-Me."

Pleased, I laughed. "Thank you."

"Don't say that in front of my mom."

"No. We won't."

When the water boiled, I filled a fat-bellied pot and added it to the tray. "Let's sit over here, shall we?"

She rose and joined me. It was true that she looked like me, but I could also see her dramatically handsome father, especially in her willowy grace and her ripe lips over even white teeth. So American, those teeth. She was clearly nervous, pulling her sleeves down over her hands.

I sat back. "Would you like to learn a little bit about the cards?"

She eyed the decks stacked neatly on one side of the table. "Sure. Like, just for fun, not for evil."

I laughed. "Of course. Just for fun. For interest." I picked up my old, worn Rider-Waite. "This is the most traditional deck. It has major and minor cards." I laid them out and then showed the suits and told her a little about each one.

She sipped her tea. Touched the Page of Wands, then the Queen of Pentacles. I smiled. "Page is a young person. Queen is an older woman." I laid them down, side by side. "You and me."

The moment ignited her imagination. I saw it flare in her dark eyes, in her quick smile. "Can you do more?"

"Of course. Would you like a reading? Something simple?"

She raised her shoulders, both not sure and sure. "Yeah. I do."

I picked up the cards, leaving out the Queen of Pentacles, the card of motherliness and nurturing, and the Page of Wands, which tells of a youth in some trouble, which wasn't hard to see. I shuffled the cards, over and over, letting them clear, then handed them to her. "Shuffle three times."

She did. I admired her long fingers, her smooth young hands, and when she returned the cards, I cut them, then offered her the deck again. "Cut them once more."

I turned them over, one by one: Page of Swords, reversed. The Empress. Nine of Swords, reversed, thank goodness. The Fool. "This is nice, actually."

"Really?"

"Page of Swords is someone who crossed you, a vindictive and maybe furious person you can't trust."

Her eyebrows lifted. "Weird. What else?"

"The Empress, which is almost certainly your mother, who is in your corner completely."

Isabel looked at it for a long moment, then blinked hard, as if to hide tears. She touched the skirts of the Empress. "She is. In my corner. That makes me feel kind of guilty for being here." She scowled. "But I don't love the look of this card."

"It looks bad, but it isn't. Nine of Swords, reversed. You are moving away from a nightmare or a terrible time."

"That's creepy."

"Why?"

She frowned again, those thick beautiful brows beetling down as she stared at the cards. "Because this"—she stabbed the Page of Swords—"is my friend Kaitlyn. And this is my mother, who would do anything to make me happier. And this"—she touched the Nine of Swords with a fingertip—"is everything lately."

"The good news is," I said with lightness in my voice, "the final card is the Fool, who represents optimism and fresh starts. That's a good thing."

She pulled her sleeves down over her hands. "I guess." She stood up. "I'm glad to meet you, but I really think I have to go now. I don't want my mom to get mad at me."

I stood, too, and carefully did not touch her. "I understand. I am so glad you came by. Come anytime."

With that, she turned and disappeared, like a hare.

Chapter Sixteen
Zoe

The morning of the sweep, I was the first one awake. I peeked in on Gran, and she was sleeping peacefully, tucked beneath her big down duvet. Her color was good, and I felt a sweet sense of relief.

And maybe a slight triumph. I couldn't believe my mother had just shown up at the door, as if she had a right, as if she hadn't been wandering around the world for nearly three decades, never bothering to check in with anybody. How dared she?

As I came into the kitchen, however, a contrary voice suggested, very quietly, that perhaps Poppy had a point. If she'd been visiting regularly, maybe I needed to at least ask Gran if she wanted her here.

A vivid red blast through my entire body said, *No! No way!*

I was saved from considering it further when Isabel came down, hollow eyed and grumpy. She hadn't washed her hair in a while, and when I brushed it off her face, she looked like she might break.

Sweet girl. "Did you have a bad night?"

"Sometimes I can't sleep," she said, and she flopped down at the table. "Mósí made it better."

"That's good." My mom radar was bleating loudly, and to give myself a minute to choose my words, I filled the kettle. "Do you want some tea?"

A shrug.

I crossed the stone floor and bent down and wrapped my arms around her from behind. I pressed my cheek into her hair. She didn't talk, and I felt her trembling, in resistance, in fear, in whatever this was. Tears burned in my throat, but I forced myself not to shed them, to swallow them back down.

A hundred times, a hundred different ways, I'd asked her to tell me what had happened. A hundred times she'd shut me down, closed off, and it was days before she'd come back. Dr. Kerry said she thought Isabel was slowly healing, beginning to find her way back after whatever trauma had so shattered her, and I had to just keep loving her, standing by her, but also giving her space.

PTSD was a tricky affliction, and when she started shrugging me off, I let her go, patted her shoulder, moved back to the counter to start my own breakfast.

Perhaps it was the exact spot I was standing in the kitchen, or the way the light fell, or the telephone that still hung on the wall with its long cord, but I suddenly remembered the last phone call I'd had with my mother.

Or rather, I felt it right in the solar plexus—that visceral recognition that she was not going to come back for me.

"Did I ever tell you that I stopped talking to my mother when I was twelve?"

"No. I thought she stopped talking to you."

Her tone was open. I turned around, arms crossed as if to protect that child I'd been, and gently felt my way through the story. "She called me every Sunday, and it was usually about now because of the time difference." I looked toward the phone, saw myself standing there with a bowl of porridge on the counter, brown sugar piled in a little pyramid on the top. "I heard a sound in the background. I heard it all the time when she called, and I asked her what it was. She said it was the call to prayer, and it happened five times a day." A wild emotion rose in my chest, and I had to blink hard. "It was so beautiful, and I wanted to be there with her so badly, and right then I realized that she wasn't coming back." I gave my own daughter a rueful smile. "I'd been waiting five years and it hadn't happened, but that's when I gave up."

"I hate that she left you," Isabel said, fiercely. But she cast a frown at the table.

I nodded. "The point is, my love, that I am right here. With you. Wide open. No matter what you need. Got it?"

She nodded. "I know."

"Good." I took a breath. "Now, what are you doing with your day? Do you want to come with me for the sweep?"

"Um . . . no. Sorry."

"That's all right. I do need a plan from you. Maybe a shower?"

"Are you saying I stink?"

I just looked at her.

"Okay, I'll shower. It's just cold in that bathroom."

"I think there are some space heaters around."

"Because that's safe! An electrical appliance plugged in, in a bathroom!"

"They're fine. I'll find you one." The tea had steeped long enough, and I wondered what to eat. Maybe a couple of eggs. I felt hollow, like I needed something substantial to get me through the grim work of the sweep ahead of me. "I might make some pancakes. Want some?"

"Sure."

"What's the rest of the plan for the day?" I repeated my query and waited at the pantry door for her answer.

She gave a huffy sigh. "I'll take a shower. And then I'll take my camera out and walk around the village and shoot some photos. And check in every hour."

"Great." I dove into the pantry and picked out baking powder, a canister of flour, and salt, then returned to the kitchen. "Don't you have some homework for Dr. Kerry and for school too?"

She nodded glumly.

"Okay, then. That works."

"Fine." She shrugged.

"I'll be back for dinner. What do you want to cook?"

"Why do I have to do it?"

"That's your job, right?"

"Yeah, at *home*."

I found a ceramic bowl under the counter and measuring cups in a drawer. "The deal was, you cooked dinner if I agreed to you changing schools."

"But this kitchen is weird. That stove is not like anything I ever saw in my life!"

"Google how to cook on a Rayburn," I said. "And there's a Crock-Pot around here somewhere. Explore the kitchen and figure out what you want to cook. It can be canned soup for all I care, but if you're going to town, you can take a backpack and get some groceries."

Another huffy sigh. But when I sneaked a glance over my shoulder, she was sitting up straighter, and she'd pulled the sleeves of the hoodie up on her arms.

Progress.

The sweep for clues to Diana's disappearance was meant to start at noon. I walked from Woodhurst to town on a metal staircase that zigzagged down the steep face to the beach, then crossed the sand, trying to keep my mind in the present, not on what I was about to do.

It was the weekend, and people were loading up their yachts and fishing boats for a good sail. I thought of Lillian's theory that there was smuggling going on and wondered if it had anything to do with Diana. Did she find something out? Did she go afoul of someone?

Smuggling would be inordinately easy. Caves and passageways riddled the coastline, and Axestowe had been a scandalously profitable smuggling site in the eighteenth century.

The people milling around the harbor were a well-kept lot, with the kind of tans bought with long hours of leisure in sunny climes. The women kept their hair short to easily dry after sailing and swimming, and they boasted the lean legs of tennis players.

These people had no need of smuggling anything. Everything they could possibly wish for was right at their fingertips. They were masters of the universe and the women of well-to-do families who'd married advantageously to provide more sons and daughters to rule the world.

If smuggling had been going on, what could such a group want that they couldn't have? I toyed with the possibilities as I climbed the stairs on the other side of the beach, trying not to think about Diana and where she might be and what I was about to do.

One of Lady Dawood's truisms was that it was human nature to always wish for more. It explained why men hunted big game and posed with dead lions and rare rhinos—the thrill of the chase. I wondered what kind of thrill seeking those rich locals could be engaged in.

Drugs? It just didn't fit.

High-stakes gambling? It was a possibility, I supposed.

I followed a dusty beaten trail from the stairs around the edge of a car park that provided space for summer visitors and headed for the edge of the forest. A group had gathered, probably fifteen people or so, all standing soberly in a knot. This was not the same forest with its hill fort that Isabel had found, but a more urbanized waste area where teenagers gathered to drink beer and have sex. The South West Coast Path wove around the high end of it, but mostly it was just a patch of trees between town and farms and the sea.

Cooper stood toward one side, looking properly dressed in an outdoor hat and canvas pants with a dozen pockets and sturdy army-colored wellies that had seen a few seasons. I thought of us at ten, striding over the moor in our hats and boots, looking for plovers and emperor moths with their feathered antennae. I'd had a passion for caterpillars and butterflies, while Cooper loved birds of all sorts, and we'd wandered everywhere to find our precious creatures. Never to capture them, only to spy them in the wild. I drew pictures; he jotted down notes in his little notebook with a pencil no larger than a pinkie finger. In those days I only wanted to be outside, all day, every day. The memory softened something in me, and I went to stand beside him.

He gave me a nod that suited the somberness of the occasion. "Hello."

"I hope we don't find a single thing," I said.

His mouth lifted on one side. "Me too."

Maybe because I'd been thinking of our childhood forays, I looked at him longer than I had been doing. More directly. He looked back, and his mouth quirked ever so slightly. Sadly. An eddy of loss swam through me.

The inspector started talking, giving us directions on what to do, how to look for clues. I'd seen the process on television, of course: a line of people side by side, walking through a forest or a field after the disappearance of someone. In horror, I suddenly imagined coming across the dead body of my lifelong friend, and all the air left my lungs. I pressed my hand over my heart, afraid I might faint if I didn't breathe.

Cooper laid a big hand on my shoulder. "It's only panic. It's normal." He offered me a mint from a roll he pulled out of his pocket. His hand, his calm voice, steadied me.

"What if we do find her?"

"In the most pragmatic terms, that's why we're here," he said, taking a mint from the roll for himself, "but even more so, what are the chances of her two oldest friends just stumbling over her body?"

We'd been the Three Musketeers as children, as close as siblings. "You know chance isn't like that."

"Come on, we'll be all right." We turned and began to shuffle through the tall grass along with everyone else. I concentrated carefully, looking for threads or discarded food or a mark that didn't seem to go with the area. I saw fungi and wildflowers, grass and fallen leaves. We walked slowly and carefully, picking up bits of debris and litter with gloved hands and dropping them into a bag each of us carried. I was glad of Cooper beside me, steady and quiet. No one talked.

Despite the grim nature of our task, I found the forest unknotting my tension. It was filled with birds chattering back and forth, whistling and chirping and making all manner of noises. I heard a squeezed note and a series of hurried chirps, a repetitive whistle. I didn't know which notes belonged to which birds, but I was sure Cooper could name them all easily. He'd always known them, all the birds and animals. The legend was that he'd spoken bird before he'd spoken English.

The air itself seemed quieter here, under the trees, the air softer. I had grown to love the austerity of Santa Fe's landscape, sketched in tones of earth and clay and sky, but it was never comfortable.

"Do you remember when we built our fort?" Cooper asked quietly.

Surprised, I laughed softly. "Yes. Do you think it's still here?"

"Doubtful." He paused, looking back toward the sea. "I believe it was that way a bit."

"Diana hated it. She was so afraid of spiders."

"Not an outside girl, that one." He resumed his slow, steady search, and I fell in beside him. "Do you still like the outdoors," he asked, "or have you grown out of it?"

"Grown out of it? Who does that?"

A half shrug. "A lot of people. They just forget what magic there is here."

I paused to pick up a cigarette butt. "Magic, all right."

He grinned, and it was the face I'd loved all my life: the high cheekbones, the straight, aggressive nose. "Not all of it, admittedly."

Dropping the butt in my bag, I said, "I was just thinking how the forest makes me feel like myself."

"Not the moor?"

"I haven't been there for a long time."

"You should come back." He untangled something from a curl of weed. "Go for a wander. Do some sketching, if you still like that."

"I do." I paused, thinking of how intimidating the open moor could be. I'd been a teenager when I'd been there last. Probably with Cooper. I remembered a day fighting bitterly about our future. Another making love in a mossy forest where the fairy queen might have seen him and arranged to take him for herself, turning his heart against me.

I remembered the taste of his mouth, the way he didn't entirely close his eyes when he kissed me. Some lost part of myself said, "After such a long time, I might need a guide."

He straightened, took off his hat, and wiped sweat from his brow. The hat had left a mark on his forehead and mashed his curls, and it didn't dent his beauty in the slightest. "You'd be fine when you got out there."

A sting of disappointment made me look away. "I'm sure."

"But I'll go with you, if you like. Give Matt a good run."

Something stirred in me, as if I'd been thickly cocooned and had suddenly glimpsed light through the walls, just a little, as they thinned. The hope was almost painful, and I wasn't sure I liked it. "I should bring Isabel. She would love it."

He slapped his hat against his thigh. Raised his head. "As we do."

The words carried a thousand hours of happiness, in childhood and preadolescence. My body softened in memory of those wide skies, the rolling, endless fields and hills.

The summer I was fifteen, I'd returned to England for the first time in three years. During my time away, we'd written hundreds of letters, sent dozens of packages, even spoken on the phone when one or the other of us could raise enough money for it.

I'd been longing to see him, burning. My grandmother had driven Diana and me out to the farm, a few miles outside the village. Cooper had been waiting outside his cottage, restless. I leapt out of the car before it had time to fully stop and flung myself into a hug.

He held me as tightly as I held him, and I buried my face into his neck, and before we let go, we were in love. As if it had been destined, as if we'd just been waiting to get old enough to make it real.

From that moment until our breakup three years later, we'd been intensely entangled. Physically, mentally, maybe even spiritually. Soul mates. We spent endless hours on the moor pursuing our hobbies of bird and butterfly, even more kissing. Kissing and kissing and kissing. We must have kissed a hundred million times that first year. Later, the kissing turned to other things. We learned to make love to each other, taking it very seriously at first, less so as time wore on.

I was deeply in love. We both were.

In the forest now, looking for our lost friend, we shuffled side by side through the grass. I spied a red ribbon that seemed too nice to have been sitting out in the forest for very long, and I dropped it in my bag, aching for those days, for those two lovers. So many things had come between us. They seemed foolish now.

Beside the ribbon was an earring. A simple gold hoop, like a million others, but I picked it up carefully, feeling terror and sorrow well up in my throat. Cooper paused, sensing my disturbance. Our eyes met. I thought of Diana laughing in the big, bold way she had, her earlobes hung with hoops.

We'd been fighting, but I still loved her. The way you love a cousin you shared your childhood with, the way you love the children you grow up with, forever.

I somberly dropped the hoop in my bag.

"A thousand girls wear earrings like that," Cooper said. "It probably isn't hers."

I nodded. We continued our sweep.

Cooper hummed a folk song I barely remembered, and the air was so much softer between us. He had been so very, very angry with me for so long. We'd never hashed it out, just finally mellowed into a different relationship over time. Those old thorns still pricked me at times, and I'm sure they did him, as well.

When it came time to choose our university paths, I wanted to go to Glasgow, to the Glasgow School of Art, one of the most famous in Europe. Cooper planned to study environmental science in Bristol.

The distance was not terrible between them, and we were sure we could navigate what everyone told us would be the end of our relationship.

A series of events served to wreck that plan. Cooper's father died, necessitating a change in his plans. He had to stay close to help his mother with the farm, and there was a perfectly acceptable program at Exeter.

For him.

But not for me. Glasgow was my dream, and I couldn't bear to give it up. Although Cooper was unhappy, he didn't stand in my way, and we promised, fervently, to put our relationship first.

It was harder than I expected to be so far from home and family. I felt lost without Cooper, especially, and found it difficult to make friends with people who all seemed to be so much more talented than me, and to top it all off, one of my teachers absolutely loathed everything I did. No matter how I approached a project or assignment, he belittled my efforts, laughed at me, taunted me in front of others. It was excruciating.

I stuck with it through most of the first term, but he flunked me on my major project, a painting I'd worked on for over a hundred hours. He not only flunked me, but he derided my talent in front of the class. Sitting there with cheeks flaming, I could tell some of the others were uncomfortable, but others snickered. A boy named Jacob who'd been kind to me stood up for me, insisted the painting was flawed, but not impossibly. The teacher roared at him, too, and Jacob stood up and grabbed my hand, and we fled together. We drank coffee for hours until I was finally calm enough to go back to my room and try to call Cooper.

He couldn't speak to me. He had exams. He had a problem on the farm.

I fell to pieces, and instead of packing everything up and going home the way I should have, I went back out to the pub and found Jacob. Predictably and foolishly, I slept with him.

It was terrible. It was stupid. I confessed the very next day to Cooper, assuming that he would understand, that he would forgive me.

He did not. Things fell apart in a bitter, passionate, desperate fight.

I'd had enough. I fled to New Mexico, heartsore and desperate to escape the things I had learned about myself. I was not the great artist I'd imagined, or even a particularly good person. I couldn't face Cooper, or the village, or even really myself.

Defiantly, I enrolled in the graphics art program at the University of New Mexico. Cooper refused to speak to me. For months.

I kept thinking he would soften, that we would find a way to come to peace and get back together, but no matter how many letters I wrote, he didn't write back.

When I flew back in the summer, he refused to talk to me. He'd taken up with one of the village girls who'd chased him endlessly. It crushed me.

It was over, and I had to come to terms with the fact that I'd killed it. Cooper might have been rigid in some ways, and I had lacked confidence, but the truth was, I'd made a mistake he couldn't forgive. I didn't think I'd have forgiven him for such a breach either. I sure hadn't forgiven Martin.

At the end of the sweep, Cooper walked with me back to the car park, where he'd left his ratty old Range Rover, which was a completely different thing here than it was in America. This one was approximately five hundred years old, the paint so faded it barely qualified as a color, with excellent tires. Colorful blankets lined the back and the passenger seat, presumably for dogs.

I thought again of the moor, the most healing place on earth. I wanted to take Isabel there, to show her the wide skies and the ponies and the owls. "Do you have any time in the next few days to take Isabel and me out to the moor?"

"Sure." He flung his hat in the back seat. "Tomorrow, maybe?"

"Really?"

A slight lift of a shoulder. "Why not?"

"Okay. I'll talk to Isabel, get back to you," I said. "Maybe I should get your mobile number."

He tugged his phone from his shirt pocket. "Ready for yours too."
I rattled mine off and he punched in it, and I returned the favor.

"I've been keeping an eye on a few nests," he said. "We might have some baby plovers if we're lucky."

A sharp longing moved through me—I could taste the wind of the moors, the flavor of wild things. "Do you ever see hares anymore?"

"I've had one at the farm around quite a bit of late, but he's especially shy."

"I miss them."

"You'll have to come up early in the morning, then, or evening. Either one. I reckon teenagers are not always ready to leap out of bed at first light."

"No."

He nodded. Abruptly he said, "I'd like to look through Diana's flat. Maybe together we'll see something."

"Now?"

"Later, after dark."

"Isn't it a crime scene?"

A slight shrug. "No. They can't really search it until they have more evidence that it's more than just a woman going away."

My heart ached. *Going away.* As if it were an adventure. "Okay. What do you want to do?"

"I don't know. Look around. See what we see. We knew her better than anyone."

"We *know* her," I said, correcting the past tense.

His celery-colored eyes were sad. "Right."

"Okay, I mean, I guess you're right about going in and looking around, but I don't want to get in trouble."

"We'll go in the back. No one will see." He slapped the hood of his truck. "See you at the Tesco at half past eight."

A shiver of nerves, both anticipation and dread, went through me. "I'll be there."

Chapter Seventeen

Isabel

It makes me feel better to do normal things like homework, so I did my assignments for Dr. Kerry (*everything that's happened today, feelings I've had*, blah blah blah). I wrote another chapter in my main Wattpad story, and I read through what I've done so far on the fairy story, which is better than I thought. It feels different, somehow, like I'm stretching my muscles.

Like when my mom first started making me cook dinner, I found out that it was fun to plan meals. It makes me feel in control of the world to know what's going to be for dinner. I like having that one thing at the end of the day that I can count on.

As I walked down the bluff to the village, I thought about my mom and how sad she was when she told that story about Poppy. It made me feel guilty, too, because I like my grandmother a lot. A *lot*. She is super kind, and it feels good to just be around her, the way it feels good to sit in a hot tub. The person my mom always talked about, the mom who'd left her like that for years and years, sounded like a completely different person.

So I hate to keep a secret, but I don't think telling this secret would make anybody happy right this second.

The village is one of the prettiest places I know about. The light is magical—sometimes soft and golden, sometimes sort of thick or something. Not like the air in Santa Fe at all, or LA, where my dad has an apartment, where everything feels extra crystal clear.

It was afternoon, and clouds were moving in. The conditions were too bright for macro shots, or even people, honestly, but I sat on a stone bench by the harbor shooting passersby anyway. My teacher made a point of saying that you have to shoot lots of faces, lots of bodies, beautiful and ugly and plain, old and young, thin and fat, to get a feeling for how the light interacts with each one. I miss Mrs. Barrow, the photography teacher. Maybe I should send her some shots if I get any really good ones.

I miss school, honestly. I liked it. I just couldn't keep going with my skin on the outside of my body, thinking about who saw what and if that person is looking at me, knowing what I look like naked or—

Ugh.

Taking pictures of people is also good for creating characters. Like, you get stuck writing the same people over and over, the same people around you. Looking at real people in the real world makes me think harder about whoever I make up.

Like right now, people were loading up boats, which I definitely have not seen in Santa Fe. A bunch of older guys were carrying stuff. One had a cooler, and I liked the way his arms strained. Click. Another had a red hat and red shoes. Click. Onboard, they slapped each other's backs, and one stripped off his shirt, showing a really hairy back and chest. Ew. But I shot it anyway.

A lady was stomping up the ramp. She had red hair and a white dress that showed off her skinny arms and legs. Even from a distance, I could hear the shouting. She was mad.

I zoomed in to capture the flailing arms of the angry woman, the way the man she'd yelled at bent his head.

Suddenly I realized that one of the other guys on the boat was glaring in my direction. He waved an angry hand at me, like *Get out of here.*

Embarrassed, I left.

And just like that, I got a flash, a disconnected memory of somebody reaching for me, laughing all around—

It kind of roared around my head, like a movie going by in my brain, really fast. It was so loud and sudden that I stumbled and had to catch myself on the railing.

It slammed through again, louder, the same clip, a face I didn't know, a hand coming toward me, laughing, and a sense of being out of control, like a nightmare where you're going too fast to stop, and you know it's a dream but you can't wake up.

Only this wasn't a dream. It was a memory.

I gripped the railing. *Five things.* Silver metal, tiny daisy growing in the wall, a bright-red scarf on one of the people on the beach, clouds like puffballs, my own hand with chipped-off fingernail polish, a thousand years old.

I was back in my body, not in my brain.

And all of a sudden I saw myself at school, hiding in my hoodie while everybody laughed at me behind my back. My friends haven't talked to me. My so-called boyfriend has dropped me. I am alone.

It is awful. And it is mean, and I *hate* them.

And I am sick of feeling like this. Sick of being alone.

I headed up to the cliff on the other side of town, thinking I would go to the store and go back home maybe, start cooking. It might be fun to cook something on that weird stove.

I had to walk through the park to get to the store. A bunch of little kids played on the swings and slide, and it seemed like a good place to grow up, with a view of the ocean always right there. I shot some of that, too, the kids and the ocean and the day.

At the edge of the park near the forest was a big tree with giant balls of seeds on it. Sitting beneath it was a knot of teenagers, three guys and two girls, sharing a bag of chips. One of the girls had a bad pink dye job, like something she did over the sink with no help, but it did the trick of setting her apart. I wondered if they knew Molly.

One of the guys saw me watching them. He was skinny and blond, wearing a coat even though it was a billion degrees. Good face with a strong nose and clean jaw. He'd photograph well.

"Hey, you, camera girl," he called, and it was so cute, the accent; even though I'm kind of used to it, it's different when it's a guy. "Come on over."

For a long minute, I didn't know what to do. I miss having friends, but that hasn't gone that well, right? I waved my hand, shook my head, kept walking.

The blond guy jogged out to walk beside me. "Hi," he said. Up close, his eyes were light green. You don't see green eyes all that often, but in Axestowe, it's pretty common, like a genetic thing in the village. "Are you shy?"

"Not exactly," I said, which is true. My mouth felt a little dry, and I swallowed a couple of times, but another part of me didn't want him to go. I am scared of the things people can do, but I am also tired of never being around people my age.

"I'm Isaac," he said.

"Isabel."

"That wasn't so hard, was it?"

I shook my head. "I'm not shy. Just careful."

"Are you visiting from America, Careful Isabel?"

"Kind of. Visiting my great-grandmother."

"Oh!" He nodded. "You're the girl Molly met the other day, right?"

"I met *a* Molly a couple of days ago, yeah." I met his glittering gaze, and an almost-forgotten something whispered up my spine. "Are you a friend of hers?"

"We all are." He pointed a thumb over his shoulder at the others. "We live in the council flats over on the other side of the river."

I had no idea what that meant, but I nodded like I knew. Maybe apartments or something.

"You should come over and hang out with us."

I looked at the group. They were looking our way, but nobody seemed hostile. Still, I couldn't seem to say yes. "I have to go to the store."

He grinned at me, coaxing, and I suddenly felt a yank of memory.

"Sorry," I said, and I hurried away.

"Next time!" he called after me.

What I suddenly wanted, more than anything, was to visit my grandmother. It felt urgent and important, and I switched directions without even giving it much thought to head into the village and the Kitchen Witch.

Chapter Eighteen

Poppy

In addition to the worry over Diana and now Jennie, and the urgency I felt over my mother, work was extremely busy. The Axestowe Festival, the biggest event of the year, would take place next weekend, and I had a lot to get ready still. The doldrums of late afternoon were our best prep times at the shop, and we were working on dry sachets. I was fretting as I worked, honestly, fretting over how to get in to see my mother, and wondering if I knew anything about Diana that hadn't really clicked.

And Jennie, damn it. Where was the girl?

With a sudden insight, I realized someone who might know. "I'll be right back," I said to Mia. "Watch the shop for a few minutes."

The sun was unexpectedly hot, but I only had a little walk, down the high street to the Rose and Crown. A chalkboard outside advertised steak pie for £10.95 and ploughman's lunch for £8.50. I smelled bread as I ducked into the cool interior, and I found the tables well occupied with a prosperous group of tourists, a good portion of them Germans of a certain age who'd come in with a coach tour and enjoyed a glass of beer with their midday meals, men and women alike.

But I wasn't interested in tourists. I wound my way through the dark rooms to the bar, where a handful of dedicated drinkers held down their favored stools. One of them was Alan, Jennie's father. So early in the day, he was still upright and tidy. I slid on a stool next to him. "Hello, Alan."

He startled a little but sat up straighter. I wasn't the belle I once was, but men over fifty still took notice. He looked at my breasts.

A burst of laughter rolled out of a corner booth, and I saw a table of well-heeled men, strangers, lingering over the remains of their lunch. No doubt one of the fishing parties that had cropped up so often lately, ready to set sail for the week ahead. The weather would be fabulous.

"Where did Jennie go?"

"How would I know?" he replied gruffly. "She ain't spoken to me in nearly a year."

"You know things anyway, don't you? Her boyfriend—"

He made a noise of disgust.

I looked over my shoulder at the room, thinking how many hours he'd sat here. "She went to Exeter. Do you have family there? Someone she might have contacted?"

"Nah. We're all here, and south."

Another big blast of laughter. I glanced over my shoulder. "What kind of fishing do they do?" I asked idly.

"Hell if I know." He raised his pint, elbow on the bar. "Don't think they're bringing in many fish."

"Why do you say that?"

He glanced toward them. "They got no coolers, not big enough for that lot."

"What are they doing, then?"

"Getting drunk. Playing poker and dice." He took an oddly delicate sip of ale. "Bunch of fat rich fucks."

The bartender came over, and I waved him away. "Your daughter is missing, Alan. I don't know where she is or why she's not answering her phone, but you might want to give it a little more attention."

"What do you want me to do? She ain't been living with me since I kicked her out over that baby."

"I just thought you'd want to know."

I walked out, wondering how many young people faced parents like this, people who abandoned a job they hadn't really wanted in the first place.

And then I heard my thought and stopped in my tracks. I had abandoned my child too. But it was different, because I'd left her with my own mother, who doted on her, who piled more love and attention on her than I ever could have.

Hadn't she?

A passerby bumped me, then uttered a quick apology. It jolted me into moving again. Not quickly, because my gut burned with something that felt very much like shame, and the pain of it radiated outward, encompassing my entire being.

I thought of my seven-year-old Zoe, with her long braids and big wide eyes and grasshopper legs, her skin so brown all summer that she looked like a chocolate Lab.

But I couldn't think about that. Not today.

A small voice said without judgment, *Then when?*

I was getting a drink of water when the bell over the door rang. I looked up to see Isabel. My heart bloomed at her beauty, the wild curls, her large brown eyes. Had the heavens ever produced a more beautiful girl? I couldn't think of a single one.

"Isabel! I am so glad to see you."

"Hi." She frowned and closed the door, and then stood there as if she didn't know what she was doing.

"Did you come for another lesson in tarot?"

"Maybe? I just"—she looked over her shoulder—"I just wanted to come here."

I inclined my head. What was this about? "All right. We're bored with ourselves here, so why don't we all sit down and play with the cards?"

Mia had been as restless as a cat all day. "Yes. I am so for that idea."

"Come, my lovelies," I said, gathering them with sweeps of my hands and moving them toward the alcove. A bay window bowed out toward the sea, and I'd covered the table with a hand-printed cloth from Jaipur, where I'd landed to study with a guru after my world had fallen to pieces. I had been so very ill, and Baba had given me the tools to heal my shredded heart.

So many teachers. I'd been blessed to find them all, one after the other, in Glastonbury and America and Jaipur and Kolkata and Kanchanaburi and Bodh Gaya.

Overhead, the speakers played ragas, music that stirred up spiritual longings and hopes. "Mia, will you pour us all glasses of lavender lemonade?" I'd made it this morning, moved by some impulse I didn't question, and now I knew why.

Isabel didn't quite roost. She sat on the edge of her chair, heels braced on the lower rung of the chair as if poised to leap away at the slightest provocation. "How is your mother?" I asked.

"Fine. Or well, not fine, because she's sad about Diana, and I think she's worried about Gigi, but you know. Fine-ish, I guess."

I gathered the decks, wondering which ones we should use. "Did she tell you I stopped by?"

"No! Did you talk to her, to my mom?"

"I did." I passed my palms over the cards, the decks, feeling them for the right energy. "She was not happy about it, but we talked."

"I'm shocked." She frowned, tucked her hands under her knees, looked over her shoulder. "Maybe I should go. Maybe this is not a great idea." But it distressed her.

"Isabel, you are not responsible for either your mother's happiness or mine. You only have to do what feels right. I will not be angry if you feel you must go. I'm sure we will have many opportunities to get to know each other."

"I asked my dad about it, and he said the same thing. That if I want to know you, I can figure out a way to do that without involving my mom." She leveled her strangely mature gaze at me. "He also said you really hurt her. Scarred her, really."

Scarred seemed a bit harsh, but I let it go. Nodded.

Mia returned with three tall glasses filled with faintly purple lemonade served with circlets of lemon. "It smells lovely," she said, settling everything and taking the empty chair.

Isabel leaned in and sipped it. "That's nice! I wouldn't have thought you could drink lavender."

Scarred, I thought, feeling the word through my heart. It burned like acid through the tenderest parts of that space, sizzling and crackling. Authentic. Had I scarred my tender and lovely daughter?

A glimmer of something broke through my careful walls, something bigger and darker than I could manage just then. I would think of it later.

On the hill I could see through the window, the search party looked for clues to Diana's disappearance. I'd read the warnings in her cards, as I'd seen death in Jennie's abbreviated life line.

Lost girls. I'd found them everywhere, all over the world, all longing for hope, for love, for an answer to their hungers in a world that did not honor them.

Mia among them. She was restless and lonely, mourning the woman she'd left behind. "Shall I read?"

Her energy was jagged, and I placed my hand over hers. "Allow me." Listening to my intuition, I laid three cards facedown in a triangle and asked Mia to turn them over, one at a time. She revealed the Three of Cups, the Ace of Coins, and, at last, the Queen of Coins. I smiled. "What do you see?"

Even Mia couldn't hold on to her resentment under the force of such a positive set of cards. "Sensuality, the physical, the material world. Fresh starts," she said. "And a woman." Her lips quirked.

"Good." I touched the Queen of Coins. "A lush, sensual woman, by the look of this. Someone very secure and comfortable in her skin."

Her body softened, all at once. "That would be awesome."

"Fresh starts, yes," I added. "Unexpected joy. Happiness and hope."

She raised her clear eyes, and I saw hope in them, which was the whole point of telling fortunes. "You're exactly where you're meant to be, dear girl. This is a rest period, that's all."

"I hope so." She took the cards, lifted the Queen, and surprised me by kissing it. "I'm so lonely. I want to find my soul mate."

"We all have so many," I said. "You're bound to find one of them very soon."

"We do?" Isabel asked. "I thought it was only one."

"Poppy!" Mia protested at the same moment. "You don't believe that! Many, not just one? That doesn't even make sense."

I thought of Ravi, standing in the doorway of a temple, his face as calm as the winter sky. "Some carry more weight than others," I agreed, "but each one brings a gift. If you're so focused on finding just the right person, you might miss the ones who bring you everything you need."

Mia narrowed her eyes, shuffling, shuffling. "You had a soul mate, though, didn't you?"

I dropped my gaze to her hands, glad to see her working with the cards as I'd taught her to do, but guarding my secret heart nonetheless. A flash of Ravi's high brow and brown throat crossed my memory, that blue kurta he wore so often. "No."

"Aha!" Isabel said. "I think you did have one. Was it my grandfather?"

"He was one of them," I said, touching her wrist. One day, she might read the cards, but for now I could touch her without her knowing that it wasn't Ben I'd loved so fiercely.

"Mmm." Mia smiled slightly and laid out a spread, facedown. "Shall we see?"

I covered her hand. "No," I said. "Not today." I left the table, set the kettle to boil. Out of the corner of my eye, I saw Mia turn the cards over anyway, but I didn't rebuke her. What would she see? What would she learn?

The Magician placed at the center of a circle. Around him the Lovers, the World, the Wheel of Fortune, the Ten of Cups, Death. "Bloody hell." She frowned. "I've never seen so many major cards in a reading."

The eyes she raised to me filled with tears. "More than a soul mate," she said softly.

I turned my back, feeling the rare baying pain rise and twist—Ravi's hand in mine, growing cold, the vastness of time before me, empty without him.

She was wise enough not to press. Looking out the tiny window to the narrow alley, I thought of the Ten of Cups, the family card, the happy card. How happy we had been in the midst of a long and terrible storm! Our tiny family of two, but a family nonetheless.

"Is that why you left my mother?" Isabel asked. "For a *guy?*"

That thin knife blade of loss and shame and confusion slid around my ribs. "In a way," I said. "But it's more complicated than that."

Isabel leveled a cool look at me, stacking cards in a way that was steady and not at all nervous. An old soul. "I'm listening."

I gave Mia a glance, and she made an excuse to leave the table. "You want to know why I left your mother."

She nodded.

I sighed, trying to gather the pieces, the right pieces, to tell her. "None of this will make it all right. And I don't offer excuses: only what I know is true for me."

"Okay."

119

"I loved your mother from the first moment she arrived in the world," I said. "But I did not love being a mother, and I most certainly did not want to be a wife."

"Then why were you?"

"That's a good question. I thought I had to. I didn't know, not for a long time, that I had any other choice."

"But it was the eighties! Not, like, the fifties."

"I know. But women were still not as free as you've become. You're not free still, but it's better."

"I don't feel free."

"There's still work to be done." I sipped lavender lemonade and let the purple scent move through me, calming and soft. "We had some freedom. The pill made it better, and I was freer than my mother had been to explore what I wanted."

"But she's a writer."

"She didn't start until she was middle aged. After my father died."

"I did sort of know that, I guess."

"Anyway, I became pregnant with your mother by accident. I was dismayed, but I was in love, and it didn't seem quite the thing to abort his child."

"Wait. So you almost had an *abortion* with my mom?"

"Well, it was one of my choices, of course. I was young and not married." I lifted a shoulder, waited, let her outrage settle back a little. "But honestly, I didn't even consider it. I loved your grandfather and we got married, even though no one in our families were happy."

"So you didn't want to get married, but you did." She stirred her tea, her demeanor very still, giving nothing away. Very much like Zoe at the door to the kitchen. Locked up tight. "Did you just get tired of being a mom, so you left?"

"I didn't know it would be for so long," I said, dodging.

"But you never came back." Again, she leveled the question with so much lack of emotion that I knew there had to be mountains of it below.

"I did come back. She has always refused to see me."

"But not until she was grown up." Her eyes narrowed ever so slightly.

"Yes." I paused. Told the truth. "I was not a good mother, Isabel. It's that simple."

"My grandma—my other grandma—says that you broke my grandpa's heart."

I nodded. "I think that's probably true."

"Do you feel bad?"

It was unexpectedly direct. I answered just as directly. "Yes," I said. "And no. I would hardly be who I am now if I went back and made a different choice."

She slumped backward. "That's not going to help."

"Oh, my dear," I said, leaning forward to touch her hand. "It's nothing for you to fix. Your mother and I will have to do it ourselves. Why don't you and I work on getting to know each other, without any of the rest of it?"

She considered for a long moment; then her eyes slid toward the worn deck of tarot on the table. "Can you teach me to read cards?"

"I would be delighted."

Chapter Nineteen

Zoe

I felt strung taut and also exhausted by the time I returned to Woodhurst after the sweep. Someone had dropped off an apple ginger cake that now rested on the surface of the Rayburn, sending a warm scent of home and comfort into the air. I shook off my mac and hung it on a hook by the door and realized I was absolutely ravenous.

From the cupboard, I took a saucer edged with lilies of the valley, my grandmother's pattern, and served myself a slab of cake. It was still warm as I cut into it, and the flavors of soft apple and sharp ginger mixed with the buttery crumb sent tiny waves of pleasure and comfort down my nerves.

Light fell through the big window over the sink, mottled by rain-drops that pattered against the glass in a replenishing rhythm. The room itself was old and worn, the boards overhead painted white to alleviate the gloom, and as familiar to me as the lines on my hands. My fingers itched, suddenly, to draw, and I ran up the back stairs, fetched the art bag that lived in my old bedroom, and settled at the table with the cake and a cup of tea, light falling through the window to make agreeable, soft shapes of the food. I drew. I used Inktense pencils to create the cake and the saucer with its tiny lilies and sharp green leaves. Soon I was humming under my breath, sketching the stove and the rafters and even the sink with the gray-green light.

It made me remember being seven and nine and eleven, when I'd experimented with every form of art supplies I could get my hands on. I'd sketched and colored and painted and drawn, in sketchbooks and on paper and canvas.

And on postcards. The thought of them lit a flame in my chest—the big, sturdy A6 cards my grandmother bought in bulk at a stationer's in a nearby village. I filled them with scenes and sunsets, butterflies, dogs, the sea, picnics, each one an incantation designed to call my mother home.

Each one destined to fail.

For dinner, Isabel made a simple supper of tomato soup and egg-salad sandwiches on a very good bread. We ate in the kitchen, where the floors sloped too hard toward the door and the cupboards sometimes hung open just the smallest bit. The old wooden table had been host to generations of meals.

Lillian seemed extremely tired, picking at her food. "Are you all right, Gran?" I asked. Guiltily, I thought of my mother wanting to come in and see her. Was I making a mistake by trying to handle it by myself?

"Fine, fine," she said airily, but she only moved her fork a quarter of an inch on her plate. "Just tired, I suppose."

"Would you like something different to eat?"

"No, this is delicious."

I glanced at Isabel, who shook her head in solidarity with me. "How about some ice cream, Gigi? With chocolate sauce?" Isabel stood up, carrying her empty plate to the sink as she always did at home. "I'm going to have some."

Lillian looked at the plate, twiddled with her fork again, and dropped her hand in her lap. "Yes, I'd like ice cream, if that's all right."

"Of course it's all right." I touched her hand. "You're the one who gets to decide what's right for you."

"Don't tell my sister Mary."

Isabel turned around and gave me a perplexed expression. I shook my head. "We won't tell anyone," I said, but fear whipped through me. She couldn't stay on her own like this. I had to figure out a long-term solution for care, with someone tender and kind and skilled.

"Mary teases me about my tummy," Gran said, and she sounded very young. "She's always been so skinny. She's lucky."

"You're nice and slim now," I said, and then redirected. "How did your work go this afternoon?"

"Very well." She leaned back as Isabel exchanged the nearly untouched soup and sandwich for a bowl of ice cream. "Nearly a thousand words."

"That's great."

Isabel sat down with her own ice cream. "You want some, Mom?" I shook my head.

Lillian said, "I really think that man is up to something."

"Who?"

"The one who keeps lurking around the balloons. I wonder if he's a spy," she said irritably.

I blinked, trying to follow the threads. "Is he a friend of Mary's?"

"Of course not. She's been dead for a year now." Her eyes welled slightly, but she dashed them away. "Mother gets impatient with me when I weep, but I do so miss her."

Mary had died in a London bomb blast, working for the war effort. Lillian had been younger, still out in the country.

"I'm sure you do," I said. "Perhaps an early night tonight, Gran."

She slammed her open palm on the table. "When I finish my ice cream."

I winced. "Of course." I carried my dishes to the sink, feeling the gut weight of my obligations. The only person in the world who knew what to tell me about this was the person I most did not want to call in all the world. Gran's cell phone was on the counter. With a hand that shook only a little, I picked it up and called up the contact list. Right there, at the top of the favorites, was Poppy.

I walked with it into the great hall, dark and cold, rainy cloud-light coming in from the enormous window that overlooked the sea. I held the phone and cloaked myself in an imaginary asbestos suit. Pressed the contact, and my mother picked up immediately.

"Mother? Are you all right?"

"This is Zoe," I said in a brisk voice. "Gran is very confused and a little agitated, and I don't know what to do."

"Oh, my dear—"

I cut her off. "No, none of that. Gran is here, and Isabel is with her. I'll wait until you arrive, but then I'm leaving. And I don't want you to be here when I get back."

"I'll be right there," she said mildly.

I hung up and let go of a breath, feeling my body for any signs of damage. Nothing.

Back in the kitchen, I said, "Gran, Poppy is coming over."

Isabel said, "What?"

I lifted my chin, placed the phone carefully on the table. "She's been looking after Gigi, and I don't know what to do."

Isabel had a strange expression on her face.

"What is it?" I asked. "I thought you wanted to get to know her."

"I did, I mean, I do, but are you ready to see your mom?"

"Oh, I'm not staying," I said, and then a hollow sense of guilt whooshed through me. "You can come with me, if you like. Or if that's weird and you want me to stay, I will." I could feel my cheeks heating up, getting hotter and hotter the longer I contemplated having to actually have a conversation with my mother.

"No, no, Mom, listen." She stood up, tucking her hands in her back pocket. "Don't get mad, but I've . . . uh . . . been visiting her already? At the shop? I just wanted to see what she was like."

Gran said, "That's nice, Isabel. I'm glad."

I stared at her. A pulse thudded against my temple, loud and painful. "What?"

"I know. I knew you would be mad, so that's why I didn't tell you."

"You've been sneaking round to see my mother?"

Her heavy brows drew down. "Well, it wasn't like you would have given me permission."

"Oh, so if I'm not going to give you permission, you can just do it behind my back?"

"No! That's not what I mean."

"Maybe you should clarify, then. I've given you a lot of freedom here, Isabel, even though I'm still worried sick about you and you still won't tell me—" I thought of my grandmother and halted, shaking my head. "You know what I mean."

She ducked her head. "I do. I'm sorry. It's just that she's my *grandmother*. Look how close you are to Gigi."

A tangled mass of sorrow and love wound through me, sticking at junctions, yanking up memories—sitting on my grandmother's lap when I was very small, staring into her eyes, decoding the colors of her irises; walking and walking and walking on the beach, for miles and miles, that very walking she could no longer do; playing board games and sitting in the window seat of her office drawing for hours. I would not have been who I was without her. Any stability I'd achieved had grown from her love for me, her steadiness.

But my mother was not like Gran. She was the opposite—unstable and flighty and untrustworthy and—

Isabel looked at me with remorse. "I'm sorry. I really didn't want you to get mad at me."

I shook my head and forced myself to let go of the hot breath burning my lungs, my belly. "I understand. It's all right." I reached for her and she let me hug her, flinging her arms around my waist, her head buried in my neck. "Just be careful. Don't get hurt."

She nodded against me, then lifted her head, wiping a tear off her cheek. "I'm really sorry."

I smoothed her hair. "I know."

"She doesn't seem like the person you talk about, Mom. Maybe she's changed."

My armor slammed closed around me, protecting all the vulnerable organs and entry points. "Maybe."

Gran dipped up a spoonful of melting ice cream. "You have to forgive her sometime, my dear." She popped the ice cream in her mouth, leaving a smear on her chin that she didn't seem to notice.

I wanted to weep, but instead I picked up her napkin and blotted her chin. She let me, as acquiescent as a child.

"You don't have to stay until she gets here, Mom," Isabel said. "I get it."

"No, I'll wait. Tell her what's happening." The heat in my face had faded, leaving only my ears burning hot.

"I can do it, Mom." Isabel touched my arm.

Gran said, "Go, my love. We'll be fine."

And of course, that was what I wanted. "Write everything down," I said. "Lists of drugs, all that."

"I will," Isabel said. "You're not mad at me?"

I shook my head. "No." I touched her smooth peach cheek. At least if Poppy was here, I wouldn't have to worry about Isabel being alone. "Text me if you need me."

I drove down to the village in a pouring rain, my emotions as wild as the weather. My mother was part of it, and Isabel going behind my back, but the worst was the decline of my grandmother. In the dark of the car, I let myself shed a few tears of sorrow and helplessness. I was going to lose her, and there was not a single bloody thing I could do about it.

The village was empty except for the odd person hurrying beneath an umbrella, and I made my way to the Tesco parking lot, where I saw Cooper's battered Range Rover. I pulled in next to it. He gestured for me to join him in the truck, and I dashed through the rain to do it, water streaming down the back of my neck. "Ack!" I said, diving in. "Gully washer!"

"Good weather for ducks."

I grinned wryly in spite of myself. It was something his mother had said every single time it rained. "How is your mom?"

"All right, I reckon. She lives in Scotland with her husband. I don't see her much."

I nodded. "We're not going to walk to Diana's, are we?"

"It's a bit wet for that. Don't really want to park on the lane either. You up for a short dash?"

"Sure."

His scent filled the cab—autumn leaves and a brisk wind, a fragrance that danced along my skin, and it made me suddenly self-conscious. I had never *not* been attracted to him, ever, even when I was married and madly in love with Martin, even when Cooper was furious with me. Why did I think it would be any different now? It didn't help that my nerves were a tangle, worried about Diana, thinking of my mother at Woodhurst with my daughter and grandmother. I worried about going into the house, about getting caught, about what we might find. I knitted my fingers together.

"Nervous?"

"Why?"

"Your hands."

"Oh." I unlaced them and immediately found myself tangling them again. "Habit." I took a breath. "I had to call my mother to come over tonight. Gran was wandering and—"

The sorrow filled my throat again, and I halted to let it subside. "I didn't know how to care for her."

He covered my hand, his big palm engulfing the area between fingernails and wrist. "That must have been hard. I'm proud of you." His hand was an anchor in the darkness and storm.

"Thank you."

"Are you all right?"

I shrugged and found myself telling him the truth. "I'm just sad. About Gran, and Diana, and Isabel and . . . life just steamrolling over people I love."

"Isabel?"

I didn't want to talk about the real things. "Well, for one thing, she's been sneaking behind my back to see my mother."

To my surprise, he chuckled. I yanked my hand away. "Why is that funny?"

"It's what you'd do, if you were forbidden."

"That's not true. I follow the rules."

He paused, his hand on the ignition. "Do you?"

Was he referring to my infidelity, or something else? I looked out the window, testing the challenge. I thought of myself as a rule follower, the one who held up the tent when nobody else did. My mother, Martin. But if someone had forbidden me from seeing my grandmother, I probably would have defied them. "Maybe not always."

"Nothing wrong with that." He turned the key, and the engine sputtered and coughed, died, and then he started it again. "She's just achy tonight."

"Well, she is a hundred and fifty years old," I said, trying to lighten the mood, for myself as much as Cooper. "It happens."

It was his turn to be startled into a laugh. Sort of. It was a quiet chuckle, a sideways glance. I had always been able to make him laugh.

"Nah," he countered. "Her last birthday, she was only a hundred and ten."

I smiled, relieved at the release of tension for even a minute.

Rain pelted the windscreen and roof and sent wide waves on either side of us as he drove up the hill. A sonata played on the radio, which was old enough to be an AM dial with white marks showing against a greenish light. The village lanes were very dark, and only the dashboard illuminated his face at all, the edges of his hair. For a moment, I was transported back to the soft quiet we'd shared, going everywhere together. I'd never been so comfortable with anyone as I'd been with Cooper. *Safe,* he'd said. *You're safe here.*

"We can dash right down the hill from here," he said, pulling beneath the branches of an ancient oak. "Will you be all right?"

"Of course. I won't melt."

"I dunno," he said lightly, eyeing the sky. "You're American now."

"I'll be fine."

"Follow me, and we'll slip between the cottages to the back garden, go in the back." He paused, hands on the steering wheel. "Do you remember it?"

I made a noise of exasperation. "She's lived there for fifteen years. I think I remember it."

"Good." He opened the door and jumped out, with the rain held off a bit by the tree. I slid out behind him, and then he dashed down the lane, through the deluge, and into a little alleyway. I held my breath, ducked my head, and followed.

I was soaked in seconds. By the time I'd reached the back door, he'd opened it, and I pushed by him. "Close the door."

He closed it quickly. "Leave your wellies."

We left them in the mud room. Cooper led the way to the kitchen, where he turned on a light.

A fist struck my gut. It was exactly the same as it had been the last time I was here last spring, a darkish cottage with whitewashed walls that she tried to brighten with a lively color scheme of yellow and red. A red kettle sat on the range.

"It looks perfectly normal."

He nodded. "I was here only a couple of weeks ago. Right before she disappeared. She made some cookies."

"It's been a while for me." The ache grew. "What should we look for?"

"I don't know. Just something. Anything."

I'd been expecting him to lead the charge, but he looked so winded I said, "Right. Nothing in here. Anything important for the business will be at her business address." I headed for the main room. The shutters were in place, and I hoped the light wasn't leaking out too much. Someone would notice and call the police, and then we'd get in trouble.

Get in trouble, I thought. Was I sixteen?

Some part of me was.

Cooper hadn't moved. "Are you okay?" I asked.

He roused himself, shook his head no.

"Why don't you check her desk?" I suggested gently. "I'll look in the bedroom."

"Yes. All right." He gathered himself and marched his body into the other room.

The bedroom was up a set of narrow stairs that creaked as I climbed them. I headed down the hall on uneven, ancient boards.

Everything was immaculately tidy—Diana's reaction to the madness of the communal childhood we'd all shared. Her hair was always freshly cut, her clothes clean and pressed, and here, in her home, everything was in its place.

In the bedroom, I had to halt again. Just as I'd found comfort in the scent of Cooper in the Range Rover, I smelled Diana here. Not perfume, but the smell of her skin and the products she used on her hair and the way she metabolized oxygen and a million other things that added up to the notes that belonged to her alone. Cooper smelled of the outdoors. Diana's scent was equal parts vanilla and fresh coriander, which wouldn't seem to go together, but they brought her presence into the room, sharp and fragrant, in a visceral, painful way. I missed her desperately, all at once, and tears sprang to my eyes. Damn it! Why had I let such a stupid thing come between us?

Where are you?

I was suddenly assailed with a vision of her dead body, lying in some wet, dank place, and something in me cracked. I couldn't do this, couldn't go through her things. Couldn't—

No.

I squared my shoulders. Everyone else could give up, but until I had exhausted every possibility, I would keep looking for her. I owed her that much. To that end, I started looking through her things. It was invasive and uncomfortable, but necessary.

I started with her drawers, where everything was folded in what I recognized as Marie Kondo order. It made me smile. I remembered our conversation not too long ago on the wonders of the Kondo method, which had made me run shuddering away but appealed to Diana's need for order and peace.

Nothing seemed amiss. Cooper was right—the police hadn't searched here at all, then, not if everything was exactly as she'd left it. I knew there were legalities about when the police could declare a missing person an investigation, but hadn't we passed that point already?

Clearly not. I opened the wardrobe with its crystal knobs and found dresses and blouses and, at one side, a pair of men's shirts, one a soft green, the other a similar tone in blue. Henry's, no doubt. Both were crisply pressed, as if she'd laundered them. I hesitated, then took one out. Henry was a big man, tall and broad, and he could afford good quality. I thought of the blurry image of the man from the boat, and he came a little clearer in my mind.

I hung it up again, hoping he would be back to wear it. Taking Diana to dinner somewhere nice, giving her the attention she deserved.

Or maybe he was the reason she'd disappeared.

Where was he, anyway? Why didn't anyone know him? Why hadn't the police talked to him yet? Even if he was in London, someone must surely have his number.

It made me think of Diana's phone again. Where was the phone? If they couldn't track it, then the battery was dead, which would make it harder to hope for a happy ending, but it was possible it had been lost. Dumped somewhere.

I continued my search—through the bedroom, peeking in the drawers of the nightstands, afraid to find anything too personal. A box of condoms was all I found.

Condoms. I held the box for a moment, trying to remember the last time I'd used them or needed them. So long that the date was lost in time. After my marriage had broken up, I'd dated a little here and there, but it was hard enough to juggle a full-time job, an adolescent child, and a home without adding men into the equation.

And really, it was all just so exhausting. Getting to know someone, starting at square one, trying to suss out who would be worth the time.

Mostly, they just were not, so I stopped trying.

I put the box back in the drawer, exactly as it had been. Nothing else in the bedroom caught my eye, and I wandered down the hall to the bathroom. It was a cramped room with a giant pink tub and a pedestal sink. The wooden medicine chest was installed in the wall, not behind a mirror, and I had to struggle to open the damp-swollen door.

The usual things—aspirin and paracetamol. Eye drops. A prescription cream for eczema. A can of manly-scented shaving cream and a razor that must have also belonged to Henry. Toiletries implied a certain expectation—of return, of stability, of settling in.

I missed that, too, the sense of coupledom and intimacy. The fact of Diana's relationship had played into the distance between us too. She'd accused me of keeping parts of myself aloof always, keeping everyone at arm's length. I was furious, wounded, and at a loss over how to overcome the distance. Martin had accused me, too, of never really allowing him true intimacy, soul intimacy.

But how did you let people in if you knew they'd always leave you?

Staring at the neat contents of the medicine chest, I blinked back more tears. Now Diana had left, too, but I'd left her first, maybe hoping it wouldn't hurt as much.

It still did.

I closed the door, aching, and went back downstairs. It was silent. Cooper sat by the desk, head in his hands. Lamplight glazed his form, edging the strong, long back, his tumble of hair, the edge of his chin. A memory of longing, or maybe something new, shimmered up my inner arms, across my throat.

I must have made a sound because he straightened, dashing tears off his face. "Sorry." He cleared his throat. "It's just so bloody sad, doing this."

My throat tight, I came to stand beside him, hesitated, then laid a hand on his shoulder. For a moment, I didn't say anything, just let my hand convey my own sorrow and my sympathy for his. It seemed strangely normal, and I found myself tempted to smooth down his hair.

Swallowing, I said, "I know. Henry's shirts are hanging in her closet, and his razor is in her bathroom. She was so happy with him, for the first time ever. Did you ever meet him?"

He shook his head. "We tried a couple of times, but he was only here on the weekends, setting up whatever it was he was doing. Fishing trips, I think."

"Yeah." I spied something on the desk and reached for it, moving away from Cooper. The paper was a business card, very simple, from an estate agent in Exeter. I wondered what she'd been doing in Exeter. I held it, frowning, and ran a finger down the numbers running down one side of the ledger. "Did you find anything here?"

"It's strange. Why would anyone use a paper ledger when you have computers? Do you see that she doesn't have a computer in here?"

I frowned. "Laptop, maybe?"

"If she had one, it's not here."

"Will you stop using past tense?" I snapped.

His jaw tightened. "You always do make up your own reality."

Stung, I glared at him, then shook my head. "How does it help to imagine she's dead, Cooper? What does that help?"

"It helps me. You saw her once a year! I saw her nearly every bloody day."

Both true and untrue. "She's still my friend."

"Not the same."

Again, the sting of truth. "I know." I shook my head, looking around the room, remembering times we'd sat in this room and talked about life, about love, about hope. I'd poured out my despair over my divorce here, and she'd shared her plan for a catering business, the millionth conversation of our lives. "I don't have many friends. Losing her is a big loss."

He took my hand.

"Until I see her body, she's alive in my mind. I want her to be happy: enjoying a relationship and having sex and going on great trips." Tears filled my eyes. "Just let me have that for a little while longer."

He softened. "I'm sorry."

I ducked my head, blinking. "What's in the ledger?"

"Accounting. Nothing seems amiss."

In Diana's square printing were categories down one side—*Picnics, Baskets, Lunches, Cold Suppers, À la Carte*. Dates ran across the top of the page. She had entered the number of each, some numbers in purple. "Why would she keep this here? And why on paper?" I frowned. "It's not like she was a technophobe."

"Not at all."

I flipped a few pages, but there were only the first two pages, dates from last summer to now. "We should check out her office and the computer there."

He smiled, albeit wanly. "Look who's getting into the spirit of it!"

"I want to find her."

"All right. I'll talk to Cora, her assistant. I'm sure she has keys."

I nodded, frowning at the page. My intuition insisted something was here. Why the paper?

"C'mon. Let's have a cup of tea. You know that's what she'd want us to do."

What I really wanted was a hug. A place to rest my head and let go of some of the tension I felt. But I followed him to the kitchen.

An array of photos was stuck to the fridge with magnets. One was of Poppy and Cooper standing in front of the bay. "You two are great friends these days," I said.

He raised an eyebrow. "We are, actually. Are you going to cut me off the way you did Diana?"

Tears of shame and loss rose again, and I blinked them back, shaking my head. "No. Lillian needs her."

He touched my shoulder, squeezed, and let go. "I know it's not easy."

I shrugged. "How did you two become friends again? I didn't think you were the type for tarot readings."

"No." He filled the kettle with water while I opened the cupboards until I found mugs. "She's doing some conservation work, counting hares, birds, and some butterflies on her farm."

"She has a farm?" In a second cupboard, I found a glass jar full of tea bags and took one out for each of the cups. "Like an actual farm, with animals?" A memory of her scattering feed for a flock of chickens rose in my mind, and with it, a sense of longing. I crushed it down. If I wanted to function at all, I couldn't let my mother in. Not right now.

Not with everything else: Isabel and Diana and what to do about my grandmother. Too much.

He turned the burner on beneath the kettle and leaned against the counter, arms folded across his chest. I found myself noticing the hollow of his throat and remembered the smell of him there, the heat. "Goats, I believe," he said, "and chickens, maybe a couple of cats. She grows most of her own herbs for the shop, and flowers. You all seem to be gardeners."

"So industrious." I always imagined my mother dancing around barefoot to a Celtic fiddle, flowers in her hair, being completely impractical. "I guess it fits, in a way. Back to the land like a proper hippie."

"Perhaps it's time to let the past go, Zoe. It's been a long time since she left you. It's not too late to have a relationship with her."

I straightened, feeling chastised by the one person who should have understood. A part of me wanted to present my arguments, my very good reasons for keeping my distance, but even the thought of it made me feel winded. If I let my mother in now, I would fall to pieces. I couldn't chance another betrayal.

"Honestly," I said wearily, "I have no desire. What would we even say to each other?"

"I suspect you'd find something."

I opened and closed a couple of drawers, looking for pencil and paper. In one, I discovered a neat collection of white packets, tea or herbal cures of some sort. Each one had *The Kitchen Witch* stamped on it, and I recoiled, shoving the door closed.

In a "junk" drawer that held a tidy stack of envelopes, I found a roll of stamps with a rubber band around it, notepaper, and a pen. I shook my head. "She's so tidy."

"Doesn't take after her mother, does she?" Cooper agreed.

I sat at the table. "Let's see if we can figure anything out about the past few months. Diana was working a lot, from the sound of things, catering to the fishing parties."

He nodded.

"Do you know if she stayed on the boats and worked the parties, or did she just drop off the food?"

"She didn't go out with the boats, no. She made picnics and sandwiches, cold chicken, things of that sort. Things they'd reheat or eat as finger food."

"Wonder why."

"The parties last a few days, out to sea. Not a lot of pleasure for a woman in that environment."

"Makes sense."

The kettle whistled, and Cooper grabbed it, poured water into our mugs. "I reckon the milk is spoiled, but there's sugar."

Her fridge. I looked at it, thinking of the food rotting within. "Do you think we should clean it out so it's not awful when—" The words stuck in my throat. *When she comes home.*

He covered my hand. "Let's not, shall we?" He nudged the sugar bowl in my direction.

"I hate to think it was Henry," I said. "But who else could it really be?"

"Honestly, it's bothered me that none of her friends had met him."

I frowned, handing him the spoon I'd used to stir my tea. "Gran thinks there's something going on in the village. Maybe Henry—and Diana—are part of whatever that is."

"Go on." The spoon looked like a toy in his big hand. He'd always been the tallest, leanest boy in our class, and he never really looked like he fit in an ordinary chair. I suddenly remembered sitting on his lap, winding my arms around him, leaning in to kiss his neck and jaw, tickling him on purpose.

I looked away. "She's getting confused sometimes, so it's hard to tell if she really means something now, or something in one of her books, or something from the war."

"Perhaps something is crossing wires, something from now reminding her of the past." He shifted, and his knee bumped mine. He immediately reached out a hand, touched my leg lightly. "Sorry."

Our eyes met fully for the first time, really, since I'd been back. Met and caught, and I was captured, a lost hunger rising in my chest. He was still as handsome as a prince from some old fairy tale, a thing he'd rejected from youngest childhood. Not only the biggest boy, but the most beautiful. Girls chased him around the playgrounds. Followed him when we all went to Exeter to shop. Left trinkets for him on his bike or car.

He hated it. It was an accident of genes, nothing to do with himself, he said, and he was a loner who preferred the company of his dogs to girls who had nothing in their minds but some fantasy.

As a woman who had known that face my entire life, it was still startling sometimes to *see* it objectively anew. It was the balance and clarity of his features, the exact measurements of what the human eye finds appealing—eyes spaced just so, with a strong, straight nose between, and cheekbones giving it shape, and his mouth, wide and full lipped. A shimmer of tears lingered in his lower lashes. A glaze of sparse beard on his chin caught the light.

His hand rested on my leg. Something filled the room, yearning then and yearning now, and without even thinking I bent close and kissed him.

For a long, long electric moment, he returned it, his free hand flying up to the back of my neck to hold me there. My hand fell on his leg, and I was leaning forward, half risen out of my chair so that I had to brace myself against him.

He pulled away, abruptly and with some vigor, turning his head. "No, not this time," he said.

Embarrassed, I flung my body out of my chair, heading for the door, imagining I would flee by diving out into the night and the pouring rain. I struggled with my wellies.

"Stay," Cooper said behind me. He stood two feet away, carefully not touching me, but one hand extended. "It's terrible out there."

I covered my mouth with my hand, my ears burning with humiliation. "I'm sorry," I said, and even as I said it, I didn't mean it. I could taste him on my lips still, could feel the silky slide of his tongue against mine. "I don't know why I did that."

He shook his head. "Forget it."

I thought of his hand on the back of my neck, felt a fluttering at the base of my throat. Stayed frozen by the door.

"Come sit down, Zoe." He gestured toward the table. "It's not fit for woman nor beast out there."

I didn't see how I could sit down in front of him with my cheeks flaming in humiliation. "I can't," I whispered.

He waited, calm and quiet.

The rain pounded overhead, splattering in bursts against the windows. I wondered just how soaked I would get if I ran back up the hill to the Tesco.

Very.

I sat. Picked up my mug to give myself something to do, a chance to let my mortification subside a little. But even in my humiliation, I felt starved and aroused. The imprint of his body and mouth, the sound of his breath against me, lingered, leaving my skin buzzing and alive.

I closed my eyes, willing myself to calm down. I thought of the way watercolor paint slides over a heavy cotton page, the depth of oil in the same color. After a minute, I could look at him.

He stirred his tea, even if it had been stirred three times. I recognized the nervousness in the gesture. "Will you bring your daughter out to the moor tomorrow?"

I grabbed the lifeline, relieved that he could return things to the new normal, that I hadn't ruined everything. "She was not interested in waking up at five, but she said dusk would be fine."

He smiled softly. "Good. We'll see what we can spot. I've been hearing a pair of tawny owls of late."

"I would love that."

"Still an owl lover?"

"Of course. You should see the great horned owls that come calling in my backyard."

"Tell me."

It gave me an easy thing to cling to, which I knew he'd given me out of kindness.

"They're enormous." I held out my hand to illustrate the height from the floor. "And they have a beautiful call." I paused and summoned the voice I used for owls, low and breathy. *"Whoo . . . whoo hoo."* I had his attention fully, and continued. *"Whoo . . . whoo hoo.* My father doesn't like them. He thinks they're unlucky, but I know you would be enchanted, as I am. In the summertime, at night, when the crickets are whirring, and there is no traffic, and the big New Mexico sky is clear, that sound is like the gods."

His eyes rested on my face, as if he had looked through me to the scene I'd sketched. It made me feel a little drunk. "You should see it someday."

"I always planned to," he said, straightening.

"That's not fair, Cooper."

"Most people call me Sage now."

Bricks made of words, making a wall. I shook my head. "I doubt I could make the change."

He nodded, rubbed a palm on his leg. The rain began to slow. I took a breath, let it out, remembered why we were there. "When do you want to check out her office?"

"Sooner the better, I suppose. Tomorrow morning, since your girl wants to sleep in?"

"I need to talk to Lillian, make sure she's okay first. Make sure Isabel has something to do. I don't want to leave her alone too much."

"All right. Text me when you're ready. I have something to do early, but I can meet you around ten."

"Okay."

He glanced at the clock, which showed five to nine. "Shall we make a run for it?"

Back home, I didn't see a strange car in the drive, and the house seemed abed. Poppy seemed to have gone. A note sat on the table. "Everything good," Isabel had written. "Xoxoxoxoxox."

Beneath the note was a neatly lettered page of care instructions from my mother. Her handwriting gave me a pang, opening a wound I really did not care to examine in my weary state, and I shoved it down. The instructions were clear and straightforward, the medicines listed in alphabetical order, with their dosages and uses also listed.

Like the idea of my mother on the farm, this evidence of her nurturing maturity went against all I knew of her. Maybe she had changed.

Maybe, I thought, wearily, turning off the lights as I made my way upstairs, I still didn't care.

I checked on Isabel and Lillian, finding both asleep. Mósí sprawled the length of his mistress, his belly open to the hand she rested there. It made me smile. Silly cat. In Gran's room, the lamp was on in the corner, and a plastic bottle of water, the type with a pull top, sat on her nightstand. She was so small now that she barely raised the covers, and my heart flipped. One day, she would no longer be in this world. I didn't know how I could bear it. She was the one through line in my life.

I made my way to my own room, at the farthest end of the wing. The corridor was dark, illuminated only by what light could sift through the cloud cover and make it through the windows lining the way. I looked out to the bay, choppy and black on such a grim night, and wondered what all the fishing-party boys were up to if they were stuck in town.

In my room, I caught up with small bits of email until our erratic Wi-Fi finally shut down completely. Too restless to sleep, I sifted through the notes I'd been collecting on my phone.

Diana had disappeared two weeks ago. Her boyfriend had been gone ever since. No one in town had seen her. The sweep had turned up no body, thank God, but maybe it would yield some other result. A spot in my heart burned with the idea of her locked away somewhere, which was at least better than imagining her body eaten by fish or tossed in a shallow grave.

I wished we could find her boyfriend, or get some sense of what she'd been doing. I made a note to see if we could find out what her most recent jobs had been.

Diana. Where are you? Help me find you.

I looked forward to taking Isabel to Dartmoor. It was a place of healing, and she'd been so much better since we'd arrived here that I had hope that the moor would take it a few steps further. It would be good for me too. My nerves were wound too tight over both Diana and Isabel, and I needed to get out in nature and breathe a bit. It would help me think of how to best proceed with my grandmother. My mother.

I really did not want to think about Poppy. Ever. At all. But especially tonight when everything felt so stirred up. My skin still rippled every time I thought of kissing Cooper, in mortification but also in longing. It was embarrassing to still want that so much.

My sketching notebooks from that time were stored here, all neatly arranged by date on the lower bookshelves. There were two dozen or more, heavyweight linen-covered sketchbooks Lillian had bought to encourage my artistic interests. She'd also bought me a flute at one time, and paid for dance lessons that lasted exactly three weeks before I realized I didn't really love the discipline as much as flying around in private dance to a waltz.

But the art turned out to be just right. After gathering a few sketchbooks, I carried them back to my bed and leaned against the wall to leaf through them. I found grasses and flowers sketched in remarkably thorough detail, cowslips and heather and dog violets. In another series, I found the various dogs who'd kept us company, and barn cats and sheep; gnarled lonely trees and windbreaks made of hawthorn. One entire notebook was devoted to glades of ancient trees, magical and green, limbs and rocks and ground covered in moss. I couldn't remember how far into the park Piles Copse was, but considering how magical Isabel had found the forest by the river, she should see it.

In some part of my mind, I'd been looking for the sketches of Cooper, and I finally found some of them. Quickly rendered figure drawings, ink and watercolors of his hands or boots. Detailed drawings of his face. Several pages of just his hair, as I tried to capture the look of curls, making hair look like hair, capturing the graded shades of blond to dark contained within a single lock.

I turned the pages, half smiling. The work was sometimes rough, the early work of an emerging artist, but I was pleased to find that quite a lot of them were very good. Hands were difficult, and the renditions of his were good, especially when I'd used pencil and had taken my time.

One book was mostly devoted to the butterflies I so loved. The green hairstreak was my favorite, with its expressive face and iridescent green wings. I drew many others, too; butterflies were a satisfying subject, particularly in colored pencil, which I'd used a lot in those days. It was a medium that required patience and the time to layer, but of course as a teenager I'd had loads of time.

I turned the page, and caught my breath. Here were more sketches of Cooper, and I remembered exactly when I'd done the series. His mother had gone somewhere, and we'd taken advantage of her absence to spend the afternoon exploring each other. I'd sketched him naked, his long lean form so poetically balanced, while he watched me do it.

Cooper, naked, in a great amount of detail.

A frisson of erotic memory ran along the edges of my shoulder blades, whispered over my palms. I looked through the page to the day itself, seeing him sprawled against the sheets, light pouring through the small window in his room.

In those days, sex had been one of our favorite pursuits. We spent hours and hours kissing, touching, looking, entwining.

As memories tumbled through my mind, I thought of kissing him tonight, thought of his thumb moving, almost unconsciously, on my thigh, his hand pulling me hard into him.

Stop it, I thought, shaking it off. I closed the sketchbook and forced myself to go to bed. Nothing was going to be solved if I didn't get some sleep.

But as I lay there in the dark, I wished for Diana, the one person who knew everything about me and about the history of Sage and me. The one who could help me sort through my inappropriate pass at him and the yearning that lingered in the hollows of my body. She would have told me what to do.

Chapter Twenty

Isabel

In the middle of the night, I woke up yelling at the top of my lungs. Anywhere else you'd think someone would hear me, but the walls in the manor are thick. In the dream, my arms were covered with letters and words made of fire, and the words burned me, traveled up my body, down my legs and stomach and back and butt.

I was fighting in my dream, fighting off the words that turned into ropes that tied me up, tied my hands and tried to lace my lips closed, but I managed to scream and flung myself upright. Even Mósí was scared by it.

My arms were clean and bare, and it was kind of stupid, but I yanked up my shirt and looked at my stomach, and for one second I flashed on that morning when I woke up and—

No.

It took a long time, maybe hours, to get back to a place where I could sleep. I used my earphones and played the soundtrack for writing, and then I went to Wattpad, where I wrote about a girl going through a doorway to the land of the fey, a magical and dangerous land where you have to be sure not to be enchanted or to eat or drink anything but berries and apples, and the most perfect pears cover the bushes and trees, and the girl is offered a golden cup of pomegranate juice, which comes from the story of Persephone, who ate a pomegranate seed from the devil, or a god who is just like the devil.

It made me hungry, all that writing, but to get to the kitchen you have to go down the back stairs, which are tight and shadowy and feel super creepy, which I didn't want to do in the middle of the night. But Mósí was still giving me a look like he didn't trust me, so I used the flashlight on my phone and made myself go through the hallway and down those narrow stairs—

Put her on the couch.

—I stopped, heart in my throat, to see if anything else would come. A smell of dust, which was both in the stairs and in memory, and—

Arms around my shoulders, my knees, a sense of falling. Laughing.

Actual memory. New memory.

I stood very still, willing more to come back to me. A face, a voice I recognized, something. Anything.

But that was all. I stood there waiting until Mósí meowed in his annoyed voice for me to hurry up and come down and give him some tuna.

Maybe all I have to do to feel better is to remember what happened. Not from the pictures, but for myself. If I can remember, then it will belong to me.

How do I do that? If I ask my therapist, it will open a big can of bullshit that I don't want to hear. A visual of a pencil pops into my mind. Write? Maybe I should write what I can remember, and then I'll remember more.

But what if I never do?

Chapter Twenty-One
Poppy

The third Sunday of the month, I often held workshops and classes in the front half of my barn, a renovated space that could hold a remarkable number of students. I taught all manner of things, from making spell candles to keeping a moon journal to creating rituals of many kinds, all based in the sacred feminine. I'd started them to supplement my thin shop income a couple of years before, and they'd proven to be well worth the time. Everyone wanted to read tarot at a party, or make a spell to bring back a straying lover, or inspire a husband to have more sex.

But in truth, the gatherings provided a chance for women to come together in ways that were becoming lost to us. Most Western women had no idea that the divine could be female, or they'd been taught that it was secondary to the male. In these workshops, which seemed to be about party tricks, I gave them the possibility that maybe Spirit could be a Mother as well as a Father.

This morning, I was still carrying the ghosts of my dreams. I'd gone back to India to visit Ravi and then sailed back to the pilgrimage in Glastonbury that had set me upon this path. In my dreams, I pressed my open palms to the Egg, that ancient ritual stone that now sits amid the ruins of Glastonbury Cathedral.

I was working with that energy today, that Egg, so the dream made sense. And Ravi, Ravi who had been so much on my mind because Zoe was back.

Zoe. She'd been gone by the time I'd arrived at Woodhurst last night, and I'd found myself absurdly disappointed. Her phone call had made me feel like there might have been a crack in the wall, and in fact, it hadn't been anything but expedient. Zoe had recognized that she needed help with Lillian, and that was something I could do easily. I'd organized the meds according to a calendar, and written out detailed instructions for what to use if, for example, Lillian became agitated or needed a sedative to sleep. Isabel had given me her full attention, and I extracted a promise from her that she would call at the slightest question or concern.

And it was plain my mother was in a state last night. Confused, which often led to her being combative. Once we got Lillian to bed, I explained to Isabel that the memory lapses were episodic—at times she functioned perfectly well, but she needed a lot of supervision.

"You've been caring for her?" she asked.

"Diana and I together."

The final dream last night had been about Isabel. I found myself at Woodhurst, watching over her as she slept.

Troubled Isabel. The sense of her, yearning and sorrowful, clung to me as I went about my chores, feeding the animals and collecting eggs and preparing myself for the day. Now, I cleared the workshop space with a ritual I'd learned from an old native woman in New Mexico, using sage to banish negative energy of all sorts.

Sage the man showed up just as I was finishing to help me put the room together. He'd pulled his hair back from his face and tucked it under a hat, and he looked tired. His dog trotted in behind him.

"Are you all right, love?" I asked.

He gave a nod. "Just tired. We looked through Diana's house last night to see if we could find any . . ." His voice cracked a little. "Anything."

"We?"

He looked at me, an unreadable disturbance in his clear eyes. The eyes of a sage. "Zoe."

"Mmm. Did you find anything?"

"No."

I touched his upper arm, rubbed it for a moment.

"What do you think happened to her?" he asked.

"It's impossible to say, isn't it?"

"Haven't you read cards or asked the spirits or something?"

It wasn't the way I used those tools, and he did know it. "If only that would give us the answers." I patted his arm. "Let's get started on these chairs, shall we? I've a crowd today."

We moved long tables from the sides of the room into the main area and then placed chairs around each one. Soft light filtered down from skylights I'd installed when I'd first done the renovation.

"What're you teaching today?" Sage asked.

"Spell work for the Hare Moon."

His lips pursed the way they always did over my subjects. He was a nonbeliever, but he liked pagan ways better than any other spiritual tradition. "What does the Hare Moon signify?"

"Oh, a good many lovely things. Growth, abundance, rebirth. Fertility." I shook out a tablecloth made of more of the hand-dyed fabric I loved from Jaipur. Each one was a different color, and I had gathered the spring colors today—soft purple and yellow and green. We spread them out over the tables. I hummed along to the Loreena McKennitt music that played on the speakers. "Perhaps you should stay and make a charm for yourself."

He clicked his tongue in mock regret. "Afraid I have to be somewhere."

Chapter Twenty-Two

Isabel

I ate breakfast with my grandmother and then helped her feed the goats, which I do with my granddad all the time.

"Tell me about your grandfather," Poppy asked.

So I told her about his little adobe house out in the desert beneath a stand of cottonwoods that have grown tall because they have their feet in a creek, and about the rugs he weaves and sells to tourists, and the plot of green chiles and tomatoes he grows.

"Sounds as if you spend a lot of time with him," Poppy commented, tossing grain out to the chickens.

"I do. He lives close by, and he's always been around a lot, even when I was a tiny baby."

"Is he still a sculptor?"

I looked up, surprised. "No. I've never seen him do that kind of art."

Poppy paused, grain for the chickens still in her hand. "Never? That's too bad. He's very good."

"He is?" I tried to fit what I knew of my grandfather into this information, or the other way around. "What did he make?"

"Animal abstracts, mostly, and he had a way of creating flow with the most difficult materials."

"Huh. No, he just weaves now."

"That's art too," Poppy said mildly.

"Why did you get divorced?"

"Oh, it's always complicated, that."

"Not always," I said. "My dad has too many women, and it made my mom sad, so she decided she'd be better off without him."

"And I'm sure she is."

I shrugged. "She's not happy, though, not really."

"Why do you think that is?" Poppy gestured for me to follow her through a gate into a big garden surrounded by a fence.

"I dunno."

"Children don't spend time trying to decide why their parents are unhappy, but parents think about their children all the time. Did you know that?"

"I guess."

Poppy picked up a basket from a sheltered bench, along with a pair of scissors from a metal container attached to the wall. We waded into the flowers, and Poppy cut this and that—a lot of one kind of pink flower, and some sprays of white—and layered them in the basket. "I suspect your mother is still looking for her place. She'll find it."

"But we've lived in Santa Fe since I was born!"

"True. I lived here from the time I was born, but I had to escape to find out who I was."

"You did? Is that how you met my grandpa?"

"Yes." She handed me the scissors and said, "Cut some of the yellow ones."

"Like this?" I felt hesitant, but how hard could it be?

"A little bit lower, below the leaves. Good. I met your grandfather when I was twenty-two. I'd been living in Glastonbury, and a friend wanted to go to the States, so I went with her."

"And was it love at first sight?"

"In a way. He was very, very handsome and was not like anyone I'd ever met. We fell in lust more than love."

I felt my ears get hot. "TMI."

"Is it, though?" She bent over to pick up a fallen rose and stood up, shaking it off. "I suspect you might have fallen in lust once or twice by now, haven't you?"

I shuddered involuntarily—a weird reaction, even for me. My stomach twisted, and I flashed on—

Hands on my head, holding me

"Are you all right?" Poppy asked.

"Just kind of dizzy," I said, and I pressed my fingers to a little twitch under my right eye.

"May I touch you, my love?"

I looked up and knew somehow that I needed that. She pressed her hands to my skull. "Close your eyes for a moment, sweetheart," she said, and I did, and my face felt hot, and my neck and my lower back, all the way to my feet. It was the strangest feeling, like almost buzzy but not quite, and I didn't even want to move, just stand there and let her touch my head.

Then I opened my eyes, and my grandmother's big blue eyes were there, kind and clear. I took a breath. She smiled.

Women started arriving. I thought it was going to be a bunch of older ladies, but it wasn't. They were all ages—young and old and in between—and I thought they were from all walks of life too. An older lady so skinny she had to be rich carried her bones to the very front of the room and plopped herself down at the table up there. She had a scarf around her neck and sporty clothes. Surreptitiously, I shot her photo.

All the tables were full by the time Poppy started. And they were so happy to be there, chatting with each other, giving each other hugs. I might have felt left out, being new, but everybody gave me hugs, especially when they found out I was Poppy's granddaughter, and they didn't seem to give me that annoying once-over that the hoodie usually brings on.

Then it got kind of weird. Poppy talked about spring and the great Egg at Glastonbury Cathedral, and fertility and women, and of all things, menstrual blood, which just seems like a gross topic, and I didn't want to listen.

But then we got to the making of the spell, a charm to wear around your neck through the summer, to bring about what you want in your life. Each table held seeds of various kinds, and beads, and string, and little pouches made of fabric, and yarn and big needles, and little slips of paper.

"To manifest the things you want this summer, take a few minutes and close your eyes," Poppy said.

I didn't close my eyes at first. I looked around the room at everyone, all the women of so many ages and ways of dress. They rested their hands in their laps and closed their eyes. The room grew very still. I felt something settling in me.

Poppy caught my eye and pulled a hand down in front of her face, nodding. Whatever. I followed directions, and with my eyes closed, I could feel a sense of something else around the room, a strange feeling that we were all holding hands, creating a circle.

"Now, think about what you want. It can be anything, big or small. Just something true, something that you feel in your heart. What seed would you like to plant in your life? What would make you happier, more at ease?"

I thought of Before, when I didn't care about the girls at school and being part of the crowd and was just happy going out to my granddad's farm and feeding the animals or spinning wool with him. But what do you call that feeling?

Peaceful.

"When you have in mind what you want, open your eyes and write it down. There's no hurry. Take all the time you need. Maybe the first thing that bubbles up isn't the one you'll write down, and that's fine. You can't get this wrong."

I thought of Thad, my boyfriend before everything happened, and the way he kissed me so long and deep, and I thought maybe I wanted that, a boyfriend again, but one who wouldn't betray me completely—

No. Not that.

Happiness. I want to be happy again and feel like a normal person. I am tired of feeling scared and sick to my stomach all the time.

I want to let go.

The words had weight. I felt them drop right into my gut and settle there. Immediately, I opened my eyes and wrote down, *Let Go.*

"Good," Poppy said. "When you have it, roll the paper into a tiny scroll and slip it inside the bag you've chosen."

Mine was a tiny blue-flowered bag that made me think of the bluebells. Poppy led us through the rest of the steps—finding a seed to represent the idea, adding herbs and flowers as we wished, both for scent and for additional power, and then sewing the bag closed with yarn and adding them to a leather string that would hang around our necks.

I loved it. It was like doing crafts at camp, only this was like Kitchen Witch camp. My bag contained a poppy seed in honor of my grandmother teaching the spell, and rose petals for sweetness and England.

And I totally love it that my grandmother is an actual witch who uses real spells. What else can she teach me?

For today, I was just happy to slip the little bag necklace on and let it fall beneath my hoodie, an incantation to bring happiness by letting go.

And in the back of my mind, I saw the good witch in my story bustling around in her white dress, trying to fix what has gone wrong.

Chapter Twenty-Three
Zoe

A text from Isabel had awakened me.

Can I go to a workshop about the Hare Moon with Poppy?

I closed my eyes, aching, and let it all move through me, then picked up my phone and texted back:

Yes. When will you be back?

Not sure. Few hours? Follow me on Find my Friends if you get worried. Srsly, I don't mind.

K, Be safe.

She sent me a red heart.

There would be no more sleeping after that, so I got up and showered. Lillian was downstairs when I got there. I kissed her head, looking for clues to her condition. She was crisply dressed in her going-to-church clothes, a pair of slacks and a silk blouse the color of cantaloupe. Her hair was done, her lipstick perfect. "Good morning, Gran."

"Good morning, my dear."

I poured coffee from the silver pot on the table. "You look lovely."

"Church this morning." She attended the local Church of England chapel, ordinary and civilized. Usually I went with her just because she liked it. "Do you want me to go with you?"

"No need," she said firmly. "My friend Gina is going to pick me up, and we shall have lunch afterward."

"Sure?" I peered at her for clues, but she seemed back to her perfectly normal self. How could I judge?

"Perfectly."

"I'm planning to meet Cooper at Diana's business to see what we might find, but I should be back in a couple of hours."

"That's fine, dear. I'm really quite good this morning. You needn't worry."

"You can call me anytime, you know. I'll drop what I'm doing."

"I appreciate that. And good idea about Diana." She slathered jam on her toast an inch thick. "I hope you find something."

"Me too. I mean, part of me wants that, but part of me wants her to just *come back*."

"I'm sure she would if she could, my dear." She delicately wiped her fingers on a cloth napkin. "Did you notice anything in particular at the gathering at the pub?"

We hadn't discussed it then, and I was surprised that it came up now, but maybe she'd just forgotten to ask me about it before, considering. "I'm not sure there was much information, really," I said, sitting back down. "There were a lot of people there, and the inspector gave us the basics, but they're flummoxed."

"People don't just disappear," she said. Her fine white brows, precisely penciled back into visibility, pulled into a frown. "Humor me, dear. Who was there, specifically?"

When she was like this, it was hard to remember that she wasn't always so sharp and clear. Maybe I was exaggerating her mental decline.

"Okay," I said. "Let me think. The usual suspects at the bar, same drinkers that are always there. A couple of people from the yacht club."

"Go on."

"Uh, a bunch of young women with tattoos—one of them I think is Diana's assistant."

"Cora."

"Yes. She and her friends. A bunch of people I don't know. Cooper, of course. Diana's mother."

Lillian shook her head. "That woman."

"I know. She asked about bank accounts."

"What did they say about Diana's boyfriend? She spoke of him, but only in general. I don't know much about him."

"No one does, it seems. I only know his first name. Henry."

Lillian tapped the side of a spoon against the table meditatively. "And no strangers? Oh, but you wouldn't know that, would you."

It stung, but I had to admit it was true. "No."

She shook her head. "There's something going on. I can feel it. Were there any drug types in the bar?"

I laughed. "Drug types?"

"Don't. You know what I mean."

"Gran, everyone is a drug type these days." I thought of the group in a back booth. "There was a group of younger guys, and I thought they'd be the pirates if the bar was in a movie."

"Good." She pointed a gnarled finger at me. "That's the sort of observation I'm looking for. Why pirates?"

I shrugged. "I'm not sure."

"Come, now. You know. Dig a little."

"Okay." I thought back to the bar, to the low light. "They were a little furtive, too skinny. Not English, I don't think."

"Ah." She waved a hand. "The Romanian boys. They come in to work the tourist trade. They're harmless." She tapped on the table a little more aggressively. "And was Poppy there?"

"Yes." I met her eyes. "We didn't speak."

She raised an eyebrow but did not comment.

I took a breath. "You think Diana's dead, don't you?"

She carefully touched her lips with her cloth napkin. "I'm afraid it's difficult to come to another conclusion. It's been nearly two weeks now."

I wanted to protest, as I had with Cooper, but it was starting to feel foolish. "But who could possibly want her dead? It doesn't make sense."

"Maybe it wasn't foul play at all, my dear. Perhaps she simply fell from a cliff and was washed out to sea."

I gave her a skeptical look. "It's not like she'd ever be close enough to a cliff to fall off. She was afraid of heights."

"Perhaps she discovered something she shouldn't have."

"Like what, though? What kind of crimes are going on around here?"

"That's what you need to find out."

I leaned back in my chair. "If you were writing the story, what would be the answer?"

For a moment, she narrowed her eyes, chewing her toast with the exaggerated completeness of a cat. "Piracy of some sort, I suppose. The coast, the coves. It's been a pirate's world here for centuries."

"Okay. So pirates might bring in what? Drugs, like OxyContin and heroin? Guns, maybe?"

"Anything valuable or expensive. Drugs, perhaps, and cigarettes. But also electronics of various sorts."

"Electronics? Like what?"

"Untraceable phones, tablets, that sort of thing."

"Untraceable phones? I would never have thought of that in a million years."

"You don't spend your days researching mystery novels, do you?"

I laughed, as she meant me to do. A woman capable of this conversation and the underlying intelligence and skill beneath it was hardly in mental decline. Maybe she'd just been tired yesterday.

Or maybe I was in denial. Emotion filled my throat, and I shook it off. "I do not."

"Well, then. I read all the newspapers, you know. Make copies of anything that might prove a good plot twist."

"Okay. I'll see what I can find out about smuggling, then." I paused. "How would I do that?"

"Ask the constable. See if there have been any indications or arrests that might shed some light on the possibilities."

"Oh, well, that's simple."

"Most things are far simpler than we believe," she said.

———— ❦ ————

I tried to keep that in mind as I walked down to the village, then up the hill on the other side to Diana's professional kitchen. I felt the hills in the backs of my thighs and my rear end. Good toning.

The heavy rain the night before had cleansed every bit of anything from the air, leaving behind the kind of day that graced every postcard in town—dazzling bright-blue skies, diamond-tipped bay with sailboats heading out to the horizon, every green thing filled to bursting with all the water it could drink. In the air was a scent of salt and sweetness, and as I came around the pink-plastered building, I discovered an old wisteria vine blooming profusely, its tentacles holding hard to the timbers between the first and second floors. The perfume hung almost visibly in the air, giving it a pale-pink cast.

Cooper's Range Rover was parked beside the building. I went inside through the back door, calling out, "Hello?"

"Hey! I'm Cora." The woman I'd seen at the pub gestured me inside. She had short blue-streaked hair and tattoos that wound their way up her arms. "You must be Zoe. Diana talks about you." A quick frown between her brows. "Talked."

"Hi." I took her hand and clasped it for a second longer than I needed to, just to convey my sense of unity. "Nice to meet you. You're her assistant, right?"

She nodded. Glanced away. "I'll—uh—leave you to it. Sage, I'll see you around."

I hadn't seen him behind a partial wall. "Wait, if you would. D'you know her password?"

"Oh, yeah. Yeah yeah." She dove back and bent over the keyboard, all lean and bendy. I rubbed the inside of my arm, wondering what I'd tattoo there if I ever became the arty person I'd once imagined.

"Thanks," Cooper said.

She whirled again. Whirled back. Pulled a large notebook off the shelf, set it down on the desk. Paused, hands in her back pockets, and looked up at him. "Hope you're okay," she said.

He nodded, gave her a polite and careful smile. "Thanks."

With a swift, biting awareness, I realized that they had something, or maybe *had* had something. It made perfect sense. She was long and lean and smart. Just his type, but young—maybe ten or so years younger than we were. It pinched. Her discomfort was vivid, but I had questions I knew she might be able to answer. "Cora, can you answer some questions before you go?"

"If I can, sure." She tucked her hair behind her ears.

"Was she working that night?"

"I dunno. The police asked me the same thing. I was in London that weekend. She gave it to me off, so I guess it was slow. She made some picnic meals, because there's a record of that, but she didn't write down where she delivered them."

I frowned. "So she made a record of who got what?"

"Of course. We had to keep track for billing. It should all be in the spreadsheet."

Cooper asked, "Did she ever make picnics and give them away or something?"

She raised her shoulders. "I mean, yes, sometimes, for the oldies in town." She nodded at me. "Your gran, for one. Mr. Hockstead, some of her other old clients." She blinked hard. "She liked caring for people, you know. She didn't like them to be alone, so she took them meals."

My throat tightened, and I looked away. "So maybe that's what she did that night? Took food to her old clients?"

"Possibly. That would be my guess."

I nodded. "She did go to Woodhurst. My gran saw her. But no one saw her after."

"Cora, do you have a list of the people she visited like that?" Cooper asked.

"Not really, but I might be able to come up with one. Should I do that?"

"Yeah."

"Well," she said, pointing at the door, giving Cooper one more longing look, "I've got somebody waiting. I'll email it to you."

"Thanks. That would be great."

"Okay, then. I'll see you. Call me if you need anything else."

"I will." He touched her shoulder. "Thanks, Cora."

She paused another moment, her face a painting of naked longing, and then dashed out.

I met his eyes. I didn't even have to add a question or a raised eyebrow. He knew that I knew, and bent his head. "She was there right after Alice died. I shouldn't have. She's not even twenty-five."

"I dated a cowboy for a few months after my divorce," I said, looking around the room, then gave him a half smile.

"A cowboy?" The word was funny in his accent, so proper. "Did he have a big buckle?"

"I guess that depends," I said, "on what you're comparing it to."

He laughed, and I just barely avoided preening. "Come on," he said. "Let's see what we can figure out."

I sat down in the chair, and he stood behind me. "I feel reluctant to look at her email. It's so personal, and I feel like I'm digging through too much of her life as it is."

"You know she'd do the same for you."

I rubbed the burn in my chest. "I wish I could talk to her about her disappearance. Isn't that weird?"

"Not at all."

I opened the books, and we scanned the entries together. She had quite a number of weddings coming up, which wrecked me. If she didn't surface sometime soon, the couples would all need to be notified, or maybe Cora would manage the orders that were already in.

We figured out her codes for birthdays, for picnics, for boxed lunches, for canapés, but not always for what event or for whom. Many of the boxed lunches were billed to a single payee, Perse Inc. "I wonder if that's a travel company, or what?" I asked.

He pulled out a chair and sat down beside me. It was tight quarters, but there was space on the desk for the book to open next to the computer. He ran his fingers over the entries, which seemed to be very similar to the entries in the ledger at her home desk.

"It's not here," I said. "Google it."

That didn't turn up anything either.

Cooper kept sorting through the notebook, while I opened file after file on the computer.

Nothing.

"We need to look at email," Cooper said.

I took a breath. "You do it. It feels weird, digging into all of her personal stuff. I know her so well."

"And I don't?"

"The things women share with each other are different than the things we share with male friends."

"Fair enough."

We both stood and shuffled around each other so he could take the chair. I was acutely aware of the way Cora's face had shown her desire, and I kept my eyes averted. He smelled of something green and growing, sunlight and chlorophyll. How could I have forgotten that fragrance? I closed my eyes for a single second to inhale it deeply. Arranged myself in my chair and pretended I didn't notice him. Our arms bumped, and I pulled mine back.

"Don't you give me any cooties," he said, brushing my touch off his arm.

I chuckled. It was a word I'd learned at grade school in Santa Fe during one of my stints there. "I can't believe you remember that."

"I know."

He took a pair of spectacles out of his shirt pocket and put them on. They were gold wire frames, round, and made him look like a bookish student, or maybe John Lennon.

It was both terrible and lovely to sit so close to him, to feel the warmth of his skin just beyond the fabric of his shirt. It had been years and years since we'd been alone—we'd been polite to each other in the company of other people, kind but never intimate. It exasperated Diana to no end. "You were bloody soul mates, and now you can't talk to each other like normal people?" she'd said more than once.

I found myself thinking about his hands, and the drawings of his naked body, and the moors and the copse where we'd made love in the moss, gloriously naked outside.

I wondered if he remembered it.

"This is a bit more challenging than I expected," he said.

"Do you feel guilty?"

"What? No." He shifted to look down at me. "Not the email business. You."

One word and I was liquid. "Me?"

"The memories of you."

I met his gaze. "I know. Me too."

"It's probably all chemical. Something about the way our bodies speak to each other."

I couldn't help smiling at that. "Everything is chemical."

"Not always like this." He looked at me. "I can't with you, even if we'd both like it."

Leave it to Cooper to put it right out there. Sharply, I replied, "You already made that very clear." A sting of tears shimmered in the corners of my eyes, and I looked away, furious and embarrassed. I would absolutely not be vulnerable as well.

"Hey," he said quietly. "I didn't mean to hurt your feelings."

I shook my head. "I'm fine."

His hand fell on my thigh. "We'll always be related, the two of us. Whatever else, that's true."

"Soul mates," I said.

"Yeah." He bumped against me, trying to jolly me out of my acute embarrassment. In a gentler voice he said, "But we tried the other way. We broke each other for a time."

I took a breath. Looked up. A fan of lines radiated from his eyes, from squinting across the moor, and a combination of wind and sun had given his face an eternal tan. "I know." But even as I said that, I felt the lure of him, the chemical pinging between us lively and loud. "It's just not easy to be around you and . . . not . . ."

"I know. Me too." He patted my leg, as if he were my uncle. "But we have to get this done. For Diana."

I nodded. Straightened my back. "Let's dig into the deep, dark secrets of email."

Of course her inbox was tidy, with clearly labeled folders down the left side of the page. Among others were files for Orders, Invoices, Personal, Inquiries, Action Required. All the folders had the numbers of unopened emails each contained. Action had seventeen.

"Open 'Action,'" I said.

We scanned the subject headings together. Nothing very illuminating, just orders and various other daily business items. I narrowed my eyes and tried to think like my grandmother.

"Maybe run a scan in email for 'Perse'?"

"Ah, good idea." He typed the name into the box, and a long line of entries turned up. He opened the first, and it was an order for sixteen box lunches, sixteen servings of roast chicken and sides, twenty-eight sous vide eggs. Delivery to the *Persephone* yacht, 24 April. "Big party for a yacht that size," Cooper said.

"You know the boat?"

"It's a local. It might be able to sleep six, tops."

"Four guys for four days?"

"Maybe. Four days is a long weekend."

"Good question." I took a screenshot of the page. "Let's look at some of the others."

Cooper took notes and I shot photos as we looked through them, one by one. Most of them were fairly straightforward, but some had instructions for particular food types, and puddings.

The invoices went to a London address. "Henry? He was the one setting up all the parties, wasn't he? I think that's how they met." I made a mental note to look through my texts about him again.

A loud deep voice broke into the room. "Oh, hail hail, fair Diana, my sweet lady. Where are you, my little love muffin? I've a present for you."

I looked at Cooper. "Henry."

He sounded so happy, so full of anticipation. Both Cooper and I stood and faced the door.

A big handsome man, a bit too stout in the way of a former footballer, came around the corner with an enormous bouquet of flowers. He was deeply tan, wearing khaki slacks and very expensive shoes. His eyes were so blue they leapt out of his face.

Oh, Diana. This is so not fair.

"Hello," he said, spying us. His tone was friendly and upbeat. "Why so quiet here today? Things are usually all abuzz on Sundays. You're new here. I'm Henry." He reached out a hand to shake, and I took it.

"I'm Zoe," I said, "and this is Cooper."

"Oh, sure, Cooper, good to meet you, lad. We've missed each other so often."

"Henry," Cooper said, moving aside. "You need to sit down."

Instantly, his guard was up. "Why? Is there something the matter? Is Diana all right? Is—"

Cooper pressed his hand on Henry's shoulder and guided him into the chair. "I'm afraid we don't know where she is, or if she's all right. She disappeared sixteen days ago, and we haven't heard from her since."

Henry looked from Cooper to me, then back again. His face showed confusion. "Disappeared how?"

"We don't know."

"But I—" He scowled, pulled out his phone. "I was fretting that she hadn't texted me, but sometimes she worried about being too needy." He cleared his throat. "Crazy woman. I've been in the Hebrides, y'see." He scrolled through his messages, just as I'd done, as if looking would make a new text appear. "But where would she go?"

"That's the trouble," Cooper said. "We don't know. I'm sure the constable would like to talk to you."

The color drained from his face all at once. I'd never seen it happen so completely before. Even his lips looked blue. "Police? Do they think she might . . . that something terrible . . . that she's dead?"

"I don't know," I said. "We don't know."

"But I brought her flowers." His voice was small. His eyes swam with tears.

Cooper said gently, "You might have information that will help them understand where she's gone. Let's have a wander over to the constable, shall we?"

"Of course." He stood up suddenly, slamming the chair against the desk. The flowers jiggled in his tight grip. "What'll I do with these?"

"Why don't I pop them in some water?" I said. "They're so beautiful. We'll want them to be nice when Diana gets back."

His face sagged as he released them. "I had such good news," he said. "It was all I could think about all the way here."

The scent of lilies filled my nose. Death flowers. My gut twisted.

Cooper waved a hand as he left. "Text me when you want to bring Isabel."

I nodded.

As they left, my entire body felt weak. I sank down into the chair Henry had vacated, holding the flowers he'd so exuberantly been bringing to Diana. Perhaps he was a great actor and really had been the reason she'd disappeared, but I no longer believed that. That draining of color in his face couldn't have been faked. Unless he was afraid of getting caught at something? Could he have killed her?

No, it just didn't feel right. He might have known something, but my instincts said he hadn't harmed her, that his arrival this morning had been sincere.

Still, he had to know something.

I carried the bouquet to the sink and looked around until I found a vase for them. As I arranged the lilies and baby's breath and roses, I imagined Diana coming back through the door and seeing them on the counter. An exuberant offering of love.

A wave of loss broke over me suddenly, deep and wide. It swamped me, soaked me, every inch of my heart and mind and body, and I stood against the counter, shaking.

Sobbing. It didn't seem fair that she should have found love, only to lose out to—what? Who?

Who would do something to Diana? And why?

It just seemed impossible that anyone would.

Chapter Twenty-Four

Zoe

Restless and unsettled when I returned to Woodhurst Hall, I sat at the kitchen table drinking hearty tea with milk and looked over the notes my mother had made last night about Gran's meds and routines. Her handwriting gave me a peculiar pang, as if seeing a letter from someone long dead. I thought of her sitting at this very table last night, with Isabel, making friends with her. It made me uncomfortable.

Because it wasn't like Isabel was at a strong point in her life. What if my mother betrayed her too? Let her down? Poppy didn't have a great record, after all.

Isabel came banging in through the back door, her camera bag on her shoulder. She was still draped in the hoodie, but at least she hadn't pulled it over her head. Her dark curls shone in the bright day.

"Hello," I said. "How was your morning?" I had tracked her on Find My Friends, and her trail had been straight to a hilltop outside the village, then back down to the hill fort.

"It was good. Do you want to hear about the workshop on the Hare Moon?"

Did I? I felt raw and emotional still after the scene at Diana's business. Maybe I didn't have to pile on anything more just this second. "No, thanks, unless you have some illumination you want to share."

"Not really." She turned on the kettle and leaned against the counter. "I did what you suggested—I went back to the hill fort and took photos anyway, even if I'm not going to post them."

"A friend of mine suggested that we could go to the next village over and see if there are some old-school scrapbooks and things."

"I need a color printer if I'm going to do that," she said.

"Gran probably has one."

"No, I checked. Old-school black-and-white laser." She indicated the size with her hands, a giant of a thing. "It would only cost a couple hundred, which I have in my savings."

"That's not necessary. I don't mind buying it. We can find something you can use with the camera."

"Okay."

"We can ask Gran—"

"Ask me what?" she said, making her way into the room with the help of her cane. She did not love using it, but it gave her a little help on the uneven floors of the ancient house.

"Where to buy a color printer for my photos. I can leave it here for when we come back to visit, and you can use it if you want." Isabel waved Gran into a chair. "I'll make your tea."

"I have one, but it won't be powerful enough for your photos. You'll need to drive into Exeter, I expect." She slid a bright floral napkin from its ring and shook it.

I nodded. "We can go Monday."

"Monday! Why not today?"

"We're going up to Dartmoor this evening, remember?"

"Oh yeah. Okay."

Gran said, "Will you make me some toast, dear Isabel? On the thick bread. And I'll need a little marmalade."

Isabel said, "Of course."

I gave her a smile and stood to fetch the fat pot of marmalade, a clear glass jar with its own spoon that had been part of my childhood.

"About that trip to Dartmoor," Isabel said. "I have something to tell you." She settled a pot of tea and an antique plate in front of Lillian.

Something in the tilt of her head made me look up. "What?"

"Um. Well, I met your friend. Sage?"

"Really, where?"

She shrugged with exaggerated nonchalance and began to make toast. "At your mom's house this morning."

A brick dropped in my gut. I knew she'd gone there, but thinking of Poppy and Sage and Isabel all cozy without me felt like a betrayal. It felt like everyone was transferring their allegiance to my mother. My enemy.

The tiniest thread of doubt snaked through my antagonism—was I wrong? Should I be taking steps toward forgiving her?

I thought of those postcards I'd sent every week, thought of that sad girl, thought of Isabel at that age and what I would have done to protect her.

No.

Everyone in the world could forgive her, party it up, but I would not. Everyone forgiving her had not suffered the unforgivable thing she'd done to me.

But I couldn't help asking, "Did Cooper participate in the workshop?"

"No, I think he was just helping her set up."

I stared at her, a thought burning in my gut. "I see."

Isabel spread marmalade on her toast, toast without butter, just as my grandmother ate it. When a thick, glistening layer was perfect from edge to edge, she picked it up. "My dad thinks it will probably be good for me to get to know Poppy."

"Ah, you talked to him about it, did you?"

A flicker of annoyance crossed her eyebrows, so slight I nearly missed it. "It wasn't like that."

"What *was* it like, Isabel? You can talk to your dad, and your grandmother, and the counselor, and whoever else in the world, but you can't talk to me?"

"I just wanted his opinion."

"Why not *my* opinion?" I could feel the emotions I'd been tamping down beginning to whip out of control. "Why not the person who has been right here, at your side through thick and thin, your whole life?"

"I don't know! I mean, I guess I knew what you would say."

"Did you, Isabel? What would I say?"

"That you didn't want me to meet her."

I stood up and walked to the stove, turning my back so that Isabel couldn't see my face. The tears threatening, which would infuriate me. I took in a deep breath, trying to calm down, but there was a cold, furious anger at my core that I couldn't shake. I turned around. "You're right. I would have told you not to meet her because you might get hurt. She isn't reliable."

"Mom! She *wasn't* reliable a long time ago. That was then. This is now."

Fury blistered my throat. "You're free to make a relationship with her," I said with some effort. "Just don't expect me to do the same." I turned, carrying my mug with me. "I have some work to do. Excuse me."

———— ⊙〜⦿ ————

It was true that I had some work to do. I'd been plugging away on a logo assignment that was finished and needed to be uploaded. When I logged in to send it, I also found an email from a magazine I loved, a literary journal that didn't pay much for my illustrations but carried a lot of prestige. I opened it eagerly to find an invitation to illustrate an article on the companionship pleasures of dogs called "All Dogs Are Therapy Dogs." They wanted six pen-and-ink drawings with light washes, something cozy and upbeat. The only problem was the deadline, which was fairly short for this kind of thing.

Then I realized I wasn't working full time on something else, and really, having something to do while we tried to solve the problem of

Diana's disappearance might not be too bad. I wrote back, accepting the assignment.

I mailed off the logo to my boss at Santa Fe Graphx and then went to the window. Thanks to the brilliant weather, a spill of watercraft had tumbled out of the harbor to the open sea—sailboats and rowboats and yachts and fishing boats dotting the vividly blue water like a scattering of child's toys, all the way to the horizon. It made me think of my youth, when Cooper and Diana and I would set out from shore in a battered but seaworthy rowboat that belonged to Diana's dad—not that he ever sailed on it, since even then he'd either been hungover or drunk. We'd take pies and biscuits and bottles of Coke and sail up to some other beach besides our own, into a cove with a tiny spit of sand, or a sandbar at the mouth of one of the rivers that emptied themselves along the coast. Diana always turned pink no matter how much sunscreen she slathered herself with, and she wore big silly hats I couldn't bear, but I tanned easily and deeply, and so did Cooper, whose arms had grown darker and his hair more tousled and bleached as the summer wore on.

A soft yearning ache moved in my limbs. Had I ever gotten over him, really? It didn't feel like it when we'd sat side by side, when I'd smelled his skin and wanted to crawl into his lap and lay my head on his shoulder.

How was it possible that after twenty years, that part of it was exactly the same? The chemistry between us was just as it had been when we were teenagers, probably the same as it had been all our lives.

I closed my eyes, thinking of a rainy day when we'd curled up in his bed and kissed and kissed and kissed, twining legs and arms, sliding skin to skin in delicious play, drawing out the pleasure. We had learned every inch of each other. I wondered how much would be different now.

We'd been so young, so inflexible, both of us.

In those days, he'd been completely antimaterialistic. Didn't believe in buying new clothes, only used ones. Didn't eat meat, darned his socks, didn't believe in television.

It was extreme, and it scared me. I didn't want to live like that forever. I liked new shoes and pretty clothes. I wanted to travel and explore the artists who'd inspired me by tracing their footsteps. There were many times I wasn't sure that I could have had that life with Cooper.

But that wasn't what had wrecked us. I'd done that. We had nearly destroyed each other. That much was true. We broke up in a great conflagration, and he did not speak to me for nearly two solid years. It still grieved me that I'd been so stupid, sabotaging such a solid relationship.

Why had I done that?

I thought of that awful week. The teacher who'd demolished me. The comfort of the boy who'd stood up for me. My anger when Cooper hadn't had time for me.

The answer whispered through me: I had to ruin it before he broke my heart.

God.

A knock came at the door. "Come in," I called.

Gran poked her head in. "I'm going to my study, my dear. Why don't you come along?"

It was an honor to be asked. Her space was off limits to everyone except me and, once a month, a cleaner who came in from the village to tidy and dust and took the job very seriously.

"Okay," I agreed and followed her to the end of the hall, where an arched door opened to a stairway that had been refitted a decade or so ago to have wider, safer steps. It was good to watch Lillian climb them so adroitly. She had to use the rail, and she wasn't the fastest human on the planet, but up she went in her pretty floral dress with its pleated hem and all her jewelry and her hair done.

The stairs led to a tower with a pair of rooms joined by an ancient brick arch. It might have once been a bedroom and sitting room, but now one side held her desk, which overlooked the countryside and her garden. The other room was a library with a generous window seat that faced the sea.

I headed straight for the window seat. It was here where I'd learned to draw by sketching everything outside while my grandmother typed in the background. An unexpected sense memory swamped me—a soap bubble of time, me at nine with my crayons and pencils. A series of sketches was still pinned to the wall, a handful of cat studies tumbling across time to me here. I touched the corner of one. "I can't believe you still have these."

Lillian stood beside me, smaller and thinner than she had been but still entirely herself. "Those were some of the happiest days of my life," she said.

"They were?"

"Mmm. I was not ready for motherhood when your mother was born. Pregnancy made me fat and stole my beauty, and then I brought forth this astonishingly beautiful child. Your grandfather doted on her, but all I saw when I looked at her were all the things I would never be able to do."

I'd never heard this before. "Like what?"

"Oh, travel the world and dance with princes. Become someone." She plucked at her necklace, lost in time. "I so desperately wanted a whirl of a life, full of adventure and excitement, and I thought your grandfather would give it to me. He was so charming when we met, the life of the party." She sighed, and I filled in the gaps. My grandfather had been a philanderer and a drunk who'd grown sloppier every year until he died of cirrhosis at the age of forty-two.

I took my grandmother's papery hand. "But you have a great career."

"I do. But I didn't start until I was forty, and by then I'm afraid your mother had borne the brunt of my bitterness." Lillian raised her eyes, took my hand between her own. "Perhaps I breathed all my longing into her somehow, and she found the courage I did not."

A thin arrow of understanding slid between my ribs, and I closed my eyes, resisting even the smallest crack in my walls.

"You do not have to forgive her, my dear," my grandmother said. "But you must allow her to know Isabel."

"Must I?"

Lillian only gave me a small, sad smile. "I have to work now. You are welcome to sit in your corner and sketch."

Unsettled, I did just that. It was a clear, beautiful spring morning, and I drew the landscape with pencils and the stubs of crayons, feeling myself at five and eight and ten, imagining I would become a great and celebrated artist with paintings hanging in galleries and museums around the world.

When had I given up so thoroughly on my dreams?

The thought was soft, whispering through my mind, blowing away dust and debris to show me a vision of myself crouching at the edges of my life, fearful of losing even more if I stepped forward.

On the paper beneath my hands, I made rough hard marks, fierce and black and powerful, as if I could change by making different art. But it didn't feel like anything, just the temper tantrum of a woman who'd missed her chance and settled for second place in all ways.

Except with Isabel. With her, I was first place.

Was I *jealous*? Afraid my mother would usurp me?

No. It just didn't seem fair. Why should my mother be able to just waltz in and do whatever she wanted after being gone for decades?

I looked out at the flat blue sea, aching, imagining my daughter and my mother engaged in a lively, cheerful conversation. I thought of myself at ten, drawing on postcards I sent around the world, and of myself at seventeen, fighting for the art school I wanted, even if Cooper had to stay behind.

And I thought of myself only five years ago, sitting at a computer screen and discovering via scandal rag that my husband was cheating on me with a singer he'd been touring with.

I pulled my knees up to my chest and wrapped my arms around them, feeling like Isabel, wishing for a hoodie of my own to hide in. The world seemed very strange and dangerous just at this moment.

Chapter Twenty-Five
Poppy

My mother called after Zoe and Isabel had gone off to meet Sage. I quickly drove to Woodhurst Hall, anxious to check on her again.

When I returned to England for good seven years ago, I lived in Glastonbury, first establishing a shop there. It felt too hard to return straightaway to Axestowe, and it gave me time to feel my way back into the village.

But primarily it had given me time to reestablish some sort of relationship with my mother. She'd never cut me off the way Zoe had, but she'd grown very chilly indeed over the years. I started slowly, bringing her bedding plants on my way through, as if it didn't mean anything, or stopping to tell her some bit of gossip I'd heard. Over time she occasionally invited me in for tea, later for a meal. It took quite a long time, but when I bought my cottage, I began to stop in every day to see if she needed anything—a little something from the village, a basket of groceries, her prescription, a drive to the GP. If Zoe came to town, I stopped for the duration, and I had never minded, but Lillian had declined in the past year, and not seeing her made me worry.

I found her in the garden, wrapped in a thick jumper, her feet in flowered wellies I'd bought her for Christmas. With a steady hand, she deadheaded the pale-pink rosebush that grew along the wall, tucking the spent heads into a pocket of her apron so they wouldn't litter the beds. "Hello, Mother," I said, kissing her head. "How do you feel today?"

"I'm well," she said, and her voice was strong, not quavery as it could be sometimes. "I wrote nearly five pages on the new book."

"Good." I squatted, rather awkwardly since my knees no longer worked the way they once did, and plucked a few weeds from the midst of the ranunculus, following a stubborn vine beneath a leaf. "How's Zoe?"

"All right." She straightened, gave me a sad shake of the head. "She's not at all ready to forgive you. Still. And now she's worried about Diana, as we all are. It's good to have her home." She moved out of the bed, rounded a particularly threatening rosebush, and began to clip a scraggly shrub. "You seem to be enjoying Isabel's company."

"She came to my shop and introduced herself." I smiled. "So much like her mother, I had to laugh."

"You didn't know her mother at this age," she said without sharpness. It still stung. "The one she reminds me of is you."

"Really? Do you think so?" I bent and yanked out tendrils of grass trying to spread into the tulips.

"She's a seeker, I believe. Restless, like you were, even then."

I nodded. "She's troubled, isn't she?"

"Oh, yes. All those clothes!"

"No idea what happened to her?"

"Zoe said it has something to do with social media, but she hasn't been able to learn what."

I thought of the number of things that could mean. Isabel didn't strike me as a nervous sort, so it must have been something substantial. It infuriated me. "Children are so cruel to each other now."

"What do you mean, now? They've always been cruel—far more cruel and conniving than adults."

I brushed my hands together. "She took part in a workshop with me this morning."

"Be careful, my dear. Zoe tried, but did not take it well."

I sighed, half-exasperated, half-understanding. "She's nearly forty. I wish she could make peace with the past."

"Oh, I think she's made peace. She just hasn't forgiven you."

"That's what peace is—forgiveness."

"Perhaps," she said mildly.

"You could help, you know."

"I do try." She moved out of the bed, swayed slightly as she stepped in the grass, and I forced myself not to reach out and urgently brace for a fall. We'd talked about falls quite a lot in recent months, and she'd agreed to safety checks, but she'd also made me promise not to fret about it all the time. I did anyway, and brewed her pots of bone broth to strengthen her thinning skeleton, but I tried not to show my concern in front of her.

She had always been so mighty when I was a girl, in constant motion while my father was alive, rushing hither and thither, hosting a tea or a party or a fundraiser while my father drank and drank and drank himself to death.

After he died, she'd only grown in power—writing her books, publishing them, and finding success, much to everyone's surprise in the village. They'd thought her a shallow female and expected her to fall apart after my father died. Instead, she became a publishing star and poured funds back into the manor, employing people to help garden and keep house and repair the inevitable issues that arose with such an old pile.

Now she was their darling, the star of Axestowe.

Even when I'd finally returned to England seven years ago, weary at last of lands that were not my own and longing for the bonds of family, she'd been sturdy and strong. The decline had arrived silently, and it had taken me some time to recognize. She was so thin and moved so slowly. Her doctor said it was nothing more than age, and we needed to help her.

Which I'd done. Diana and I had cooked up the plan to hire a housekeeper, and we took turns making sure she was safe and fed and looked after. Now it had fallen to me entirely. I did not wish to return to the Hall and the site of some of my loneliest memories. The girl I'd been had not been loved enough, and look at the damage that had caused over time!

"I am quite severely missing Diana," she said. "It isn't the same without her."

"I know, Mum."

"Who could want to hurt such a good woman?"

"I wish I knew." I glanced at the lowering sun and brushed off my sadness for the moment. It would be there when I finished here. "Shall we head inside and make sure you have everything you need?"

"Zoe can do it," she said.

"I know," I said, swallowing the hurt her words delivered. "But I'd like to, if you don't mind."

She allowed me to lead her inside. As we walked slowly, her arm linked in mine, I thought maybe my actions were all for me. That I was trying to make it up to her for running away.

"We talked this afternoon," Lillian said. "Your daughter and I." She paused and faced me. "I told her that I was not the mother you deserved, but it occurs to me that I've never told you that."

A swell of something blue and dark and sad bubbled up through my chest. I clenched my teeth together to stem the tide of tears. "You were good."

"No," she said. "Look at me."

I did. She raised a hand to my cheek. "I resented you. I wanted a different life, a bigger life." She dropped her hand. "Perhaps I breathed that into you, and off you went into the world to see what it held."

I closed my eyes, unable to speak. Emotion boiled up and through me, and I breathed through my nose, calming it all down. Finally, I said, "Thank you."

"I love you, my dear. I hope you know that."

"I do," I said, and I did. But the words carried great weight. They soaked into my soul, rich and thick, a bulwark against the sorrows of the world.

I tried not to wish she'd said so before.

She took my arm again. "I am trying to help move things along with your daughter too. Before I die, I'd like to see this family reunited."

"Me too, Mum." I tucked my hand around hers. "But I'd like you to hang around for a lot longer. Wouldn't it be lovely to see Isa married?"

"Oh," she said with a sigh. "I suppose."

I left it at that. What did I know of great age?

Chapter Twenty-Six

Zoe

Just after seven, Isabel and I drove up to the farm to meet Cooper. Poppy had gone to stay with Lillian, so I didn't have to worry about her, and I felt an urgent need to be out on the moor in nature, away from all the madness.

It was a beautiful drive, on winding roads that twisted between hedgerows that would suddenly part to make way for an old farmhouse, its door so close to the road you could reach out and touch it. The hedgerows themselves bloomed just now with wood sorrel and campion, the colors popping out of the ancient earthen walls that had been here since the Celts and Saxons had first farmed the hills.

We had always done our best talking in the car, and for a long stretch of moments, I wondered if I might be able to nudge her into confessing her secret.

But she was showing signs of healing, and my own anger at what felt like a betrayal had eased a bit. Sometimes it was best to let sleeping dogs lie.

I gathered myself and gestured to the landscape opening up as we topped a hill. Around us spilled the fields and hedgerows and ditches of my childhood. Queen Anne's lace bobbed along the road as we turned into the drive. "This was my world until I was seven."

The farm sat against the back of a hill, the house looking toward Axestowe and, in the distance, the sea. The house sat amid a cottage garden I remembered my mother working, long ago. It was two stories, with small windows to keep the heat in. A thousand threads of memory and emotion wound through me as I stepped out—the years I'd lived there as a child, the years I'd spent there with Cooper.

Diana, too, was everywhere. A longing to see her, touch her, apologize for everything, moved through me.

A dog barked, and Cooper came from the back garden, feet in worn green boots, his hair loosely tied away from his face so that curls escaped to catch the breeze. I parked and took a slow breath to calm my reaction. This was the Cooper I'd loved so wildly, his long body framed against the sky and clouds, everything about him capable and calm and strong. In my memory was the day I'd tumbled out of the car to run to him when we were both fifteen, and I wished that I could do it again, that he would catch me up and hug me for so long it would become embarrassing for anyone watching us.

He raised a hand in greeting and then waved to give the dog permission to run toward us. Matt, from the pub the other night, trotted over eagerly, giving our hands licks. "Hello, Matt," I said. "This is my daughter, Isabel."

Cooper joined us. "Hello."

"I guess you've met," I said.

He gave a nod. With a glance at the sky, he said, "We should get moving so we can get out to the moor by sunset." He'd wanted us to meet him at the farm. "You have your camera?"

Isabel patted the case.

"You bring waterproofs?"

"Of course." I had a pack over my shoulder, filled with bottles of water, raincoats, and woolen scarves.

He gave me the faintest of smiles. Our eyes snagged, held. "Good."

We followed him around the house and up the hill to a level spot where we'd always parked. From here you could see the farm itself, the vegetable plot, and the barns and sheds and pens. "Do you work this all yourself?" I asked.

"I have a man. He lives in the second house." He opened the door to the Range Rover. "We bring in more hands when we need them, for shearing and the like."

Isabel looked around. "I can see why Grandad liked it here," she said. "It's kinda like his land, isn't it? Sort of lonely, different trees, but you know what I mean?"

I'd never thought about it, but she was right. "I guess so. He lived here a fairly long time, I think. Six or seven years."

She nodded and asked Cooper, "What kind of sheep do you have?"

Cooper hid his surprise quickly. "Dartmoor whites, mostly, and some longwools. You know sheep, do you?"

"My granddad has merinos. He let me raise one for 4H a couple of years ago."

He gave me a quizzical glance. "4H?"

"County fair."

"That's great, Isabel. Not so many girls like farming work these days."

"I don't love it, honestly." She climbed into the back seat. "But I like to know about things."

He gave me an actual smile this time, one that made it to his eyes. "Still good."

I sat in the passenger seat, as I had the other day, and Matt climbed in next to Isabel, who rested her hand on his neck and scratched his ears. Cooper watched her in the mirror for a moment, then started the car. "How is your dad?" he asked me. "He was one of my favorite people when we were small."

"I remember. He's good."

"Why did my grandparents get divorced, anyway?" Isabel asked as we bumped down the lane. Sunlight blasted over the top of the hill into the car, and I put on my sunglasses. "They're really kind of alike."

"I wouldn't know," I said in my frosty voice. I was so tired of my mother being everywhere, in every conversation since we'd gotten here.

Isabel ignored me. "They both live in the country. They both teach classes on these earth-based things. They both have land and animals and gardens. Like, it seems crazy."

I stared out the window, thinking of the days before my mom took off, when we all lived on the same land where Cooper still lived. My mother had specialized in breads and teas, and she milked the goats while she sang a little song. The tune haunted me sometimes, and in odd moments I found myself humming it.

It always irked me.

The children had tumbled in a little pack all day, roving up and down the hills, scaling hedgerows, sleeping in the woods. On Saturdays we'd drive to the Axestowe market to sell vegetables and crafts and farm goods, and the children played in the woods. Often I stayed with my grandmother, along with Diana and Cooper, who had been "Sage" then.

"Do you prefer to be called Sage?" I asked.

"It doesn't matter, Zoe. You can call me whatever you like."

Isabel persisted. "It just seems kind of sad, doesn't it, that both of them live alone, a whole world apart, doing the exact same things?"

I gave her a look over my shoulder. "That's enough."

"Fine," she said. "But it is interesting."

"Maybe to you. For those of us who lived through everything, it doesn't feel interesting. It feels painful. She broke his heart, Isabel. Don't dredge up old pain." I turned around to look at her fully. "Don't get any ideas."

Her big eyes blinked. "What kind of ideas?"

"I mean it."

She flipped her hair. "I won't."

"Do we want some music?" Cooper asked.

"I know how much you love small talk." I smiled at him. "Go ahead."

He glanced in the rearview mirror. "Any requests, Isabel?"

"You won't have the music I like. Play whatever you want."

He nodded. "Pick something," he said, pointing at a case of cassette tapes.

"I can't believe you still have this," I said. "How do you even make cassette tapes now?"

"Same way as before."

"They have new technology, you know," I said, "where you just plug your phone into the speakers, and whatever music you want comes out." I flipped through, pulling out one and another. Some of them were really old, from the days when we'd first been together. "Mix tapes. Wow."

We listened as scenery rolled by, the Cranberries and Toni Braxton and Foo Fighters. When my raw heart reminded me that Diana might be dead, I forced myself to just look out the window at the old trees and brooks and bridges, all ancient and beautiful, fields and sheep and the odd estate tucked back in a copse of trees. Next to me, Cooper drove with one hand on the wheel, the other resting on the gear stick. Light broke from the west through the windscreen, dancing over the dashboard and his hands and my legs.

It took most of an hour to get there, to the spot I knew he'd choose, parking nearby a bridge that crossed a wide stream. As if the gods had arranged the scene just for Isabel, a Dartmoor pony bent over the river. "Oh, my God. Wait. Let me get my camera ready."

Her excitement had been missing for so long that I wanted to cheer. My instincts to bring her here had been spot on. Maybe I wasn't failing as a mother after all. "We're not going anywhere," I said. "Take your time."

"He's a beauty," Cooper said.

The pony was small, traditionally colored with a shaggy brown coat and long black mane. As Isabel stepped carefully out of the truck, the pony lifted his head, but when there appeared to be no threat, he bent his head to the water once more. The water caught the sky and his head and the muscles in his haunches.

Eventually, he meandered on, and we got out. The air was cool, layered with moisture. I was glad of my wool socks and jeans as we wandered toward the moor, spreading up and over the horizon. Buttery light hung in a soft ball just above the hills, casting a gold glaze over everything.

I paused for a moment, urgently seized again with a hunger to paint. The names of colors rolled through my mind, and I found myself visualizing which brush to use, how to make it less of an ordinary landscape and more of something breathing, a being waiting to awaken.

And like me, Isabel was seized by the mystery and beauty. I smiled, watching her shoot everything. She got down on her knees and found a new angle for the trees twisting over the stream. I watched her, stunned by a depth of emotion that could still wipe me out. I loved that face more than any other in the world. Watching her dive into joy like this, after so many weeks of depression, lifted my spirits in a way nothing else could.

"She's so beautiful, isn't she?" I said.

Cooper nodded. "She looks a lot like your mom. And her dad, to be fair."

"She does."

He pointed at a bird lifting from a tree, making a sound I didn't know. "Willow warbler."

"I found my sketchbooks," I said. "So many birds I'd forgotten. You knew them all."

"Still do."

"I was going to ask about them when we were in the woods looking for . . . well, you know."

"Why didn't you?"

"It seemed disrespectful."

He cocked his head, then returned his attention to the landscape, lifting his hands and imitating another bird whistle. From the trees came an answer. I laughed softly in delight.

"Do it again!"

He grinned at me, the full, unselfconscious one that showed teeth and made his eyes crinkle at the corners. I made myself stand there like it was nothing, pretending that I hadn't missed that particular smile for twenty years and had never even known it.

"What bird is that?"

"A wood pigeon." Matt the dog suddenly went on alert, and Cooper gave him a hand signal that made him sit. But he stayed alert, ears up, back straight.

Isabel joined us. "What does he see?" she asked in a soft voice.

Cooper scanned the trees. "Not sure."

"Coyotes?" she asked. "Are there coyotes here?"

He shook his head sadly. "Nothing like that, not wolves or mountain lions. Not for centuries. Might be an otter."

"Otters live here?"

"They do. They nearly went extinct in the eighties, but it's a good population now." He gestured for us to move along the trail, and we followed. "We don't want to go too far when it's going to get dark, since you're unfamiliar, but I'd like to check a couple of nests while I'm here."

"Egg stealers again?" I asked.

He nodded grimly. "It was better for a while, but the past couple of years, they've been raiding all sorts of nests."

"Why do they steal eggs?" Isabel asked. She stopped and held up her camera, shooting a quick series of a twisted tree standing on the rise against the bright sky.

"It's a foodie thing," he said. "People want rare eggs to cook up for their friends, and those yacht-club trips are full of foodies trying to impress each other."

"That's disgusting."

"It is. Just greed," Cooper said. "It doesn't matter what you destroy, if you're the richest one, have the rarest egg to serve."

"What kind of eggs?"

"The rarer the better." He crossed a stile, then turned back to help us over, one at a time.

Isabel had never crossed one, and before she did so, she had to kneel and shoot a photo of it. "That would be a great Insta," she said, almost to herself, and then remembered her vow. "Or not."

Oh, my sweet girl! I thought. *What the hell did they do to you? Why won't you let me in to help you fix it?*

Seeing her at peace for once made me realize more viscerally just how hard this past month had been.

But not tonight. Tonight, she seemed happy.

We kept walking, and in a copse of trees Cooper stopped, looked all around, then strode into the shadows and presumably checked a nest. He emerged a couple of minutes later, offering a thumbs-up.

Isabel snapped his photo. It made my chest hurt. I knew exactly why she'd done it—the way the light caught half his form, his hair and one shoulder, and the trees behind making shapes against the sky, made him look like something ethereal, a creature of the forest, not quite human.

"He kinda looks like Legolas," she said. "From *The Lord of the Rings*."

"Or Tam Lin," I said. "The Pamela Dean version."

"I don't think I've read that one."

"It might be at the library." We started walking at his gesture, the trail between tufts of growth growing quite thin as we left the main area and strode into the moor itself. Wind, unstoppable, blew across the tops

189

of the trees and set a whirling dervish in motion, a dust devil rising like a genie from a bottle.

We walked in silence for quite some time while the sun fell lower and lower, the color of the light growing more and more saturated with gold, gilding grasses and fences and tree branches and each of us.

"Oh, look! Look!" Isabel cried, grabbing my arm. "Look!"

On a rise only a few yards away were three ponies, staring us down. Their long black manes and tails blew in the strong breeze, fluttering over their faces. The one in the front had an arrogant expression, and the other two stuck close behind her. They made soft whuffling noises but seemed unafraid.

Moving with quiet ease, Isabel changed lenses and knelt in the hillocks of grass, shooting quickly, the camera whirring as she captured the images.

"As long as you don't run at them, you can get closer," Sage said.

"Okay." The word was whispered, and she moved like a cat, one step at a time, shooting and shooting. They watched her but didn't move.

"She's quite something," Cooper commented.

"I completely agree. This was such a good idea." A sudden gust of wind blew up my back and caught my hair. Before it could tangle a million ways, I captured it and wound it into a rope that I tied into a knot at the back of my neck, an automatic habit.

I could feel Cooper looking at me. "What?" I said.

"Your hair is beautiful. Sometimes people cut it by our age."

"I see you didn't get that memo either."

"I tried," he said, shoving fingers through the curls. "Alice liked it short. It just didn't feel like my hair."

"I like it long."

He met my gaze. "I know."

Beneath the vast sky, adorned with fluffy clouds as painted by Constable, I felt our old selves standing with us. Seven-year-olds and ten-year-olds, then fourteen and fifteen and eighteen. Those ghosts of us wound around us, unable to see the future, and I felt them all, playing and doing experiments and then experimenting ourselves, mouth to mouth and body to body. The knowledge of them filled me. Their ghostly hair brushed my lips and my neck.

I wondered if he felt them, too, but he'd always been more sensible than I in most ways. If he did feel them, he wouldn't acknowledge it.

But he didn't exactly put distance between us either. He just looked at my face, and I felt the drag of his gaze across my brow, my earlobes, my mouth. I took a breath and forced myself to look away.

And attempted to change the energy by changing the subject. "Did Henry give a statement?"

"Yeah." He tucked his hands in his jacket pockets. "Don't know what he said."

"I thought he might have been responsible," I said, "but that felt pretty real to me. His whole face lost color when we said she was missing."

Cooper nodded, his gaze in the distance. "That worried me."

"Worried you? Why?"

He dipped his head sideways. Wind caught his hair and flung it over his face, but he just let it be. "It seemed a bit too much. For the information he had."

I waited.

"If your dog got out of the garden," he said slowly, "and someone told you about it, you wouldn't immediately fear he was dead, would you?"

"But a woman isn't a dog." I frowned. "I do see your point—if she's missing, maybe the reason he's worried is because he knows something?"

"Yeah."

"I hadn't thought of it that way."

"Maybe he's not entirely blameless. Perhaps he knows things she only discovered by accident."

"Or"—my stomach roiled with a recognition of possibilities—"she's not blameless herself. Maybe she was meddling in something or wanted to save the world somehow." It had gotten her in trouble often enough before. *Save the whales, save the oceans, never buy plastic.*

He sighed. "Maybe all of the above."

I moved my hand over that burning in my belly. Above us, the sky began to shift more dramatically, the sun dropping below the line of the earth, the atmosphere going softly purple while the clouds began their show—soft pink now, some coral along the scalloped edge of a cottony group to the east, a dazzling streak of orange along the bottom of the other.

It coaxed me to forget daily mortal sorrows and invited me to dive into the brilliance, dance in the eternal colors, and rub them all over me.

A noise cut through the hush of sunset. Something flitted through the air, two and three, then four and five. "Bats!" I cried. "Isabel! Look!"

They wheeled out of their den, primitive shapes, such an old species, and I tipped backward to watch them.

"Wow!" Isabel's face shone, and she raised her camera to shoot the heavens, the clouds, the bats, and then the two of us, standing on the hillside.

My heart sailed with the bats, buoyed by the extravagant beauty of my beloved moor, and Isabel's happiness and even standing beside Cooper. Sage. I glanced at him. The name suited him now; he had weathered the storms of youth and young adulthood and loss, and he now stood armed with wisdom to grapple with whatever else life had to offer.

Matt came trotting down from the hilltop as if to let us know it was all safe ahead. I scratched his smiling face. "I miss having a dog," I said.

"You said you lost one recently."

"Yes. Simba. Six months ago." Even saying his name made my eyes water. "I haven't been able to get another one yet. He was a puppy when

Isabel was born, and he was totally my dog in a way no other dog ever has been."

"What breed?"

"Oh, I don't know. Some kind of mutt—retriever and chow and husky. He had a lot of fur and great ears that were half-floppy, half-standing, so when he walked, the top half flopped along." I could see him, orange fur and black face and weirdly curly tail that fell in a spray along his lower back at all times, and I suddenly missed him so desperately that it felt like a hole right through my chest. "He was very small when I took him home."

"You were his mum, then."

"Yeah." I took a breath.

"You mean Simba?" Isabel said, coming up to us.

"Yes."

"I miss him too. The house is too quiet. I brought my cat with me, though. He hates to be left alone, so we trained him to be able to fly."

Cooper gave her a soft smile. "That's thoughtful."

We walked to the top of the hill, which was farther than I thought it would be, and I started getting nervous. "Will you be able to lead us back to the car? It's going to get dark."

"I doubt it. I'll get lost and we'll have to sleep out here with the piskies and the ghosts."

Isabel laughed.

"I want to go up to the top so you can see the view, and then we'll turn back." He glanced at Isabel over his shoulder. "If you'll come in the morning, we'd have more time."

"Hmm. I'll think about it."

We walked in silence for a time. I let myself drift in the magic of the changing sky, watching the landscape turn softer and softer as we climbed. At the top, we halted, each of us facing a different direction. Isabel faced the sunset, far to the west. I faced north, where the moor stretched in vast emptiness for miles and miles. Cooper faced east, toward the sea and civilization. The sky filled with light and life—birds diving for insects, and bats wheeling, lavender and red and aubergine joining the show of clouds. It all seeped into me, into my pores, and I felt soft and quiet within, an emotion that had become almost alien.

When had I lost the knowledge that nature could heal? As I stood there, the wild filled me up, eased my spine, made me forget all the wounds and sorrows of daily life. I could think of Lillian with a sense of calm, and Diana without wanting to shatter. Somehow the vastness of life here made it all seem more manageable.

From the corner of my eye, I caught a movement and turned my head in time to see a hare outlined against the light, long ears unmistakable, his paws in front of him, and then another dashed out and they both disappeared. "Oh!" I cried. "I just saw a hare!"

Isabel whirled. "Where?"

I pointed. "He's gone now."

"Tonight's moon is called the Hare Moon," Cooper said.

"Is it a full moon?"

He nodded, and as if it were as natural as breathing, he rested a hand on my shoulder. I wanted to lean against him and did not, just let that warmth and steadiness ground me.

Isabel only stood in the light, staring out over the moor. She took something from beneath her hoodie and kissed it, then let it drop back below.

I didn't ask her to explain.

Chapter Twenty-Seven
Poppy

As the moon rose that evening, I wandered outside to the garden, along the path between fields. I'd left the grass long for the hares, joining a push by the conservation society to provide more habitat for the Devon native, and I loved the way it shone against the silvering of the moon rising on the eastern horizon.

I was uneasy. The night was calm, but just beyond the bright moonlight, a spirit of something dark lurked. I couldn't shake the sense that things had come undone.

My mother's unexpected confession had unsettled me: just one more thing to add to the swirling apprehension I'd been feeling for more than two weeks since Diana's disappearance. She had been gone so long now that I knew she would not be coming back. A part of me reached through the night, seeking her body, wondering if I could sense it if I just let myself be open to it.

Darkness, darkness. It made me ache for all the things that break and all the evil afoot in the world.

Isa was on my mind too. She was everything fifteen made wondrous and strange—as fey as the fairies, all limbs and hair and shining eyes, and a quick temper, and so easily offended and chased away. Fifteen was mercurial and shimmering, and I was glad I could know her at this stage.

But something hanging about her disturbed me. A secret, something she was hiding, perhaps, but maybe something else. Danger, perhaps, or only foolishness. The trouble with being only slightly gifted in the realm of the spirit was that one could never decide whether there was genuine trouble or only the vague worries we all felt at times.

Like Diana, who was so alight with new love, but every time I read for her, the secrets were showing. She had been hiding something. At first I thought perhaps her lover had had a wife, but as time went by it seemed to be something more, something she herself was hiding.

Now my granddaughter. She'd been wounded. Anyone could see that, with her oversize clothes and skittishness. But was that a sense of danger clinging to her, or was I only on high alert because of whatever was going on in the village?

The rising moon leaked bright-white light into the landscape, throwing everything—house, garden, fence, barn—into sharp, defined shadow. The cool light bathed me and all the land around me as it emerged like a sacred egg from the womb of the earth.

Once upon a time I had believed that the moon had called me, called me to be an earth witch, a wise woman. I'd followed it around the world, to Glastonbury and New Mexico and India and Thailand and back to Glastonbury before wandering, at last, back to my home village.

Now I was of an age when I longed for wisdom and had no idea what that meant. I sometimes wondered if I'd wasted my entire life on a quixotic quest. Had I done anyone any good, ever?

Dark thoughts indeed.

Some of the thoughts stemmed from Isa's questions about my exhusband. Ben of the beautiful eyes, which both my daughter and her daughter had inherited. Long velvet eyes with arched brows over them. I could see him on the land, as he'd been once upon a time, feeding the chickens and clucking his tongue to bring them close. All animals loved him, dogs to pigs to sheep to birds, which would practically fall out of the air for him. They sensed his love and kindness.

Only I had resisted that loving care. It felt smothering, impossible. I dreamed of the far away, and he wanted only to return to his home in New Mexico, where he could visit a hundred relatives each day. He believed in the land, his land, and in family, and in hard work. He believed in art, but not very much in his own. He believed in making love to smooth fights over, and he'd been very right on that front.

What did I believe in?

The weight of that question made it hard to breathe. What did I believe in? After all this time, after all the trouble and wandering and study and teachers, what did I believe? What had been true, and what had proved to be false, over time?

The question centered me. I believed in nature. In the moon, rising like something brand new and something ancient—all over the world the same. Sunrise. The chuckle of a brook and the sharp cry of a woodpecker and lunchtime.

Love. Sexual love and motherly love and sister love and friend love. Love for the earth and all that was sacred.

I believed in wisdom, though I did not own it.

I believed in my daughter. She'd been born with a thick shock of dark hair, so much hair it made her look six months old. I had adored her. That's the truth. I spent hours just looking at her, smelling the crown of her head, nibbling on her fingers.

I'd been bored too. Bored with the endless sunshine of the desert, bored with the same chores and tasks day in and day out, bored with Ben and his serious nature, bored with myself. His family did not love me, with good reason, as it turned out, and that made me feel judged and even more alone. After a year I was ready to chew off my foot to get out of New Mexico. We moved to Devon and found the farm, and there we stayed.

But Ben was as unhappy in England as I'd been in New Mexico. He loved me and loved his daughter, so he did his best to adjust, making a place for himself among the locals, who admired his knowledge and his grit.

Moving did not solve my unhappiness. I was unhappy with *him*. Everything about him that had seemed interesting now only irritated me. His quiet seemed dour. His moodiness, once so romantic and artistic, only exasperated me. By the end, we loathed each other.

Why did I leave my Zoe, though? That's the part that's hard to remember. How could I have left her behind?

I was pulled to India, just as I'd been lured to Glastonbury and then to New Mexico and back to Devon.

For years, India had called to me. This was the late eighties, well past the days of the great hippie tour, but plenty of people I knew had gone or were going. They talked about it. Sometimes I dreamed of it at night, of what I might see, who I might meet. It started to burn in me, and when one of my girlfriends announced that she was going in a month, I made up my mind to go with her.

But I couldn't take Zoe. I asked my mother, who doted on the child, to watch her for a month, and she agreed. We both knew Ben was drinking and smoking too much weed to be a good father—and to his credit, he knew it too. When I asked him to go back to New Mexico and give the relationship some time, he agreed.

How selfish I'd been! So breathlessly, cheekily selfish!

I thought it would be a month, maybe two. A woman had as much right as a man to explore the world and herself and her choices, after all. I was desperate to avoid the stale repetitive lives of the mothers I saw around me.

And left my daughter to grapple with the world on her own.

Before that bit of recognition could settle, I shoved it away. I'd done what I had to do to escape the life the world had told me I should have, and indeed, I'd walked a path of adventure.

I couldn't imagine who I would be if my life had not taken me around the world, to my teachers, to Ravi. Would I even be myself at all? I didn't see how.

I'd been selfish, it was true. But standing there under the light of that enormous moon, I knew that I'd also been brave. It had taken courage for me to reject the life girls of my generation were taught to want, and then take steps to find something else.

But I was beginning to understand that my freedom had come at a great price for my daughter. What had I stolen from her?

And how in the world could I ever hope to make amends?

Chapter Twenty-Eight

Isabel

I've always thought moors are like the prairies, grasslands that are open and vast. They are nothing like that. The moor is wild and full of animal life, and I shot a billion photos out there.

But what I was dying to do by the time we got back to Woodhurst was write. I dropped my camera on the bed and fired up my laptop and started writing about the girl in the forest and her Dartmoor ponies. I wrote a character description that is my grandmother as a wise woman on the human side, and about Sage, who is an elf, on the other side.

My FaceTime app dinged with my granddad's face, and I opened it eagerly. "Hey, Grandad!"

He snapped into focus, sitting at his desk in his house, his long black and silver hair in one long braid down his back. "Hi, Isa. It's nice to see your face!"

"You too. How are you doing?"

He looked over his shoulder when the dog barked, and he picked up the iPad to show me a slim brown dog. "Jesse wants to say hi. He misses you. Nobody to spoil him."

"*You* should spoil him!"

"Nah, you can't teach old dogs new tricks."

I laughed, rolling my eyes. "Ha ha, old dog." He always makes silly puns like that. It made me miss being in his house, eating whatever amazing thing he's cooked.

"You look happier, kiddo. England must be agreeing with you."

I paused, cocking my head. "Maybe so. Guess what I saw today?" I said. "Ponies! They were amazing. Do you remember them?"

"Sure. The Dartmoor ponies, right?"

"I loved them." My eyes filled with tears in a strange way. "Like, I feel like I should have known they were in the world before this."

"They're proud and strong, like you."

I felt the opposite of proud and strong, and I'm pretty sure he knew it. "Thanks."

"You like it there, I can tell. The bluebells and the ponies." He gave me a sad smile. "Like your mom. She loved it there."

"And," I said, smiling, "guess who I met?"

He shook his head. "I don't know. Tell me."

"Poppy!"

His expression didn't change.

"Poppy Fairchild," I said. "Your ex-wife? My mom's mother?"

Still he didn't even flicker an eyelash.

"Don't you care?"

"I care if you care. Is she nice to you?"

"I wanted to hate her," I said slowly, "because of how she treated you and my mom, but when I went to her shop, I liked her. A lot."

"How is she doing?"

"Good. She has a house on top of a hill, and a gigantic garden, and goats. And some sheep!"

Something changed in my grandfather's face. Not quite a smile, but everything lightened. "She fat?"

"A little, like all old ladies, but not that much." I raised an eyebrow. "She's really pretty."

"You're like her in a way. Same energy."

"Really? You never told me that."

"I forgot." He drank something out of a mug. "How is your mom? Did they find Diana?"

"No. But she's okay. She's been looking for her every day, with her friend Sage."

"Sage, huh? Boy, those two have been friends since they were tiny babies." The dog started barking behind him. "I gotta go, kid. My sister is here. Be good. Send me a picture of the ponies."

"I will. Love you!"

But he was already gone.

Chapter Twenty-Nine
Zoe

Poppy showed up early the next morning, by arrangement. I knew she was coming and steeled myself to open the door to her without speaking. She wore a white wool coat and carried a basket of what smelled like fresh croissants. To her credit, she didn't try to make conversation, but I could see that she was very comfortable in this kitchen. That she spent a lot of time there. I picked up my jacket.

"You don't have to leave," she said.

I shrugged. "I need some exercise and didn't want to leave Gran alone." I buttoned my coat. "Isabel is asleep, and I just checked on Gran, who was writing in her office."

"Good."

"How long will you be here?"

For the first time I saw how sad she was. "A couple of hours, I suppose. I have to open the shop at ten."

"Make sure Isabel eats breakfast." I pulled on my gloves and stepped up close. "And just a warning. If you break my daughter's heart, I will pluck your fingernails out with pliers."

"Zoe!"

"Just so we're clear."

The encounter left me feeling slightly breathless. In the crater where I kept my memories, I had a sense of things trying to climb out, but I'd ignored them for a long time, and they knew better than to bother me. Shoving the zombies back down into the dark, I set out walking.

It was a sharp, brisk sort of day, and I found my body easing as I hiked along the South West Coast Path for an hour, putting my mother out of my mind by focusing on all the information I had collected about Diana, every scrap of everything I'd heard. I shook it apart and worked it one way, then another, but no matter how I pieced the facts together, nothing made sense. I'd honestly believed that once we talked to Henry, everything would become clear, and now it was foggier than ever.

I wondered if he was still in town. I wanted to ask him some more questions.

The morning was cool and foggy, threatening rain, and by the time I made my way back toward the village, I was chilled to the bone. Poppy would still be at Woodhurst Hall, so I'd find a cup of coffee and waste a bit more time before I went back.

As I rounded the last turn, it was plain something was happening on the beach. A small knot of people, along with a pair of constables, was gathered around something I couldn't see.

Dread gripped me. I walked as close as I dared. "What's happening?" I asked a fisherman, his head covered in a navy stocking cap.

"Found a body." His accent was thick, local. "Right here on the beach. Girl, looks like."

A chill ran up my spine. "Do they know who it is?"

"Nah. Body's pretty chewed up. Probably been in the water awhile."

I pushed forward, feeling my gut roiling, but a constable stopped me. "Stay back, please."

"Wait, I'm a friend of Diana Brooking, the woman who went missing two weeks ago. Is it her?"

"Sorry, Miss. You have to stay back."

I tried to peer over his shoulder. "You don't know?"

"We don't know anything yet." He glanced toward the body, mostly obscured by the legs of the examiners or whatever they were, then took pity on me. "Too young for the woman who went missing."

Too young.

Relief rushed through me that it wasn't Diana, followed by pity for the young victim.

I stood back to observe whatever was going to happen and then took out my phone. I texted Cooper. Body on the beach. Not Diana, but do you think it might be connected?

A text came right back. I'm here on the beach. Where are you?

I lowered the phone and looked around, and there he stood, head and shoulders above the others, not ten feet away. He saw me at the same moment, and I gave him a half smile as he approached. "I didn't even see you," I said. "What are you doing in town so early?"

"I came down to see if I could talk to Henry."

"Did you?"

"Not yet. Saw all the commotion."

"Who found the body?"

"Some fishermen, I heard."

"It's not Diana?" I wanted to be sure.

He shook his head. "No. Smaller. Dark hair." His eyes had shadows, and he suddenly wiped a hand down his face. "Christ."

"Let's go find Henry."

"I know where he is—at the Barrow Harbour Hotel. I dropped him off there after the trip to the constable."

We walked up the hill in silence. The mist hushed the world, and by the time we'd climbed half the stairs from the beach to the village, the noise of the investigation had been swallowed. At the top of the stairs, I turned and looked back. A row of multicolored beach houses stood against one side of the cliffs, facing the jagged rocks on the other side of the beach. In between was the milling investigation. Lying on the beach, looking very small, was a body, facedown. Red coat. A fist squeezed the air from my lungs. Where was her mother? "She looks so young."

"They think maybe a drug overdose."

"Is that a big thing in Axestowe?"

"It's a big thing everywhere, Zoe."

Chastened, I silently walked with him. Had drugs played a part in what had happened to Isabel? Could that be part of why she didn't want to tell me? I knew she'd been hanging around with a new crowd, and I also wasn't naive enough to believe that teenagers didn't experiment, but Isabel was a great student, and she'd seen enough alcohol and drug abuse among her father's set to know it wasn't a cakewalk.

Martin had said he'd talked to her about her secret, too, and also hadn't gotten anywhere. It did seem logical, honestly, that she might have been roofied or blacked out or—

A vision of her, so vulnerable, doubled the fist around my lungs. Damn.

A scent of coffee curled in the air and snagged my desire, but we walked past the coffee shop and around the corner and up another slope to the hotel. It was a classic 1960s tourist spot, sitting high on the cliff overlooking the sea. Glass enclosed the main level. A tour bus waited in the parking lot.

"That's his car," Sage said, pointing to a sporty black BMW.

Inside the lobby, a group of older German tourists milled around, finishing breakfast or maybe getting ready to go in. Sage went to the desk. "Hey ya, Bill. How're you?"

"Great, man. How y'been?"

He nodded. "I dropped Henry off here last night . . . don't know his last name. He was my friend Diana's boyfriend, you know who I mean? Big guy, solid." He jabbed a thumb backward over his shoulder. "The BMW is his car."

"Oh, sure." He punched something into the keyboard. "Room twenty-six, right up at the top of the stairs."

Sage slapped a palm down on the counter. "Thanks."

As we came around the corner, he flashed me a surprised expression. "That was easier than I expected."

"The boys always wanted to please you."

"Not the girls?" He was just behind me on the steps, which put our faces on nearly the same elevation. His eyes glittered, though his mouth showed no smile.

I inclined my head. "The girls too. So much charm."

For an instant, we connected again. Just us, stripped of all the bullshit and all the years and judgments. Mine and his.

Then we were walking down a clean hallway that smelled faintly of boiled cabbage, and the moment was gone. Sage knocked on the door. "Henry? It's Sage Cooper."

The door opened, revealing a Henry who was considerably more haggard than he'd been the day before. It was as if the air had been let out of him—he had bags under his eyes, his jowls sagged, and his shoulders slumped. "Hello. What can I do for you?"

"Can we come in?" I asked. "I'm hoping we can figure something out about Diana's disappearance if we share what we know with each other."

He swung the door open. "Sure. I just ordered some coffee. I'll ask for another cup."

"None for me," Sage said, pointing at the kettle. "I'd have a cup of tea, though."

Heavily, he nodded and stood in the middle of the room, as if he'd forgotten what he was doing. "Sit down, Henry," I said, touching his shoulder. I flashed on his toothbrush in Diana's bathroom, the sharply pressed shirts that hung in her wardrobe. "Sage can get his own water. I'll call down for the cup, shall I?"

He nodded wearily and sank down onto the bed, his hands open on his thighs, and slumped as if his grief were a heavy cloak.

I called down for the extra coffee, and then thought to ask, "Have you eaten, Henry?"

He waved a hand.

"Bring a bowl of fruit and some toast too," I said.

"I'm gutted," he said roughly, staring through the long windows that faced the sea. Mist ribboned along the balcony, moved in an unseen wind. For a moment it parted, and I saw the spire of Hyrne Rock. It reminded me of the smuggling aspects we'd talked about earlier.

Could Diana somehow be connected to some kind of smuggling? It seemed far fetched, but at this point I was willing to consider any idea.

A knock on the door announced the coffee. I opened the door, and a uniformed young man brought in a tray. I waited until he left and then poured a cup for Henry.

We sat down. Sage said, "It's a bloody awful thing, Henry. But maybe if we all compare notes, we can figure out what happened."

He nodded. "Whatever you like."

"When did you meet Diana?"

"Last August. My usual caterer fell through for a big trip I'd worked on for months, and she stepped in. Brilliantly."

"How did you find her?" I asked.

"Google. It was an emergency, and I was in London. She had good reviews, so I called her."

I remembered the job and how excited she'd been to land it. It was one of the few FaceTimes we'd shared before everything fell apart—or rather before I became the worst friend in the world. She'd been practically bouncing in her chair, the freckles across her nose more visible after a day of strawberry picking. I'd teased her a little about it, but she didn't mind.

Sage asked, "And you started dating her right away?"

Tears welled in his eyes, and he used his thumbs to pinch them away. "She had the most dazzling smile. I'm so tired of women who put on airs and have to carry designer bags. She isn't like that. She makes me laugh." He paused. "I just liked her, that first day."

"She liked you too," I said. "I have the texts to prove it."

He nodded, his head bowed, and I could see he was struggling. I gave Sage a look, and we busied ourselves with our cups for a moment. I watched the mist eddy and swirl, giving glimpses of a portion of the coast I hadn't seen from my grandmother's house. A lighthouse stood on a point, and farther on, I knew the cliffs curved around to another string of small villages.

"Henry," Sage said quietly. "Do you have any idea of something she might have stumbled on, some crime or something she shouldn't have known about?"

He shook his head, still bowed. "Like what?"

"I don't know," Sage said, clearly frustrated. He flung up his hand, let it fall. "The girl on the beach this morning looks like a drug overdose, so maybe drugs? Gambling? Smuggling?"

Henry raised his head. Coughed. "Not that I know of. They gamble, for certain. I've heard of some big pots, but these men—they can afford it."

"Who takes these trips?" I asked.

"Businessmen, mostly, getting away from their wives and responsibilities, having a laugh for a long weekend."

"What kind of businessmen?"

He shrugged, looked at the wall as if the answer were there. "Bankers. CEOs of all kinds, I reckon."

"Masters of the universe," I said.

He nodded. "I'm sure they're not particularly nice fellows, all told, but they're not smuggling. Why would they bother?"

I frowned, examining his face carefully for signs of lying. As if I knew what those signs would be.

I realized that I did think he was lying, however. An intuition, something that my body picked up that I didn't know I was reading.

Sage must have felt the same way, because he asked quietly, "Why did you immediately assume she was dead, Henry?"

He started, visibly, and coffee sloshed out of his cup and over his fingers. He shook them off, and I handed him a napkin from the tea caddy. "What d'you mean?"

"When we said she was missing, you immediately looked like you would die. Almost as if you were not surprised."

"That's not true!" He looked shaken. "I was in love with her! Ask anyone."

"No one has met you in town. Not me, and I was one of her best friends," Sage said. His persistence surprised me. "Why didn't you make time for us?"

"We had so little time together. No matter how I tried, I couldn't get down here every weekend. It wasn't personal. I just . . . wanted to be with her."

And then a tsunami of grief slammed him. He bent his head and began to weep. It made me like him more, that he was so lost without her, and I rested my hand at the top of his back, feeling an internal shiver, my own fear and grief, wanting outlet. Surely we all knew she was dead by now. I knew the reality would sink in at some point.

The thought met a fierce resistance. No. I would not give up. Not yet.

Sage ducked into the bathroom and brought back a snowy-white towel he then handed over to Henry. He cocked his head toward the door.

"We'll leave you alone, Henry," I said. "I'm so sorry we bothered you."

He didn't speak as we let ourselves out.

In the hallway, I stopped halfway to the stairs and leaned against the wall, my heart aching as the sound of his tears followed us. "He's wrecked," I said.

"He didn't answer the question." Sage leaned next to me, our arms just touching. "He knows something."

"Agreed. But what?"

"I dunno." He looked down at me. "Let's go for a walk. I have an idea."

"Can we get some coffee first? I'm dying of cold and hunger."

One side of his mouth lifted. "Done."

A sense of history moved around us, a wash of air and time and ourselves, and I held his gaze.

He lifted one hand and brushed a damp lock of hair out of my face. "You're kind of a mess."

"Thank you."

"I missed you." His hand touched mine, knuckles to knuckles.

"Me too," I said, and then I straightened, pulling away, putting myself in my place. "Coffee."

Chapter Thirty

Zoe

At the coffee shop while we waited in line, I texted Isabel and my grandmother to let them know I was still out walking. Neither replied, so it was safe to assume that Gran was lost in her work, and Isabel was still sleeping. Tucking the phone back in my pocket, I commented, "I'm the only lark in the family."

"Poppy is a lark," he said.

I narrowed my eyes. "She's not my family."

"Don't be ridiculous." He stepped up to the counter and ordered muffins and coffee for both of us, glancing back to ask how I took it. "You might want to disown her, but genes will out."

"Whatever." I twitched my shoulders as I went over to stand by the fogged-up window. The café was full, and I heard snippets of conversation here and there, most of it revolving around the body on the beach.

Sage stood next to me, completely at ease, and said not a single word. Not to needle me, not to draw me out, not anything. I noticed that he was listening, too, and I focused on collecting whatever information we might learn like this.

Approximately nothing. It was all speculation. We took our muffins and coffee and walked toward the playground, where he gestured for us to sit on a bench that was beaded with water from the mist. I wiped it off with my sleeve and sat. "What's your idea?"

"Let's play with scenarios, shall we?"

"Okay."

"We have the fishing parties, which Diana started catering after she met her new boyfriend."

"Right."

"We have the dead girl on the beach, and I'm going to predict it's drugs that killed her."

"Mmm." I was starving, and the muffin was studded perfectly with big grains of brown sugar. There wasn't much room in my mouth for talking.

"Henry said they're all out to have a good time, so drinking, gambling, fishing." He peeled the paper from the muffin carefully. "But what if not all of the parties are fishing parties? What if some of them are not the—what did you call them? The masters of the universe—but something else? Drug traffickers or whatever."

"My gran thought maybe electronics, like cheap phones."

"Right. The actual goods are less important than the active smuggling. What if Diana found out somehow, and somebody killed her to hush her up?"

"But how would we find that out?"

He frowned, studying the cliff. "Surely she'd have left us some sort of clue. She documented everything."

I thought of the bedroom and wondered if she had a journal or diary somewhere. "She wouldn't have been foolish enough to write down something like 'I'm suspicious of the fishing party I just catered.'"

"No, you're right." He took a bite of his muffin and brushed crumbs from his jeans. I found myself watching him chew. I noticed a scar high on his cheekbone that I didn't recognize, and the length of his throat, and how smooth his jaw was this morning in comparison to the glitter of beard that had been there the other night.

He looked at me. "What? Do I have crumbs?" He brushed his mouth.

"No." I wanted to touch the same path, his cheek and jaw, but more compelling was the sense that we'd done something very stupid all these years. "How did we let all that time go by without talking, Sage?"

He shook his head. "We were so young back then. We thought we knew everything, didn't we?"

"Not me. I was pretty sure I didn't know anything." I kicked my feet out in front of me, moving them back and forth against the backdrop of misty sea, trying to make sure I didn't say the wrong thing. I looked at him. "And after everything, I didn't even stick with my art."

"Why didn't you come back to Axestowe, instead of going to New Mexico?"

"You know why. We broke up in such a bad way."

"But Woodhurst is your home."

I nodded. I thought of the apoplectic face of the teacher who'd hated me, the humiliation of the smirks of the other students, my own overwhelming sense of insecurity, and my terrible, terrible mistake. I couldn't face Sage and Axestowe after that. "It's a long story, and really not that interesting."

"It's interesting to me," he said quietly.

I held up a hand, feeling more emotional than I would have expected. "I'm not sure I can talk about it, even now."

"You're right." I heard him take a breath, then let it go. "I'm sorry." He took my hand. "We're here now, right?"

I looked up. Nodded.

To my surprise, he lifted my hand and kissed the knuckles. "I'm sorry, Zoe. For all of it."

I didn't trust myself to speak. All the things I wanted, all the things I'd lost, all the things that could have been welled up in my throat, and I just nodded.

"Let's go have another look at the ledger."

"All right."

In my pocket, my phone buzzed. "Sorry. I have to check."

"Of course."

It was from Isabel:

Gigi is very agitated. She needs you. Poppy is still here, but she says she will go when you arrive.

"Damn." I texted back:

Be right there.

"I have to go. Gran is having an episode."

"Of course. Do you need help?"

"No, thanks. Do you want to go over to Diana's and maybe send me files so we can compare them side by side or something?"

"Uh . . . sure." He stood too.

"That doesn't sound sure."

He took a breath. "It'll be hard to be in her house by myself."

I thought what it would be like to be in her house alone, with all the things she'd left behind waiting for her return. "I get it. We can go over later if you want."

"I'd prefer that. But I'll head over to her business. Look through those files. Text me your email."

"Okay." I started to turn away, then turned back. "Sage, I'm glad we're talking again."

He nodded and gave me a sad smile.

———— ❦ ————

I avoided the climb down to the beach by walking along the high street and the bluff that marked the edge of town, walking as urgently as possible. I still had to climb down toward the town and then up the path toward Woodhurst, and from the top I could see a big knot of people down on the beach, swirling around the crime scene. I couldn't tell if the body was still there, but it didn't seem so.

Poppy and Isabel were in the kitchen, with Mósí at Isabel's feet, tail wrapped tidily around his paws. "Where's Gran? Has she eaten this morning?" I hated seeing Poppy there with Isabel, looking so cozy, but I had to admit to a sneaking sense of relief too. It was much less terrifying to face whatever was happening if I wasn't entirely on my own.

"She wouldn't eat," Poppy said. She gave me a bottle of pills. "Try to get some protein in her if you can, and if she keeps getting more agitated, give her a Valium."

She smelled of lavender, and up close, I could see the lines around her eyes. Some dark thing moved through me, ran down my spine. In the distance, that keening sound rose, a lost girl pining for her mother. Shards of emotion stuck in my skin from head to toe, and I had to grab the pills and turn away. "Okay." I swallowed. "Thanks for your help."

Light flickered over her face, and she raised a hand as if to pat my arm, but I shrank away. "Call if you need anything."

"Yep."

"She's out in the garden."

My mother left. Isabel stood quietly nearby. I realized that she was wearing normal clothes, clothes appropriate for the climate and the area, and completely ordinary—a jumper over a turtleneck, jeans, boots. I hadn't even realized that she'd packed them.

What had wrought such a big change? My mother? A very nasty twist of jealousy squeezed away some of my happiness, and when I realized how ugly that was, I forced myself to ask in an even tone, "Are those my Doc Martens?"

"Yeah." She grinned, holding up a foot. "So cute. Is it okay?"

Eyeing the well-worn oxblood boots, I felt a soft puff of nostalgia. "Yeah, they're too small for me now. They look great on you."

"Thanks." Even her hair was done, washed and calmed into beautiful ringlets with product. "I'm going out to shoot."

"Only shoot?"

She lifted a shoulder. "I'm going to look for some of the people I met the other day. Is that okay? Molly texted me a while ago."

"Molly is . . . ?"

"The girl I met a few days ago. I told you about her. She's good."

I knew she'd been desperately lonely. "Okay. Be careful. And—"

"Check in regularly. I know." She shrugged into a puffy jacket the color of the shoes, tossed her camera bag over her shoulder, and tugged her hair out to freedom.

I nodded. "You look great," I said. "It's nice to see my girl again."

"Thanks." She lifted a hand as she headed for the front door, which was closer to the path to town.

"Wait!" I called. "Stay clear of the beach. Something is going on."

"What?" she said, stopping.

"They found a body. Someone drowned."

She frowned. "Diana?"

"No. Not her, for sure. That's all I know."

"Okay."

"Be careful."

"Mom!" Exasperated. "I've got it."

"Okay."

I found Gran in the garden, sitting on a stool so she could weed. She wore her dressing gown, and her hair had not been done. A little child part of me burst into tears, but I was perfectly calm as I sat down beside her on the grass. "Hello," I said. "You must have been in a big hurry to get out to the garden."

"Oh, I couldn't sleep all night. I just couldn't be bothered."

"Have you eaten?"

She paused, dirty fingers in the air. "I can't remember."

"Are you hungry?"

"No. I just want to get this bit done. I wish you'd stop nagging me. You're worse than your father—both of you so needy. A body barely has a chance to take a breath."

At first I was taken aback. She didn't speak to me with that tone—and . . .

"My father?"

"Stinks of cigars, chokes me out," she muttered.

My grandfather, whom I'd never met. I crossed my arms over my ribs, wondering what to do. And what we would need to do long term. We would have to find actual nurses, figure out some kind of plan to keep her safe.

Her fine white hair stuck up, some of it pressed to her temple. A sense of painful tenderness made me lift a hand and smooth it down. The woman she'd always been would be horrified to be caught out so untidy. "What if I bring you something?"

"Leave me alone!" she cried. "I just want to think!"

It wounded me, even if she didn't really mean it. For the moment, she was safe enough in the garden. She could wander off, I supposed, but not far, considering her frailty. I went in and made a pot of strong tea, arranged a plate of biscuits on a saucer, and then stuck my head back out the door. "Gran, would you like some tea? I've just made a pot."

By the way she startled, I realized that she'd fallen asleep. "What? What?"

I hurried out. "Come inside," I said gently. "I've just made some tea."

She stood willingly and then looked at her dressing gown. "Why am I outside in my gown?"

I remembered what I'd read about dementia: just to stay kind and in the moment. "Well, it's a lovely morning for weeding, isn't it? I expect you were simply eager to get out here."

"I was plotting. The mistress of a wealthy man is murdered."

It was the plot of my grandmother's most famous book, the first of the Lady Dawood books.

"Mmm," I said, noncommittal. "Lady Dawood?"

"Oh, no," she said with some of the same irritability that had marked her early tone. "I wrote that book already. This one will have Diana at the center."

"A mistress?"

"I have never believed that man was not married. Why would he only come on weekends?"

She was utterly rational now, completely in the here and now. In dismay, I said, "You really think so?"

"It doesn't matter now, does it," she said, and she sank into her chair with a huff. "I'm shattered today."

"Eat," I said, pushing the plate and cup closer. "I'll make you an egg."

"Oh, yes, please."

As I took out eggs and butter and the heavy pan, my phone stuttered the sound for a text. Sage:

You haven't sent your email.

Sorry. Zoefairchild@emailtime.com.

I wrote:

I can't leave Gran. Can you possibly just drop in to Diana's house, grab the ledger, and bring it here?

No response right away. I added butter to the pan and watched it begin to melt.

The phone stuttered.

The sun is coming out. That will make it easier to go to the house.

I sent a smiley face back.

See you when you get here, then.

Anything you need?

No. But thanks for asking.

No worries.

I set the phone down on the counter and looked out the window for one long moment, feeling the shocks and switches and turnarounds of the morning swirling through me. Then I picked up an egg and cracked it into the pan.

As Diana would have said, people always have to eat.

Chapter Thirty-One

Isabel

It made me really sad that Gigi was so out of her head when I got up. She made no sense, talking about people I'd never heard of, and it was impossible to get her to sit down and have her tea.

Gigi is really smart, and it's sad to think she'll lose all those pieces of herself.

So I took my camera out and walked along the cliff and shot photos of the milling cops and onlookers gathered on the beach. I never had a clear view to tell if there was even a body down there, but it was the first time I'd ever seen an actual crime scene. How do you make something like that interesting?

I shot a few focusing on color—red coat, red boat, blue uniforms, blue car. Another of arrangements of people, some kneeling, some hovering. It's a good telephoto lens, so I could catch a few expressions, though not many good ones, honestly.

After I was finished, I headed for the old church where Molly said she'd be. It seemed like a weird place to meet until I saw it, just a sort of ordinary ruin surrounded by trees and tall stands of grass. A graveyard stretched out from the church, the headstones mostly just gray shapes, erased of any identifying information. The place felt empty as I walked through it, as if nothing was really here at all, but I couldn't help imagining all the bones below my feet, the skeletons in their rotted clothes, the human beings who had once walked around the world just like I was right now.

I spied a blue sleeve in the opening of what was once a door, and then I heard a couple of people talking. As I came around the wall, I felt suddenly shy without my big hoodie. I pulled my sleeves down over my hands.

A few kids were there, but I only recognized two of them—Molly and the guy from the Tesco crowd. Isaac. He saw me first and jumped to his feet. "Hiya! Isabel, right?"

"Yeah." I measured the others, suddenly feeling a sense of panic in my throat. Three guys, two girls, plus Molly and Isaac. Most of them white, one brown girl with a nose ring, and a black guy with hair cut short. "Hi."

Molly, smoking a rolled something, patted the space beside her. I sat, but I passed on the weed when I realized that's what it was. "I'll get paranoid," I said, handing it to the guy next to her.

"Just because you're paranoid doesn't mean they're not out to get you," he said with an accent I didn't recognize. "I'm Marcu. You are American."

She nodded.

"I want to go to America," he said.

"Not me," one of the girls said. She was blonde and raw looking, like she never ate anything healthy. Her eyes were rimmed in pink. "I'd be afraid to get shot, like at the movies or a mall or something." Her accent was thick and hard to understand, half of it swallowed, the *th* pronounced as an *f*, and the *g* like a *k*. *Somefink.*

I lifted a shoulder. What could I say to that? It's not like it isn't true.

"D'you know anybody who got shot?"

"No. It hasn't happened around me."

"Don't mean it won't, though, does it?"

I shrugged. And had to crush a rise of memory, that morning walking home. Finding my phone on the front porch—

This was a bad idea. I wanted to escape.

Isaac rescued me. "Did you see the body on the beach?"

"No. There's a bunch of cops. You can't see anything."

The girl with the nose ring said, "Yeah, they wouldn't tell us nothing, just shooed us off to school." She snickered. "We been thinking it's this girl who lived near us. Jennie. She was living with Diana, and nobody's seen her in weeks."

"Why?"

She shrugged. "I dunno. It was weird, right? Like, I talked to her every day, and she just disappears?" She held up her phone. "Nothing."

"Have you told the cops?" I asked. It seemed like something they should know.

For a second they all stared at me like I'd sprouted horns. Then, all at once, they started to laugh. "Like they'd listen to the lot of us."

I snapped to reality. They were smoking weed in the ruins of a church on a school day. I gave them a rueful smile, embarrassed. "Right. Sorry."

Molly bumped me with an elbow. "S'all right."

For a minute, I was tempted to take a hit. I could feel the zigzaggy sensation of anxiety running along my veins. Weed would calm that down.

But my dad told me a long time ago that the reason a lot of people fall on their faces is because they can't handle big things without booze or drugs. You have to figure out how you can face things that hurt or burn or even make you really happy.

So I sat there, mentally going through a five, four, three, two, one, naming what I saw, what I smelled, what I felt physically. After a couple of minutes my breath didn't feel like it was stuck at the back of my throat anymore, and I didn't feel like I had to run away.

After another ten minutes, I felt myself just starting to relax, being myself, listening to the back and forth. It felt good to be laughing at stupid jokes and feeling a guy's eyes on me, trying to impress me.

Maybe life will be okay again.

Chapter Thirty-Two

Zoe

I settled Gran in her bedroom and covered her with a soft, thick blanket. As she looked out the window to the sea, now glittering and calm, I read to her from a Jacqueline Winspear novel she'd left in progress on her bedside table. Eventually, she fell asleep.

Leaving her tucked in, I looked in her medicine cabinet for the meds she'd been taking and then compared them with the chart Poppy had made. There was a considerable number of them, and I gathered the lot into a box to carry back into her bedroom so I could go through them, one by one.

I sat in a chair by the window and looked each one up on the internet. Blood thinner, blood pressure medicine, serious antacid, cholesterol control, all of which were fairly normal for a woman of eighty-seven, I supposed. I also found an antianxiety medicine, the bottle hardly touched, and one for Aricept, which I found to my dismay was used to treat dementia.

I sat with the bottles in my lap and watched Lillian sleep. How long had she known? How long had she been taking it?

And why hadn't Diana said anything to me? We hadn't been completely out of touch, after all. A nudge would have been the right thing to do.

Unless my grandmother had sworn her to silence, which was entirely likely.

For now, Lillian was sleeping, but I wasn't sure how much antianxiety medicine she could safely take, or what to do if she still seemed so lost when she woke up. I knew I should probably call my mother, but—

I remembered that pharmacists would give advice here, especially in a village where the prescribing pharmacy would know my grandmother. I punched in the number on the label with a vast sense of relief. When the man picked up the phone, I explained who I was and what the situation was and asked if I could give her antianxiety meds. "She's been very agitated today, and I'm worried about her."

He was quiet for a long moment. "Yes. I'm sorry. You need to meet with her GP as soon as you can."

"Yes, we have an appointment at the end of the week, according to the medical info I have here. But I'm most concerned about today, and if it's safe to give her the antianxiety meds."

"I'm reluctant to say yes or no, Ms. Fairchild. Your mother is listed here as the main contact. Perhaps it would be best to speak with her first?"

I sighed. "Of course."

It wasn't like he didn't know we'd had a longtime war. In a village as small and insular as this one, such a story would have been discussed a million times, in a million variations. "I'm sorry I couldn't be of more help."

"It's all right."

Across the room, my grandmother snored. I needed to talk with my mother about long-term plans, about whether she'd seen doctors and been treated, about all of it.

When I absolutely had to, I would. At the moment, Lillian was okay. With any luck, she'd sleep awhile and get herself right, and I wouldn't have to make a phone call I did not want to make.

In the meantime, I left a message with her GP, then looked up carer services. She needed more than occasional help and family looking in on her. She would need a full-time carer, and the great news about her fortune was that she could afford to pay for the best. I made three calls and lined up as many interviews for tomorrow.

When I hung up the phone, I simply sat in her chair and watched her sleep.

Cooper showed up midafternoon. The clouds were moving back in, shouldering into the sky like a noisy crowd, the tops rising high into thunderheads. It reminded me that I hadn't heard from Isabel for a bit. I texted her.

Looks like a storm.

I'm with Molly at a house by the Tesco. It's fine.

I found her on Find My Friends, a dot not far from the high street, less than a mile away.

Ok

He arrived at the kitchen door as I was preparing a stew for dinner, and the scent of browning onions gave the air a homey smell. It had been a while since I'd had a chance to cook. It calmed me to skin carrots and chop celery and crush whole spices, and with the radio turned to a classical station, I felt a soft sense of normality ease the taut skin of my face. So many things were wrong, but this was something I could control.

"Hey," I said as he came in. "Looks like you found a few things."

He carried a canvas bag that looked pretty heavy, and he settled it on the table. Mósí ran into the room, meowing in greeting, and swirled around his legs.

"Hello, you," Cooper said, bending to scoop the big cat up in his arms as easily as if he were a kitten. "You're a little dog of a cat, aren't you?"

Joyfully, Mósí headbutted his chin, and Cooper greeted him in return by rubbing along the cat's forehead, back and forth, while holding his big body without any apparent effort. I ached a little, watching them.

"He loves men," I said. "My ex raised him when his mother was killed, and he thinks men will nurse him."

"Is that right?" Cooper said to the cat, who meowed in response.

While he was busy, I said, "I need your help with something."

"Sure."

"You won't feel that way when I ask."

"Must be to do with your mother, then."

I nodded, stirring mirepoix over low heat. "She was here this morning, but I'm worried that I don't have enough information. I'm afraid of giving her too much Valium, and the pharmacist said my mother is the person listed."

"Ah." He set the cat free and straightened before going to the sink to wash his hands. "Diana was holding up the tent, wasn't she?"

"It looks that way." I stirred, watching the cubed carrots and celery and onion in the pan. "Gran was very agitated and confused this afternoon. She mistook me for my mother, and her plots are mixed up with the current village trouble. She was quite combative, honestly."

"I'm sorry. It's been happening for a while."

"Why didn't anyone tell me she had dementia?"

"It was never mine to do." He leaned on the counter, crossed his arms. "And you don't speak to your mother."

I absorbed that. Nodded. "Damn it, I'm just so sad."

"Understandable."

"Will you call my mother and ask her about the drugs?"

He smiled. "I will. What do you need to know?"

"I just want to ask about the Valium and the general protocols for how to soothe her when she's agitated." Saying this aloud made my throat ache.

Cooper held his phone up, waiting for me to finish. "Anything else?"

"No." I knew it was ridiculous, but I also knew I would not be able to dial the phone, or even speak if she answered. We'd spoken in person, but the phone was different. The thought of it made it hard to breathe, the memories of my lost self having a panic attack.

PTSD was a bear.

"I need to get you a pencil."

"Might be helpful." He touched the screen and lifted the phone immediately to his ear, so I knew she must be in his favorites, though why not? He'd known her as long as I had. I remembered the pair of us sitting in her lap as she read the story of the Velveteen Rabbit, her beautiful voice acting out all the parts, and the way she cut off the edges of a too-brown potato casserole for him.

I added cubed sweet potatoes to the pot and stirred slowly as he listened to the phone ring. I could hear it ring on the other end, *ring-ring, ring-ring*. And then her voice, which I could hear quite clearly. "Hello, Sage."

Something about the way it sounded made my heart squeeze so hard I felt I lost a few beats. Her fluting vowels, her breathy softness. All the nerves on my arms rustled, and I had to rub them.

"Hiya, Poppy," he said. "I have a favor to ask."

"Go ahead."

"Your daughter has asked me to find out how much Valium she can give Lillian. She's worried about giving her too much."

"Oh, dear. Shall I come over?"

"No!" I said.

Cooper switched to speaker and laid the phone down on the table. "I guess she can hear me, then," Poppy said. She might have sighed. "You don't have to speak, Zoe, but I hope you will listen."

"I am." I tried to make the words hard, but they sounded slightly pathetic.

"Gran has been in decline for nearly a year. She can be very mean when she doesn't know where she is, so you might want to warn Isabel."

After a pause, she continued. "In addition to the chart I left, which does have the dosage on Valium, there's a more complete medical history and helpful tips in the top-left drawer of the desk in the small parlor. She never goes in that room, so I hoped she wouldn't tear them up. She's done that several times."

I waved for Cooper to follow me. He picked up the phone, and we traipsed through the house, through the great hall, then into the hearth room, a large sitting room, and then the small one. It was cold and smelled dusty.

The desk creaked as I opened the narrow upper drawer and took out a file folder, neatly labeled in a hand I recognized as Poppy's—a spidery, slanted cursive. Again, the look of it stabbed me oddly, as if she'd already died and I was looking through old letters.

Would I mourn her when she died? It was an entirely new thought. I had no idea of the answer.

I held up the file, and Sage said, "We've got it."

"Good. Everything you need is there. She's often fine for many weeks on end, and then she'll have a bad day or two. I worried yesterday that she might be slipping."

There were questions I wanted to ask, and it would be stupid to tell Sage to ask them when I was standing right there, but the first thing out of my mouth was, "Yesterday?"

A short pause. "I stopped by to see her when you and Isa went to the moor."

"Really." I looked at Sage. "And how did you know I was going?"

"Your gran told me, Zoe. I am trying to be respectful of your wish to avoid me."

A thousand retorts crowded into my mouth, but all of them had the ring of adolescence, and I refused to indulge. One of us had grown up. "I appreciate that."

Silence buzzed in the room. The floor creaked below Sage's left foot as he shifted his weight.

"Is there anything else?" Poppy asked.

How about *Why did you leave me?* Instead some meanness in me lashed out. Isabel had told me that Poppy was worried about the girl who'd been staying with Diana. "Did you hear about the girl who washed up on the beach?"

"What? No. What body?"

"How did you miss it?" I asked. "There's been a crowd on the beach all day, looking for clues. Beach was closed."

"The shop is closed on Mondays. Mia and I have been in the workshop all day making charms for the festival." Her voice cracked as she asked, "Do they know who it is?"

Sage said, "She's young, Poppy. Dark hair. That's all we know."

"Oh, no." Her voice was hushed, and I almost felt sorry for her. "Oh, I hope it isn't Jennie. Thank you for telling me."

"I'm sorry, Poppy," Sage said. "Don't lose hope. It might not be her."

"It's terrible, no matter who it is," she said, and she sounded so very weary. "Zoe, if you have any questions, you can text or have Isa call me on your behalf. We do not have to speak again."

She hung up.

A brick of guilt fell into my gut. I stared at the phone for a long moment, burning with shame and fury and a little shattering thing at the back of it all that made me feel breathless, as if shrapnel had lodged in my lungs. I pressed a hand to my diaphragm, reminding myself that it was just an emotion. Nothing I hadn't felt a thousand times before.

"That was a bit unsporting."

I looked at him. Flushed. "Probably."

He licked his bottom lip and picked up the phone. "No one is perfect, I suppose."

His meaning was clear—that I expected her to be perfect when I was mean myself. With a swift and bitter fury, I said, "The sainted Sage knows everything."

"That's not what I meant."

"I don't want to talk about it. You never understood. You thought it was the same, you losing her. Diana losing her. It wasn't."

I thought it would make him angry, but instead, he bowed his head. "You're right, Zoe."

"Let's go see if we can figure anything out with all the material from Diana before Gran wakes up," I said. "I'll need to focus on her then."

We walked back to the kitchen through the dark, cold rooms, some of which I couldn't remember ever using. The hearth, as tall as my shoulder, stood cold and empty before a long wooden table that in my lifetime had never seen big family gatherings or parties of any kind. "What's the point of these houses in the modern era?" I wondered aloud.

"History?"

"Cold comfort, isn't it?" I paused, looking at the view of the garden in the half-purple twilight. A white rose blazed against the dusk. I wondered where Isabel was. She'd been out a long time. I pulled the phone out of my pocket to text her. "Maybe the manor should be flats."

"Would you really want to do that?"

"I don't know." That sense of desperate sadness clawed at me again, a sense of time passing, of nothing having any permanence or reliability. I blinked back tears. "I'm just in a mood. Let's have some tea and see if we can figure out what Diana might have discovered."

He touched my upper back for one moment, then dropped his hand as I moved away, into the light of the kitchen, where the Rayburn warmed the air and a kettle waited. As I walked, a text from Isabel came in.

Every hour on the hour, and I'm fine. I'll be home in a bit.

Sooner rather than later. It's getting dark

k

Chapter Thirty-Three
Poppy

After Zoe's call, I stood with the phone in my hand for fully five minutes, feeling a thousand memories move through my body, my heart. Zoe as a baby, and Ben playing with a goat, and Sage and Zoe heading out to explore, shoulder to shoulder.

Her voice now was mature and cold, so different from the girl who'd informed me that she would never speak to me again unless I came home to her. Had I believed she would stick to it?

Not at all.

What surprised me was how deep my longing for her went. I wanted to look at her face, watch expressions move over it. I wanted to trace the path of time across her brow and chin, and listen to her spin stories about her life, about Sage and art and her husband and Isabel's birth. I wanted to listen to the sound of her voice, both American and English, and make special meals to make her smile.

I deeply, painfully wanted to *know* her, and it appeared that perhaps that would never happen. It was the price I would have to pay for leaving her.

Abandoning her.

Scarring her.

I closed my eyes and let the pain and shame fill me for the space of three breaths. Yearning. Sorrow. Pain. Whatever she doled out now, I had certainly earned.

With a heavy heart, I headed to the village and the constabulary. It was a rush of motion and discussion, everyone busy after the discovery of the body, but I knew who I wanted to talk to. Although the front line tried to hold me off, Inspector Hannaford heard me and came forward to wave me into his office.

"What can I help you with, Poppy?" he asked. We'd attended school together until my mother had sent me off to boarding school, though he'd been a year or two behind me.

"Was it Jennie on the beach?"

"Poppy, you know it's too early."

"No, you have an idea right now."

"Did you know the girl?" he asked, slightly askance.

"She came to me every week for a reading." Her palm had broken my heart the first time I saw it, the shortest life line I'd ever seen, and yet I'd tried to jolly her into action. Ways to save her life.

"I'm sorry," he said.

"So tell me, was it her?"

He sighed, rubbed the bridge of his nose. "We honestly don't know yet. The body was pretty badly decomposed."

"How long was it in the water?"

"Hard to say. A couple of weeks, probably."

A little of the pressure on my heart eased. "I saw Jennie last Tuesday. Almost a week."

"Right." His attitude was guarded. "I promise I'll let you know as soon as we identify her."

I slumped, my shoulders suddenly tired of carrying the weight of sorrow. "What is going on in this village, George?"

"Wish I knew." He picked up a pencil and made it do pirouettes over a sheet of paper. "Your mother thinks it might be smuggling."

"Is anyone monitoring the coast for that kind of activity?"

"Of course they are." He sighed. "We haven't found anything. If you know a spell to draw out the bad guys, I'd love to see you offer it."

I smiled sadly as I stood and smoothed my tunic. My bracelets clattered down my arm. "Thanks for the vote of confidence."

"Me gran was a witch, you know. She had a cure for everything. Lived to be ninety-nine, she did."

"Is that right?" I paused. "Was she local? What was her name?"

"Lived down by the river, with a smallholding. Mary Hooper."

"Oh, aye. She came from a long line of wise women. Well known for her cures, your grandmother. They say she held a line against smallpox in the thirties, and not a soul in the village fell ill."

His cheeks shone red with pleasure. "I've never heard that before. Thank you."

"Maybe you've a touch of her gifts," I said, cocking my head. He did have that look about him, now that I took the time to pay attention. Great pale-blue eyes and a thick head of hair that grew almost unnaturally well for a man well into his fifties. I let myself go still, studying him, and reached out for his aura, testing—

But he shut me right down, walls as thick and opaque as gold bars. I wondered if he knew he'd done it. "Come see me, George," I said. "I'll make you a pot of tea."

"Good night, Ms. Fairchild," he said, erecting more distance between us. "I'll let you know when we learn the identity of the body."

Out in the night, I lingered. Where was Jennie? Where was her baby?

Suddenly I realized that I was more worried over a village girl than I'd ever been over my own daughter when she was making her way through all the challenges of growing up. Around the world, I had collected lost and lonely girls, offering them insight and a place to sit and tell their stories, opening my heart to them in ways—

Oh, Zoe, what have I done?

And how could I never have put the two things together? The fact that I'd filled the emptiness of being away from my daughter with girls other people had abandoned. What terrible twistedness was that?

Why hadn't I come home to her after Ravi died?

I couldn't remember. The years following his death were a blur of temples and ashrams and wanderings. I felt I'd been shattered and all the pieces of myself had to be reassembled, one shard and then another. It had taken a long time.

The sound of her voice on the phone this afternoon echoed in my mind as I made my way slowly up the high street. In the restaurants, people laughed and made merry. Through the windows of the Golden Mermaid, I spied a pair of local couples, well to do and polished, eating oysters and drinking martinis.

Once, I had dreamed of a family of my own. A husband to tease me indulgently and children to be exasperated with me. A long table I would set with cloth napkins in rings everyone would choose to be their own.

I'd longed for that as a child, too, but we never sat down at the same time to dinner. At the time we kept staff—not a lot, but a cook/housekeeper and a gardener and a nanny until I was ten. Maisy, our cook, fed me at the same kitchen table where my mother now took her meals, me on my own while my mother stormed around or fought with my father, or drank martinis alone, listening to Frank Sinatra records.

My father died when I was thirteen, and after that I didn't go home from school much at all, except at Christmas. Other holidays, I found a way to be with friends who traveled to Zurich for the holidays, or to their homes in the South of France. My best girlfriend's father ran a slew of international shoe-manufacturing centers, and I traipsed around a bit with her over summers, to the Black Sea and Amsterdam and once, thrillingly, to Thailand. I'd been madly in love with Yul Brenner in *The King and I*, and I'd hoped to see his counterpart somewhere in the villages of the old Siam.

I realized I'd been staring into the restaurant window for far too long and made myself move.

By the time I'd finished school, I knew I was absolutely not going to go off to university for any reason. My mother threw a fit, of course—how else would I find a husband of good standing?—but I refused. It was the seventies, and I wanted a life of beauty and choice, not like my mother's staid existence, she in her pressed trousers and discreet strings of pearls, so I followed the hippie train to Glastonbury and donned my india cotton skirts and long earrings and grew my hair to my waist and smoked weed and ate mushrooms.

Meeting Ben had steered my cart for a time. Girls of my generation were so encultured to expect that, to be good helpmeets to the men who thought they'd chosen us.

I loved him. I genuinely did. He was kind and quietly brilliant, and his abstract sculptures wrecked me—they were the air, the desert, the morning sun, all without direct reference. We were sexually very good together, which I thought meant we were soul mates and learned later was just good chemistry, but it made a beautiful daughter.

Who hated me, with good reason. I heard it in her voice tonight, the struggle she'd had to keep her tone from breaking. As she spoke in a voice so unlike the one she'd had as a child, this one as musically toned as her father's, it occurred to me that I did not know her at all. I'd heard about her life from my mother, and I'd stalked her online as I was able, though, unlike most of her age group, she wasn't really very present on social media.

But I did not know my own daughter, because I'd chosen someone else.

———— ⚬⚬⚬ ————

On the eighteenth day of my sojourn across Rajasthan, on what was meant to be a monthlong trip with my girlfriend, then back home to England, I met Ravi. My friend and I had landed in Udaipur, a busy city with an old town and a lake with a hotel in the middle of it. We had no money and all our belongings were on our backs, but I ached to see that hotel. We polished ourselves up as well as we were able, dressed in the prettiest of the outfits we'd splurged on at the markets, and took a boat ride over. Young pretty women always got dispensation, and today was no exception.

It was so lovely. From the hotel you could see a great white palace that spread across one edge of the lake in splendor. Windows looked out over the mountains behind us, and the water and the hotel, and I was enchanted.

I'd lost Annie, my friend, and was wandering the hotel trying to find her when I saw Ravi. He stood in an arched doorway near the edge of the island, with the mountains rising behind him. The sun hung low, spreading a deep-orange light across the stones and the building and casting him in a compelling light. He wore a tunic and trousers and had sandals on his tanned feet. He was not, as Ben was, a beautiful creature. His face was harsh, his nose too large, but he had large dark eyes, and they looked right at me, steadily, plainly.

I would like to say that I felt the world shift, but I didn't. I looked away and primly kept walking. We'd been warned not to give the wrong messages to men here, and I took that seriously.

But he fell in beside me. "Do you speak English?" he asked in an exquisite, well-educated accent.

"I do." Up close, he smelled of spice and morning, and his nose was a marvel. I suddenly thought I must have met him before, even if I didn't remember, because his face and voice were as familiar to me as my own hands. "Where have we met?"

"I would have remembered," he said, and paused, making me stop too. "Perhaps it was another incarnation."

"Perhaps," I agreed.

We fell in love. It was instant and deep. Not lust, for we did not think we would be lovers. He was a married man, a writer and scholar who'd come to Udaipur to pen stories of the great Mughals. Adventure stories, full of swords and drama and beautiful women sacrificed to honor. At first, my task was to facilitate communications with his English publishers: the same, by the way, who'd published my mother's mysteries.

Right away we made each other laugh, and we could fall into discussions of literature and folktales that would last for hours. I read to him from a book of English folktales and sang some of the old ballads to him. He sang the folk songs of his world, translating their stories for me and nearly always making me cry.

From the very start, the connection was deep and inexplicable. From the first conversation we were not strangers, and the weaving of our minds commenced instantly and never ceased. Years later, I still found ribbons of Ravi's thoughts woven through my own.

We spent nearly every waking hour together, and then one day he returned from his wife and children and brought me inside to his rooms and kissed me. It was a kiss so transforming, so completely *other*, that I realized I had only been a caterpillar all this time, and his lips cracked open my cocoon so I could emerge as a butterfly. It was as if I'd been called to India for just this moment. For Ravi and our connection, which remained to this day as inexplicable as anything that had ever happened to me.

We made love as if we had invented it, lingering over each other's bodies for so long sometimes that we would be faint with hunger and would have to stagger out to find sustenance.

As I walked the ordinary streets of Axestowe, I let the memories of Ravi flood back into my body. His long limbs, his big hands moving over my body. His mouth. How I sank into it.

And more. It was as if we shared one mind, one soul, and only upon finding each other were we whole.

He loved me. I loved him. It was terrible to say so, but I forgot everything else.

We were together for nine years, half of eighteen, a sacred Vedic number. In those years, we lived together in Udaipur, and he traveled home to his small town every few weeks to spend time with his wife and his children. His wife knew about me, and it sometimes made me ache with guilt, but I could no more have left him than cut off my own foot.

Summers, we traveled north to Kashmir, to live on a shabby houseboat on Dal Lake. Winds blew down from the Himalayas and across the water to cool our bodies but never our ardor.

It was an enchanted time.

And yet I'd left my daughter to do it. I took no pride in that, nor in the fact that Ravi had a wife and children who missed him when he was with me.

But life is not an orderly thing, and rules of conduct do not always tell us how to proceed. I could not turn from Ravi. Our connection, the vast love that had bloomed between us, was the reason I'd been called to India. It was precious, and holy, even if that word seemed wrong.

I spoke to Zoe every week by phone, although it was horrifically expensive in those days before cell phones, so we wrote letters. Long, chatty letters, and hers had drawings of all sorts, postcards she painted or drew herself, big murals of the countryside that she rolled up and mailed in cardboard tubes. I kept them, all of them. Even now, I had every last one of them.

I had learned, over time, to tell the truth, even when it was painful. The truth of this was that I knew my daughter missed me desperately, and I missed her, too, but I'd chosen Ravi over her, just as he'd chosen me over his children.

I never once considered returning to England, and my mother refused to let Zoe come to India. She thought it was dangerous and horrifying, especially when I had malaria and could not speak for weeks.

My love affair with Ravi was doomed to be short lived. It happened slowly at first. He was easily tired and did not make the trip to his town so often. As the months passed, we learned that he could not be cured.

It seemed impossible that I would lose him, impossible that the vigorous man he was could ever die.

I nursed him in an apartment open to the breezes off the lake in Udaipur. We read aloud from the great classics of both India and England, Shakespeare and the bhakti poems of Mira Bai, and the Ramayana. He loved the earthy poetry of the cavalier poets. I read him mysteries and war stories and whatever else he wished. I read so much aloud that my voice changed.

As his big frame melted away to almost nothing, I fed him broth and teas brought by a local healer. I bathed him and sang folk songs from my childhood.

And back home, Zoe was becoming a teenager, with righteous anger shifting her sorrow into power. She refused to speak to me, and returned my letters unopened.

It shook me. I still could not go home. Not while he was dying.

Which he did. Much too fast. The last thing he said to me was, "You are my heart and soul and greatest love." He held my hand as he drew his last breath.

It had been twenty-three years since that day, but the memory of it could still bring me to my knees.

After that, I dressed in white, the color of widows. I could not think or breathe for my pain. For two years I lived in an ashram near Kolkata, taking refuge in the daily prayers and chores. There was no requirement to be anything but who I was, a woman shattered by grief. By then, Zoe would never talk to me, and I had no energy to make my way back to her.

I wished now that I had.

Chapter Thirty-Four

Zoe

Sage and I pored over the ledger and the other papers he'd gathered from Diana's desk, as well as the screenshots he'd taken of the books on her computer. I checked on Gran several times, but she continued to sleep in what appeared to be a natural, deep kind of sleep. Once she awakened and I helped her to the loo, but she didn't speak and I couldn't check her mental state. She just wanted to go back to bed.

Isabel texted, telling me she was going with a friend to another friend's house, right in the village. I wavered, but it was important that she'd start feeling like a normal kid again.

Be home by nine, I texted back. And keep your ringer on.

She sent me a thumbs-up emoticon.

After two hours, Sage flung down the papers he held. "I don't see a bloody thing out of place."

I shook my head. There were plenty of notes about customers and orders and preferences, notes on big orders of salmon, notes on when the repairmen would be coming to service the refrigeration system. "I keep coming back to the initials or whatever she's using for Perse. Did we cross-reference the numbers and labels on that one?"

He leafed back through, running his finger down the notations. Against my will, I was charmed by the sight of him sitting in my grandmother's kitchen in a worn-soft cotton shirt with small green lines through it, his hair caught back from his face in a rubber band, his round spectacles on his face. "I don't see anything."

I sighed. "Okay, maybe that was a wild goose chase."

"Perhaps." He straightened, stretching his long arms over his head. "Are you saving the stew for a special occasion?"

I laughed. "Not at all. Would you like some?"

"Yes, please."

I stood. "Get that stacked up, and I'll dish up the stew. Will you also go check on Gran? She's in her bedroom. Do you know where it is?"

"No worries."

I reached in the cupboard for bowls and came back short—everything was in the dishwasher. Extra dishes were kept in the pantry, so I padded across the stone floor in my stocking feet to find some spares. I snagged a stack of bowls and carried them back through into the other room, then rinsed the dust out.

I remembered these bowls from youngest childhood, deep ceramic bowls with an elephant pattern around the outside. As I held one, the raised pattern imprinting my fingers, I was flooded with memories. Of myself at four or five, trying to pour my own cereal; of my mother, hair impossibly long and loose over her shoulders; of Gran dressed for a meeting in her crisp best. Bright morning sun lit the memory, a sense of happiness.

I shoved the memory away and ladled generous portions into the bowls.

Sage came back. "Gran is sleeping soundly."

"Good." I swallowed, picked up one bowl and handed it to him and then got my own, and I walked as if I were not crumbling inside to the table and sat down. "Do you want milk or something?"

"No." I could feel him looking at me.

I took a bite of stew, wiped the memories away as if I were washing a counter, but a brand-new group fell in behind them. My mother in her swirling red scarf, dancing with me. Her voice over the phone from India, thin and sometimes interrupted by static—*I'll be home soon, my love,* she said, over and over, and over and over. Lies, and she'd known it even then. She'd never had any intention of coming home.

Sage reached over and covered my wrist with his hand, and with the other he offered his handkerchief. "It's clean."

I hadn't realized there were tears dripping off my chin until that moment, didn't notice that the subterranean river of my losses had risen to the level of my eyes and spilled over. When I did, it was as if I'd given them permission, because they fell thicker and faster, even as I willed them to stop. I had no connection to the tears, exactly, just those memories rolling through, one after the other after the other.

"I used to pray every day that she would come home," I said, mopping my face. "Every day, for years and years." The memory of my small self kneeling before a Catholic statue slid in, with me lighting a candle in some obscure place. "I lit candles at the Magdalene chapel and wrote notes to the piskies on the moor and petitioned every deity I knew by name."

His hand stayed on my arm, steady. Calming. He'd taken his glasses off, and I could see the clear celery color of his eyes. He was entirely present, right here, in this moment.

"It's so much harder than I expected, having to deal with her," I whispered. "To feel . . . I didn't know—"

The wave washed over me, and I put my head down on my arms and wept silently for my little-girl self. Sage settled his hand between my shoulder blades and moved it in gentle circles. It released some switch, and I let it all flow through me, all those days I'd wanted her, all those evenings I'd spent waiting for her to walk back through the door.

I don't know how long I cried. Long enough to get a very sloppy face that I was too embarrassed to show to Sage, so I sat up, turning toward the sink. I ran cold water and splashed it on my hot eyes, washed away the tears and snot, and then just stood there, calming myself. "I'm so sorry. I didn't know—"

"Every grief brings back all the old ones," he said.

Startled, I looked at him. "I've been feeling raw for days. Just missing Diana so much and wishing I could talk to her about missing her, and having to deal with my mom, and now Gran, and I still haven't figured out what's going on with Isabel."

He nodded. "Come eat," he said quietly.

I carried myself to the table and sat. Like many good ideas, it was simple and true. As the stew settled in my belly, my whole being felt more centered. We didn't speak. In the background, the same radio station I'd been listening to while I cooked played violin sonatas, melancholy and sweet.

Sage finished his stew and went back to the pot for more, taking my bowl with him. When he came back, he said, "When Alice died, there were weeks when I wondered why human beings even bother to keep going—like if you live, you're going to face loss after loss after loss, forever, and why would you do that?"

I nodded. "I felt that way after I got divorced."

His smile was sad. "You always make it sound like it was nothing."

I shrugged, ate a perfectly round carrot from my spoon, pleased that I had made this meal with my own hands, that the depth of the flavors was so good. "I just didn't want people feeling sorry for me. 'Poor old Zoe, no one ever stays.'" A welter of sorrow welled up, and I forced it back in place, blinking. "It was humiliating, you know, but I also really did love him."

He nodded.

We ate in silence for a while. "I'm sorry I was hard on you about your mother. I do remember how you missed her."

"If we start apologizing, it could go on for a while."

His chuckle, low and warm, surprised me. "True enough. Do you still have that scar from the tree?"

I straightened my arm. "This one?"

"Bad day, that." He'd pushed me, playing around, and I'd fallen out of an apple tree and needed seven stitches to close the wound.

"I lived."

Isabel suddenly came in through the back door, bringing with her a scent of night air and ocean. "Hi."

"Hi." She still had a generally cheery aspect, and the loose body language I'd missed so much. "Do you want some dinner? I made a vegetable stew."

"No, thanks. I ate some cheese pasties. OMG, they are so amazing!" She leaned against the counter, picking grapes from a bowl. Her hair had curled crazily in the damp, and now that she'd climbed out of the hoodie and sweats, you could see her figure, all legs and breasts and that beautiful face.

She looked just like my mother, I realized. *Just* like her.

"What have you guys been doing?" she asked.

"Same thing. Trying to figure out something about Diana."

"That's all anybody was talking about tonight at this party—the girl on the beach and Diana."

"Party?" I asked, alerts leaping through my brain.

"Well, not exactly. It was a bunch of kids in somebody's 'lounge.'" She pulled more grapes off the bunch and tossed them up, one at a time, catching them in her mouth. "Nothing like before."

This was my Isabel, the girl I'd lost a few months ago, and I wanted to see her continuing to evolve. "What did they say?"

"They all knew Diana, because I guess she volunteered at the school or something? And they think the body on the beach is going to be this other girl who ran away a little while back, Jennie."

I nodded.

"I'm going to my room," Isabel said.

"Hey, you should know Gran is having a few issues. If she gets combative or mean, let me know. Don't argue with her or try to change her mind; just go with it."

"Issues? As in dementia issues?"

"Yes. I'm sorry. I'm going to look for a new carer right away, but it might take a couple of days."

"Why not ask your mother? She took care of her all the time before we got here."

I took a sharp breath. "I don't want to."

"You're being really stubborn," she said, and the words sliced my skin in neat little marks. She picked up her earphones from her neck and started to plug them into her ears.

My throat tightened, and I stood, holding my hand out.

"What?"

"Give me the headphones."

Her shock opened her eyes wide. "Why?"

"Because you were very rude just now. I've been too lenient with you."

She huffed, throwing a look toward Sage before she hissed, "Are you seriously going to do this right now? In front of other people?"

"It didn't stop you."

With a furious gesture, she yanked the earphones out and stabbed them into my palm, then stomped off.

With a sigh, I turned back and dropped them on the table. Rubbing my face, I said, "I'm sorry. Welcome to the madness."

He moved the bowls out of the way and tugged the sheaf of papers back to the space between us. "Are you okay?"

"Fine, why?"

His face went blank. "Just seem a little tense."

"I guess."

He flipped through several pages, then tapped an entry. "There're two payments to an Exeter address here, both for the same sum."

I frowned. "That *is* interesting. What happened to that business card?"

He shook his head with confusion. "I don't know what you're talking about."

I shuffled through the papers he'd taken from her home desk, but it wasn't there. "It was from an estate agent in Exeter. Maybe that person would know something."

"That's good. Maybe it's still on her desk." He closed the ledger and leaned back, rubbing his temples. "I should probably go, get a fresh start on all of this tomorrow."

I felt bereft, but I took a breath. "Okay. Thanks for coming."

He regarded me silently for a long moment. "I could stay. Trounce you in a game of Mille Bornes?" He raised an eyebrow. "Or Yahtzee?"

I smiled. "Oh, yes, please. Yahtzee."

"I'm shocked." It had been a joke that I'd do almost anything to get people to play Yahtzee with me. Something about the dice and the sound of them rolling made me happy every time.

"Is it in the closet?" he asked, standing.

"I have no idea." I carried our dishes to the sink and set the kettle to boil again. We moved around each other easily, and after I rinsed the cups, I crossed my arms to watch him sort through the debris in the closet.

Those shoulders had always been so pleasingly wide and square, a bulwark against the world. And I liked his long legs, and even his ridiculous hair, which on anyone else would have seemed strange, but on Sage was just . . . him. I wanted to touch it, see if it retained the softness it had always held, and in my exhausted state, I realized dimly that I wanted to touch all of him.

"Here it is," he said, blowing a loose ringlet from his face, and then stopped. He looked at me across the room, and I had no will to hide anything, and it seemed to shift something between us.

He gently set the game on the table but kept coming forward until he stood right in front of me. I kept my hands on the sink behind me, fingertips itching, as he lifted a hand and brushed hair over my shoulder.

"You're a magnet," he said quietly, and he stepped into my space until our bodies were lightly touching, chest to chest, thigh to thigh, his hands braced on either side of me on the sink.

He bent closer, holding my gaze, which forced me to lift my chin to hold that intense connection, and then he dipped in that last small distance, and our lips met. I made a soft noise and our mouths opened and our tongues met, and he kissed me as delicately and softly as a prayer. I raised my hands to his shoulders, and he cupped my face and took a half step, meshing our bodies even more.

It was green and fresh, and I fell adrift in the taste of him, the solidness of his shoulders, the legs scissored between mine. He smelled of himself, of sunlight and limes and his own skin, and my body reacted, coming alive to sensations I'd shut down hard.

After a little while, he lifted his head and looked at my face, touched my hair, smoothed it back from my face, and then he sighed, resting his forehead against mine.

We simply stood there like that for a long time, heads pressed together, hands in innocent positions. I absorbed him, the nearness of him, the sound of his breath, the tangle of his fingers in mine.

And then, in unspoken agreement, we moved toward the table and played Yahtzee, as if nothing had ever happened.

As if it would never happen again.

Chapter Thirty-Five
Isabel

Gah! I can't believe my mother took away my headphones! For what? For practically nothing! All I did was roll my eyes, but she said I was disrespectful. She acts different here. I don't know how to explain it, but it's way different. Especially when she's around her friend Sage.

Tonight I went to a party with Molly and Isaac. It wasn't much of a party, I have to admit, just a bunch of kids lying around a living room with ugly carpet, smoking weed and listening to music I don't know. I felt like I do sometimes when I'm with my cousins in New Mexico, like they're speaking in code. My grandpa says I'm too sensitive, but sometimes, those cousins are kind of mean about me, and they call me "white girl" even though I'm multiracial.

Isaac kissed me. I like him. He's not as stoner-stupid as he pretends he is, but I get the feeling his life at home is not great. He made me laugh three times, which is a record. Once was a play on words, once was a joke about numbers, and one was just a funny quip he made to somebody else, super fast.

He's not the kind of guy I'd pick as a boyfriend or anything, but when he kissed me, I liked it.

For about three seconds, and then the panic attack started blazing through me, sucking the air out of my lungs and making it feel like I couldn't breathe. So I bailed, and he probably thinks I'm an idiot. All the way home I thought about that. About fitting in or not fitting in.

I stopped and took some photos of the moon over the bay, and something hot and mean struck me right through the chest, this giant ugly weird emotion. I heard a bunch of voices, laughing, and—

I stopped and tried to hear. Let the memories surface. I would feel so much better if I could *remember*. I know what happened because I saw the photos and saw all the writing, but they gave me something, and I can't remember the actual events. I hate that I can't remember!

Listen.

Me. I heard me, crying but in a weird way.

My heart sped up again, and I had to start counting. In the dark, it was hard to see, and I started feeling really scared being out by myself in a town where my mom's friend is missing and another girl has washed up on the beach, and I practically ran the rest of the way home.

Running blew away the bad feeling, and by the time I got to the kitchen door, I wasn't scared, but not exactly normal either, and I just wanted to get to my room and write, but there was my mom in the kitchen with Sage, and they had their heads bent over some papers. I saw him raise his head and *look* at her, and it was an expression I've never seen on anybody's face before, like love to the twelfth power.

I like him, so I don't know why it felt so weird. It's just that everything is different. Everything, everything, everything.

I hated it when my parents got divorced. They weren't happy for a few years, but so what? Nobody has happy parents, except maybe our neighbors the Rodriguezes, and they even got married really young and had a bunch of kids, and they don't make a lot of money, but that's a very happy family. Mr. Rodriguez will steal kisses right in front of everybody.

I changed into my pajamas and brushed my teeth and wrote for a couple of hours. It kept me from stalking all my old friends—not that I'm friends with them anymore.

But you can't exactly be in the world without social media now, and now that I'm away from the old crowd, I've joined everything with a new identity, witchesgranddaughter333. I have zero friends, and I like it that way. I've followed a bunch of generic photography accounts and cat people so I'll look like a complete nerd. And then I can stalk people I want to follow, just randomly. If anyone notices, they'll only see the weird cat person with no followers.

Which maybe they'll figure out is me, but I haven't decided what to do about that.

The dream showed up right after I fell asleep. I was standing on the beach under a full moon. A bunch of people stood around me, dressed in weird old-school clothes, and somebody was reading something out loud.

I was myself, but not exactly, and I was trying to explain that my friends were lying about me, that they had set me up, but no one was listening. I saw my friend Kaitlyn in the back of the group, half smiling, and I yelled, *I didn't want your stupid boyfriend! He was the one who wanted me!*

But it didn't matter. Strong arms dragged me into a boat and held on to me as they rowed out to sea. They tied my hands and feet, then muttered more damning things over me about witchcraft and sorcery. Even in my dream I knew this was about my ancestor, Hannah, who was drowned as a witch, but it was also about me. I tried to wake up, but I couldn't move.

The moon was full, letting me see everything, even when they threw me overboard, and I sank, struggling to move my body in some way so that I could swim, could surface, could breathe, but I sank and sank and sank, the moon growing more and more watery the farther I fell.

I bolted awake, gasping for breath and sitting up in my bed. Mósí, disturbed by my movement, resettled with a little grumpy meow. I was surprised to find that his hair was not wet.

It was the worst nightmare yet, and I was so scared I couldn't even move for a while. When I got my courage up, I grabbed Mósí and dashed down the hall to my mother's room. For a second, I was afraid that Sage might be in there, and that would be so weird, but I had to try. I flung open the door, and there was my mom, fast asleep, her long hair woven into a braid that snaked over her pillow. I dove in beside her, finding warmth and comfort and a wall against fear.

"Isabel!" she said sleepily. "Are you okay?"

"Now I am," I said, and with Mósí and my mom, I could fall asleep.

Chapter Thirty-Six
Zoe

Gran was back to her normal self on Tuesday morning. She slept straight through, and it was as if the sleep had scrubbed her brain clean. When she came down for breakfast, she was her usual self—hair done, dressed in crisp blouse and polyester slacks with a crease, and shoes with a little heel. Her lipstick was perfect, the berry color following the curve of her lip exactly.

It was as if the incident yesterday had never happened. "Good morning," I said. "How are you feeling?"

"I am very well, thank you." She plucked at the napkin in front of her. "I miss Diana."

"I know. The service is sending out some women to interview." I stood. "I'll make some scrambled eggs, shall I? And toast?"

"That would be nice." But she looked into the distance—sadly, I thought. "Zoe, I can't really be alone."

"Oh, Gran, I know! I'm here, and Isabel is here, and we'll get a nurse who knows the ropes." I didn't say that we were working on long-term plans, but we were.

"I need Poppy."

My heart dropped. I couldn't think of anything to say, so I broke a couple of eggs into a bowl and scrambled them with a fork.

"She doesn't have to stay here all the time. She won't sleep here."

I watched the butter melt in the pan.

"She's been doing a lot for me, my love."

What could I say? "Whatever you need, Gran."

"I'll call her, then. Perhaps she can come over later today and help me sort things out. If you like, you can go for a walk or—whatever you need."

I nodded, but there was a buzzing in my head, a sense of doom or endings or something. I wanted to weep, but I'd done quite enough of that last night.

Isabel burst into the kitchen. Her hair was wild. She'd slept with me last night after a bad dream, and I'd left her asleep in my bed. "I had the worst nightmare!"

I leaned my head into hers. "Do you want to tell me about it?"

"No." She nuzzled her face into my neck. "I want a different room."

"What does the room have to do with it?"

"That's the haunted room. Poppy even told me it was."

I rolled my eyes. "There's no such thing as hauntings, but whatever." I lifted the pan off the stove, and she let her arms drop. "Gran, what would be best?"

"Take your pick," she said. "Anything but Rowan, which does have a problem. We've got to get someone in here to look at that."

The place was crumbling. It needed a caretaker and at least a handful of servants. There was money enough. "Why don't you have anyone to clean more often?" I asked Gran, bringing her plate over. "Tea is brewing. Do you want something, Isabel?"

"Yeah, that looks good."

Gran said, "The last girl quit, and I haven't had time to replace her. The interviews, the conversations." She waved a hand. "Too much trouble."

"I'll take care of it." I picked up my phone and made notes as I talked. "You have a gardener, is that right?"

She ate with gusto, smearing her toast with jam. "I do need a cook. I simply forget to eat if there's not someone to make my meals."

"Got it. Cook, someone to clean, and a nurse to stay twenty-four seven."

"And Poppy, don't forget."

Isabel's eyes widened.

"And Poppy," I repeated. "I'll deal with the others. She's all yours."

After breakfast, Lillian went upstairs to work, and I sat down with Isabel. "Another nightmare, huh?"

"Don't read all kinds of stuff into it, Mom. It was just that witch stuff. Poppy and I were talking about her, and that girl washed up on the beach, and my brain just made a movie."

I examined her face but found only calm. "Nothing happened at the party?"

She lowered her eyelids. "No."

"Isabel."

"Okay, I met this guy and he kissed me, but that's it, and there was nothing bad about it, just normal, okay?"

I took a breath, feeling impotence and a sense of urgency. "I really need to know what happened to you, Isabel. I'm getting to the point that I can't relax, and I can't trust you if you don't trust me."

"I do trust you!"

"Then what?"

She bowed her head, and I saw the depression descend on her, weighting her shoulders, her long neck. "I don't want to talk about it. I just want to leave it behind."

Two sides of me warred—the part that wanted to restrict her until she talked, but wouldn't that feel as if I was punishing her? And the part that wanted to let her figure out how to heal herself. It was a powerful skill.

And the problem was, I hadn't had a mother to show me how to mother, so how would I know what was right and wrong? I'd felt my way through every moment of her childhood, and I would trust my gut through this too. "When do you talk to Dr. Kerry again?"

"Tomorrow."

"Okay." I reached out and held her wrist. "Maybe you can't tell me, for whatever reason. But I want you to really think about who you might be able to tell. Your counselor. Your dad. Whoever."

Isabel took a breath and tossed her hair out of her eyes. "Okay. I promise I'll think about it."

When she'd gone upstairs, I called Sage. "When are you going to Exeter?"

"I don't know, exactly. Why?"

"I'd like to come with you, if you don't mind. My mother is coming over to help sort things out with Gran, and I don't want to be here."

A soft silence. "Is that wise?"

"What do you mean? What does wise have to do with it?"

"Well, it would seem you need to know what's going on with Lillian, and your mother has that information."

The closer she came, the more panicky I felt. "I just . . . I . . . no." I pressed a palm to the pain in my gut. I felt myself reverting to the child I had been in all manner of ways, but I couldn't seem to halt it. "I can't. Unless you want to go alone."

"Not at all, Zoe. I'll text you when I'm on my way. I'll pick you up."

"Thank you."

I spent the morning engaging a nurse, a woman by the name of Margaret. She had kind eyes, like Mary Poppins, and when I coaxed

Gran out of her office, Margaret took both of her hands into her own and said the magic words. "I am such a fan of your work, Ms. Fairchild. You give the genre such a refreshing feminist bent."

With so many things settled, I found time to do some work of my own, sketching out my illustration ideas for the dog story that was due in a few weeks—a series of poignant and sweet and funny dogs of various sizes. I drew Simba three ways, his beautiful head and floppy ears and that gorgeous red-gold fur. I missed that dog like a limb.

Martin and I had found him at a garage sale, of all places. We'd only been married six or eight months, and everything felt golden. I was as happy as I'd ever been in my life, traveling with him and his band on the weekends when I could, working at my graphic arts job the rest of the time. We had a sweet little cottage near the Plaza, and I loved the courtyard bound by adobe walls. It was my first garden, and it was a hard learning curve to discover that what had worked in my grandmother's garden did not work in the high-desert sun. Simba grew up trotting beside me, garden to kitchen to bed. When Isabel was born, he adopted her as his very own child, sleeping by her crib, growling when flies buzzed around her head.

The ache returned, that ache of longing and loss all mingled together. Every loss brought back all the others, Sage had said.

Maybe I needed to stop fighting it. Fighting the terror I felt over Diana, fighting the fury I felt over my mother, fighting to fix Isabel's loss, whatever it was, and just feel my grief.

My phone buzzed.

Pick you up in five, Sage texted.

I grabbed my sweater and my bag. Isabel was reading in the sunroom. "Poppy will be here in twenty minutes. Gigi is upstairs. If you go anywhere, text me."

"I will. You don't have to worry."

"I'll see if I can find a color printer in Exeter," I said. "Unless you just wanted to be there."

"No. I'm reading this book I found in the Whitethorn Room." She flashed the cover, a very thick paperback from the nineties, fantasy of a sort I'd loved as a teen.

"You'll have to let me know what you think."

"Yep." She opened the book again. "I'll text you specs for the printer."

"I'm leaving, Gran!" I called up the stairs. "Call my evil mother as you wish."

"Yes, dear," was all she said.

As I left through the front door to meet Sage on the road, I noticed the beach was quite empty for such a bright day. A handful of boats was out on the bay, but most were gloomily moored, and only a scattered number of people sat or strolled along the sand. Superstition? Respect for the dead? With the festival coming up in just a few days, I hoped whatever it was would pass.

The Range Rover pulled up alongside me. Sage tugged the hand brake for safety so I could climb in. "Hi," I said, settling. "Thanks."

"You're welcome. I don't mind the company."

He wore a soft cotton shirt, many years old, that was the exact color of his pale-green irises. "Did Alice buy you that shirt?"

"Huh." He opened his palm over the fabric, looking down with a frown. "I can't remember. Perhaps. It's the right era. Why?"

For one second, I hesitated, realizing too late that my observation would give away how closely I watched him. "It matches your eyes. That's something a wife would notice."

"Maybe it was an accident." He looked at me directly, as if to give me time to admire those peepers. "Or maybe I did it myself."

I shook my head. "No. You've never been vain in the slightest."

"That you know of."

"I seem to recall you hating girls chasing you."

"I did." He dropped the brake as soon as I fastened the seat belt and pulled in a circle to head back to the main road up to Exeter. "We'll need to get out of there by four or so if we want to avoid the commuter traffic."

"So early!"

"Better safe than sorry." He checked behind him, pulled into traffic. "I didn't like the girls because they were silly. They wanted something shallow. Dates. Prince Charming."

"Such wretched longings!"

He gave me a reluctant smile. "You were never like that."

"Chasing you for your beauty?"

"You're deliberately misunderstanding me."

"No," I said. "I'm sorry. I was only teasing." I looked at him, with the green countryside rushing by his side of the window. "Did you wear it on purpose?"

His mouth turned up the slightest bit.

I looked at his hands on the steering wheel, strong and sinewy with all the work he did, and at the careful way he'd rolled the long sleeves up his forearm, not yet brown with summer sunshine, but they would be. A rustling stirred in my heart, feeling suspiciously like hope.

He glanced at me. "A woman told me once that I should play up my eyes more."

"She was right."

A blanket of quiet settled between us. The radio played an alternative station. Little of it was familiar to me, but I knew the odd song and hummed along. I wished I could talk to Diana about what was happening here in the car. What would I say?

I think something is happening between Cooper and me.

What????

I kissed him. And then he kissed me last night, and it was . . . it was the way it always was, D.

Which is?

I paused, looking out the window toward the sea. What was it?

Like . . . I found something I lost. No, that's not it. Like I found something someone else was holding.

A tear welled up in the corner of my eye. She wasn't here to listen or offer advice or laugh at me. "God, I miss Diana so much!" I said.

He reached for my hand. "I was just texting her in my head."

"Me too!"

"What were you telling her?"

"Oh, no. You first."

He squeezed my fingers. Shook his head.

It was always much farther to Exeter in my mind than it was in real life, and we were there within twenty minutes. Sage asked me to navigate with my phone to the address he'd copied from Diana's papers. The payments had been substantial, thousands of pounds each, but there'd been nothing to point to what they might have been or been for.

"Did you talk to Henry about this?" I asked. "Turn right at the next intersection."

"He hasn't answered my calls."

"Is he still at the hotel?"

"No." He turned where I'd indicated. It was a neighborhood of terraced houses, all a little weary looking, too close to the street for much of a front garden, not that anyone seemed to bother. A pot of petunias bloomed on one front step, and a small fruit tree had blossomed, but there was little else.

"Surely the police want him close by," I said. "Henry, that is."

"I would think so, but that doesn't change the fact that I haven't reached him."

It made the anxiety in my chest grow three times its size. "Damn." I looked at the address. "One more right, and it should be about halfway down the block."

More of the same brick-terraced houses. A little nicer here, as if the invalid had begun to respond to treatment. Grass grew in clumps, and a cat wandered lazily down the pavement.

The address we sought had nothing to set it apart. A few tulips grew by the door. We went to the step and knocked, but from there I could see straight into the big front window, and the place was empty.

"What the hell?" I said. "Surely she wasn't going to move to Exeter. She hates it here." I thought about correcting myself to *hated*, but I didn't.

"Maybe it was meant for someone else? Or a rental, maybe?"

"But why buy a rental here?" I peered into the front room. "A holiday rental in Axestowe would make a fortune."

He nodded. Looked at the piece of paper in his hand, as if to double-check. "I don't know."

We stood there, flummoxed. "Now what?" I asked.

"I don't know. Maybe we just follow the string wherever it goes and keep doing that until we get answers that take us farther."

"You're right. Sorry."

"Not necessary. Let's get some lunch somewhere with Wi-Fi, and I'll see what I can track down on my phone."

"I haven't had fish and chips since I've been here."

His smile was easy. "Well, let's find you some, then."

First I had to find a shop to pick up a color printer for Isabel, which we accomplished without a lot of drama. I texted to be sure it was powerful enough but would also work with her laptop, and I got a thumbs-up.

Which left us free to find a fish and chips shop just a block from the Exe. We carried our lunches down to a bench overlooking the river. The sun played hide-and-seek with clouds, and a fairly stiff breeze blew off the water, making it too chilly for most to sit and picnic. Aside from a few walkers out on a weekday afternoon with their dogs, we had the spot to ourselves. Rows of houses crouched behind us, and across the river were blocks of apartment houses. Everything was red brick, sturdy, unlovely, although the trees and water added some beauty.

But on our bench, the world was good. The fish was fresh haddock, cooked crisply, and I splashed it with vinegar and salt. "This is heaven," I said, licking my fingers. "You just can't get this kind of fish and chips in America."

"Especially in New Mexico, I would imagine. It's pretty far inland, isn't it?"

I shrugged, taking another bite and savoring it completely as I watched a stick bob along on the current. "These days, they fly things in same day from the coast, so everyone has fresh fish."

"Still. This was probably taken off a boat this morning over in Brixham and filleted in his back room."

"Mmm."

We sat relatively close together, partly for warmth. Partly because there was something brewing between us, something that had been there from the first day, there in the grocery store. I wasn't sure what it would be, exactly, or even what I wanted, except that I wanted, very badly, to touch him. As we ate, I found myself admiring his thumbs with their square, well-tended nails, and the turn of his knee, and the length of his thigh. I was aware, in turn, of my body. Of my waist and my ankles and my lips.

The air of knowledge thickened between us until it had weight and heft and color. I finished my chips and dropped the refuse into the white bag it had come in, and he took it from me and walked it down to a bin. As he walked back, I thought I'd never really stopped missing him, not ever, that swing of his arms and the loose-limbed cadence of his long legs.

He sat down again beside me, and the air of expectation swallowed us. He picked up my hand between both of his palms, making a sandwich of my fingers. His palm lay against mine, and when he moved it very slowly, I felt the skin-to-skin slide as a shiver through my arms and down my spine.

I looked up, and his eyes were lowered, focused on our hands, then my breasts and neck and face. I raised my hand and touched his cheek, shaved cleanly, and his cheekbone. My thumb gravitated to his lower lip, and I brushed the pad over it, back and forth.

The air was still. All the days we had spent together and all the days we had lost were there with us, part of this moment when we were trying to get the nerve to take the leap.

With a quick moment, he captured my thumb in his mouth, pulling it into the wet and heat of it, and I couldn't help making a soft noise.

"Mmm," he said, "salty."

And finally he slid closer and pulled me into the circle of his arms and bent his head and kissed me.

It was like coming home after a very long, wearying trip to a hostile place. The color behind my eyelids was a soft green, and I snuggled in closer beneath his arm, into the warmth of his body. He felt sinewy, strong, beneath my hands.

We angled to fit our lips into a position that would allow us to kiss long and deep, lips sliding, smoothing, bumping, tongues meeting, dancing, flickering, diving.

We kissed. Sitting in the cool wind of a May afternoon on a river that smelled coppery and more than a little dank, on a bench that was cold beneath my legs. We kissed.

Kissed until we were both panting a little, and shaking with desire. He discreetly moved his hand up my ribs until my breast rested against his fingers, and I edged my hand inside his shirt, stroking hot skin.

"Jesus," he whispered, lifting his head slightly, murmuring the words against my mouth. "I'm about to spontaneously combust."

"Is that what it's called?"

"Will you come back to my house with me?"

"I thought you didn't want to get mixed up with me again."

He touched my face with one fingertip. "That ship sailed a while back."

I nodded, rubbing his bare skin with my fingertips. "I wish we could find a transporter."

He kissed my mouth, then my chin, then my forehead. "It won't take long."

"Let's go."

Chapter Thirty-Seven
Poppy

I was feeling emotional and exhausted, unprepared for the festival in just a few days, when Lillian called. She didn't sound querulous, which could be patted into quiet, but imperious, which was always a sign that she was frightened.

"Poppy, my love," she said. "I need you to come over. I've managed to get Zoe out of the house for a few hours."

"Now, then?"

"Yes."

I looked at the shop work surface, strewn with flower buds and herbs and bottles and little velvet bags, and took a breath. She was my mother. She took precedence over anything else. "Is Isa there?"

"Yes."

I promised her I'd be there within an hour. Foot traffic was slowing, thanks to a storm gathering on the horizon, and Mia could keep an eye on things by herself while continuing to work on potions. We'd finished the love potions, the money potions, and the sleep potions. Today we'd been working on those that would help retrieve lost things, dream manifestation (which came with a spell: the more steps the better, when one wished to build belief), and a handful of others I'd felt moved to include, prompted by something tickling me. One was strangely specific—the retrieval of a passport. I assumed whoever needed it would pick it up. I'd mixed it in a yellow bottle.

I packed up tiny bags and envelopes, powdered herbs and flower petals, and an array of possible extras and carried it all to my car, then drove up the hill. Flashes of lightning laced through distant clouds, but by the feel of the wind, it was on its way here.

My mother needed me. Me, specifically, which made everything I'd done the past seven years make sense. At least one of my relationships might be healed.

She brought me upstairs to her tower and showed me a page she'd written the day before. It seemed, at first, to make sense, with commas and periods and a regular cadence of words. And the words themselves were actual words, just arranged in an order that didn't immediately make sense.

Her eyes filled with tears. "What will become of me?"

"Oh, Mother!" I bent and hugged her tiny, shrinking form. "You're going to stay right here, writing away, with people who love you."

"I'm frightened. I don't know who I'll be without my brain. It's been everything."

I thought of Ravi, his body disappearing bit by bit, and his fear that I would leave once he became a wizened version of himself. "I'll be here to remember everything for you," I said, rocking her a little back and forth. Suddenly, my wish to stay at Greencombe held no weight against my mother's needs. "I'll move back in and we can have meals together, and I'll make sure you don't wander off, and you can entertain me with flights of fancy."

"I don't deserve that, the way I treated you."

"Oh, Mother, you don't have to earn my love. You've just got it."

She wept a little then. "No one ever wants to face death," she said at last, pushing me away to wipe her eyes. "And yet, it's the one thing that we will all know."

"Or not know, in your case," I said, and laughed.

For one long second, she stared at me, then joined me in a good belly laugh. "Poppy, my dear," she said, taking my hand. "I do not deserve you."

"You made me," I said, brushing the hair from her forehead. "And I love you."

Love, I thought. *It takes so many forms.*

I found Isa in the kitchen, editing photos on a tablet. "What are you up to, my dear?"

She raised an eyebrow, and in the gesture, I saw with a jolt my own face. It wasn't vanity, just recognition, like seeing yourself in a strange time mirror. "Just going through some of my photos." She gave me a mischievous grin. "Want to see one of my granddad?"

"Sure." I bent over to share the screen with her. She smelled like strawberries and herbal shampoo, such a young and exhilarating scent, and I inhaled it with pleasure. People always complained about teenagers, but I liked them—all the angst and drama and rolling eyes. They charmed me, each and every one.

She clicked on a thumbnail, and a photo of Ben filled the screen. He was laughing, and he had that look in his eye that let me know he'd told a joke he didn't think anyone would get.

He was devastatingly handsome, still.

"Wow," I said. A sweetness moved through me. He was such a kind and gentle man, and I had hurt him badly. "He *is* very handsome, isn't he?"

"Yep. But he never has a girlfriend, even though they try. Pretty hard."

I chuckled. "I'm sure they do." I pointed. "Why don't you show me what you've been working on?"

"Okay." She clicked to a new folder, then opened a bunch of pictures of the hill fort in bluebell splendor.

I leaned in to see the thumbnails. "Ooh, I love the close-ups of the flowers. Looks magical."

"Right? The whole time I was there, I kept thinking it seemed like a place fairies would be, like the trees were alive and having conversations when I wasn't looking." She clicked through, showing me various shots—close shots of bluebells and through the grass to the trees. I saw a thumbnail of two men. "Who is that?"

"Just some random guys," she said, but she clicked on it. "I only shot their picture because I was by myself, and if they dragged me off into the woods to rape me and kill me, I wanted evidence."

I touched her shoulder. "Let me see it."

She clicked on the series of the men, going slowly through it. One of them wore a yellow-checked shirt and had the worn face of an old coyote, a Romanian I'd seen around. He worked at the yacht club.

"Do you know them?" Isa asked.

"Not really. This one works in the kitchen at the club, I think. What were they doing?"

"Nothing. They just talked in another language—Romanian, I guess—and then that guy"—the yellow shirt—"went back toward town, and this guy went to the parking lot."

I studied the photo, trying to discern what my gut wanted me to see. I kept looking back to the man I knew, sorting through any other images I had of him in my memory. Just seeing him. At the grocery store, smoking in the street, talking to some of his friends. Nothing very much.

But my gut was insisting there was something here. "Leave that photo up, will you? I'll be right back."

In my car, I kept a tarot deck in the glove compartment. It was one I'd used for a long time, and it was wrapped in a piece of a sari scarf that I'd worn with Ravi. I kept it cleansed for moments just like this. I grabbed it and headed back inside, and as I turned to face the sea, wind slapped me, sent my hair into a spiral over my head. I smelled angry ocean and the freshness of rain. Thunder boomed, still in the distance. It was going to be quite a storm.

Lillian had come down, her face repaired, and she stood at the sink filling the kettle. "Quite a wind out there."

I smoothed my hair back. "It is." I wiped the table off and dried it, then sat down next to Isa and her computer, which was floating with screen saver pictures. "Can you get that photo of the men back full screen?"

She slid her finger along the touch square, and I looked at it for a long moment, absorbing whatever it was I needed to see, and then shuffled the tarot. It was old and soft and responded easily to my energy. Going with the prompts, I laid out three cards, side by side. Eight of Cups, Ten of Swords, the Fool.

I frowned, feeling the heaviness. Cups were a cheery suit, but this was a card of exile or leaving. The Fool often indicated a young person, eager and untested and unaware of danger.

Ten of Swords. I sighed. One of the darkest cards of all, a knight flat on his face with swords—

I flashed on a vision of a body, floating.

—Shot in the back.

"What?" Isa asked. "You look like you've seen a ghost."

"Maybe," I said, and I looked at the photo again. In the distance, almost too distant to make out, was the shape of a person in the trees behind the man I didn't know. "Can you zoom in on this part?"

Isa zoomed in on the figure, but it still wasn't very clear. A person, that was all you could really see. "He might have shown up in another picture," she said, and she clicked through the others, looking closely. Nothing until: "Oh, hey. This is better."

She zoomed in on the figure, and a lot more detail showed up, though still not clear enough to recognize a particular feature. A girl, probably, with very long dark hair, and jeans. "I didn't see her, but maybe she was trying to keep out of sight."

"It might not mean anything," I said, and I turned over three cards because my gut disagreed. Queen of Cups, King of Pentacles, Six of Cups. One more. The Tower.

The image of the floating body returned, and I let it in this time instead of wincing it away. Hair floating, arms. No face.

But the cards told me who it was. Cups were the homely arts, happiness and family. Diana. The Tower was there again, as it ever was in her readings. A tightness burned in my throat, because I would not say aloud what I saw.

Six of Cups showed children. Reversed. I frowned but didn't see how it fit. Diana didn't have children.

Children. Lost children? Abused children?

And the King of Pentacles. "This is an interesting card," I said to Isa. "It's a man of wealth and power who loves his material comforts." I wondered to myself if it might mean Henry, because it seemed this reading was about Diana in some way.

I looked at the cards again, searching for other patterns. Youth, maybe. Exile. Death.

"If it's telling me anything, I don't know what it is," I admitted. "It was worth a try." I stuffed the cards together and dropped one on the floor.

Isa retrieved it. The King of Pentacles again. Maybe I needed to find Henry. Perhaps Sage had a phone number for him. Or . . . even more likely, Inspector Hannaford.

Chapter Thirty-Eight

Zoe

As we climbed into the Range Rover, Sage said, "One rule on the way."

"Okay?"

"No talking about anything bad. Not now, and not in the past."

"I wasn't really thinking about talking," I said, running a hand up his thigh.

He caught my hand with a laugh. "I have to drive." He kissed my palm. "I'm so glad you're here."

"Me too," I whispered.

In the end, we didn't talk much. He played the radio, and we drove toward the farm on a back road, watching as clouds billowed up on the horizon, thick and serious clouds. "I should tell my family where I am," I said. "But I don't really want to let anyone else in."

"Just tell them we have to make a stop at the farm to pick something up."

"What?"

"I don't know. Make it up."

"Matt?"

"Sure."

I texted Isabel. And added:

Is Poppy still there? Everything good with Gigi?

Yes. Gigi is good. Poppy is here.

I hesitated. Then texted simply:

K

At the farm, I suddenly felt shy and strange. "Is this a good idea?"

He came around, took my hand, and pulled me toward the front door. "Yes. No thinking."

Without a word, he led me inside and up the stairs to a bedroom that had once been his mother's. I'd never been inside it, but the second we were there, Sage was unbuttoning his shirt, and then he'd stripped it off and was standing there in only his jeans, and I was stunned into a hush of desire. His body was mature now, his shoulders broad, his belly lean. His skin was the color of honey, with hair the same pale wheat across his chest.

"Are you going to undress?" he asked, unbuckling his belt. Before I could respond, he was standing there naked, aroused, beautiful, and I was frozen, my arms crossed over my chest.

"Romance was never your strong suit," I said.

He spread his arms in offering. "I'm all yours."

But I felt terrified. The last time he'd seen my body, I'd been seventeen and perfect. "I've had a child, you know. And I don't weigh a hundred fifteen pounds anymore."

"I don't care." He inclined his head. "Are you shy with me, Zoe Fairchild?"

"Yes!"

A slow, very wicked grin bloomed on his mouth. "That's silly." He crossed the small space between us. "Don't you want to touch me?"

"Of course."

"Go ahead." He settled his hands on my shoulders, stepped in a little closer, and angled his head to kiss me.

And there he was, more than six feet of naked, sinewy male, smelling of musk and heat. I raised my hand and skimmed his hip, raising my mouth to his.

"There you go," he said, and he tugged the hem of my shirt. I raised my hands and let him take it off, and then I kicked off my jeans. He bent and kissed my shoulder, the curve of my neck, and I reached around and unhooked my bra. He let my underwear alone for the moment, gathering me up, bending in to kiss my mouth, my shoulders, my breasts, his big hands on my rear end. I was trembling with emotion and desire, but I touched him, too, exploring his long back, his hips.

"You're never a stranger," he said.

"No."

We kissed, again and again, skin to skin, and found our way to the bed and tumbled down. Outside, it began to rain. Hard. Inside, we renewed our knowledge of each other's bodies, slowly, and quickly, and in every possible way. When we were spent, weary and sweaty and shaking with expending so much energy, we collapsed into a position we knew already—Sage on his back, me curled into him, my head in the curve of his shoulder, his arm around me. He pulled the duvet over us, tucking us together like kittens.

"I don't believe I shall be moving for a month or two," he said.

"I know." I stretched a leg over his luxuriously, taking pleasure in the crisp rustle of hair against my inner knee. "I'm having trouble even bringing up words for a sentence."

"That won't last long." He scratched my shoulder softly.

I laughed a little. It was true that having sex often turned a talking switch for me. "I used to feel so alight after we had sex," I said, tracing a circle around the middle of his chest. "Like I could see all the connections in the world, all the molecules."

"Not anymore?"

I sighed, tilted my head so that I could look at his face. "Honestly, I haven't had sex in . . . I don't even know."

"Me either," he said quietly.

"What about Cora?"

"Mmm. I forgot about that. Still, it was a while ago."

"Not as long as me."

He tumbled me over sideways. Kissed me. "Why now?"

"Because . . ." I dug my finger into his hair, silky and soft, the curls winding around my fingers like ivy. I met his eyes. "Because you're you, Sage."

He closed his eyes and bent into my neck. "I planned to keep you at arm's length while you were here, but the minute I saw you at the market, I knew we'd end up here."

"You didn't act like it."

"I missed you, Zoe. I had so much pride, back in the day."

"I missed you too." I wanted to say more, that the world felt right with him beside me, in a way it never did without him, as if he were some key to the universe that I couldn't access any other way.

But that would have been too rash, too much.

I tangled my hands in his glorious curls, still as soft as they'd ever been. "I'm so glad you let your hair grow out."

"I guess we're still hippie children at heart."

"No. We're just ourselves."

He crept up closer, sliding his body over mine. "I can't believe you're here in my bed, Zoe Fairchild. But, Jesus, I'm glad."

"Me too," I whispered, pushing back all the things that threatened to rise between us and ruin everything. I reached between us. "Let's do it again."

At one point, the lightning was so brutal that it knocked the lights off, and I texted Isabel:

At the farm still. Road is running like a river. Lightning insane. How is it there?

Same. Super violent storm. Gigi says don't try to come home.

Are you guys okay alone?

We aren't alone. Poppy is still here.

Wrapped in a sheet, with my limbs shivering in sexual exhaustion, I had no right to feel mad about anything, but I hated to imagine my mother and Isabel and my grandmother all there bonding without me. Except, I didn't want to bond with my mother under any circumstances, so there was that.

A sad plucking thing moved through me, leaving me on the outside. *Who put you there?* a voice asked in a reasonable tone. I swallowed it.

Call me if you need me.

Sage came back to the bedroom, wearing sweats and a sweater, the same soft heather-colored one he'd had on the night at the pub. "I've got a fire going in the stove downstairs. With the power out, it'll get cold very quickly." He turned around to rustle through the small wardrobe tucked under the eaves and brought me a flannel shirt. From a drawer, he pulled out socks. "My sweats are too big for you, but these will help."

"Hand knitted," I said as I pulled them on my cold feet. They were thick and long, up to my knees.

"Alice knitted a lot when she was ill. It gave her something to do." I squeezed his arm. "They're very nice socks."

Downstairs, settled by the warm stove, with candles lit all around the room and a tray of food to graze on, we talked. He told me about the years he'd spent setting up the farm properly again, and going back and forth to study business and marketing in Exeter. "I always knew you'd stick to your plan," I said, plucking a piece of cheese from the plate.

"And I'm surprised that you didn't." My feet were in his lap, and his legs were tossed over a big soft ottoman. His hand circled my ankle. "You were so determined to be an artist."

"Yeah, turns out nobody thought much of that plan except me." I shrugged. "I'm still doing art, just not quite the way I thought I would."

He sipped his tea. "I was one of those opposing you," he said, and he kneaded the bottom of my foot.

"I remember," I said.

"I was so afraid I would lose you," he said, his thumb moving on my knee. His smile was sad. "Turned out I did anyway."

"It was all a long time ago." I shook my head. "We all take different turns than we think we will when we're making plans. And anyway, I wouldn't have Isabel if it weren't for that."

"Still. I'm sorry for my part in keeping you from what you wanted."

"I was an idiot, Sage," I said, reaching for his hand. "That guy didn't mean anything at all. I was so crushed by flunking out, and then you weren't there to talk to and—"

"Zoe." He curled his fingers around mine. "You flunked out?"

I sighed. "Yep. That teacher, remember? The one who hated me?"

"I thought you were imagining things."

"No." I shook my head, remembering his gray face, his spluttering fury. "I don't know why he hated me so much, but it was from the very first day, and he made fun of my work, and belittled my questions, and made me feel like a giant fake, and I was already feeling that way, that maybe I was in the wrong place, and—"

He said, "Go on."

"We had a big project, a painting in the style of our favorite artist, and I spent over a hundred hours on a painting in the style of Maxfield

Parrish. So many layers," I said. "It was the moor at dusk, with all that soft light, you know?"

He nodded.

I remembered the endless hours, the thin glazes that were Parrish's hallmark, each one bringing the light higher and brighter. I'd been so desperately proud of it. "He hated it. Put it up on the easel and tore it to shreds. It was so mean that some of the other kids were embarrassed."

"I'm so sorry."

"So this guy stood up for me, and when I left, we went to the pub together, and I just cried my eyes out. I couldn't get hold of you, and my grandmother was in the hospital, which I didn't know—that was the second bout of breast cancer, remember? The first one was when I had to go home to New Mexico when I was twelve."

He didn't meet my eyes. "But we'd been together for almost four years, Zoe. How could you have just—"

"I don't know!" I whispered. "I was lost and sad and so insecure, and I was so very, very humiliated. It didn't seem like I would ever have the life I wanted, and—" I lifted my shoulders. "There was Jacob." I sighed. "And I made the biggest mistake of my life."

His mouth looked sad. "Damn. And then you had to confess."

"I loved you. I didn't want to lie."

He nodded. "I know. And I was such a prig about it. I just couldn't get over it. I felt like I'd been gutted."

"We were so young."

"Yes." Our fingers laced and unlaced. The candle flames flickered. One cast his eyelashes into shadows across the bridge of his nose. "I still try to live simply. It seems more important than ever."

"It does."

"How do you live, in Santa Fe?" He let go of my hand to sip tea. "You were married to a wealthy man. Do you live in a big house?"

I measured him for a moment, suddenly seeing that judgmental side anew. "What if I did? What if I had a big house and a closet full of clothes and drove a new car?"

He just waited. A trick I'd never mastered.

"Okay, I don't. I live in a two-bedroom adobe in Old Town in Santa Fe, which is not a cheap place to live, but it's not a lavish house. At all. It's over three hundred years old, and it needs a lot of tender loving care. I don't have closets big enough to hold a lot of clothes, and honestly, I don't like to shop, anyway."

A smile edged over his mouth. "I knew it."

"I'm not the hippie you are, though. I recycle, but I do buy new clothes, and my car is a hybrid—oh, wait. You drive a Range Rover. How many petrol stations to the mile do you get in that, Mr. Cooper?"

"Three or four, depending."

I laughed. The taut moment passed. "Do you have any games around here?"

"Cards."

"Fine with me."

Abruptly, he leaned forward and kissed me hard. "I'm glad you're here tonight."

A swift pluck of sadness moved through me. It wouldn't last, this sweetness. I gripped his face between my hands. "Me too."

Chapter Thirty-Nine
Poppy

After dinner, I sat with my granddaughter in the warm kitchen, a fire flickering on the hearth. Gran had gone to bed, her color so much better that I was relieved.

"I have something I need to tell someone," Isa said, out of the blue.

I looked at her, stirring my tea. "All right."

"My mom wants me to tell somebody, but I just can't tell her . . . it would make her so sad. But I do need to tell someone."

Alert, I leaned in, made my body soft, tuned in to the agitation in her jiggling knee and the way she twisted her hair around a finger. "Of course. Whatever you need. I'm listening."

Behind me, the storm began to crash and rumble and pound, a fitting backdrop, as it turned out.

"Okay. I'm just going to barf it out."

I nodded.

"Last year, I started high school, and there were a lot more kids, and it's a really mixed school, too, like Anglo, Indian, and Mexican, or I guess Latinx and Native American, but nobody in my class ever says that. They say Indian."

"I remember that mix."

She looked out the window, her dark eyes reflecting the turmoil of the sea. "So me and these two girls, Katrina and Madison, have been best friends since fourth grade. We live in the same neighborhood and went to all the schools together, and we are—were—like best, best, best friends.

"When we started high school, things changed." Her leg started to jiggle harder. "Like, last year, in ninth grade, it was kind of okay. They both had boyfriends, when nobody even wanted to be with me at all, because I grew, like, seven inches when I was fourteen, and the guys called me 'beanpole' and 'pancake chest' and all kinds of mean things like that."

"And then?"

"Over the summer last year, I got these." She pulled her shirt back to show her generous breasts. "And everybody noticed, let me tell you."

I smiled, patted my own chest. "I had that experience too."

"Did you? My mom tries to be sympathetic about how much people stare, but she's not exactly . . ." She made a gesture of enormity with her hands. "It happened so fast, too, like one day I was pancake girl, and two weeks later, every guy in the universe was staring at my boobs."

I nodded. I remembered the bewilderment of wondering what the hell was happening with the world all of a sudden, how often people accidentally bumped into me, touched me. It shamed me when I was fifteen, because I'd been taught to believe my body belonged to other people and it was all my fault the way people acted with me. I had the power, suddenly, to drive men mad with lust.

It was my fault. I hoped that had not been Isabel's experience.

"So anyway, when I went back to school last fall, all of a sudden, things were different. Like really popular guys wanted to talk to me, and even girls were nicer to me, and it was completely weird—that it was just my chest, and everybody acted different, but they did. And Katrina and Madison started saying I was stuck-up and conceited and all this stuff that was just not fair, because I was *exactly the same*. It was them who'd started acting so different."

She chewed on the inside of her cheek for a minute, the jiggling of her right thigh going double time. I took her hand, wrapped it in mine, settled myself into a place of calm. "Okay, so this part I'm not proud of, but I have to tell the whole story. So don't be mad or judge, okay?"

"I promise," I said. That was easy.

"I started hanging out with some other kids. They were nicer to me. But they also were kind of partiers. Not bad, not like super stoners or anything, but they vaped out behind the school, and sometimes at parties, there was weed and some beer. Like that."

"Okay." *A girl needs someone to listen,* I thought.

A sharp voice asked, *Who listened to Zoe?*

Not now.

"Katrina and Madison were still my best friends, and we still talked every day, but Katrina's boyfriend, Robert, started hanging out with the other crowd I was with, and I could tell that he was sort of into me. I kept him at arm's length, but he was, like, always there, right? I wasn't sure what I should do. Like, tell Katrina? Tell Madison? Not tell anybody? Ignore it?"

"That's hard."

"Yeah, so, this one day, it was just me and him out in the smoking place, and he offered me some weed, and I smoked it and it was fine, but then he kissed me. Like totally leaned in and gave me some tongue.

"I was high and I kissed him back, but only for a minute, because I swear to God, he got so grabby, so fast. I hadn't even really had a boyfriend then, right? So I shoved him and told him to fuck off, and that was that."

"He sounds like an asshole."

"Definitely." She nodded. "The whole year goes by, right? Like everything settles down, and I think it's all fine. I had an actual boyfriend—a different guy—who seemed like he actually liked me for me, and we hung out. Not a lot, really, because my mom is kind of strict and she didn't really like him, so I had curfews and stuff that got in the way.

"But one night, Katrina and Madison and I were going to have a sleepover. I thought it was just going to be us, but Madison's mom went out, and then all these people came over—older kids, too, like seniors, and even a couple of college guys—and there was a lot of alcohol, like lemon vodka and stuff like that, and I was careful, but I got pretty drunk. My boyfriend was there, and he kept telling me it was okay, that he'd take care of me."

Her voice broke. She curled over her body and tucked her hands between her thighs, all the way up to her midforearm. My heart surged out to her, wanting to pat the jagged edges of her pain into softer angles. Knowing I could not. "It's all right, sweetheart. I'm right here."

"I don't remember what happened, like, at all. It's just blank, like somebody erased my brain, so I kinda think somebody gave me a roofie or something." She took a breath.

"Take your time." I touched her knee, but she flinched, and I got the message. She couldn't be touched right now. A wave of warning pushed through me.

"The next morning, everybody was gone, even Katrina and Madison. I had, like, the worst headache of all time. And I was completely naked. But I couldn't remember anything." She bent over, making a soft noise, and rocked a little. I left her in her bubble of protective space and didn't even make any sympathetic noises. "They wrote all over me. All over me. With Sharpies."

She choked, put her head down. Very, very gently, I brushed my hand over her hair, her shoulder. For a long moment, she just sobbed, heartbroken. The keening sound rocketed through my body and roused a thousand furious reactions—I wanted to murder those kids, and wrap her up in a cocoon, and scream like a banshee for all the terrible things that happened to innocent girls.

But she'd chosen me for a reason, because I was trained in listening and I had sat with hundreds of girls and women while they told their stories. It was what I did. "Oh, baby, I am so sorry that happened to you."

She let me stroke her hair while she cried. After a minute, she wiped her face on her arm and sniffed hard. "I got dressed and walked home. I lost my phone, too, so I was feeling, like, so bad, and so hung over, and I couldn't text anybody to find out what happened, and I just had this sense of . . . disaster . . . in my gut."

Oh, my girl, I thought, and I let her keep talking.

"My phone was on the porch when I got home, and when I opened it, I saw all the social media notifications, and I threw up. I knew it would be bad." Her voice sank to a whisper. "They *posed* me. All . . . open . . . and naked, with different boys, all of them . . . touching me in all kinds of different ways. And then they wrote all that stuff on me. Mean things." She closed her eyes and pressed the heels of her palms into her eyes, as if that could make it all go away.

My entire body was shaking with rage. "Those fucking bastards," I said, low and fierce.

"Right?" She used her sleeve to wipe her face. "It was all over social media, everywhere. I didn't know what to do. Like, I kind of felt like it was my fault, and if I told my mom, it would make her so sad, and she's always kind of sad anyway." She started to cry again.

A wave of shame slammed me. Shame and guilt and sorrow, so many dark emotions that I didn't even know how to name them all.

Zoe was always sad. A lump of something I couldn't quite identify stuck in my throat.

But it was Isabel who needed me right now. "You know this is not your fault, right?" I asked. "They assaulted you. It was a crime."

"Yeah," she said without conviction.

"Sweetheart, why didn't you tell your mother? She loves you so much."

Her eyelids fell, and her hands twisted together. "She might have killed somebody. Like, she's so protective, and it would be like it had happened to her, too, right? Because"—her voice broke—"she takes such good care of me. Me and her against the world, that's what we say, and she would have just been so devastated that she hadn't protected me."

"Oh, honey. You don't have to protect her. She wants to be there for you."

She squeezed her eyes tight and bent over from the waist, making a keening noise. "It was just so humiliating," she said with a moan. "I couldn't go to school anymore, and I erased all of my social media accounts, and I asked my mom to homeschool me until next year, and maybe even then I'm going to go to another school."

I kept my voice calm, even as I felt my hands shaking.

"And she doesn't know what happened?"

"No. I didn't tell her. I promised her that I wasn't raped—"

"But how do you know, if you can't remember?"

"I'm a virgin. I could tell they didn't do anything like that."

I thought the top of my head might shoot off.

"I wish I could strip the skin off of each and every one of them." I took her into my arms. She wept against my neck, her hands in fists at my sides.

Then she let go and sobbed, which is the whole purpose of a generously proportioned shoulder. I rocked her and held her and made soft, soft sounds and wanted to string every single one of her torturers up by their feet. Or make them sit in the village square in stocks while I pelted them with rotten fruit. Or dog shit.

They deserved to pay for their crime, and I would talk to Isabel about that another time. Somehow Zoe had to hear this story. But I had promised. I would keep that promise. Only Isabel could decide what to do.

In the meantime, my healer's mind went to work to think of things to salve this wound.

I fought back my own tears, closing my eyes tight. My poor love.

A vision of Zoe waving goodbye to me that last day rose in my mind. So small, so trusting.

Oh, my girl. My sorrow and shame rose like a wave, smashing all my illusions of finding myself and living a bigger life and all the other lies I'd told myself. I'd left my daughter. Scarred her for life, and never taken one minute of responsibility for it. If Zoe had experienced something like Isabel had, who would she have turned to? In fact, she very well could have, and I wouldn't even have known. While I'd been out in the world, comforting lost girls, my own daughter had lived her life as a motherless child.

Shame burned me.

I rocked her daughter, the daughter even all the most passionate protection in the world couldn't protect. "I love you, sweet girl. I'm so glad you could tell your secret at last."

Against my neck, she shuddered. "Me too."

Chapter Forty

Zoe

I woke up early, coming to awareness slowly. First, a sense of pleasure and peace that had been missing in my life. Next, the sensation of being warm next to a body. A naked body, I realized.

Sage.

My eyes popped open, and there was his face right in front of me, asleep on the other pillow on the bed. He was deeply asleep, mouth open slightly, and his breath made a soft whuffling sound as it moved in and out. His hand was wrapped around mine.

I didn't move. The moment was too precious, and I wanted to stay in it as long as possible, suspended between the dark errand that had brought me to England and the losses that had plagued my child, and me, and my grandmother, and the reality of whatever this day would bring. In between was Sage asleep and at peace. My body was sated on a level I'd barely known was possible, and yet I wanted to awaken him with kisses, with touches, with exploration.

An emotion I didn't want to examine rustled through my veins, ran through my heart, and then back through my limbs, a gilded, glittery sense of possibility.

To be honest, I'd never loved anyone else but Sage Cooper. I'd loved him when we were three, playing with worms in the garden and sleeping together for our naps. I'd loved him as my best friend when we were six and seven and eight, chasing butterflies and reading animal stories and building forts and tree houses. I'd loved him from afar when I'd had to go back to New Mexico, and we wrote letters every week, sending photos and feathers and stories back and forth. And my romantic love had bloomed entirely when I'd returned to England at last when I was fifteen. Erotic discovery had bonded us, but only because there had been such a groundwork before.

As if he felt me staring at him, his eyes opened and there we were, staring into each other's faces on the morning after.

"I thought it was a dream," he said, and he touched my face.

"A good dream?"

"Yes," he said simply, and he kissed me. We began again, as if this were all the time we had, as if the life that awaited us on the other side of the door would shatter it all again.

And with Sage, kisses and touches had always been more than their parts, too, carrying the layers and layers and layers of union we'd known together.

I let myself fall adrift in it, be lost in it, in the soft green land of Sage and Zoe, where our childhood selves roamed free and our souls were eternally connected. "I missed you so much," he breathed.

"Me too."

Could we start again? Would it be real, or was this just nostalgia and our shared grief? At the moment, I didn't care. For once, maybe I could just be where I was and not try to decide the entire course of the future.

It was slightly awkward when he drove me up to the house. I sat in the truck for a moment, wondering what I should say, or if he would say something. And then neither of us did—we just stared at the house.

"I'll need to get the printer from the back," I said, remembering at the last minute.

"Of course." He parked and then politely opened the back door.

I'd started to get the printer and would just leave everything in its awkward state, but then I stopped. "Sage, what was that? Last night?"

He looked at the house, then back at me. "Let's be careful with each other, shall we?"

"What does that mean?"

His smile was gentle. "Do you want to go to the festival with me on Friday night?"

A whoosh of relief moved through me. "Yes. I do."

"Good. In the meantime, I'm kissing you with my heart, but I don't want any eyes to see us and speculate that we were up to more than waiting out the storm."

"I'm kissing you with my heart too," I said.

I made my way to the house, not realizing there was a car parked in the side garden until I got there and had to shove the heavy wooden doors open. "Let me get that for you," said a voice.

My mother's voice. She stood there in the hall as if she belonged there, in her flowy tunic and leggings. "Why do you always wear white?" I snapped irritably.

"Long story."

I hauled the printer box into the kitchen, where Isabel was sitting with her computer. "Oh, yay! I can't wait to get started."

"I bought photo paper, too, a couple of different sizes, so you can play with the best formats."

She flung her arms around me, hugging me very tightly for such a mundane sort of purchase. I hugged her back. "Is everything okay?"

"Not exactly," she said. "You should sit down, Mom."

It was only then that I realized that Gran had come into the room, and my mother hadn't left, the way I expected her to do, and even Isabel had a grave expression on her young, young face. "What is it?"

"I'm afraid they've found Diana's body," Gran said. "She washed ashore in the storm last night."

Tears welled up in my eyes, but I protested, "How can they know for sure so fast? They didn't know who that girl on the beach was for . . . days!"

My mother spoke. "It was her jewelry, and her phone, which they found in her pocket. I'm so sorry."

Rage rocketed through me. "You need to go. Just leave." I pointed at the door, my hand shaking. "I don't need your sympathy or your kindness or anything else. Nothing, do you hear me? Go."

"Mom!" Isabel cried.

"Don't," I said in a tight, hot voice. "Don't defend her, and don't make me forgive her, and don't get in the middle of this at all. You just don't know." Emotion like a tidal wave was coming, and I jumped up to flee the kitchen before it could fling me down. It was my gran who stood in my way.

"Sit down, my love. Your mother is leaving, but we're here. Your girl and I are here."

I wailed, covering my face with my hands. In all things, since I could remember, Diana had always been there. Beside me, or in a letter, or phone call, or text. I had been so petty, pushing her away this past year, and now I would never see her again.

And she had just found happiness!

The wave took me. With a wail, I collapsed to the floor . . .

Oh, Diana! I'm so sorry! Gran and Isabel did their best to comfort me, but it was only Diana I wanted. I wanted to pour out my stories and tell her about Sage and to have dinner parties with her and Henry. I wanted to go back in time and move back home before Isabel had been wounded and Diana had gotten mixed up in something she shouldn't have and fall in love with Sage all over again and start fresh. I wanted to apologize for cutting her out of my life.

But fresh starts never really happened, did they?

When Sage came over, I was lying on my bed with a cold washcloth over my face, courtesy of the new nurse, who insisted I take a pill she'd produced from somewhere. It didn't stop the leak of tears—again that river of grief was overflowing its banks—but it made me care less about them.

He didn't say anything, but he crawled up on the bed beside me and wrapped his long arms and legs around me, and we wept silently together.

"We have to do something beautiful," I said after a long time.

"Yeah." He wiped his face with a hand.

I offered him the towel in my hand. "Isabel brought it to me."

He laughed a little and then used it, falling back down beside me. "Jesus, I'm gutted."

"Me too. The nurse gave me something, however, and it is kicking in quite nicely."

Isabel came into the room, carrying her tablet. "Oh, sorry," she said, and she started to back out.

"No, come on in." I sat up. "What's up?"

She shot me a dark look. "Grandad wants to talk to you."

"Okay."

Sage started to get up, but I stopped him with a hand on his arm. "I'm sure he'd love to see you."

"See me?"

Isabel brought the tablet over, and there was my dad, in his house outside Santa Fe. It was an old territorial, with a kiva fireplace and adobe benches built into the walls. He kept the doors and window frames painted turquoise to protect against evil spirits, as was the custom.

"Hi, Zoe," he said. Then, "Cooper! You look just the same."

"Hi, Ben." Sage waved. "I'm going to give you guys some privacy." He headed out, and he touched Isabel's back to turn her too. She crossed her arms and ducked away, but after throwing some more shade toward me, she flounced out.

"I'm sorry about Diana," he said when I looked back to the screen.

I nodded, feeling more tears leak out of my eyes. I wiped them off with the towel that now had mine and Sage's tears mingled. It felt like maybe I'd drained enough from the grief river that they might stop for a while. "Thanks. It's so sad."

"It really is. She was a good person."

We sat there for a minute. I couldn't really think of anything to say. "No offense, Dad, but I have nothing."

"I know. Isabel called me. I just wanted to be sure you're okay."

I nodded. "Thanks."

"You saw your mom, huh?"

Oh, that's what this was about. "I don't want to talk about it. She was here because Gran wanted her, and that's fine, but that doesn't change anything for me."

"Mmm," he said, like he was some wise man in a movie. "Isabel really likes her."

"Great. Maybe she'll leave her, too, and we can both be scarred forever."

He had the grace to chuckle. "Maybe things are not all black and white, kiddo. People change."

"Do they, Dad? I don't know if that's really true."

"Are you the same person you were twenty years ago?"

"No, of course not. I was nineteen."

He nodded. "I'm not the same as I was then either."

The anger river, running side by side with grief, suddenly took over, spilling fire into my body. "You know, Dad, speaking of that. Why the hell didn't you talk me into going to art school in New Mexico?"

"I tried," he said in his calm way. "It was a mistake, you leaving Scotland, but you wouldn't listen to me."

"What? Yes, I would have listened."

He shook his head, his mouth turned down at the corners. "You didn't listen to anybody. You talked yourself out of it. You were afraid. You decided you wanted a 'more stable life.'" He put the phrase in air quotes.

And suddenly I remembered the moment of decision. A woman I knew had come into the restaurant where I worked all the time. She was an artist, a painter who had a good reputation. Her studio was in some little hovel near the freeway, and she always had paint under her nails.

She was poor. Always scrabbling for money, paying with dollar bills and change for a meager breakfast of one egg and toast and coffee, which she would stay and drink for a long time while she sketched.

I didn't want that life. No way.

"Oh, my God," I said aloud. Even through the haze of Valium, I felt my own shock. "You're right."

"It's not too late," he said. "Go now."

I closed my eyes. It was many years too late. "I don't know about anything right now. I have to go, Dad. Thanks for calling."

"Anytime. Love you."

"Love you too."

For a long while, I sat on my teenage bed staring out to the sea where Diana had drowned. I'd thought about cutting her out of my life in a fit of—what? Jealousy? Control? Thought about the sabotage I'd employed when Sage hadn't responded immediately to my freak-out at school. I'd pushed them both away.

And maybe I'd pushed Martin away, too, just as he'd said I had, afraid that if I didn't, he'd break my heart.

The only person I hadn't pushed away was Isabel.

Or, well, I suppose I hadn't pushed Gran away either. I trusted them both to love me as me.

What a mess.

There was nothing left in my body, no emotion, nothing. Soon, I would try to sort out what I thought of all this. Figure out, maybe, what I actually wanted.

I needed to check on my gran and bring Isabel back her tablet. Maybe we all needed to get some food. With some effort, I washed my face and carried the tablet downstairs.

Gran, Isabel, and Sage were grouped around the table. Isabel had plugged in the printer, and it whirred away, printing photos. "What's this?"

"We're going to solve a murder," Gran said calmly, looking over a piece of paper. "Why don't you make a cup of tea and come help?"

Chapter Forty-One
Poppy

Because she asked me to, I accompanied Diana's mother to make the official identification. Joan had never been made of anything more than putty, and she smoked three cigarettes between her flat and the coroner's office. When we went downstairs to view the remains, she stopped cold. "I can't," she said. "Will you do it, Poppy?" Her eyes filled with tears. "I want to remember her the way she was."

Who could say no to such a request? "Of course."

It was an unpleasant task, but not as terrible as I'd feared. Because the sea was so cold, a certain lack of decomposition had made her identity plain, though if she'd been in the water much longer, it would have been much more difficult.

I recognized her coat first of all: that leather coat she'd been so proud of buying for herself once her business had begun to prosper. She'd bought it on a trip to Bristol, and it had been very nice indeed—black leather with zippers and buckles that had survived a week at sea perfectly well. Her hair, so proudly clipped into a mod asymmetrical style, was tangled.

But in the end, I'd had to look at her face. Not terribly decomposed, only bloated and discolored. Unmistakably Diana, poor child.

My heart ached with sorrow, with all the things she would never do, or know. I would miss her terribly.

I gave them a nod, and they led me away. Her mother had gone outside to smoke, and the inspector walked up the stairs with me.

"She was the prettiest baby," I said, blotting my eyes. "Fat and happy."

"I liked her," he said. "She was a kind woman."

"When will they know the cause of death?" I asked.

"We already know, more or less. She was shot."

"Shot?" It was not at all what I'd expected. I'd only seen a drowned body.

His expression was grim. "She must have found something. I'm going to London to talk to that boyfriend of hers again."

I squeezed his arm. "Be careful."

"You too."

The rest of the afternoon I accompanied Joan on the many errands required when someone died—to the funeral home to choose a casket and the chapel to arrange a funeral and then to find out about flowers. "I wish she could cater her funeral," Joan said, lighting another cigarette, then coughing out the smoke.

I finally dropped her off at dinnertime and made my way home to the goats and the empty house.

Please, I petitioned the heavens, *no more.*

I made a simple supper of bread and cheese and carried it out to the bench in the garden. The sun had broken through the clouds at last, and it stretched gold fingers out to caress flower heads and the tips of the grasses. The goats munched hay happily. The air smelled of humus and rich earth, and I let the scent and the silence settle me.

Into the softness tumbled images of the girl Diana had been, a chubby toddler who grew into a sturdy girl who liked reading and cooking but never anything outside. When I had returned seven years ago, it was easy to recognize her—still plump and rosy and cheerful.

I'd hungrily pumped her for news of Zoe, who was then married and a mother, living near her father in Santa Fe. In a way, I suppose Diana had been a surrogate daughter.

Zoe. What have I done?

I had so often imagined how my daughter and I might finally come face to face again. I had treasured the idea that she might simply just love me after so long a time, that she would see things in my face that would erase the grudge she held against me.

I'd come home to make things right, carrying with me decades of spiritual study. And in many ways, that study had made me a better woman. I'd learned to help heal those in pain, to listen to their stories, to absorb the sorrow they carried, help relieve their burdens.

But I had never faced the fact that I'd delivered a terrible pain to my own daughter. I had left her, and then I had not cared enough to take the time to fetch her from my mother and bring her to live with me.

I had wronged her.

And I'd wronged Ravi's family too. Taken their husband and father away for my own selfish desires.

The knot of wrongs sat against my heart day and night, and I didn't know yet how to dislodge it. How to atone and begin to perhaps make things right.

Her disdain this morning had been painful enough, but the hatred in her eyes had nearly shattered me. I could see that it had shocked Isa. Not my mother, who stood on the sidelines with no opinion. For the first time, I understood that I deserved it.

The churning of my emotions and thoughts would do no good for anyone or any situation. I carried my dishes with me to the workshop, where I'd dropped the material for the festival herbal packets. I thought I might as well work on those.

But in the work space, I found my thoughts still so chaotic that I dared not put together spells for other people. We had one more day until the festival began on Friday. I could finish them tomorrow.

Or not finish them at all. Mia said she'd completed all the spell bottles, and we'd already stocked a great many crystals and earrings and bracelets. We would offer readings all day both days, and Mia had invited a friend of hers to come in and do henna tattoos. We'd split the profits in half. It would be a prosperous weekend, no matter what. Maybe I could let the rest go.

I washed my dishes and set them in the drainer to dry. The house seemed extraordinarily quiet after I'd been among family at my mother's house. I'd stayed at Woodhurst Hall at Isa's urging. I couldn't have driven home anyway, not in the deluge.

With some dread, I'd made up the bed in the Oak Room, and Isa asked if she could sleep with me. We saged the room for good measure and then played a rousing game of gin to chase off any spirits. I was relieved to see that her confession had left no lingering stain on her mood—in fact, it seemed to have given light to some space in her heart.

Before we climbed into the bed together, I secretly placed a dinner plate full of dry rice on the bureau, because ghosts liked to count things, and rice was hard to count.

She fell asleep quickly. I did not. Nor did I find myself on edge, fretting about what I might feel or dream in this big, old, empty house. Lying there in the dark, smelling that sweet herbal scent of her hair, I was swamped with such love that I thought it might carry me away right there. It was as if life had saved a special, wild surprise for me late in life, the gift of a love so sweet and pure I hardly knew what to call it. I did not have to do anything for her, or shape her, or earn her love or even *have* her love. I was free to simply, wholly adore her, just as she was. I'd never experienced such an emotion in my life. Closing my eyes, I twined a lock of her hair around my finger and whispered, *Thank you.*

We slept well and deeply, my granddaughter and I.

Now tonight, I missed her. I worried about what kind of toll the assault would take on her over the course of her life, and I wanted to talk with Zoe, and perhaps Martin, about strategies to heal her as fully as possible.

Not that it was my place. But it was until Zoe knew.

Apart from my worry, I wanted to hear Isabel laughing again, and to show her more about tarot, which she was eager to learn. I wanted to know every thought in her brain. I wanted to avenge the abuse she'd suffered at the hands of her so-called friends, but more, I wanted to teach her how not to mind, to live her own life and not carry shame like a cross on her back.

But to do it, I would have to make peace with Zoe.

Idly, I picked up the soft old tarot deck I'd not yet returned to my glove box and shuffled it. The cards knew her heart, or at least they could help me think of ways to soften her.

A moth fluttered hard around my head, startling me, and I dropped the cards with a little cry. They scattered across the floor, all facedown but two. The King of Pentacles and the Tower. I looked up at the moth fluttering about the kitchen, small and white. It alit on the windowsill and moved its wings, as if speaking to me; then it fluttered through the window and out into the garden.

I looked at the cards again. Who was the King of Pentacles, the powerful man behind all of this?

Chapter Forty-Two

Zoe

I was the first one awake Thursday morning. The view out my windows was gloomy, the sea a surly dark gray. The working fishing boats were already out, but I wondered about the yacht cruises. With so much going on, two deaths in a week, would they still go out?

I could see the festival grounds from my window, high on the opposite cliff, and it was plain that it was still on. It would open tonight with a big food festival. Booths and tents were being set up, and what looked like a carnival had moved in overnight, occupying a wide space nearby, by the woods.

Where we'd searched for Diana. Memory made my gut feel hollow. We hadn't gotten very far last night in our quest to solve the murder, even with the expert Lillian and her clever, puzzle-piecing brain. We were all exhausted with emotion and events, and when it became clear we weren't getting anywhere, we all went to bed. I'd asked Sage if he wanted to stay, but he'd had to get back to his animals.

As a farmer must.

In the stillness, I padded downstairs in the socks Sage had let me keep and put the kettle on. I'd tucked my art bag into a corner and now picked it up, thinking that maybe I'd be able to focus better if I drew for a while. As the tea brewed, I opened the bag and took out the Inktense pencils and a sketchbook.

Isabel had left a stack of her photos on the table, some of which we'd combed through last night, searching for possible clues, looking at photos and combing back through the spreadsheets. The vague figure in the background of Isabel's photograph in the bluebell wood proved to be more frustrating than helpful, and even Lillian finally tossed it aside with a grunt. "Nothing to be seen here," she said.

Now I looked at the other photos, the artistic group, of bluebells and the trees, and chose one to draw. Just below it were a few others I hadn't seen last night, shots of the harbor and of a boat being loaded for a trip.

A man glared at the camera, and right below him was the name of the boat: *Persephone.*

Persephone.

Urgently, I looked for the ledger that Sage had brought from Diana's house. Hadn't the strange notations been for Perse? Could that have been an abbreviation for *Persephone*?

I texted Sage:

Did you take the ledger back?

Yes. Thought I'd go through it again. Problem?

No.

I stirred sugar in my tea and called him. "Hey," I said. "This is easier."

"Sure. What's going on?"

I realized he probably had a million chores. "Are you busy? I just had a couple of thoughts about the clues."

"I'm working but I've got headphones. Tell me."

"Isabel has some photos here of a boat named *Persephone*. Maybe that's the business we were wondering about."

"Maybe." He sounded hopeful, then made a noise I recognized as a dog command. *Hoi!* "The ledger is out here. I can bring it into town later."

"Or I'll drive out there," I said before I realized how forward it sounded. And when did I care about being forward, anyway? What was this, 1962? Before he could respond, I said, "Or not. I'm just thinking aloud."

"I'd be glad of the company. I've just been so bloody sad."

"Me too."

"I would cook you dinner if you came to get the ledger."

I smiled. "I'll bring bread."

"Good." He gave a long whistle. "Sorry, I have to go."

"No worries."

I sat down at the table, bringing my tea, a banana, and an enormous muffin. I drew the bluebell and its stem, and then, in small letters, I began writing in a spiral, starting at the bottom corner of the page and going around.

> Dear Diana,
>
> I just can't seem to think clearly without being able to talk to you. I miss you, so much. I want to tell you everything. About Isabel and the way she's blooming here and how hard it is to see my mother like this, just right there, like she's just an ordinary person, which of course she is, but you know what I mean. But mostly I want to tell you about Sage, and how real this feels. Again. I wonder what you would say? Be careful? No, that's not you at all. You'd say go for it, be happy, you've always loved him. OMG, how will I live without you?
>
> Love,
> Zoe

The words curled into the flower and turned into a bee with a little coaxing. For the first time, I realized, I hadn't wept while I'd drawn it. The ache was there, deep and painful, but maybe I'd wept enough yesterday that I could function today. There was much to do.

One of the first things was to go to the website the constabulary had set up. We'd read through it last night, but I'd been so exhausted that not much had sunk in. This morning, fortified by strong tea and my substantial breakfast, I scrolled through the notes left by the community. Much of it was speculation—that her boyfriend had killed her, that the "Londoners" flooding the town all summer must be the responsible parties, that drugs were obviously involved. As ever, the rhetoric took a xenophobic tone, blaming everyone for mysterious things.

Impatient, I clicked off. This was not going to solve the problem. But maybe going back to Diana's house would. What had she been hiding?

I left a note for Isabel, letting her know I'd be back later and to stay in touch. The nurse had settled into the apartment just off the kitchen, so no matter how Gran woke up, stable or unstable, she'd be covered. Last night she'd been sharper than ever, so I hoped it would be the same today.

I headed for Diana's house, wondering if it would be closed off now that she'd been found, but it looked exactly the same. If it had been named a crime scene, I didn't see any sign of it, and if anyone came, I'd just say I was looking for her will. I let myself in the back door, only realizing as I did so that it was going to be very different this time. It would probably count as evidence tampering at this point. I'd just feign ignorance.

But also, I now knew that she was dead. Knew that she would never be coming back here. Emotion rose in my throat, but I swallowed it back down. She deserved justice, and maybe I could help get that for her.

I took my time, going through her bedroom carefully, looking in all the drawers all the way to the bottom for something hidden. I found racy lingerie and some sex toys that made me laugh, but nothing else. I didn't know what I expected. Notes on what she'd been thinking? A journal? A will?

Nothing like that turned up. Not in the bedroom or the kitchen or the desk in the living room. Flummoxed, I was about to leave when I remembered an old show we'd seen about how to keep things safe from thieves. One place we'd both thought brilliant was the freezer.

I hesitated. By now everything in the refrigerator would've been spoiled, and I fancied I could even smell rotten food, but the freezer would be fine. I opened it to find the usual things—frozen peas and single-serving meals and ice cream. Boxes of frozen vegetables. Carrots, potatoes, okra.

I paused. Okra? She hated it, in every variety. I pulled the box out and opened it. Behind a thin layer of freezer-burned vegetables was an envelope. I shook the veggies into the sink and extracted the envelope.

It was money. A thick stack of £50 notes. Good God. I opened the freezer again and started checking all the boxes. Every single box and bag contained more notes, thousands and thousands of pounds. For long agonized moments, I had no idea what I should do with it. Tell the constable? Put it back? Stash it somewhere safe?

What I was afraid of was that it might mean she'd been mixed up in something criminal. Why hide bills? It wasn't the way you saved carefully. And it was certainly not what the fastidious Diana would have done. She saved in high-interest accounts.

In the end, I went upstairs to get a bag from her bedroom and started stuffing the money into it. I was almost finished when I heard someone at the front door.

My heart slammed into my ribs, and I grabbed the bag and dashed to stand against the wall of the kitchen, a place I knew would be out of the line of sight. Whoever it was knocked, waited, knocked again.

Holding the money made me feel guilty. I couldn't quite catch my breath, and when they rattled the door handle, I slid down the wall and tried to make my body very small. What if they came to the back door?

I jumped up, staying low, and locked the back door, then hid against the wall, keeping my body crouched, the bag in my hands. I nearly jumped out of my skin when the back door rattled and someone called out, "Hello?" A man with an accent that was not Devonshire.

It suddenly occurred to me that whoever had killed her already knew she was dead and they were coming to find something, just as I was. The sound of my amped-up heart filled my ears, and I tried to think what I would do if they broke in the back, but I heard someone shouting. "Hey, you, what are you doing? That woman is dead! Have some respect!"

Whoever it was abandoned their quest. Afraid the neighbor might call the police, I ran to the front door and slipped out, hoping no one saw me. I walked as naturally as possible, then ran to my car in the Tesco lot and drove home as quickly as I could.

Chapter Forty-Three

Isabel

I was supposed to talk to Dr. Kerry this morning, but I didn't think I could do it and hide the truth from her, so I pretended I forgot. She pinged my cell phone, but I'll say I was in the shower. Or sleeping. Or something.

I feel guilty that I told Poppy about the stuff with Katrina and Madison and I haven't told my mom. Poppy—I still don't really know what to call her, and everybody else calls her Poppy—is really easy to talk to, and you just get the feeling that she's not judgmental at all. Like she's lived this crazy life and she's done a bunch of things wrong and would get it if you screwed up.

Which makes it sound like my mom is judgy, and she's not. Well, she is, kinda, about her mom, but they have some stuff between them I can't quite figure out. Like, my grandmother left her, but now she's back.

And my grandmother is the person everybody really loves. She's kind. She listens. She has this way about her that just makes it easy to be yourself. I want to tell my mom that, but she *hates* Poppy. Hates her.

But how would I feel if my mom had left me when I was seven? It makes my stomach hurt to even think about it. We are really, really close. Like, I can't stand it when she's disappointed in me, but living in the modern world isn't that easy, and I sometimes just want to fit in, so a little partying doesn't seem that bad, and I don't want her to know about it.

So why can't I tell her about the pictures?

It just makes me want to cry to think about it. I think about the words they wrote on me, stupid things, mostly, but in very personal places, and they were looking at my private, personal body when they did it, all of them, invading my privacy in such a bad way . . . and I just can't. Not yet.

But if she finds out I told her mom first, she's going to be furious.

Anyway, I'm going out tonight with Molly and Isaac and some of the other people. We're going to the festival, which tonight is mainly about the carnival and the foodie stuff, not the art yet. But tomorrow I'm totally going to look at all the photos and think about how I'll do that someday maybe.

In the meantime, I need to write a little bit more on the fairy story.

Chapter Forty-Four
Zoe

I drove to the farm in the late afternoon, armed with a fresh loaf of bread that filled the car with a mouthwatering aroma and the bagful of cash I'd taken from the freezer. I'd been jumpy all afternoon, second-guessing myself and wondering what the hell I was doing.

Gran and Isabel spent the rainy afternoon making collages with her photos and a stack of magazines Isabel had found somewhere. I offered my art supplies to give them more to work with, and they cooed like doves. Isabel told me that she planned to go to the festival if it stopped raining. I told her to text me when she left and to stay in touch.

"Mom. I'm fine," she said, rolling her eyes.

"I know." I kissed her head. She seemed a hundred times better in just a week's time. For a moment, I paused, wondering if she'd just swept her pain under a rug and if, in bringing her here, I was letting her run away.

"Really," she said. "I'm fine."

"Be home by nine thirty."

"Fine."

I checked in with Margaret, the nurse, on my way out. She said she'd be sure to be in the room with Gran or check on her regularly until

I returned, just to be safe. "But she's having a good day. You needn't worry."

I wanted to say *My oldest friend was just murdered. I'm worried about everything,* but I didn't. "Thanks. You have my mobile if you need me."

The farm was only ten minutes out of town, but down looping lanes that moved you from the civilized, village- and town-centered coast to the open expanse of fields and livestock. As I drove, I felt my anxiety sliding away, letting my shoulders ease away from my ears, my heart slowing to a more normal rhythm.

When I pulled into the drive, Sage came out, still wearing his muddy wellies, and Matt came running down the hill. It was so much like the day I'd first come here again when I was fifteen that I wanted to get out and run over to give him a hug.

I was too shy. "Hi."

He kicked one foot out in front of him, hooking his thumbs through his belt loops. "Hello." He inclined his head "Are you getting shy on me again, Zoe Fairchild?"

"Maybe?"

He left his spot and came toward me. "Where's the shameless girl who leapt out of her grandmother's car and flung herself into my arms, eh?"

"I just thought about that!"

He opened his arms. "Give her a try."

So I did. I felt silly and then I didn't, because when I launched myself, he caught me, and it was exactly right. He smelled exactly right. He felt exactly right, and when he spun me around, it put the world exactly right. "Come on in," he said. "I've got supper in the oven."

"I brought bread. And something to show you."

He kissed me, then pressed his forehead against mine. "My heart is so heavy."

"Mine too."

We took comfort in each other, in the quiet of the land. When Matt came over and leaned against us, we laughed softly. "Good dog," I said, reaching for his ears.

We went inside to feast on baked pasta with cheese and a rich tomato sauce along with the crusty bread I'd brought with me. Sage lit candles and poured big glasses of milk. "You can bring wine if you like. It doesn't bother me."

He'd never been a drinker. "I don't care that much." The milk was cold and refreshing, and it gave me the courage to say, "I went to Diana's house today. I found something strange."

"Yeah?"

My phone stuttered a text alert. "Sorry. Isabel is under orders to text me."

On my way to the Festival

Ok. Be safe! Home by nine thirty.

I know!

"What did you find?" Sage asked.

I picked up the bag and handed it to him. "Look."

He wiped his fingers and unzipped it, then looked inside. "What the—?" He pulled out a fistful of notes. "Where was it?"

"In the freezer. I didn't know what to do, but it feels like she might have been in trouble, to stash this much money. Like, why else would she need cash?"

"We're going to have to tell the inspector."

"I know. I just don't want her to be—"

"In trouble?"

"I know. It's ridiculous."

He pulled out the envelopes, frowning. "Did you count how much was in each one? Is it the same, different?"

"I didn't. Someone came to the door and scared the hell out of me."

"Who?"

I shook my head. "Somebody who might have been trying to get in if it hadn't been for a neighbor."

Sage looked at the money, then tossed me an envelope. "Count yours."

We both counted and came up with the same sum: £2,500.

"A lot of money," he said. "How many envelopes?" He eyed them. "Maybe a dozen?"

"What was she *doing*, Sage?"

He tossed the bag on the ground. "I don't know. Jesus." He rubbed his face. "How could all of this be happening to her and I had no idea?"

"I didn't either!"

"But you lived a long way away. I saw her all the time. You'd think I would have noticed something."

"I just thought she seemed happy."

"Me too."

We fell silent, then started eating again, each of us lost in our own thoughts.

"There has to be an answer," I said. "Let's look at this logically. What's the first thing that happened? She met Henry, and her business started booming with his fishing trips."

"Right. And then, she and Henry fell in love."

"She kept building her business with the fishing trips, and—wait. Didn't you say you thought the *Persephone* might be the answer to the weird business entries?"

"Yes. Let's see if we can figure that part out."

"First let's finish this. They fell in love. He seemed pretty serious about her."

"Where did all this money come from?" he asked, looking both bewildered and frustrated.

"Maybe Henry's gig is gambling. A couple of different people have said that there are some high-stakes poker parties on the fishing trips. They're very wealthy men—maybe they're buying into the games, and he gets a cut?"

He nodded, frowning. "But why stash it in the freezer?"

"Drug money, tech money?"

"Maybe." He tapped a foot. "I keep thinking about the girl who died of a drug overdose. How did she get in the water?"

"Huh. That's a very good question. Was she on one of the boats?"

"She was a runaway, right?"

"That's what Gran said the inspector told her. Do you want me to text her?"

"No, that's not necessary." He stood up, walked to the stove, walked back. "Why did Diana have that house in Exeter? What was she going to do with it?"

I shook my head. "We don't know."

"What if what's being smuggled isn't phones or drugs, but girls?"

"Oh, my God." A sense of horror mixed with recognition poured through me. "The *Persephone*," I said. "Who owns that yacht?"

"I don't know. But I think we need to go to town. To see the police."

"Yeah. And I need to know where my daughter is." I suddenly felt sick to my stomach. We both stood, carried the bowls to the sink, and headed for the door. Sage picked up the cash as he passed.

Sage was by far the better driver, so I climbed into the Range Rover. Matt jumped up in the back seat, ready for adventure. I texted Isabel:

What are you doing?

Her answer didn't come right away, and my stomach squeezed. I'd learned that she didn't always reply when she was with her friends, so I gave it five minutes, then texted again:

Isabel, I'm worried. You need to answer me now.

Still no answer. "She's not picking up." I stared at the phone as if to make it light up with her text. "Probably irritated."

"To be honest, I don't know. Where do the girls come from?"

"We don't even know if that's what it is!" I scowled at the phone, resisting, then caved and checked the Find My Friends app. Isabel was squarely where she should have been, right on top of the bluff where the carnival was. Relief and irritation filled me. "I just can't stop worrying about her," I said. "Something awful happened to her, and she won't tell me what it was."

"Something awful like what?"

"I don't know. She was bullied somehow. Her friends turned on her." In the dark cab, hurtling down the hill to the village, it was easier to talk about it. "Something happened one night when she spent the night with her girlfriends. The next day, she was a different person. She got off all social media and trashed her phone—she said she lost it, but I don't believe her—and flat out refused to go to school."

"Wow. And you couldn't find out what it was?"

"Believe me, I tried everything I could think of. I talked to the parents of the girls, and I had the principal do an investigation, but nothing. Nothing," I said again. "I don't even know how that's possible, that there could be no trace of anything."

My phone, right on time, buzzed.

MOM! STOP THIS! YOU ARE STRANGLING ME!!!!!!!!!!!!!

I snapped.

Then maybe you should have let me in and told me the truth about what happened. I can't stop worrying.

why are you doing this right now????????

I realized, with a stinging sense of idiocy, that it *was* weird.

I don't know. Worried about that girl, about everything.

Three dots hung on the screen for a long time, then disappeared. Came back. Then:

I will tell you. Just give me a break. I'm having fun! I'm happy!

Promise?

YES. OK??? Now leave me alone. I have to go home in an hour. :)

"Argh." I dropped my head against the seat. "She really is happy again. I hate to make her go home."

"I would never have figured you for a fretful mum."

"I'm actually not. Well, I am right now, but mostly, I want her to make decisions while I'm right here," I began. "You never learn to make good decisions if nobody lets you make them. If she falls on her face now, it'll be a lot easier to pick up the pieces than it will be later."

"Are we still talking about Isabel?"

"I don't know. No. I wish my mother and Gran and Dad would have let me make more choices. Somebody else always decided." I watched the lights swoop across the hedgerows, casting shadows short and long, like a cartoon. "And then, when I did make a choice, to go to Glasgow on my own, I didn't have the grounding I needed. I was so insecure, and then I just blew it all up and ran home."

"We all make mistakes, Zoe. It's part of living."

"I know." I sighed. "I think that's part of my problem, though, that I'm always trying to make it just right."

"So that your mum won't leave you?"

I ducked my head. "Maybe."

He squeezed my hand. "I'd go back and make different choices too," he said.

"What choices?"

"I thought I hated you, Zoe. Like real hate." He shook his head. "The second I saw you at the market this time, I knew that was just a big lie."

"I know. Me too. Except—"

"Except?"

"I wouldn't have Isabel, and she's everything to me. If I think about going back, I can't do one thing that would mean I didn't have her."

For a moment, he was silent. When he spoke again, his voice was husky with emotion. "And I wouldn't have had the time with Alice." He cleared his throat. "Being there for her while she died was one of the most powerful times in my life. I would not trade it."

Deeply moved, I covered his hand. "I love her socks," I said, and as I'd meant him to, he gave me a smile.

"Are we starting again?" I asked. "Me and you?"

"I hope so." He raised my hand to his lips. "I was afraid of it, but now—"

"Now?"

He let go of a breath. "I'm more afraid of not taking the chances life offers."

"Me too," I whispered.

"What about your life in Santa Fe?"

I snorted. "Some life. The only person I'd miss is my father. And—" I looked out the window, acknowledging the truth. "Gran is dying. I need to be here with her."

"Yes."

As we drove into town, the lights of the carnival glittered against the still-heavy sky. "Looks beautiful, doesn't it?"

"I guess. It's a lot of wasted energy."

"What?" I slapped his chest with the back of my hand. "Are you serious?"

"Well, a little serious. We have to reduce our consumption on every level if we want a world worth living in. Maybe fewer carnivals wouldn't be so bad."

I stared at him for a minute. "This is actually one of the reasons I was afraid to be with you before."

He grinned in the dark. "Because I'm a conservationist?"

"Because you're kind of priggish about it." He kissed my fingers, and I relented. "But I have to admit you're right. I mean, how much worse is it since we were together then?"

"Some things are worse, but some are better." He pulled into a parking space in front of the constabulary. "But right now, we need to face the music over this cash."

"I'm scared."

"I'll tell them we were both there. And they know she was our best friend. What charges would they even press?"

"Breaking and entering? Tampering?"

"Not going to happen. I've known Hannaford since he had a crush on my mom after my dad died. He knows me better than that. C'mon."

Chapter Forty-Five

Zoe

We walked into the station, and I felt guilty instantly. "Is Inspector Hannaford around?" I asked.

"He's in his office," said the man behind the desk, a beefy guy I hadn't seen before. "Big break in the case today."

"Really? What kind of break?"

The man cocked his head, gesturing toward the back. "That boyfriend of hers is singing."

Startled, I looked toward the back, and there was Henry, head in his hands, sitting on a bench. Hannaford was on the phone, writing something down. "May I talk to Henry?"

"No. You can sit and wait."

Sage and I sat gingerly on the bench. He held the bag with the money between his legs, as if a thief might come along and rip it out of his hands. I looked at the phone in my hand, wondering if I should text Isabel again or leave her alone for an hour.

The inspector made the choice for me by coming out of the office and waving a hand in our direction. Henry raised his head, and he looked utterly haggard.

"What can I do for you?" Inspector Hannaford asked, gesturing us into the office.

"Do you mind if I close the door?" I asked, pointing.

"Not at all."

I closed the door and perched on the edge of the chair. "I don't know if you're aware that Diana was one of our best friends, both of us, from childhood."

He nodded. He looked as weary as Henry, and it seemed it had been a very bad day for them.

Sage said, "We wanted to look through the house one more time, see if we missed anything, if something might point us in the right direction." He heaved the multicolored bag onto the desk. "We found something in the freezer."

The inspector frowned and stood up to open it and look inside. Upon seeing the bills, he looked at us. "What were you doing in there?"

"It was my idea," I said. "I just needed to see if there was anything I missed. Something I might understand that you—or anyone else— might not understand."

"It was in the freezer?"

"Yes."

"Did you count it?"

Sage said, "Not all of it, but the packages we did count were all twenty-five hundred pounds."

He wiped his face. "All right. Christ. You've put yourselves in a position. How'm I to know if you kept some of the money for yourself?"

"You know we didn't," Sage said. "And there's more. We found some notes in her business accounts about a property in Exeter. We went there, and it was empty."

"Look, I've got a big witness out there who's waiting for his solicitor and a case about to crack wide open. Diana's murder might be connected, but it's bigger than that, and I need to keep my wits about me." He looked in the bag again. "Christ. I hate that she was mixed up in this."

"Gambling?" I offered.

"How did you hear that?"

"It's logical. Everyone's been talking about it in town, and the men on those charters have deep pockets, right?" I leaned forward.

Sage caught my arm. I took the hint. "I guess that's your job, isn't it?"

"Thank you, Ms. Fairchild. You have been very helpful. I'll let you know if I need anything else."

"What if," Sage said casually, standing up, "it's girls?"

Hannaford frowned. "I don't follow."

"What if the gambling has been hiding a sex-trafficking ring?"

For a long moment, Hannaford only looked at Sage, his expression unreadable. Then he swore. "Jesus fucking Christ." He picked up the phone. "Grayson, get in here."

A constable with a trim waist and crisp uniform came in.

"Bring in the commodore."

"Sir?"

"Just do it." His polite manner broke, and he waved a hand at us. "You need to get out of here. Go home. We'll let you know if we need you. And stay out of the way."

I leapt to my feet. "Absolutely. Thank you."

As we headed out, I stopped. "Henry, was it girls? Was she trying to save them?"

He only hung his head. I wondered what he knew, what he'd mixed her up in, and rage burned through my veins. "She loved you," I said.

Sage pulled me away.

Chapter Forty-Six

Isabel

The carnival—which everybody calls a fair—was kind of lame, and after we tried to win teddy bears and had ridden the loser-size Ferris wheel and eaten a bunch of cotton candy, or "candy floss," as they called it, we detoured into the woods. It was dark, but we used our phone flashlights to find a good spot, and we settled in for the real purpose of the evening. To party.

I really wasn't all that sure I wanted to stay. My curfew was in a half hour, my mom was in freak-out mode, and I didn't really want to get on her bad side. But the balance of girls to boys was not great. Too many boys to three girls. I didn't want to leave Molly.

I was feeling guilty about partying when I knew my mom would hate it, but mainly because I should never have told Poppy about the pictures before I told my mom. Poppy is her mortal enemy, like in a Shakespeare play or something—a vow to the death to hate somebody.

I think Poppy is one of the best people I've ever met. Not just kind, or not kind in that soapy, fake way, but genuinely interested in other people. It seems like she really likes people, all of them.

But my mom has a point. Poppy left her. Loving all the other people in the world doesn't really make up for that.

"You want some?" Molly asked, passing the joint.

"Nah." I passed it on and stood. "I'm gonna go. My mom's been freaking out. You want to walk back with me?"

"Yeah," Molly said, and she handed off the joint. "Maybe I'll buy some more candy floss."

"I'll walk you guys back to the fair," Isaac said. "It's dark."

"Thanks." We turned on our phones and walked back through the trees. The fair glowed bright against the night, and it looked beautiful from here. "I'm looking forward to seeing the art booths."

"Yeah, it's not bad," Isaac said. "I have to work tomorrow, but maybe I'll see you Sunday?"

"Maybe." We reached the edge of the woods. "I've got it from here."

He nodded, lifting a hand, but he didn't try to kiss me again, maybe because Molly was there.

"Isaac likes you," Molly said after he'd left. "You like him?"

I shrugged. "I'm taking a break from guys, really."

Molly nodded. "Somebody hurt you?"

I looked out over the black ocean, appearing dangerous behind the bright lights of the carnival. "Not like you think."

"Girls are worse sometimes." Molly lit a cigarette. "Wait for me a sec while I go to the loo?"

"Sure."

Molly peeled away and loped behind a bank of booths that hadn't been completely set up yet. I shivered a little in the cold and watched the Ferris wheel spin around. My phone beeped, and it was Molly.

Weird guys over here. Meet me

OMW

I rounded the booths, but there was no one there. The porta potties were all in a line, but nobody was around. "Molly?" I called, looking around.

No answer.

The hair on the back of my neck stood up, and I turned around and ran back to the front of the booths before I texted her:

Hey, where are u?

My phone stayed silent. I turned in a circle, looking around carefully. Maybe she was playing a joke on me, trying to scare me. It was pretty busy, families and teens and even some tourists.

I texted again:

Hey, this isn't funny. Text me back

Nothing. I walked around the main area, looking for her, but nothing. I wished I had Isaac's number, but we hadn't gotten that far yet. Then I saw a flash of red, the color of Molly's blouse, and I ran after her.

But when I got there, she was gone.

It was dark and getting kind of lonely, and I didn't know what to do. I thought about running back to the woods, but I wasn't sure I could find the others that easily, and honestly, I was getting pretty creeped out.

I called my mom.

She picked up before the first ring was finished. "Isabel. What's wrong?"

"I don't know. My friend went to the bathroom and texted me that there were some weird guys hanging around, and then she just disappeared, and now I'm really scared and I don't want to walk in the dark."

"Stay right where you are. We'll come find you." Her steady, calm voice made me feel calm too. "Do you want to keep talking to me?"

"Yes, please."

"We're in the truck already, so it'll only be two minutes. Where are you, exactly?"

I looked around, over my shoulder. "I'm standing right by a game booth that's giving away teddy bears and stuff like that. The carousel is to my left."

"On the way."

I had an idea. "Hang on, Mom. I want to check something." I opened the Find My Friends app and looked for Molly. My hands were shaking, afraid I'd see that it was just around the corner, and I'd go over there and find the phone on the ground.

But the dot was moving.

Chapter Forty-Seven

Zoe

My heart was racing as Sage drove up to the car park by the fair, and I was out of the truck and running toward the carousel before we had even properly stopped. "Isabel!" I cried.

A figure peeled away from the shadows, dressed in jeans and a top I recognized. "Mom!" she cried.

I hugged her hard, but she shook me off. "I think somebody took her!" She held out her phone in a hand that was shaking so hard that she could hardly keep it straight. I wrapped my hand around her wrist. "This is her on Find My Friends," she said, and now tears streamed over her face. "It's moving. We have to find her!"

Sage joined us and took the phone. "What the hell?" He scowled. "Come on. Let's follow." He gave Isabel a look. "You're all right?"

"Yes."

We ran back to the truck, and Sage said, "Isabel, you sit in back with Matt and keep him company, all right, and your mom can hold the phone where I can see it." We climbed in and slammed the doors. "Zoe, call Inspector Hannaford."

"Do you know the number?"

He shook his head. "You'll have to look it up."

"Do you know where to go?"

"More or less. They're on the Old Coach Road. Some vacation homes out there, but not many occupied until June."

Isabel hugged Matt, who took his job as comforter very seriously. She leaned into him, burying her face in his fur.

We had to loop around the village and then head out into the extremely dark country lanes that led out to farms and grazing land. The road was approximately two inches wider than the truck, and all I could see was the narrow path between hedgerows below a dark, dark sky. The lane itself was bumpy, tossing us around as he took curves and corners. It felt like we were racing, but when I looked at the speedometer, I saw that it read twenty-five miles per hour.

I set Isabel's phone beside me and googled the number for the police in Axestowe. The screen stuck for long minutes, and I had to start again. Now *my* hands were shaking. The dot on Isabel's phone still moved, and we followed, all of us locked in the terrifying dark.

"God, what if it's just her dad or something?" Isabel suddenly moaned. "I'm an idiot!"

"No, you're not," Sage said. "Trust me."

"I have the number."

"Dial it and hand it to me."

I did, and when it started to ring, he said, "Hello. I need Inspector Hannaford. This is Sage Cooper. It's urgent."

He glanced at us, nodded. "I think we might have found something," Sage said, and he gave the background and where we were. "Yes, sir. We'll stay put."

"I'm scared," Isabel said.

"I know. Me too." I looked over my shoulder. "You've just proven yourself to be a good friend. I'm so proud of you."

Isabel wailed. I reached over the seat and took her hand. She let me.

"They stopped," Sage said. "We're about two miles behind them."

We drove down one narrow lane after another, twisting this way and that, passing cottages sitting right against the road, and others set a bit of a way off, then plunging back into the inky dark. "Do you know where you are?" I asked.

"Not far from the Grimsell farm. Just to the east, if that helps."

"No. But I trust you."

He glanced at the phone and said, "I don't need that anymore. We're going to the top of that hill."

I couldn't see a hill, and then I did, a hump of black against the star-bright sky. He drove around the back of it and, near the top, turned off his lights, and we parked near a pile of boulders. "Come on," he said, opening his door.

Isabel and I stepped out. In front of us was a vast expanse of blackness broken at intervals by the lights of a house or farm. Just below us was a large house, with many windows lit. A faint sound of music drifted toward us.

Sage fetched blankets from the truck, spread a few of them on the ground, and then wrapped each of us in one.

I looped one arm around Isabel, and Sage had one arm around me. Matt settled across all of our feet, as if to make sure we were protected. Overhead the sky held so many stars that they looked painted. A cold wind burned my earlobes.

Below, at the house with too many lights on, music pulsed, and in the distance, I saw a trail of lights looping through the Devon lanes. The police were on their way.

Chapter Forty-Eight

Zoe

We met the police back at the station. The raid had yielded eleven girls, all between the ages of fourteen and seventeen, some of whom had been kidnapped over a year ago to provide sex for the yacht parties. Molly was among them, and when she found out Isabel had followed her, she burst into tears and flung her arms around Isabel's neck. "I am your friend for the rest of my life," Molly said.

"I'm good with that," Isabel said. Her eyes were closed, and I could tell she was trying not to cry.

Most of the girls had been kidnapped from London or Romania, but two had been captured locally, including Jennie, who'd left her baby with an aunt and then deliberately set out to get herself kidnapped to see if she could find Diana. She'd fallen in way over her head. They were in poor physical shape, most of them high, and they were taken into Exeter to a hospital for observation while their families were contacted.

Jennie was the one who'd solved the mystery of the Exeter house. Diana had planned to open the Exeter place as a safe house for girls to escape the sex trafficking, and the money would help them start new lives.

It wasn't clear exactly where the money had come from, though it did seem to be profits from gambling that she'd shared with Henry, or rather, he'd shared with her.

Inspector Hannaford allowed me to talk to Henry when we returned, for just five minutes. He would be charged with racketeering in exchange for revealing the head of the trafficking ring, the commodore of the yacht club, who would be charged with a list of crimes as long as my arm.

I met him in a holding cell, where we had to talk through the bars. Blue hollows ringed his eyes, and his entire face seemed to have sagged a mile over the past few days. "What was she doing, Henry, with the money?"

He shook his head. "I don't even know. I thought we were getting ready to get out of the whole mess, move up north to Scotland and retire. That was what I was doing in the Hebrides—finding us a place. We'd live there in the summers and travel in the winters." He broke down, hanging his head. "I was never involved in the girls, but she found out about them and wanted to do something to rescue them."

A part of me was relieved that at least the relationship had been true, that Henry had honestly loved her. I couldn't have borne knowing he'd played her.

"When I heard she'd gone missing, I knew it had to be about that. That she'd done something and been found out. That's not a lot you want to cross, and she did it." He let go of a sob. "Oh, my poor girl!"

"I'm sorry, Henry. I do know you made her happy."

"Never as she made me," he said.

Sage drove us home and promised to bring Lillian's car back the next day. Isabel and I, exhausted but wired, sat down in the kitchen for tea and apple cake. "Are you all right?" I asked.

"Yeah. I'm glad Molly is safe." She buried her face. "That scared me so much!"

"You were so brave, Isabel. I'm so proud of you. You saved a lot of girls tonight."

"I helped, anyway." She raised her eyes and took a breath. "I'm ready to tell you what happened. I want to tell you what happened, Mom."

I swallowed, and my heart started thudding. "I'm listening."

She poured it out to me, and although I wanted to howl, to scream invectives, I just listened. At the end, I said, "Come here."

She flung herself into my arms, all legs and elbows and hair, and buried her face in my shoulder. "I wanted to tell you, but I had to work it out in my head first."

"It's all right." I could feel tears on my neck, and as much as I wanted to be a different sort of mother, I found tears streaming down my own face. I thought of her horror and her humiliation, and I wanted to shield her from everything, all of it. Anything in life that would hurt her.

And I couldn't.

"I'm so, so sorry this happened to you, Isabel. It's awful and mean and petty. Together, we'll make sure you find whatever you need."

She nodded against me and wept harder. I held her and held her and held her while she let go of months of sorrow and fear and shame. When the tears were finished, we simply clung to each other.

At last, she raised her head, using her fingers to wipe tears away. "I've thought so much about what I would have done if I didn't have you through all this, and I can't even stand to think about it." She swallowed, her big eyes luminescent. "I don't ever want to be in a world where I don't have you. I'm strong and I'm going to get through this, because you made me strong."

I let her see my tears as I took her hand and twined our fingers together. "I believe in you one hundred percent. But you never have to pretend to be strong, either, right?"

"I know." She sniffed. "I want to press charges against them, the whole group."

Yes! "I'd like to pluck their toenails out one by one, but charges will probably be better."

She smiled.

I knew that she had miles to go, that we would both need counseling to get through the layers of pain she had endured, and I would have my own set of horrors when I left her and the reality of what she'd endured would come back to me, but for now, it had been a long enough night that I said, "We need ice cream."

"Oh, yeah."

The next morning, after we'd all had a long, long sleep, Isabel, Gran, and I sat at the table in the kitchen.

"I really don't want to go back to Santa Fe, Mom," Isabel said. "I don't think you do either."

"What do you mean?"

"You know how when you're out somewhere and you see a couple and they're just *with* each other? Like they're a couple in some way you can't even see? That's how it is with you and Sage. You're a couple, period."

It startled me that she'd noticed us at all. "Well, we've been friends since we were born—"

"Not like that," she said. "You love each other."

"Yes," Gran said, spreading marmalade over her toast. "You've always been that way."

"I don't—"

My mother swanned in through the back door carrying a basket of what looked to be muffins. Smelled like chocolate chip muffins, not that I would eat something she'd baked. "I brought breakfast," she said. "Since the festival is canceled, we may as well enjoy ourselves." After taking a plate from the cupboard, she arranged seven or eight muffins in circles and placed it on the table.

"Zoe," Poppy said, "will you give me one hour to talk?"

If Isabel had not been in the room, I might have said no. No matter how much help she'd been through everything with Diana, no matter how much my daughter and my mother loved her, she had deserted me, and I really didn't care what she had to say. It couldn't be fixed.

But there were Gran and Isabel staring at me. The little girl who'd watched her mother dance away ached to hear what that mother had to say, but my adolescent self was still furious. "Fine," I said. "One hour, no more."

Poppy nodded, crossed her hands over her heart. "I have to get something from the car. Will you meet me in the hearth room?"

Without looking at either of them, I headed for the hearth room. On such a bright day, sunlight splashed in through the giant window, making squares of light over an ancient rug that must have cost thousands of pounds when it was purchased.

I had hardly been in here this trip, though Isabel had discovered it as her reading nook. Paperbacks and empty cups were stacked on the floor by the window seat. I picked up the cups and set them on the table so I wouldn't forget them. The table, too, deserved more attention, I thought. It could seat a banquet, though the chair seats were dusty and worn. I tested them, wondering—

It was all distraction from my pounding heart. My long-held walls had grown crumbly, and without those defenses, I didn't know how to keep myself safe from her.

My mother breezed into the room. I wondered how she did that, breezed, when she was not terribly tall and was so very busty, but she did. Light on her feet, I supposed.

Nerves made me fold my hands in front of me. She carried a large bag with her and put it on the table.

"Well," she said. "Shall we sit down?" She gestured to the end of the table, and I moved down there, pulled out a chair. Sat.

"This is an illustrated journey," she said, "and I set most of it up, but I might need a minute now and then."

"Do we have to do some big dramatic thing? Can't you just say what you need to say and be done?"

"I could," she said, sitting down, "but this will be better."

"For who?" I asked, weary already.

"For you." She reached into the bag and brought out a postcard. An arrow stabbed me, and I reached for it without even knowing I would. It was colored green, with crayon, and I'd ironed it to make the crayon smooth, then dripped melted crayon dots, red and yellow and blue, on the green to make flowers. On the back, I'd written, "Today, Gran and I cut daisies. We miss you! Come back soon! Love, Zoe." I'd made the *Z* a decorated vine.

I remembered making it. Sitting at the kitchen table under the supervision of my grandmother using a candle and the iron to make my postcard. I must have been ten or so, still hopeful the alchemy of love and art would bring her back to me.

My throat tightened. "I don't think I can do this." I started to stand, and she covered my hand with hers, holding me in place with the most gentle of touches. Brittle bits of wall shattered within me, and I trembled from head to toe, unable to stop it.

"I left you, Zoe," she said. "I didn't mean to. I was only going to be gone for a month. It was still reckless to leave you like that, when I knew you'd be lonely up here without Sage and Diana, but—" She took a breath, cleared her throat, met my gaze.

"When I was a girl, one of the things that appalled me was the way the cycle of life just repeated and repeated and repeated in this boring way. A child is born, has dreams and talents, grows up and gets married and has a child who has dreams and talents, et cetera." She moved her shoulders. "Endlessly."

I made a choked noise. "Sorry to get in your way."

"Not you. Your dad. I didn't want to be married. I had to shake it up, somehow."

"So you left me."

"I know it doesn't help, but it really was only going to be a month. And then—" She reached into the bag and brought out a photograph.

It was faded the way old color photos always fade, of a man with a severe expression and thick black hair. "I met Ravi." She added another photo, this one of the two of them, he much taller, she as tiny as a little princess with yards of hair. They looked happy, laughing at the camera, but it didn't move me. My trembling ceased.

"Oh, my God!" I yanked my hand out from beneath hers. "So you only planned to go for a month, and then you met a man and stayed for twenty years, and it didn't matter that you left your child?"

"It still wasn't like that," she said.

"It was, actually."

"I got malaria and I couldn't travel, and then your grandmother wouldn't send you to me, and then—" She bowed her head. "I stayed."

"Okay." I stood up. "So you fell in love and got malaria and then my gran wouldn't send me, so you just gave up on being a mother. Got it."

"Zoe!"

"No. Do you know that the day I decided never to talk to you again, I got my period? And Gran is lovely, but she was old, and I was embarrassed and I wanted to tell *you*."

She closed her eyes. "I'm so sorry."

"Yeah, well, it's too late." I started to leave and shoved the chair into the side of the table, lost in a whirl of emotions I really did not want to experience.

"Zoe," she said in a reasonable voice. "Sit down. You gave me an hour. Let me tell the story, will you?"

I yanked the chair back out and sat, arms crossed in the sulky manner of a seven-year-old.

"All these years, I've been telling myself that I made the only choice I could make," she said. "I fell so deeply in love that it seemed like the only thing in the world, and I stayed to help him die, which is still one of the most influential experiences of my life. It made me who I am, loving him and then helping him die. I told myself that justified everything I did.

"Even when you first came back this time, I wondered how I could reach you to change your mind about me, never once thinking that perhaps you were *right*."

She paused. "I dug out all of these cards and letters the night they found Diana's body, and as I read them, I was horrified by the breathtakingly selfish actions of a woman I have to claim as myself."

"Why didn't you *take* me?" I asked before I could stop myself. "I missed you so much!"

Poppy just shook her head. "I know." She pulled the postcards out of the bag a handful at a time, lining them up in little piles in front of me. Each one a prayer, sent to the goddess who could grant my happiness. *Mommy, I love you. Mommy come home.*

I chose one at random. The front showed a green hairstreak butterfly, drawn in exquisite detail. The skill surprised me, and I turned the card over to check the postmarked date. June 1991. I'd been eleven years old. I remembered drawing it, using colored pencil to create the lines of the butterflies, painstakingly rendered.

I picked up another, this one a watercolor of the ocean. Small figures sat on a bench in the foreground, and I flashed on the day I'd drawn it. "You have no idea," I said quietly, "how much I missed you."

"I was a breathlessly selfish woman, Zoe. I betrayed you, my only child, in a cruel and terrible way. I don't deserve your forgiveness, but I hope you can one day find a way to give it."

My walls were heaps of rubble, leaving me as exposed and vulnerable as a pupa, halfway between caterpillar and butterfly. I made a soft noise. "The only way I survived was by hating you."

"I know," she said without rancor. "Still." She shoved a giant pile of my postcards toward me. "You need to make art your life."

There must have been hundreds of them. "I didn't realize I'd sent so many," I said, leafing through them.

"Once a week for six years."

It pierced me. That subterranean river of sorrow swamped me again, and I almost choked holding back the tears. I bit the inside of my lip, willing myself not to show how much this hurt. She didn't deserve it.

And even as I sat there, I felt ridiculous over how much it hurt still. I was a grown woman. I hadn't had her in my life since I was seven. Why would it even matter after so much time? I'd been lucky to have my gran and my dad, Sage and Diana, then Isabel.

How could something so old hurt so intensely?

"I missed so much," she said in a whisper. Her lower lip trembled.

"You should have come to get me," I said. "That was all you had to do."

She nodded. Her enormous, beautiful blue eyes were shimmery with tears, and I realized with some not-heartless part of me that she was struggling with this, too, that she was working hard to be self-controlled, and I was grateful for it.

"Thanks for these."

"I love you, Zoe. I hope we can find a way to have some kind of relationship. Maybe not mother and daughter, but maybe distant cousins?"

It surprised a laugh from me, and then I sobered. "I don't know. I just don't know if I can put it all aside."

"Fair enough." She stood.

"You don't have to avoid the house," I said, "and you and Isabel are free to have whatever relationship you want. My relationship with my grandmother is very important to me, and I don't want to keep that from her."

"Thank you," she said, and her voice cracked a little. "I'll leave you alone now."

"Okay." As she started to leave, I said, "Why do you always wear white?"

She touched the trousers she wore, with a soft rayon top. "It's the color of widows in India."

"When did he die?"

"July sixteenth, 1992." She folded her hands in that way that she had, as if she had all the time in the world. "You were sixteen."

We had not spoken in four years by then. I had Sage and my dreams and didn't think I needed my mother. It had become so patently, ridiculously obvious that she was never going to come home. "You really loved him."

"I did," she said in a matter-of-fact way. "That doesn't excuse what I did to you."

"No," I said. "It doesn't."

She left then, and I let her go and looked through all the postcards. So much hunger, so much love. As a mother myself now, I could see where I'd been damaged, how desperately she'd let down this little girl.

Would I forgive her? I really didn't see how.

A postcard slipped out of a stack, and I picked it up. My seven-year-old self and my teenage self and my adult, broken and mended and mostly whole self came together and touched the face I'd drawn. It was Sage, fishing, his hair exaggerated ringlets, the sky full of puffy clouds.

I needed to tell him about this. He would be glad.

But first, I sorted through all the postcards, remembering, remembering, remembering. I let the grief of that child, that girl, that abandoned teenager rise and overflow. In the quiet room, alone with bits of myself, I could grieve.

It took a long time, but when I finally stood, cold and headachy, I had let a heavy burden go. Maybe I would never love her, but I didn't have to hate her.

After gathering the postcards back into the bag, I went to find Sage.

Epilogue

Zoe

Nineteen months later, Boxing Day

A swirling storm had blown in overnight, roiling the sea into a wild, noisy thing that crashed against the rocks and sent spray against the long windows of the hearth room. Inside, an enormous fire crackled in the massive hearth, and I placed the last of the silver on individual place mats sewn by the girls rescued from the raid. The fabrics were as unique as the girls themselves, bright peaches and pinks in some, chintzes and flowers in others, big bold geometrics in still others. We'd hosted the girls—who'd been staying at the halfway house—early last week, at this very table, and they'd presented us with the gift of the place mats. It choked me up, but then everything choked me up these days.

Isabel bounced into the room with Molly, the pair of them inseparable after the rescue. Even after the incident, Molly's mother had not been able to step up enough to take care of her daughter, and over the course of a few months, Molly had begun living with us. Goaded by Isabel, Molly had raised her grades to the point that she would be taking her GCSEs. "We are starving!" Isabel said. "We hiked five miles this morning!"

"In this weather?"

"If you're going to walk five hundred miles around the West Country," she declared, sitting down and raiding a plate of fluffy white rolls, "you'd better be able to take the weather."

She had announced that she was going to conquer the South West Coast Path. "I suppose so. But don't eat all the rolls. Go get a snack from the kitchen."

They danced away, all fresh-smelling good health. Our case against the people who'd assaulted Isabel had still not been resolved, although investigators were tracking the erased photos via cell phone companies and sophisticated tracking software. The case was moving forward, and in the meantime, she'd become very active online in groups devoted to people recovering from bullying and other social media issues. I was quite proud of her. She still spoke to Dr. Kerry once a week, and she participated in a group chat with assault survivors her age.

One by one, everyone assembled around the table. Gran was having a semidecent day; though they were few and far between, we tried to make sure she felt as normal as possible. Poppy had been key in figuring out ways to do that, actually, which had gone a long way toward giving us a chance to work out at least a polite relationship. Isabel was crazy about her, just as I'd loved my grandmother, and I had to admit it was a healthy, strong relationship for my daughter.

And my mother. She flat out adored Isabel.

I gazed around the table. Gran and Isabel and Molly. Poppy and Mia and her partner, Beatrice; Sage and my father, Ben, who was visiting for the holiday. I had no idea where the possible reunion between him and Poppy might go, but whatever. Isabel was thrilled with her machinations. I didn't have the heart to tell her that Ben never gave in to anything he didn't want.

When everyone was seated, I stood from my place as matriarch at the table and lifted a glass. Mine was filled with water, but there were plenty of spirits around the table. "Welcome, everybody! This is a new tradition here at Woodhurst Hall—our Boxing Day celebration."

"Hear! Hear!" cried Poppy.

"We're going to celebrate all the best events of the year, and I think we have a lot of them today. Who would like to start?"

Sage stood up. "I will! I married my sweetheart this year, and I could not be happier."

Even knowing he was going to do it, I felt a rush of pleasure. "Hear! Hear!" I cried. "Best year of my life thus far."

Isabel stood. "A publisher approached me to publish my book about the bluebell woods after reading it on Wattpad, and I took the deal!"

Molly whooped. "Best story ever!"

Others marked their stories, including a mention for my grandmother's mystery novels as some of the best feminist works of the century and my father's recognition as a weaver.

When they were all finished, I said, "I have two things to celebrate." Sage stood and picked up a canvas that had been carefully placed against the wall. He carried it over and turned it around, and again I felt a wild sense of accomplishment over the piece. I'd used the postcards my mother had returned to me to create a portrait of her.

The piece had taken more than a year, both because I'd been uncovering my voice and because it had forced me to deal with my feelings about my mother and about being abandoned. The collage showed her standing on the shores of a lake, wearing white. It was pieced in colors I'd cut from butterfly wings and ocean waves and grass and moor. In the shadows and making the lines of her hair and the wavy lines of the lake were words—*dear mum, mummy, mother, I love you. Come home. Come back. I love you. I miss you, I miss you, I miss you.*

It had won first prize at an exhibition. "This piece has earned me an honorable mention at the Hurley Awards," I said, "and will be entered in a major competition next spring."

The table was entirely silent. It was unnerving, and I glanced at Sage, who smiled. He'd been saying the piece was more than I thought it was. My father stood and began to applaud. Isabel leapt to her feet and joined in, and then the entire table was applauding.

I only looked at my mother, who sat in her place with her hands in her lap. Tears streamed down her face.

I realized that her approval was the only thing I wanted. That I'd created it for her.

She stood and left her place, coming up to examine the collage closely. Her fingertips floated above the words, the longing expressed so nakedly across her shoulders, my love across her mouth. "I am so proud of you, Zoe. It's remarkable."

Something broke loose, and I found emotion welling up in me, something that felt very like love. "Thank you," I said, and I looked into her eyes, letting her see me, letting myself see her.

"I have another surprise," I whispered, and I took her hand and placed it over my belly. "You have another grandchild on the way."

She burst into tears. My mother, my enemy, the grandmother of my children. I hugged her. For the first time in thirty-two years. She clung to me, smaller than I could believe, softer, warmer.

It felt strange and painful and healing.

It felt like forgiveness.

Acknowledgments

So many people contributed to this book that I barely know where to begin.

First up are my West Country relatives: Ander and Jeanie Barlow in the north, who flung open their doors warmly and offered their stories of life in Somerset. I often remember the view over the hills and fields to Glastonbury Tor in the distance. I owe so much of Poppy's character to that visit! Thanks to their daughter, Brinna, a brilliant and questing woman I admire deeply, for help with language. In the south are Frances and Charles Holme, who showed us another angle of life in the West Country in their little village and in the forest. Thanks for the village cricket match and the ginger apple cake, and always the sense of love and family.

I also had the good luck to find excellent and knowledgeable guides to the West Country: first John Flanagan, from Divine Light Tours, who opened doors to discovery on a tour of the spiritual side of Glastonbury. His thoughtful authenticity and historical knowledge proved invaluable. I am more grateful than I can say. In the south, photographer and local native Mark Lakeman from Unique Devon Tours drove us through narrow lanes and along tall cliffs and through a dozen villages so that I could build one of my own. I will never forget the day on Dartmoor with Ken the shepherd, which—books and research aside—provided one of my favorite days of travel, ever. Thanks, too, for the bluebell wood, an enchanting place indeed.

Thanks to the inimitable Ellen Kushner for the watercolor of a hare, who kept me company through the toughest stretches, a cheerful companion.

I am insanely, deeply grateful to my entire team at Lake Union— Alicia Clancy, Danielle Marshall, Gabe Dumpit, and the entire marketing team. I can't say enough about how much I love writing for this imprint.

Enormous, vast buckets of thanks to developmental editor Tiffany Yates Martin, who pushed me hard to do my best work, and to Meg Ruley, who is, let's face it, the greatest agent of all time.

Finally, thanks to my partner, Neal Barlow, who is steady, funny, and kind, and is a great travel companion, even when we get lost in the forest. I know I can always trust him to lead me home.

About the Author

Photo © 2009 Blue Fox Photography

Barbara O'Neal is the *Wall Street Journal, Washington Post,* and Amazon Charts bestselling author of more than a dozen novels, including *When We Believed in Mermaids, The Art of Inheriting Secrets,* and *How to Bake a Perfect Life.* She lives in the beautiful city of Colorado Springs with her beloved—a British endurance athlete who vows he'll never lose his accent.

To learn more about O'Neal and her works, visit her online at www.barbaraoneal.com.